The Mysteries of Florence

George Lippard

Alpha Editions

This edition published in 2024

ISBN : 9789361479366

Design and Setting By
Alpha Editions
www.alphaedis.com
Email - info@alphaedis.com

Contents

The Scene of the Romance.

THE moon arose!

Reposing on the porch of an ancient mansion,—which, deserted and falling to ruins, was pitched on the brow of a dizzy steep;—a traveller, who had journeyed far and long, looked forth upon the night, through an opening in the trees crowning the verge of the cliff, and, with a soul filled with silent awe, beheld this scene of the grandeur of nature, combined with the glories of art, and the stern memories of a long past age.

A lovely valley lay sleeping in the moonbeams: ancient towers, Gothic temples, domes of religion, palaces of pleasure, rose clearly in the air, from amid gardens gay with flowers, or forests heavy with foliage, while around the scene of slumbering grandeur, swept the mighty Apennines, lifting their blue peaks into the universe of azure that arched above, silvered and tinted and mellowed by the midnight moon.

A stream of tremulous silver wandered brightly through the valley, like a banner waving along the blackness of night. The domes of an ancient city, baptized by the strains of the Minstrel, and consecrated by the words of the Romancer, were seen looming over the forest trees, from the dim distance of the vale.

The moon arose!

There was softness, and beauty, and power, written on the wide sweep of that boundless sky, with its horizon of blue mountains; there was solemn silence resting on the night, and the angels of God might look down upon the scene, and weep to think that a land so like heaven in its gorgeousness of beauty, should be stamped with the footsteps of crimes too mighty for belief, wrongs too dark for the page of history, woes steeped in the very bitterness of death.

It was the valley of the Arno, and the traveler gazed from the height upon the distant City of Florence, surnamed the "Fair."

Arising in the calm moonbeams from the very centre of the valley, the gray towers of a ruined castle broke abruptly into the dark azure of night, looming from the distance like stern monuments of a past age, lifting to heaven their testimony of the glory and the gloom of the Gothic Era.

It was the Castle of Albarone, the home of a mighty race who flourished in long past centuries. Within the walls of the lonely {xi} castle,—lonely because in ruins,—rising from the bosom of the Arno, and along the shores of a mountain lake, not many leagues away, the tragedy of the race of Albarone found its theatre of action, with vast multitudes of men looking on, spectators or actors in its scene of varied and contrasted horror.

And as the traveller, wearied with his day's journey, athirst from fatigue and toil, uprose from his resting-place, and looked yet once more upon the night, ere he hastened on his path to the Fair City of Florence, his eye was again met by the stern vision of the castle towering in ruins, and over his soul came a feeling of awe and horror, as he mused upon the crimes and mysteries of the House of Albarone, while the night around him grew more still, and the sky above more shadowy in its beauty.

And as he mused, a dark cloud covered the face of the moon, hovering like a vast bird, with wings of night, and form of omen, right above the ruined towers of Albarone. A moment passed, the sky was again all glory and light, while still—

The moon arose!

BOOK THE FIRST.
THE RED CHAMBER

CHAPTER THE FIRST.

THE SIGNET RING OF ALBARONE.

HIGH NOON AMID THE OLD CASTLE WALLS.

FROM the clear azure of the summer sky, the mid-day sun shone over the lofty battlements and massive towers of an ancient castle, which, rising amid the heights of a precipitous rock, lay basking in the warm atmosphere; while along the spacious court-yard, and among the nooks and crevices of the dark gray walls, the mellow beams fell lazily, gilding each point they touched, and turning the blackened rocks to brightened gold, with the voluptuous light of a summer noon.

The massive cliff, from whose stern foundations the castle arose, sank suddenly, with a precipitous descent, into the bed of the valley, while around, venerable with the grandeur of ages, swept the magnificent forest, with its mass of verdure mellowing in the sunlight; and, winding on its way of silver, a broad and rapid stream, gleaming from the deep green foliage, now gave each wave and ripple to the kiss of day, and now, sweeping in its shadowy nooks, sheltered its beauty from the dazzling light.

Far along the view, forest towered over forest, and sloping meadows, dotted with cottages, succeeded shelving fields, golden with wheat, or gay with vines; while many a pleasant hill-side arose from amid the embowering woods, with the peaceful summit sleeping in the sun-light, and the straight shadows of the still noon resting along the depths of the valley, from which it greenly ascended.

Along the edge of the horizon, amid the tall peaks of the far-off mountains, summer clouds, vast and gorgeous, lay basking in the sunlight, with their fantastic forms, of every hue and shape—now dark, now bright, now golden, now gray, and again white as the new-fallen snow—all clearly and delicately relieved by the back-ground of azure, transparent and glassy as the sky of some voluptuous dream.

The hour was still and solemn, with the peculiar silence and solemnity of the high noon; the broad banner floated heavily from the loftiest tower of the castle, unruffled by a whisper of the wind; and along the court-yard, and throughout the castle, a death-like silence reigned, which betokened any thing save the presence of numerous bodies of armed men within the castle walls.

The sentinels who waited at the castle gate, rested indolently upon their pikes, and glancing over the spacious court-yard, marked, with a look of discontent, the absence of all signs of animation from those walls which had so often rung with sounds of gay carousal and shouts of merriment. All was still and solemn where, in days by-gone, not a sound had awoke the echoes of the time-darkened walls save the loud laugh of the careless reveller, the merry carol of the minstrel, or the glee-song of the banquet hall.

A footstep—a mailed and booted footstep—broke the silence of the air, and presently, appearing from the shadow of the lofty hall door of the castle, a stout and strong-limbed soldier emerged into the light of the sun. As he descended the steps of stone, he paused for a moment, and glanced around the court-yard. Stout, without being bulky in figure, the person of the yeoman was marked by broad shoulders, a chest massive and prominent, arms that were all bone and muscle, and legs that discovered the bold and rugged outline of strong physical power, hardened by fatigue and toil.

He raised his cap of buff, surmounted by a dark plume, and plated with steel, from his brow, and the sunbeams fell upon a rugged countenance, darkened by the sun, and seamed by innumerable wrinkles, with a low, yet massive forehead, a nose short, straight, yet prominent, a wide mouth, with thin lips, and cheek-bones high and bold in outline, while his clear blue eyes, with their quick and varying glance, afforded a strange contrast to his toil-hardened and sunburnt features. Around his throat, and over his prominent chin, grew a thick and rugged beard, dark as his eyebrows in hue, while his hair, slightly touched by age, and worn short and close, gave a marked outline to his head, that completed the expression of dogged courage and blunt frankness visible in every lineament of his countenance.

Attired in doublet and hose of buff, defended by a plate of massive steel on the breast, with smaller plates on each arm and leg, the yeoman wore boots of slouching buckskin, while a broad belt of darkened leather, thrown over his manly chest, supported the short, straight sword, which depended from his left side.

Having glanced along the court-yard, and marked the sentinels waiting lazily beside the castle gate, the yeoman's eye wandered to the banner which clung heavily around the towering staff, and then depositing his cap on his head with an air of discontent, as he again surveyed the castle yard—

"St. Withold!" he cried, in a voice as rugged as his face—"St. Withold! but some foul spell of the fiend's own making has fallen upon these old walls! All dull—all dead—all leaden! Even yon flag, which kissed the breeze of the Holy Land, not three months agone, looks dull and drowsy. 'Slife! a man might as well be dead as live in this manner. No feasting—no songs—no carousing! Ugh! A pest take it all, I say! No jousts—no tournaments—no mellays! The foul fiend take it, I say; and Sathanas wither the heathen hand that winged the poisoned javelin at my knightly Lord—Julian, Count of this gallant castle Di Albarone! The foul fiend wither the hand of the paynim dog, I say!"

"Ha, ha, ha! my good Robin," laughed a clear and youthful voice, "by my troth, thou'rt sadly out of temper! What has ruffled thee, my buff-and-buckskin? Holy Mary—*what* a face!"

Robin turned, and beheld the slender form of a daintily appareled youth, whose full cheeks were wrinkled with laughter, while his merry hazel eyes seemed dancing in the light of their own glee.

"Out of temper!" exclaimed rough Robin, as he glanced at the laughing youth; "out of temper! By St. Withold! there's good reason for't, too. Look ye, my bird of a page, never since I left the service of mine own native prince, the brave Richard, of the Lion Heart—never since the day when the gallant Geoffrey o' th' Longsword drew his sword in the wars of Palestine, under the banner of Count Julian Di Albarone, have I felt so sick, so wearied in heart, as I do this day—mark ye, my page! 'Out of temper,' forsooth! Answer me, then, popinjay—does not our gallant Lord Julian lie wasting away in yon sick-chamber, with the poison of an incurable wound eating his very heart? Answer me that, Guiseppo."

"Ay, marry does he, my good Robin," the page answered, as he played with a jeweled chain that hung from his neck; "but then thou knowest he will recover. He will again mount his war-horse! Ay, my good Lord Julian will again lead armies to battle in the wilds of Palestine! He will, by my troth, Rough Robin!"

"I fear me, never, never," the yeoman replied, in a subdued tone. "Look ye, Guiseppo, what dost think of this thin-faced half-brother of the Count, the scholar Aldarin? There's a mystery about the man—I like him not. Thy master, the Duke of Florence, hath now been three days at this good castle of Albarone—why is he so much in the company of this keen-eyed Aldarin? By St. Withold! I like it not. Marry, boy, but the devil's a-brewing a pretty pot of yeast for somebody's bread! Guiseppo, canst tell me naught concerning the object of the visit of thy master, the Duke, to this castle—hey, boy?"

"Why, Robin," replied the page, as, placing one small hand on either side of his slender waist, he glanced at the yeoman with a sidelong look; "why, Robin, didst ever hear of—of—the fair Ladye Annabel? Eh, Robin?"

"The fair Ladye Annabel! Tut! boy, thou triflest with me. The fair Ladye Annabel—she is the lovely daughter of this crusty old scholar. Her mother was an Eastern woman; and the fair girl first saw the light in the wilds of Palestine, when the scholar Aldarin accompanied his brother thither. Marry, 'tis more than sixteen—seventeen years since. 'Tis long ago—very long. By

St. Withold! those were merry days. But come, sir page, why name the Ladye Annabel and the Duke in the same breath?"

The restless Guiseppo sprang aside with a nimble movement, and then folding his arms, stood at the distance of a few paces, regarding the stout yeoman with a look of mock gravity and solemn humor.

"What wouldst give to know, Robin?" he exclaimed, with a peculiar contortion of his mirthful face. "Hark ye, my stout yeoman, 'My Lord Duke of Florence and the Ladye Annabel, Duchess of Florence.' Dost like the sound? What says my rough soldier, now?"

"I see a light," slowly responded Robin; "I see a light!" and he slowly drew his sword half-way from the scabbard. "But as yet 'tis but a pestilent Jack o' lanthorn light, dancing about a tangled marsh of pits and bogs, with plenty o'hidden traps to catch honest men by the heels, i' faith. Annabel and the Duke! Ho—ho! Then the game's up with the son o' th' Count—my Lord Adrian?"

"Wag that clumsy tongue o' thine with a spice o' caution, Robin," whispered the merry page. "See, the sharp-faced steward o' th' castle draws nigh, and with him a group of sworn grumblers. The four old esquires who followed our lord to battle in the wilds o' Palestine—a soldier, with a carbuncled visage, and a lounging servitor, the huntsman o' th' castle. Hark! didst ever hear such eloquent growling?"

And as Robin turned to listen, he beheld the strangely contrasted party lounging slowly along the castle yard, with the indolent gait of men having little to do save to eat, to drink, to sleep, and to gossip, while around them the lazy hours of the silent castle-walls dragged onward with wings of lead.

"Talk not to me of thrift, sir steward," cried the bluff-faced and thick-headed huntsman. "When my Lord, Count Julian, was well—not a day passed but a lusty buck was steaming on the castle hearth—"

"Wine flowed like water," chimed in the soldier with the fiery nose. "Your true soldier swore by his beaker alone—"

"*Now!*" interrupted the sharp-faced steward, waving his thin hands, and with an expressive shrug of the shoulders; "*now*, my lord the Count is *sick*. The scholar Aldarin hath the rule. Tell me, sir huntsman, and you, sir, of the fiery nose, is there any waste o' flesh or liquor in the castle? Is not the signer careful of the beeves of my lord. No longer are we quiet folks disturbed by your carousings: no silly dances, no rude catches o' vile camp-follower songs! By the Virgin, no!"

"By the true wood o' th' cross, sir steward, thou'rt a rare one!" growled a white-haired esquire, as his scarred and sunburnt visage was turned angrily toward the sharp-faced steward. "Dost think men o' mettle are made o' such broomstick bones and mud-puddle blood as thou? Body o' Bacchus, no! 'No carousing!' I'd e'en like to see thee on a jolly carouse!"

"Say rather, sir esquire," Robin the Rough exclaimed, as the party reached his side, "say rather, you'd e'en wish to see a death's-head making mirth at a feast, or a funeral procession strike up a jolly fandango! Sir steward at a feast!—the owl at a gathering o' nightingales!"

The sharped-faced steward was about to make an angry reply, when a sudden thrill ran through the party. Each tongue was stilled, and each man stood motionless in the full glare of the noon-day sun.

"Hist! The Signor Aldarin approaches," whispered the page Guiseppo. "He comes from the castle gate along to the castle hall."

And as each head was stealthily turned over the shoulder toward the castle gate, there came gliding along, with cat-like steps and downcast look, a man of severe aspect, whose gray eye—cold, flashing, and clear, in its unchangeable glance—seemed as though it could read the very heart.

A tunic of dark velvet, disclosing the spare outlines of his slim figure, reached to his ankles, and over this garment, depending from his right shoulder, he wore a robe of similar color, passed under his left arm, joined in front by a chain of gold, and then falling in sweeping folds to his sandaled feet.

A cap of dark fur, bright with a single gem of strange lustre, gave a striking relief to his high, pale forehead, seamed by a single deep wrinkle, shooting upward from between the eyebrows, while his gray hair fell in slight masses down along the hollow cheeks and over his neck and shoulders.

"This is the—scholar!" growled one of the white-haired esquires. "His days have been passed in the laboratory, while his brother's sword hath flashed at the head of armies."

"The saints preserve me from the wizard-tribe, say I!" muttered Robin the Rough; and as he spoke, with an involuntary movement of fear, the party separated on either side of the castle hall, leaving room for the passage of the Signor Aldarin.

He came slowly onward, with his head downcast, neither looking to the one side nor to the other. He ascended the steps of stone, and in a moment was lost to the view of the loiterers in the castle yard.

The hall of the castle passed, a passage traversed, and another stairway ascended, the stooping scholar stood in a small ante-chamber, with the light of the noon-day sun subdued to a twilight obscurity by the absence of windows from the place, while an evening gloom hung around the narrow walls, the arching ceiling of darkened stone, and the floor of tesselated marble. A single casement, long and narrow, reaching from floor to arch, gave entrance to a straggling beam of daylight, disclosing the stout and muscular form of a man-at-arms, with armor and helmet of steel, who, pike in hand, waited beside a massive door, opening into one of the principal apartments of the castle.

With a soft, gliding footstep, the Signor Aldarin glided along the tesselated floor, and stood beside the man-at-arms, ere he was aware of his approach.

"Ha! Balvardo, thou keepest strict watch beside the sick chamber of my lord." The words broke from the Signor Aldarin. "Hast obeyed my behest?"

"E'en so, my lord," the sentinel began, in a rough, surly tone.

"How, vassal! Dost name me with the title of my brother? Have a care, good Balvardo, have a care!"

"He chides me in a rough voice," murmured the sentinel, as though speaking to his own ear; "and yet a wild light flashes over his features at the word. Signor, I but mistook the word—a slip o' th' tongue," he exclaimed aloud. "Thy behests have been obeyed. No one has been suffered to pass into the chamber of my Lord Di Albarone since morning dawn, save the fair Ladye Annabel, who waits beside the couch of the wounded knight."

"Come hither, Balvardo. Look from this narrow window: mark you well the dial-plate in the castle yard. In a few moments the shadow will sweep across the path of high noon. When high noon and the shadow meet, thy charge is over. The soothing potion which I gave my brother at daybreak, will have taken its proper effect. Until that moment, keep strict watch: let not a soul enter the Red Chamber on the peril of thy life!"

And with the command, the Signor swept from the ante-chamber, gliding along a corridor opposite the one from which he had just emerged, and his low footsteps in a moment had ceased to echo along the dark old arches.

"He is gone," the sentinel murmured, slowly pacing the tesselated floor. "He comes like a cat—he glides hence like a ghost. Hark! footsteps from opposite corridors meeting in this ante-chamber. By'r Lady! here comes Adrian, the son of this sick lord, and from the opposite gallery emerges the monk Albertine, the tool and counsellor of my Lord of Florence. 'Tis a moody monk and a shrewd boy. I'faith, there's a pair o' 'em."

And as he spoke, sweeping from the shadows of the northern gallery came a dark-robed monk, walking with hastened step, his arms folded on his breast, and his head drooped low, as if in thought, while the outlines of his face were enveloped in the folds of his priestly cowl. And as he swept onward toward the centre of the ante-chamber, from the southern gallery, with slow and solemn steps, advanced a youth of some twenty summers, attired in the gay dress of a cavalier, with a frank, open visage, marked by the lines of premature thought, and relieved by rich and luxuriant locks of golden hair sweeping along each cheek down to the shoulders.

"Whither speed ye, Lord Adrian?" exclaimed the deep, sonorous voice of the monk, as the twain met breast to breast in the centre of the rich mosaic floor. "Whither speed ye, heir of Albarone, at this hour?"

"Whither do I speed?" cried the cavalier, starting with sudden surprise. "Sir monk, I wend to the sick-chamber of my father."

The monk grasped the cavalier suddenly by the right hand, and raised it as suddenly in the light of the sunbeams streaming through the solitary window.

"An hour since, this hand was graced by a signet ring: the signet ring which has been an heirloom in thy house for centuries. Dost remember the prophecy spoken of that strange ring? Dost remember the rude lines of the vandal seer:

'While treasured and holily worn,
An omen of glory and good:
When from the hand the ruby is torn,
An omen of doom and of blood.'"

"Sir monk, the lines are rude; yet I mind me well the words of the prophecy, are an household sound to an heir of Albarone. Yet why this sudden grasp of my hand? Why thus urgent? The fire in thine eye seems not of earth."

"Lord Adrian, by the Virgin tell me how long since parted this finger from the ruby signet ring of thy house? Never parted that ring from the hand of heir of Albarone, without sudden evil, fearful doom, or unheard of death, gathering thick and dark around thy house!"

"I missed not the signet ring till this moment. An instant ago, I was in my chamber. Thy air is strange and solemn for the confessor of this jovial Duke, yet I will turn me, and seek the signet without delay. Thy warning may be well-timed."

"Boy, a word in thine ear. My life has been strange and dark. I have loved the shadow rather than the light. I have courted the glare of corruption in the midnight charnel-house, rather than the blaze of the noon-day sun. I have made me a home amid strange mysteries, and from the tomes of darksome lore I have wrung the secrets of the hidden world."

"To what tends all this, sir monk? By'r Ladye, thou'rt strangely moved!"

"And from my hidden lore have I learned this mystery of mysteries. When the stillness of midnight hangs like lead over the noon-day hour—when, at mid-noon, a strange, solemn, and voiceless silence pervades the air, spreads through the universe, and impresses the heart of each living thing with a feeling of unutterable AWE, then wicked men are doing, in the sight of heaven, with the laughter of fiends in their ears, some deed of horror, that the fiends tremble 'mid their laughter to behold. Some deed of nameless horror, which thrills the universe with AWE, making the hour of noon more terrible than midnight in the charnel-house. Look abroad, Adrian—'tis high noon. Dost hear a sound, a whisper of the wind? All silent as death—all still as the grave! The silence of this nameless AWE is upon the noon-day hour. Adrian, to thy chamber, to thy chamber, and rest not till the signet ring again encircles thy finger! There is a doom upon this hour!"

And with these words, uttered in a low, yet deep and piercing tone, the monk glided from the ante-chamber; and the cavalier, without a word, as hastily retraced his steps, and in an instant had disappeared in the shadow of the southern gallery.

"Whispered words!" muttered the bull-headed man-at-arms. "A ring! What about a ring? Ha—ha! The Monk and the Springald commune together—well! I could not make out their secret, but—but, the ring!"

And raising his sturdy form to its full height, with a grim smile on his bearded face, Balvardo glanced around the ante-chamber, and then, with a low chuckle, he let his pike fall heavily upon the pavement of stone.

CHAPTER THE SECOND.

THE WHITE DUST IN THE GOBLET OF GOLD.

IN a lofty apartment of the castle, hung with rich folds of crimson tapestry, and designated from time past memory as the Red Chamber, on a couch of gorgeous hangings, lay the once muscular, but now disease-stricken, Julian, Count of Albarone, shorn of his warrior strength, divested of the glory of his manhood's prime.

The warm sunlight which filled the place, fell with a golden glow over the outlines of his lofty brow, indented with wrinkles, the long gray hair parted on either side, the eyebrows, snow-white, overarching the clear, bold eyes, that sent forth their glance with all the fire and intensity of youth, rendered more vivid and flame-like by the contrast of sunken eyelid and hollow cheek.

And by the bedside of the warrior, bending like an angel of good, as she ministered to his slightest wants, the form of a fair and lovely maiden was disclosed in the noon-day light, while her flaxen curls fell lightly, and with a waving motion, over the rich bloom of her cheek, glowing with the warmth of fifteen summers, and her full, large eyes of liquid blue, gleamed with the expression of a soul, whose fruits were pure and happy thoughts, the buds and blossoms of innocence and youth.

"Annabel,"—said the warrior, in a voice faint with disease—"Methinks I feel the strength of youth again returning; the sleeping potion of my good brother, Aldarin, has done me wondrous service. Assist me to the casement, child of mine heart, that I may gaze once more upon the broad lands and green woods of my own domain of Albarone."——

As he spoke, the Count rose on his feet, with a tottering movement, and had fallen to the floor, but for the fair arm of the maiden wound around his waist, while his muscular hand rested upon her shoulder.

"Lean upon my arm, my uncle,—tread with a careful footstep. In a moment we will reach the casement."

They stood within the recess of the emblazoned window, the warrior and the maiden, while around them floated and shimmered the golden sunshine, falling over the tesselated stone of the pavement, throwing a glaring light around the hangings of the bed, and streaming in flashes of brightness among the distant corners and nooks of the Red Chamber.

'Tis a fair land, niece of mine,—a fair and lovely land.—"

"A land of dreams, a land of magnificent visions, overshadowed by yon blue mountains of romance. Look, my uncle, how the noon-day sun is showering his light over the deep woods that encircle the rock of Albarone—yonder, beyond the verdure of the trees, winds the silvery Arno; yonder are hills and rugged steeps, and far away tower the blue heights of the Apennines!"

"And here, niece of mine, in my youthful prime I stood, when my aged father's hand had dubbed me—knight. 'Twas such a quiet noon-day hour, on a calm and dream-like day as this, that, from the recess of this window, I gazed upon yon gorgeous land. How the blood swelled in my youthful veins; how dreams of ambition fired my boyish fancy, as the words broke from my lips,—'Here they ruled, my fathers, in days by-gone, with the iron sword of the Goth; here they reigned as sovereign princes—as Dukes of Florence.'"

"Since that noon-day hour thy sword has flashed in the van of a thousand battles!"

"It has—it has! And yet what am I now? Old before my time, swept away from the path of glory, as I neared the goal! A warrior should never utter a word of complaint—and yet—by the Sacrament of Heaven, I had much rather died with sword in hand, at the head of my hosts, than to wither away with this festering wound on yonder couch. I like not to count the pulsations of my dying heart."

"Nay, my uncle,—chide not so bitterly. Thou wilt recover—thy sword will again flash at the head of armies!"

"My sword, Annabel, my sword,"—cried the warrior, as his eyes lit up with a strange brilliancy, and his wan features were crimsoned by a ruddy flush.

In a moment, the fair hands of the maiden bore the sword from its resting-place, in a nook of the Red Chamber, with a slow and weary movement, as though the massive piece of iron which she trailed along the marble floor, exceeded her maidenly strength to lift on high.

"It is my sword, it is my sword"—shrieked the warrior, as he flung the robes of purple back from his muscular, though attenuated shoulder, and raised his proud form to its full height—"Look, Annabel, how it gleams in the light! So it gleamed on the walls of Jerusalem, so it shone aloft over the desert-sands of the Syrian wilderness! It will gleam over the battle-field again! Ay, again will the snow-white plume of Julian Di Albarone wave over the ranks of the fray, while ten thousand warriors hail that plume as their beacon-light!"

He swung the sword aloft in the air; his whole form was moved by excitement; every vein filled and every pulse throbbed; his eye flashed like a thing of flame, and his whitened lip trembled with the glorious expression of battle-scorn.

Thrice he waved the sword around his head; but when the impulse of this sudden excitement died away, his eyes lost their flashing brightness, his limbs their vigor, and Julian of Albarone tottered as he stood upon the marble floor, and stepping hurriedly backward, fell heavily upon the couch of the Red Chamber.

"The goblet, fair niece—the goblet on the beaufet. Haste thee—I am faint."

As the words broke gaspingly from the sick man's lips, the Ladye Annabel turned hastily to bring the goblet, and as she turned, she beheld the head of Lord Julian resting uneasily on his pillow, while his left arm hung heavily over the side of the couch.

She turned again with trembling footsteps, and hastened to arrange the pillow of the sick warrior. Her fair hands smoothed the pillow of down, and she gently raised his head from the couch.

At the very instant, the tapestry in a dark corner of the Red Chamber rustled quickly to and fro, as a figure, muffled in a sweeping cloak of crimson, emerged into view, and treading across the tesselated pavement, with a footstep like a spirit of the unreal air, it approached the beaufet of ebony, and a white hand, glittering with a single ring, was extended for a moment over the goblet of gold.

The Ladye Annabel placed the head of Lord Julian gently upon the pillow of down.

The glittering ring shone in the sun, as it fell in the goblet of gold, and the hand of the figure, white as alabaster, was again concealed in the thick folds of the crimson robe.

The Ladye Annabel, with her delicate hands, parted the gray hairs from the sick man's face, and swept them back from his brow.

The figure in robes of crimson, strode with a noiseless footstep across the apartment, and sought the shelter of the hangings of tapestry, with as strange a silence as it had emerged from their folds.

Without taking notice of the white dust that covered the bottom of the empty goblet, Annabel filled it with generous wine, and approached the bedside of her uncle. The Count raised himself from the pillow, and lifted the goblet to his lips. As his wan face was reflected in the ruddy wavelets of the wine, he fixed his full large eyes upon the lovely face of Annabel, with a look of affection, mingled with an expression so strange, so solemn and dread, that it dwelt in the soul of the maiden for years.

He drank, and drained the goblet to the dregs.

"Thank thee—fair niece—thank thee."

He paused suddenly, his arms he flung wildly from him, a thin, glassy film gathered over his eyes, a gurgling noise sounded in his throat, and he fell heavily upon the couch.

His features were knit in a fearful expression of pain and suffering, his mouth opened with a ghastly grimace, leaving the teeth visible, the lips were agitated by a convulsive pang, and his eyes, sternly fixed, glared wildly from beneath the eyebrows woven in a frown.

"My uncle—my father,"—shrieked the Ladye Annabel, rushing to the bedside—"Look not so wildly, gaze not so sternly upon me. Speak, my uncle, oh, speak!"

Her utterance failed, and an indistinct murmur broke from her lips. Her hands ran hurriedly over the brow of the warrior—it was cold with beaded drops of moisture. She bent hastily over the form of Lord Julian, she imprinted a kiss on his parted lips. She kissed the lips of the dead!

Then the tapestry, the hangings of the Red Chamber, the couch, with its ghastly corse, all swam round her in a fearful dance, and the Ladye Annabel fell insensible on the floor.

The great bell of the Castle of Albarone tolled forth the hour of noon. The shadow of death had been flung across the dial-plate in the castle-yard.

While the thunder-like tones of the bell went swinging and quivering, and echoing among the old castle halls, a footstep was heard without the Red Chamber, and the door was flung suddenly open.

A young Cavalier, with a face marked by frank, open features, locks of rich gold, and an eye of blue, while his handsome form was clad in a gay dress of velvet, entered the apartment, and strode with hurried steps to the couch.

He cast one look at the face of the corse, marked by the ghastly grimace of death; he cast one quick and hasty glance at the form of the Ladye Annabel, thrown insensible along the floor of stone, and then he covered his face with his trembling hands, and his manly form was convulsed by a shuddering tremor, that shook the folds of his blue doublet, as though every sinew writhed in agony beneath the gay apparel.

The heavy sob, which unutterable anguish alone can bring from the heart of a proud man, broke on the deep silence of the room, and the big heavy tear-drops of man's despair came trickling between the clasped fingers, pressed over his countenance.

"He is dead—my father—he is dead!"

He mastered the first terrible impulse of grief, and raised the swooning maiden from the floor.

"He is dead—my father"—again sounded the husky voice of the Cavalier. "Thou, Annabel, art all that is left to me—I am—"

"*A murderer—a parricide!*" cried a sharp and piercing voice, that thrilled to the very heart of the cavalier.

He turned hurriedly as he grasped the maiden with his good right arm, he turned and beheld—*the Scholar Aldarin.*

His glance was fixed and stern, while, with one hand half-upraised, with his thick eyebrows darkening in a frown, he stood regarding the Cavalier with a look that was meant to rend his inmost heart.

"What means this outcry in the presence of the dead?" exclaimed Adrian in a determined tone—"Let our past disputes be forgotten, old man, in this terrible hour. See you not, my father lies stark and dead?"

"Murdered by *thee*, vile parricide!"—rang out the voice of the Signior Aldarin, as, with a determined step, he advanced to the bedside—"Ho! Guards, I say"—he shouted, raising his voice—"Vassals of Albarone, to the rescue!"

The eye of the young Cavalier brightened, his brow was knit, and his form erected to its full height as he spoke, in a quiet, determined tone.

"Look ye, old man, thou mayst taunt and gibe with thy magpie tongue, as long as the humor pleases thee. My father's brother need fear no wrong from me—this maiden's father can fear no harm from Adrian Di Albarone. Heap taunt on taunt, good Signior, but see that this spirit of insult is not carried into action. I am lord in the castle of my fathers!"

"Father, what mean those wild words, these looks of anger?" shrieked the Ladye Annabel, as she awoke from her swoon of terror, and, supported by the arm of Adrian, glanced round the scene—"Surely, my father, you speak not aught against Lord Adrian?"

And as she spoke, the chamber was filled with men-at-arms, in their glittering armor, and servitors of Albarone, all attired in the livery of the house, who came thronging into the apartment, and circled round the scene, while their mouths were agape, and their eyes protruding with astonishment.

Aldarin glanced around the throng, he marked each stalwart man-at-arms, each strong-limbed yeoman of the guard, and then his chest heaved and his eye flashed as he shouted—

"Seize him, men of Albarone, *seize the murderer of your lord!*"

He pointed to Adrian Di Albarone as he spoke. There was one wild thrill of terror and amazement, spreading through the group, a confused murmur, bursting involuntarily from every lip, and then all was still as death.

Not a man stirred, not a servitor moved, but all remained like statues, clustering round the group in their centre, where Aldarin stood with his slender form raised to its full stature, his arm outstretched and his eye flashing like a flame-coal, while Adrian gathered the Ladye Annabel in his good right arm, and gazed upon the Signor with a look of concentrated scorn.

"Seize him, guards"—again shouted Aldarin—"seize the Parricide!"

There was the sound of a heavy footstep, and the form of the stout yeoman emerged from the group.

"Not quite so fast—marry, my good Signor, not quite so fast"—he cried as he advanced. "By St. Withold, I have followed my old lord to many a hard-fought fight, I have served him by night and by day, with hand and heart, for a score of long years. Shall I stand by, and see his brave son suffer wrong?"

"What means this wild uproar?" exclaimed a calm yet half-indignant voice, as the stately dame of the Lord Di Albarone, yet unaware of her bereavement, crossed the threshold with a lofty step and an extended arm, advancing, with the port of a queen, to the centre of the group. "Vassals—what means this wild uproar? Know ye not that your lord lies deadly sick? Brother Aldarin, I take it ill of you to suffer the clamor! What can our liege of Florence think of ye, vassals, when he beholds ye thus assail the sick-chamber of your lord with noise and outcry!"

The stately dame pointed to a richly attired cavalier, who had followed her into the apartment. He was a well-formed man, with a face marked by no definite expression. His dark hair gathered, in short, stiff curls around a low and unmeaning forehead; his small dark eyes, protruding from his head, seemed to be trying their utmost to outstrip his faintly delineated eyebrows; the nose, neither aquiline, classic, or Judaic, seemed composed of all the varieties of nasal organ; his upper lip was garnished with a portion of the wiry beard that flourished on his prominent chin; his lips were thick and sensual, while his entire face was as inexpressive as might be. The throng bowed low, as they became aware of the presence of the guest of their late lord. They bowed to the Duke of Florence.

"Adrian, my son," cried the Lady of Albarone, turning to her son in utter amazement, "what means this scene of confusion and alarm?"

Adrian took his mother by the hand, and led her to the couch. He spoke not a word, but waved his hand toward the couch. Her form was concealed for a moment amid the hangings of the bed, and then a shriek of wild emphasis startled the ears of the bystanders.

"He is dead," exclaimed the Lady of Albarone, in a voice of unnatural calmness, as she again appeared from amid the hangings of the bed, with a face ghastly and livid as the face of death. "Vassals of Albarone, your lord is dead!"

There was a cry of horror echoing through the chamber, and the Lady of Albarone sank, leaning for support upon the arm of her son, while Annabel, in the intervals of her own sobs and sighs, whispered hurried words of consolation in her ear.

Aldarin stood regarding the group with a glance of deep and searching meaning. He gazed upon the vacant features of the Duke, distended by surprise, the countenance of Adrian, marked by a settled frown of indignation, the visage of the Countess, livid as death; and then the fair face of his daughter Annabel, her eyes swimming in tears, the parted lips and the cheek pale and flushed by turns, met the glance of Aldarin, and a strange expression trembled on his compressed lip, and darkened over his high forehead.

"Lady of Albarone," exclaimed the Scholar, advancing,—"Lady of Albarone, my brother died not through the course of nature, he died not by the hand of disease—he was murdered!"

"Murdered!" repeated the Countess with a hollow echo.

And the Duke took up the word, echoing, with a trembling voice, that word of fear, "murdered," while the Servitors of Albarone sent the cry shrieking around the nooks and corners of the Red Chamber.

Adrian of Albarone looked around the scene and smiled as if in scorn, but said not a word.

Aldarin made one stride to the couch of death.

"Behold the corse," he shrieked; "behold the blackened face, the sunken eyelids and the livid lips; behold the ghastly remains of the Lord of Albarone!"

Another stride, and he reached the beaufet. He seized the goblet of gold, and held it aloft.

"Behold," he cried, "behold the instrument of his murder!"

"God save me now," shrieked the Countess.—"There has been foul work here—Adrian—oh, Adrian, thy sire hath been poisoned!"

"This is some new mysterie, Sir Scholar," exclaimed Adrian, with a look of scorn.

The Lady fell insensible, and the goblet rung with a clanging sound upon the marble floor, while from its depths there rolled a small compact substance, encrusted in some chemical compound, white as snow in hue.

The Duke of Florence stooped hurriedly to the very floor, and seized both the goblet and the encrusted substance, with an eager grasp.

"Ha! There is a white sediment deposited at the bottom of this goblet. Albertine, advance; thou art skilled in such mysteries. Tell me, Sir Monk, the nature of this white powder."

The Monk Albertine, whose dark eyes had for a moment been gleaming over the shoulders of the bystanders, now advanced with a slow and measured footstep, and confronted the Signor Aldarin, with a look full of meaning and thought. Aldarin returned the look, with a keen and searching glance, and their eyes then mingled in one long and ardent gaze, as though each man wished to read the heart of his fellow.

With a look of calmness and perfect self-possession, Albertine turned to the Duke and took the goblet from his hand.

He gazed at its depths for a moment; he was about to speak, when the heart of every man in the Red Chamber was thrilled by a wild and terrific howl, more fearful even than the yell of the dying, which proceeded from among the curtains of the death-couch, and echoed around the apartment.

"That sound," exclaimed Aldarin, with a nervous start—"That sound is from the couch of death! It means, it means—"

A ruddy glow passed over his pale countenance, and, suddenly pausing, he gazed round the group in silence.

"It is the poor hound of our good Lord;" muttered Robin the Rough, advancing. "The hound, with skin black as death, which Lord Julian brought from Palestine—he is howling over the dead corse of his master. So have I heard him howl for three days past, as the castle-bell tolled the hour of high noon, beside the panels of yonder door. Come hither, brute; come hither, Saladin."

The hound, black as night, with an eye like fire, came leaping through the throng, and crouched, whining, at the feet of the stout yeoman.

It was, in sooth, a noble hound, with full chest, slender limbs, long neck, and tapering body, marked by all that delicacy of proportion, that beauty of shape, and grace of motion, which tradition ascribes to the bloodhounds of the Eastern lands. The head was like the head of a snake, while the eye seemed almost instinct with a human soul.

"Sir Monk," cried the Duke, in an imperious tone, "were it not better for thee to tell us at once whether the white powder in the goblet is poison? or shall we wait thy pleasure while thou dost weary thine eyes with gazing at yonder hound?"

The monk Albertine made a solemn inclination of his head, and kneeling on the marble floor in the centre of the group, he struck the edge of the goblet upon the tesselated stone with a quick and sudden motion of his hand.

The diamond-shaped stone of black marble was strewn with the white sediment deposited in the bottom of the goblet.

The hound sprang forward, and while his wild eyes flashed and blazed, his nostrils dilated, and the sable animal snuffed the atmosphere of the Red Chamber, as he leaped quickly around the group.

"He snuffs the smell of human blood!" muttered the stout yeoman.

And while all was intense interest and suspense, while a mingled feeling of surprise and terror and nameless fear ran around the group, while every eye was fixed upon the kneeling form of Albertine, with the goblet upraised in his hand, the hound Saladin passed from man to man, scenting the garments of the bystanders, and glancing wildly from face to face, from eye to eye.

He paused for a moment in front of the Signor Aldarin, and uttered a low whining sound as he gazed in the scholar's face.

"How long is this mummery to last?" exclaimed Aldarin, advancing with a sudden step—"Tell me, Sir Monk, is thy study over?"

The hound Saladin sprang suddenly aside from the robes of the Signor, and eagerly snuffing the marble floor, approached the monk Albertine, and with a moaning sound licked the white substance from the diamond-shaped stone.

"Is it poison?" asked the Duke, and the interest of the group clustered around became absorbing and intense.

"Some new mysterie of thine, learned scholar!" exclaimed Adrian Di Albarone, with a smile of incredulity. "The man does not live, so false in heart as to place a death-bowl to the lips of a warrior like Julian of Albarone!"

"Is it poison!" exclaimed Albertine, gazing round upon the group— "Behold!"

And as he spoke, the hound Saladin fell stiffened and dead, upon the marble pavement, with a single fearful struggle, a single terrible howl.—His limbs were fearfully distorted, and his eyes were starting from their sockets, while a thin white foam hung round his serpent-like jaw.

A confused cry of horror thundered around the apartment, and then you might have heard the footsteps of the Invisible Death, all was so fearfully silent and still.

"As God lives, my father has been murdered!" shouted Adrian Di Albarone, as the expression of incredulity lately visible in his manly face changed to a look of pallid horror—"Now, by the Sacrament of God, he shall be avenged as never was murdered man avenged before! Who," he shrieked in a husky voice, turning to the throng—"Who hath done this murder?"

"Sir Duke," exclaimed Aldarin, as though he had not heard Adrian, "the encrusted substance which fell from the death-bowl may be poisonous—"

The small white ball, which the Duke had absently clenched in his fingers, fell to the floor, and every ear heard a ringing sound as it fell, and every eye beheld the fragments splintering as it touched the floor. The whole substance had vanished, and along the floor there rolled a massive signet ring, glittering with a single ruby.

The Duke of Florence stooped hastily and again grasped the ring; he held it aloft, and shouted, in a tone of amazement and horror—

"It is the ring of the murderer, dropped by accident into the death-bowl! It bears a crest and an inscription—look, Signor Aldarin—canst make out crest or inscription?"

Aldarin replied with a look of horror—

"The crest, 'tis a Winged Leopard—the motto—'*Grasp boldly, and bravely strike!*' Both crest and motto are those of Albarone"—his voice sank to a death-like whisper—"Lord Adrian—behold—*it is, it is the signet-ring of Albarone!*"

Aldarin turned with a voice of fierce emphasis—

"Thy question has its answer—let the signet-ring tell the tale. Adrian, oh, Adrian," he continued, as his voice changed with mingled compassion and anguish—"what moved thee to this fearful deed? Oh, that I, a weak old man, should live to see my brother's son accused of that brother's murder!"

"This is some damning plot!" calmly responded Adrian, though his chest heaved and swelled with the tempest aroused in his soul—"Tell me, Signor Aldarin, what were the contents of the 'soothing' potion administered by thee to the late Lord Julian at daybreak?"

"Tell me, good Albertine, thou didst aid in its composition, and thou canst witness when I gave it to my murdered brother."

"I aided in its composition—it was harmless—I saw thee minister the potion to Lord Julian."

"Thou alone, Aldarin, thou alone hast had access to this chamber since daybreak"—spoke Adrian, with his calm eye fixed full on the Signor's visage—"Now tell me who it was that drugged yon bowl with death?"

"Balvardo, thou didst stand sentinel at yon door from daybreak until high noon—did a soul enter the Red Chamber from the first moment to the last second of thy watch?"

"Not a living man"—muttered the hoarse voice of Balvardo from the crowd—"not a soul save the Ladye Annabel."

"Search the apartment!" shouted the Duke; "the assassin may be yet lurking in some dark nook or corner!"

The doors were closed, the search commenced. Every nook was ransacked, every corner thrown open to the light, not even the bed of death, with its pillows of down and its hangings of purple, was spared.

While the search was in progress, the Countess of Albarone awoke from her swoon, and striding from the recess of an emblazoned window, where the Ladye Annabel remained glancing with a vacant look over the strange scene progressing in the Red Chamber, she was soon made aware of the fearful crime charged upon her son, the signet-ring and the terrible mystery.

"There is mystery," she cried with a proud voice, "there is mystery, but—no dishonor!—Who can believe Adrian Di Albarone guilty of so accursed an act!"

"For one, I do not!" bluntly cried the stout yeoman.

"Nor I!" cried one of the servitors; and the cry went round the apartment,—

"Nor I"—"Nor I"—"He is guiltless."

A shrill and prolonged shriek, echoing from a nook of the Red Chamber near the death-couch, sent a sudden thrill through the group assembled in this terrible mystery.

Every form wheeled suddenly round, every eye was fixed in the direction from whence issued the shriek, and the aged Steward of the Castle was seen, upholding with one trembling hand the folds of the gorgeous crimson tapestry, while his aged face grew livid as death, as he pointed with the other hand to a dark recess.

"A secret passage—the door cut into the solid wall is flung wide open—a robe laid across the threshold—a robe of crimson faced with gold."

And as he spoke he flung the hangings yet farther aside, and the bright sunshine gleamed over the panel of the secret door, flung wide open; the crimson robe was thrown over the threshold, but no beam lighted up the gloom of the passage beyond.

The Lady of Albarone rushed hurriedly forward, she seized the robe, she held it aloft in the sunbeams, and—*every eye beheld the robe of Adrian Di Albarone!*

"Adrian!" shrieked the Countess, "Adrian of Albarone—yonder secret passage leads to thy sleeping chamber—thy departed sire, myself and thou, alone were aware of its existence. It has ever been a secret of our house. Tell me, by yon murdered corse, I implore thee, tell me who flung this door open, who laid thy robe across the threshold?"

Adrian passed his hand wildly over his forehead, and with a cry of horror fell insensible upon the floor.

CHAPTER THE THIRD.

THE EMBRACE OF A BROTHER.

THE sun was setting, calmly and solemnly setting, behind a gorgeous pile of rainbow-hued clouds, magnificent with airy castle and pinnacle, while the full warmth of his beams shone through the arching window of the Red Chamber, its casement panels thrown wide open, filling that place of death with light and splendor.

In the recess of the lofty casement, with the sunshine falling all around, and the shadow of her slender figure thrown like a belt of gloom over the mosaic floor, stood the Ladye Annabel, silent and motionless; her rounded arms half raised, with the slender hands crossed over her bosom, her robe of pale blue velvet, with the inner vest of undimmed white made radiant by the sunbeams; while, swept aside from her features, the golden hair fell with a floating motion down over her shoulders, and along the breast of snow.

And as she stood thus still and immovable, gazing with one unvarying glance along the courtyard, the sunshine revealed her face of beauty, every lineament and feature disclosed in the golden light, seeming more like the face of a dream-spirit, than the countenance of a mortal maiden. The soul shone from her face. The eyes full, large, and lustrous with their undimmed blue, dilating and enlarging with one wild glance; the cheek white as alabaster, yet tinted by the bloom, and swelled with the fullness of the budding rose; the lips small, and curvingly shaped, slightly parted, revealing a glimpse of the ivory teeth; the chin, with its dimple; the brow, with its clear surface, marked by the parted hair, waving aside like clustered sunbeams—such was the face of the Ladye Annabel, all vision, all loveliness, and soul.

"He is bound; yes, bound with the cord and thong! They gather around him with looks of insult; they place him on the steed; they move—oh, mother of Heaven!—they move toward the castle gate! And shall I never see him again—never, never? It is a dream; it is no reality. It is a dream! Was it a dream, yesterday, when he stood in this recess, his hand clasped in mine, his eyes calm and eloquent, gazing in mine, while his voice spoke of the sunset glories of the summer sky?"

One long, wild glance at the scene in the courtyard, and then veiling her eyes from the sight, she started wildly from the window.

"It is a dream," murmured the Ladye Annabel, as she hurriedly glided from the room, and the echoes returned her whisper. "It is, it is a dream!"

Her footsteps had scarce ceased to echo along the ante-chamber, when another footstep was heard, and ere a moment passed, Aldarin stood in the recess of the lofty window of the Red Chamber. His face was agitated by strange and varying expressions, as with a keen and anxious eye he glanced over the spears and pennons of along line of men-at-arms, passing under the raised portcullis of the castle gate.

The portcullis was lowered with a thundering clang, the spears and pennons, the gallant steeds and their stalwart riders, were lost to sight, but presently came bursting into view again, beyond the castle gate, where the highway to Florence, appearing from amid surrounding woods, led up a steep and precipitous hill. And there, flashing with gold and glowing with embroidery, the broad banner of the Duke of Florence was borne in the van of the cavalcade. Then came four men-at-arms, in armor of blazing gold; and then, distinguished by his rich array, rode the Duke, mounted upon a snow-white charger, and behind him, environed by guards, his arms lashed behind his back, came Lord Adrian Di Albarone, accused of the most foul and atrocious murder of his sire. Beside her son, her face closely veiled, and her form bowed low, the Countess rode; and in the rear, their steeds gaily prancing, their spears flashing, and their pennons glancing in the sun, came the men-at-arms in long and gallant array.

With parted lips and strained eyes did Signior Aldarin watch the movements of this company.

As the steed of the last man-at-arms was lost in the shades of the forest, Aldarin smiled grimly, and, extended his shrivelled hand, shouted in tones of exultation:

"One hour ago, I was the stooping scholar,—The *Signior* Aldarin. *Now!*" full boldly did he swell that little word; "Now, I am the *Count Aldarin Di Albarone*, lord of the wide domains of Albarone!"

He laughed the short, husky laugh which was peculiar to him.

"Adrian swept from my path—and is he not already swept from my path?—that brainless idiot, *my liege* of Florence, swallowed the charge against that forward boy as greedily as the fish swallows the tempting bait; the signet and the robe will bring the changeling to the block, and thus, my only obstacle swept away, I, as next heir, succeed to the titles and estates of Albarone! And Annabel, my fair daughter! thy brow shall be decked with a coronet; thou shall reign Duchess of Florence! Ha—ha!"

And here, as the wide prospect of ambition opened to his mind's eye, he became silent, and, hurriedly pacing the floor, resigned his soul to the dreams of his excited fancy.

Suddenly his visions were interrupted by a deep sigh, that seemed to proceed from the corse upon the couch.

Aldarin started, and for a moment stood still as a statue, his ear inclined toward the couch, as if intently listening; his lips apart, and his quivering hands stretched forth as though he would defend himself from some unreal foe.

At last, gaining courage, he approached the bed. There, without the slightest signs of animation, lay the faded form of the gallant warrior; the eyes closed, the stern expression of the features vanished, and the whole attitude that of unconscious repose.

Turning away, Aldarin was chiding himself for his childish terror, when a deep, sonorous groan met his ear. With a swelling heart he once more turned, and beheld a sight that caused the cold sweat of intense terror to ooze from his person, and every nerve to quake with alarm.

The eyes of the Count were wide open; a slight flush pervaded his cheeks, and his entire attitude was changed. A voice came from his pallid lips:

"Annabel, dearest Annabel! a fearful dream but now possessed my fancy! Methought I lay dead—dead, Annabel, dead; and that I died ere thy nuptials were solemnized—thy nuptials, Annabel, and thine Adrian!"

A fearful expression came over the scholar Aldarin's features, as though he was stringing his mind to one great effort. In an instant his countenance became calm again, and approaching the bedside, he enquired, in a soft voice, if his dear brother wanted anything?

The Count answered hurriedly, as if a sudden light burst upon him:

"Ah! the Virgin save us! good Aldarin, art thou here? Surely, I saw Adrian and Annabel but a moment since? Surely—"

"Nay, my brother;" answered Aldarin, "'twas but mere phantasy. Annabel is not with us, nor is my Lord Adrian here; but I, dear brother, I am by your side."

Speaking these words in a voice tremulous with affection, Signior Aldarin passed his left arm around the body of the Count, while the other enclosed his neck. He clasped him in an ardent embrace, as he continued:

"I am with you, dear brother; I will minister to your slightest wish; I, Aldarin, your own devoted friend."

Here he inserted his right hand beneath the long gray locks of the Count, and clasping his neck, pressed him yet closer to his bosom.

"Kind Aldarin," the Count began, but the sentence was cut short by a piercing cry, and the right hand of Aldarin clutched tighter and tighter around his brother's throat.

"Nay, brother, thou shalt have rest, an' thou wishest it," cried Signor Aldarin. "There, sleep softly, and pleasant dreams attend you!"

The Count fell heavily upon the bed; his blood-shot eyes protruded from his blackened face, a livid circle was around his throat, and a thin line of blood trickled from his mouth. A sigh, heavy, deep, and prolonged came from his chest, and the murdered man ceased to live.

"The fiend be thanked!—it is *done!*"

Having thus spoken, in a voice that came through his clenched teeth, the murderer looked up and saw—the dogged, rough, yet honest visage of the stout yeoman peeping from among the curtains on the opposite side of the bed, his eyes steadily fixed on the corse, and a curious look of inquiry visible in every feature of his face.

The Signior drew back, trembling in every limb, and pale as death. It was a moment ere he recovered his speech, when, assuming a haughty air, he exclaimed:

"Slave, what do you here? Is it thus you intrude upon my privacy? Speak, sir—your excuse!"

The stout yeoman replied in his usual manners speaking in the Italian, but with a sharp English accent:

"Why, most worshipful Signior, you will please to bear in mind that for twenty long years have I followed my lord, he who now lies cold and senseless, to the wars. That withered arm have I seen bearing down upon the foe in the thickest of the fight; that sunken eye have I beheld glance with the stern look of command. By his side have I fought and bled; for him did I leave my own native land—merrie, merrie England,—and I will say, a more generous, true-hearted, and valiant knight, never wore spurs, or broke a lance, than my lord, the noble Count Julian Di Albarone."

The yeoman passed the sleeve of his blue doublet across his eyes.

"Well sirrah," cried the Signior, "to what tends all this?"

"Marry, to this does it tend: that wishing to behold that noble face yet once more, I stole silently to this chamber, thinking to be a little while alone with my brave lord. I did not discover your presence, till I looked through the curtains and saw—"

The stout Englishman suddenly stopped; there was a curious twitch in his left eye, and a grim smile upon his lip.

"Saw what, sirrah?" hurriedly asked the scholar Aldarin.

"Marry, I saw thee, worshipful Signior, in the act of embracing the Count; and such a warm, kind, brotherly embrace as it was! By St. Withold! it did me more good than a hundred of Father Antonio's homilies—by my faith, it did!"

The thin visage of Aldarin became white as snow and red as crimson by turns. Making an effort to conceal his agitation, he replied:

"Well, well, Robin, thou art a good fellow after all, though, to be sure, thy manners are somewhat rough. I tell thee, brave yeoman, I have long had it in my mind to advance thy condition. Follow me to the Round Room, good Robin, where I will speak further to thee of this matter."

"*The Round Room!*" murmured Robin, as he followed the scholar Aldarin from the Red Chamber. "Ha! 'tis the secret chamber o' th' scholar; many, many have been seen entering its confines—never a single man has been seen emerging from its narrow door, save the scholar Aldarin! I'll beware the serpent's pangs! I'll drink no goblets o' wine, touch no food or dainty viands while in this Round Room; or else, by St. Withold, Rough Robin's place may be vacant in the hall, forever and a day!"

With these thoughts traversing his mind, the yeoman followed the scholar over the floor of the ante-chamber, and as they entered the confines of a gloomy corridor, a spectacle was visible, which, to say the least, was marked by curious and singular features.

Imagine the solemn scholar striding slowly along the corridor with measured and gliding footsteps, while behind him walks Robin the Rough, describing various eccentric figures in the air with his clenched hands; now brandishing them above the Signior's head, now exhibiting a remarkable display of muscular vigor at the very back of Aldarin; and again, making a pass with all his strength apparently at the body of the alchemist, but in reality at the intangible atmosphere. These demonstrations did not appear to give the stout yeoman much pain, for his cheeks were very much agitated, and from his eyes were rolling thick, large tears of laughter.

The corridor terminated in a long, dark gallery hung with pictures colored by age, and framed in massive oak. Traversing this gallery, they ascended a staircase of stone, and passing along another corridor, terminated by a winding staircase. This, the scholar and the yeoman descended, and then came another gallery, another ascending stairway, and then various labyrinthine passages traversed, Rough Robin at last found himself standing side by side with Aldarin, in front of the dark panels of the narrow door leading into the Round Room.

This room was scarce ever visited by any living being in the castle save Aldarin, and strange legends concerning its mysterious secrets were current among the servitors of Albarone.

Many had been seen entering its confines with the Signior, but never was any one, save Aldarin, seen to emerge from its gloomy door.

CHAPTER THE FOURTH.

THE DEATH-TRAP.

ROBIN THE ROUGH IS ADVANCED TO HONOR, WHILE THE SKELETON-GOD LAUGHS OVER HIS SHOULDER.

THE door flew suddenly open, and Robin, gazing around, found himself standing in a small room, circular in form, with an arched ceiling, and floor of stone. The walls were lined with shelves, piled with massive books, clasped by fastenings of silver and of gold, thrown among scrolls of parchment, richly illuminated, and emblazoned with strange figures, relieving pictures of dark and hidden meaning.

The apartment having no casement, light was supplied by a small lamp of curious workmanship, depending from the arched ceiling, and diffusing its intense and radiant beams all around the place, making the lonely room as bright as though the noonday sun shone over its shelves and walls.

Around the chamber were scattered strange instruments pertaining to the science of astrology or mysteries of alchemy; here richly emblazoned parchments, inscribed with curious characters, glittered in the light; and yonder, the ghastly skull, with its hideous grin of mockery, was strown along the floor, mingled with the bones of the human skeleton, the last fragments of the tenement of the living soul.

While Robin's eyes distended in wonder, as he hastily glanced around the room, he stumbled and fell against an object reared in the centre of the floor.

"The foul fiend take thee, slave!" shouted Aldarin, as, with his extended arms, he stayed the soldier in his fall. "Wouldst thou destroy the labor of thrice seven long years? Wouldst thou destroy a Mighty Thought? Stand aside from the altar, and come not near it again, or by the body of * * *, I will brain thee with this dagger! Thou slave!" he shrieked, in tones of wild indignation, as his blazing eye was fixed upon the face of the yeoman, who stood confused and silent, "for what dost thou suppose I have watched yon beechen flame, by day and night, for twenty-one long years? For what have I wasted the youth and the vigor of my days before yon altar? Was it to have my labor, the mighty thought, for which I have dared what mortal never dared before, destroyed by thy clumsy carcass? Dost think so, slave?"

Rough Robin murmured an excuse for his awkwardness, and, while the Signior's features subsided into their usual deep and solemn expression, he again gazed around the room.

From the centre of the oaken floor arose a small altar, built of snow-white marble, with a light blue flame arising from a vessel of gold on its surface: the fire sweeping along the sides of an alembic, suspended over the altar by four chains, attached to as many rods of gold placed at each corner of the structure.

There was something so strange and solemn in the entire aspect of the place—the light blue flame arising in tongues of fire from the vessel of gold on the snow-white altar, burning for ever beneath the hanging alembic, the chains and rods of gold, the pure and undimmed white of the marble, varied by no sculpturing or ornament, combined with the utter stillness and solitude of the room—that Robin felt awed, he scarce knew why; and dark forebodings crept like shadows over his brain.

The scholar seated himself upon a small stool placed near the other, and pointing to another, in a mild voice, desired Robin to follow his example. The yeoman hesitated.

"It is not meet for a poor yeoman o' th' Guard to rest himself in the presence of so great a scholar."

"Nay, nay, good Robin, rest thyself. I was angered with thee a moment hence, but now it is all past. Seat thyself, brave yeoman."

The soldier complied, and rested his stout person upon a stool of oak, placed some six feet from the spot where sat the Signior Aldarin. Robin had but time to note a singular circumstance, ere the scholar spoke. *The stool upon which the stout yeoman sat, was firmly jointed in a large slab of red stone, which, spreading before him for the space of some six feet, was curiously fixed in the planks of the oaken floor.*

With a mild and smiling look, the scholar spoke:—

"Robin, thou hast been a true and faithful vassal to my late brother. Thou didst right carefully attend Lord Julian, when forced by the incurable wound of a poisoned arrow, some three months since, he returned from Palestine, leaving Sir Geoffrey o' th' Long-sword, at the head of his men-at-arms. Robin, I have long designed to testify the good opinion in which I hold thee by some substantial gift—thou shall be Seneschal of this mighty castle of Albarone!"

"Marry, good Signior—"

"How, sir!—dost thou address *me* as Signior? Vassal, I am the Lord of Albarone!"

"But Adrian—"

"What sayest thou of Adrian? A murderer—a parricide—his death is certain. The Duke of Florence hath sworn it."

"Well, my Lord Count, then, an' it pleases you better, I was about to say that if I had my choice I would sooner be made an esquire."

"This thou shalt be:—first promise to serve me faithfully in all that I shall command."

"Well, as far as an honest man may, so far do I promise."

The scholar Aldarin mused a moment and then said carelessly—"Was it not an exceeding wicked deed, this murder of my good brother?"

"Aye, marry was it," replied Robin, looking fixedly at Aldarin—"and the fiend of hell, himself, could not have done a more damned, or a more accursed thing."

"True good Robin,—'twas a horrid murder. What could have prompted Adrian to raise his hand against his father, eh? good Robin?"

The Yeoman did not reply. He cast his eyes to the floor and confusedly fingered his cap.

The Count Aldarin—so must I style him—reached a folded parchment from a writing desk and then asked—

"Why dost thou not speak, good Robin? What art thinking of?"

"Why, heaven save your *lordship*," said Robin, speaking in a whisper, and gazing full in Aldarin's face, "*I was just wondering whether the murderer embraced the Count ere he strangled him?*"

Aldarin started aside—his features were writhen into a fearful contortion, and his whole frame shook like a leaf of the aspen tree. Again he turned his visage, it was calm, as the face of innocence, and a smile was on his pinched lip.

"Receive thy warrant as Seneschal of the Castle of Albarone," said Aldarin, as he held forth the parchment—"nay, kneel not, good Robin; keep thy seat."

Robin held forth his hand to reach the parchment—his fingers touched it, when Aldarin stamped his foot upon the floor, and the slab of red stone fell quick as lightning beneath the yeoman. A deep and dark well was discovered. In an instant the stool affixed to the stone was empty, and far below, in the depths of the pit the echo of the falling slab, sunk with a sound like the rushing of the winter wind through the corridors of a deserted mansion.

A face, with eyes rolling ghastly, with the lower jaw sunken and the tongue protruding from the mouth, appeared above the side of the cavity, at the very feet of Aldarin, and a muscular hand convulsively clutched the oaken plank, while the body of the stout Yeoman, was seen through the darkness of the pit, as he clung with the grasp of despair, to the floor of the room.

"Devil—" shouted the desperate soldier, as he made a convulsive effort to lighten the grasp of his hand on the smooth plank. "I'll foil thee yet. 'Tis not the fate of an honest man to die thus! My doom—"

"Is DEATH!" shrieked the scholar, and drawing the glittering dagger from his robe, he smote the fingers of the Yeoman, with its unerring steel. The joints of the hand were severed.

The grasp of the soldier failed, he gave one dying look, and then far, far down in the pit, a whizzing noise like the sound of a falling body was heard, and as it grew fainter and fainter did Aldarin stand in attitude of listening, gazing down into the shadow void, his arms outstretched, his eyes wildly glaring, his lips apart, and every lineament of his face expressive of triumph, mingled with hate and scorn.

A wild, maniac laugh came from the murder's lips:

"Ha—ha—ha! caitiff and slave! Thou hast met thy fate. The scholar hath enemies, but—ha—ha!—they all *disappear*!"

Again he cast his eyes into the well. All was still as death. A single look into the dark cavity, and, with his bitter smile, Aldarin pictured the mangled corse of the yeoman, lying in bloody fragments, strewn over the vaults of the castle, amid the corses of the unburied dead.

He stamped his foot on the floor, and the red slab, bearing the empty stool, slowly arose on its hinges, and was again fixed in the oaken planks.

"Silent forever, prying fool! My secret is safe. Thou shalt no more prate of a certain *warm* embrace. Nay, nay; now for my schemes. I must send on to Florence fresh proofs of Adrian's guilt: witnesses, and so on, and so on. That matter arranged, then comes the marriage of Annabel and the Duke. Ha—ha! Let me think."

Here he fell into a musing fit, and having newly fed the beechen flame upon the altar of marble, he approached a point of the Round Room, where a small knob of iron projected from the oaken floor.

Stamping upon the knob, a division of the shelving receded, and a portion of the wall, leaving an open space, while a passage was disclosed into a secret chamber, beyond the Round Room.

A door of dark and solid wood, painted in imitation of the walls of the Round Room, had been made in an aperture of the wall, with shelving placed on its panels, and every sign or mark of the existence of such a door, carefully and effectually erased. It bore a complete resemblance to the other parts of the walls, and no one, save Aldarin, could have dreamed of its existence. The small knob in the oaken floor, communicated with a spring, and the secret door rolled into the adjoining room on grooves fixed in the floor.

Aldarin stepped through the secret passage, the door rolled back, and the Round Room was left to the silent flame and the grinning skull.

CHAPTER THE FIFTH.

THE CHAMBER OF MYSTERIES.

FEAR * * * AND GIVE GLORY TO HIM, FOR THE HOUR OF HIS
JUDGMENT IS COME—THE SMOKE OF THEIR TORMENT
ASCENDETH UP FOR EVER AND EVER.—*The Book.*

A CHAMBER with a low, dark ceiling, supported by massive rafters of oak;
floor and wall of dark stone, unrelieved by wainscot or plaster—bare, rugged
and destitute—in form, an oblong square, narrow in width, and extensive in
length, with the impression of a coffin-like gloom and confinement, resting
upon each dark stone and rugged rafter, while the air was insupportable with
the scent of decaying mortality.

In the centre arose a rough table of massive oak, with a smoking light,
burning in a vessel of iron, placed at each corner, flinging a dreary radiance
through the darkness of the chamber.

The light threw its red and murky beams over the fearful burden of the table.
It was piled with the unsightly forms of the dead. There were lifeless trunks,
all hewn and hacked; there were discolored faces, green with decay; with the
eyes scooped from the sockets, the livid skin dropping from the forehead,
the jaw torn from its socket, and the brain, once the resting place of the
mighty soul, protruding in all its discoloration and corruption over the bared
brow; there were arms and limbs torn from the body, some yet wearing the
hue of life, others rendered hideous and disgusting by the revel of the worm;
there, in that lone room were piled up all these ghastly remains of humanity,
these fearful mockeries of life, there rotting relics of what had once
enthroned the GIANT SOUL.

The form of a muscular man, with chest of iron, and arms of brass, lay on
the centre of the table, side by side with the figure of a fragile woman. The
scanty locks of gray hair surmounted the half peeled forehead of the warrior,
while the copious tresses of the woman drooped over the white cheek, the
alabaster neck, and fell twining over the bosom, yet untainted by decay.

"Here," cried Aldarin, with dilating eye—"Here, for twenty-one long years
have I toiled. The sun shone over the beauty of spring, the luxury of summer,
and yet I beheld him not. Autumn came with its decay, and winter with its
cold, and yet Aldarin went not forth. Toil, toil, toil, while youth died in my
veins, and age came wrinkling over my brow; toil, toil, toil, unceasing and
eternal toil.

"Julian went to war, his plume waved over the ranks of battle. Aldarin toiled on, over the carcasses of the dead. Others have made friends among the living, and won honor from the great—it was mine to build a home amid the corses of the unburied dead, and to wring knowledge, wild and terrible, it is true, yet mighty knowledge, from the grasp of death. Toil, toil, toil, but not forever. It will come at last—the glorious secret.

"A few more weary days, a few more dreary nights, and the corse will speak, the alembic will give fort was! h the secret. The future speaks two words that fill my heart with fire—*unbounded wealth*—IMMORTAL LIFE!"

He looked around with a blazing eye and extended arm—"They rise before me, the host of victims—ghastly with the dead hue, gory with blood they rise, they raise their hands, and shriek my name? And yet, it was to be, it was to be, and *it was*! And *he*, the last, the most dread and fearful sacrifice—oh, FIEND, wring not my heart with throes of intolerable torture nor point to yon wan and pallid form! I tell thee when the last secret shall have been wrung from the lips of Death, then, then, *he*, aye, *he* may, may——"

He paused, he drooped his head low on his breast, a scarcely audible murmur broke from his lips. Two phrases of doubtful purport might alone be heard——

"Live again—" and then the murmur—"mighty secret——from *his* body—"

Aldarin turned from his dread and mystic reveries, he seized the scalpel, he commenced the work of knowledge, among the carcasses of the dead. Long he labored, and eagerly he toiled, but at last, as the solemn hours of the night wore on, he slept and dreamed a dream. Prostrate among the bodies of the dead, his arms flung carelessly on either side over the torn and mangled faces, Aldarin slept and dreamed.

And this was the DREAM OF ALDARIN THE FRATRICIDE.

CHAPTER THE SIXTH.

THE DREAM OF THE DAMNED.

HE stood upon a lonely isle. His feet were tortured by the sensation of burning, he looked beneath in wonder, and discovered that he stood upon a rock of fire.

He looked around—he beheld an ocean of fire; as far as eye could see, nothing met his vision but the waves of crimson flame, undulating to and fro, with a gentle, yet solemn motion.

Had the waves arisen around him, in giant billows, or swept above in mountains of liquid flame, the dreamer would have rejoiced, his spirit would have joined in the tumult, his soul become the incarnation of the storm.

But that strange calmness of the waves, that quiet undulation, awed him, chilled him to the heart. He looked again over the shoreless sea, and saw with straining eyes a sight of woe—unutterable woe.

From the surface of every wave, from the waves breaking in spiral flames at his feet—afar and near, on every side—from the surface of every wave was thrust a discolored face, with burning eyes, that gleamed with a strange life, while the lips were colorless, the cheeks livid, and the brow green with decay. As the Dreamer looked, low, faint murmurs, unutterable sighs and sobs, broke on the air, and a hollow whisper, more like the echo of a thought than a sound, came to his ear—THESE ARE THE FACES OF THE DAMNED—every face you see, is the face of a *Lost-soul*—THESE ARE THE FACES OF THE DAMNED.

Aldarin turned from side to side with a horror he had never felt before. All around seemed turning to fire, fire in every shape and form, fire intangible and fire incarnate. Above, no sky with Sun of Glory gave light to that ocean of flame, with the faces of the damned, thrust from every billow. A roof of brass, vast and awful, and magnificent, arched over the waves of fire; it was heated to a burning heat, and the eye of Aldarin seemed turning to flame, as he looked upon the brazen sky.

The horizon of this fearful sky, was concealed by great clouds, rolling slowly on, and on, and on, over the waves of fire, far, far, from the isle where stood Aldarin.

And while the hollow murmur broke over the scene, and the whispering of subdued voices, and the sobs of soft voiced women, shrieking that unutterable wail, Aldarin felt the very air burn into his flesh hotter, and more torturing than the air of the simoon, he felt the rock beneath him turning molted fire, his feet were crumbling into fragments, while agony and intense pain, quivered along his veins, and the flame lapped up his blood. He burned, and yet—he burned not.

The air penetrated into his flesh, entered the pores, burning along his veins; he felt the fire at his very heart; he drank in the flame with every breath, and yet—he burned not.

No sooner did his feet crumble with the agonizing influence of the fire, than another portion of his frame, seemed renewing its life, his heart became young, and his brain flowed with healthy blood.

Again his feet renewed their flesh, and then, with a hollow voice, he shrieked, mingling in that unutterable wail of the damned, "I burn, I burn, my heart is on fire, my brain is turned to flame, and yet I am not consumed."

A sudden change in the shape of the islet on which he stood, attracted his attention. At first wide and extensive in form, it was now narrow and contracted. Every moment it grew smaller, and yet smaller, and the waves of fire came rolling wave after wave over its surface. Aldarin started with a new and strange horror. Terrible it was to stand on the rock of fire, his feet consuming, his brain on fire, his heart a flame; air, sky and ocean, all burning into his very soul, terrible, most terrible, but those hollow murmurs, those fearful whispers of the damned came breaking on his ear, speaking of mysteries, yet more terrible, in the VAST BEYOND.

The wretched man clung to the rock. Oh! God, how fearful was the first touch of the waves of molten flame; how the liquid fire ate into his flesh and corrupted his blood, as the spiral flames cresting, each wave came hissing and curling round his limbs!

The waves rose higher and higher; the bodies of the lost, offensive with decay, the loathsome, and worm-eaten came floating around Aldarin. He raised his hands, he pushed the ghastly carcasses aside, but still they came floating on, and on, throwing their crumbling arms around his neck and fixing their livid lips upon his burning cheek, in the kiss of the damned.

They hailed him—brother—with a hollow welcome, and as innumerable voices whispered forth the sound of awful welcome, Aldarin missed his footing on the rock, he felt his form changing with decay, he raised his hands in the effort to keep on the surface of the waves, and saw his fingers with the flesh dropping from the bones; he floated on the surface of the boundless sea, he became one of the damned.

Forever and forever lost.

They were floating on and on, the boundless legion of the lost, and with them floated Aldarin.

A strange distant sound burst on the ear, he heard it grow louder and louder, now it was like the roaring of a mighty ocean, now it was like the hissing of a thousand furnaces.

Floating on the waves of fire, crowded by legion of the lost, Aldarin turned with a feeling of intense awe, and murmured the question—"What means yon sound of terror—yon murmur of fear?"

"We are floating on and on, toward the Cataract of Hell—" was the hoarse murmur of the living corse floating by his side, and a million tongues, speaking from livid lips returned the echo—"On and on toward the Cataract of Hell!"

Aldarin was carried on without the power of resistance, with no object to stay his career, on and on, every moment nearing the fearful Cataract, whose omnipresent thunder now deafened his ears, and fell upon his very brain, like the awful echo of an unrelenting Judgment.

Then came a pause of strange unconsciousness, from which Aldarin presently awoke; and opening his eyes, gazed around.

He hung on the verge of a rock, a rock of melting bitumen, that burned his hands to masses of crisped and blackened flesh as he hung. The rock flung its projecting form over a gulf, to which the cataracts of earth might compare, as the rivulet to the vast ocean.

It seemed to Aldarin as though the universe, with all the boundless fields of space, was comprised in the sweep of that awful cataract with its rocks of bitumen and red-hot ore extending for miles and miles innumerable, on either side, with the waves of fire—each wave bearing its awful burden of a damned soul—surging and foaming over the edge of the precipice, while a hissing and crackling sound, like the noise of ten thousand forests, ravaged by flame, startled the very air of hell, and mingled with the shrieks of the ******.

Aldarin looked below.

God of Heaven, what a sight! A gulf, like the space occupied by a thousand worlds—deep, vast, immense, and yet perceptible to the eye—sunk beneath him, with its surface of fiery waves, all convulsed and foaming with innumerable whirlpools, all crimsoned by bubbles of flame, each whirlpool swallowing the millions of the lost, each bubble bearing on its surface the face of a soul, damned and damned forever. Forever and forever.

And as the lost were borne on by the waves and swallowed by the whirlpools, they raised their hands and cast their burning eyes to the brazen sky, and shrieked, with low and muttering voices, the eternal death-wail of the lost.

Over the cataract, shrieking and wailing, were precipitated the millions and ten thousand millions of living-dead; each one swelling that unutterable murmur as he fell, each soul yelling with a more intense horror as it sank into night and all around, innumerable echoes bursting from the rocks or bitumen and melting ore breaking from the very air gave back the shriek, the wail and murmur of the lost. Forever and forever lost.

And over this scene, awful and vast, towered a figure of ebony darkness; his blackened brow concealed in the clouds, his extended arms grasping the infinitude of the cataract, while his feet rested upon islands of bitumen far in the gulf below.

The eyes of the figure were fixed upon Aldarin, as he clung with the nervous grasp of despair, to the rock of melting bitumen, and their gaze curdled his heated blood.

Every moment he was losing his grasp, sliding and sliding from the rock, now his feet were loosened and hung dangling over the gulf.

There was no hope for him, he must fall—fall, and fall forever.

At this moment, when his burning hands clung to the rock, when his feet were dangling in the air, when his blood-shot eyes, protruding from their sockets, glared ghastily above, a new wonder attracted the gaze of Aldarin.

A stairway, built of white marble, wide, roomy, and secure, seemed to spring from the very rock to which he clung, and winding up from the cataract, encircled by white and rainbow-hued clouds, was lost in the distance, far, far above.

Aldarin beheld two figures slowly descending the stairway from the distance—the figure of a warrior and the form of a dark-eyed woman.

As they drew near and nearer, he felt a strange feeling of awe gathering round his heart.

He knew the figures, he knew them well.

Her face of beauty wore a smile, her dark eyes were brilliant as ever, brilliant as when first he wooed and won her in the wilds of Palestine. Yet there was blood upon her vestments near the heart; and *his* lip was spotted with one drop of thick red blood.

It was most fearful to see them thus calmly approach; it was most terrible to recognize every line of their features, every part of their vestments.

"This," muttered Aldarin, "this indeed, is Hell.—And yet he must call for aid, and call to the warrior and the woman. How the thought writhed like a serpent round his very heart!"

He was sliding from the rock, slowly, yet certainly sliding. Another moment and he would plunge below. There was but one hope. He might, by a desperate effort, drag his carcass along the pointed rock: by a single extension of his arm, his hand would grasp the lowest step of the stairway.

He prepared himself for the effort, his feet hung dangling below, it is true, and his body was gradually slipping, but he gathered all the strength of his living corse for that single effort.

Slowly he passed his hand along the rock of bitumen, clutching the red-hot masses of ore in the action, and with his heart all aflame, he supported his trembling carcass with the other hand, and passed the extended hand yet farther along the rock.

It wanted but a single inch, a little inch, and his hand would grasp the marble of the stairway. And, yet that inch he could not compass with the hand so nervously outstretched, all his strength had been expended in the effort, and there he hung trembling on the verge of the abyss, when had he but the additional vigor of a mere child, he might grasp the stairway—he might be saved.

Another and a desperate effort! His fingers touched the carved marble-work of the stair-way, but his strength was gone—he could not hold it in his grasp.

With an eye of horrible intensity he looked above him, ere he made the last effort. The figures stood before him on the second step of the stairway. The woman, beautiful and bright-eyed, smiled, and the stern warrior shared her smile.

"Thou, thou wilt save me Ilmerine—my wife, my love, thou wilt—drag—drag—my hand to thee, and I can reach the staircase."

She stooped, the beautiful woman, she reached forth a fair and lily hand, she grasped the blackened fingers of Aldarin.

"Thanks, beautiful Ilmerine. I have wronged thee, but—the SECRET—a little nearer—drag—drag my hand—a moment—and I will grasp the staircase—I will be saved."

She placed his fingers round a projecting ornament of the staircase, his grasp was tight and desperate.

"Ascend!" she cried in a sweet and soft-toned voice.

"Julian—oh, Julian—grasp this hand—aid me, oh Julian my brother!"

The figure of the Warrior slowly stooped and seized the other hand, and drawing it towards the staircase, wound the fingers round another piece of the carved work of the staircase.

"Ascend, Aldarin, brother of mine, ascend!" cried his deep toned and awful voice.

"Ascend, brother of mine, I would, but my strength fails—seize me, by the body, and drag me from this rock of terror—oh, seize me."

The Warrior seized Aldarin by the shoulder, and dragged him slowly along the rock, but the flesh he clenched, crumbled in his grasp. Aldarin again trembled over the verge of the abyss—the blow of a single straw, might suffice to hurl him into the world below.

"Julian my brother. Ilmerine my wife, save me—oh, save me!"

The woman, dark-haired and beautiful, stooped, she slowly unwound the fingers of Aldarin from the ornament of the staircase. And as she unwound finger after finger, she looked upon his horror-stricken face and smiled, and pointed to the red-wound near her heart. He returned her smile with a ghastly grimace, he looked to the Warrior, and tightened the grasp of his other hand.

"Thou Julian, wilt save me—thou wilt not unwind my fingers, thou wilt hurl this beautiful demon aside."

"Aldarin my brother!" said the Figure in a voice of awe, as kneeling on the lowest step of the staircase, he cast the glance of his full and burning eyes upon the livid visage of Aldarin, while for a moment he wound the folds of his robe yet closer around his warrior-form.—"Aldarin, my brother, I will save thee."

He smiled—Aldarin returned his smile.

"Reach me thy hand, Julian, thy hand, or I perish."

The Warrior slowly reached forth his hand, from beneath the folds of his cloak, he held it before the face of Aldarin, and the eyes of the doomed man saw that the fingers clenched a Goblet of Gold, that shone and glimmered thro' the air, like a beacon-fire of hell.

"Oh—FIEND—THE DEATH-BOWL!"

As these words shrieked from Aldarin's livid lips, he drew back from the maddening sight, with horror, he missed his hold, he slid from the rock—HE FELL.

A thousand fires burned before his eyes, ten thousand horrid sounds fell on his very brain, serpents loathsome and noxious crawled thro' his hair, all around, above and beneath was fire, waves of flame eating into his soul, sky of brass, burning his eyes from their sockets, all was fire and horror and death, and—still he fell.

And a hoarse hollow voice, rising above the murmurs of the damned, spoke forth the words—"*Forever and Forever*—" and all hell gave back the echo— "EVER, EVER, EVER!"

Still he fell! The whirlpool sucked him within its circles of flame, around and around he dashed, with the bodies of the living dead floating over him, with ghastly faces, upturned to his vision, with foul arms, clenching him in a loathsome embrace, around and around he dashed, joining in the low, deep murmur of the damned, and his heart gave back the murmur. This, This, is hell!

Suddenly all was dark. Aldarin heard no sound, no murmur of the lost. All was dark, all was still. He touched his brow, and was amazed to find it untortured by flame. Yet big beaded drops of sweat stood from his forehead, his frame was chilled, a feeling of unutterable AWE was upon him, he feared to stir. He had been dreaming. His dream was past, his consciousness gradually returned, he found himself reclining among the foul remnants of decay, amid the carcasses of the dead.

He drooped his head low on his bosom, his face rested on his knees, his arms were folded across his eyes, and there in that lone chamber, while the silent hours of the night wore on, with his own weird soul, communed ALDARIN THE FRATRICIDE.

CHAPTER THE SEVENTH.

THE CELL OF THE DOOMED.

THE DOOMSMAN.

"HE dies at daybreak—ha, ha, ha—he dies by the wheel."

And as he laughed, the man-at-arms, Hugo, let fall the end of his pike upon the dark pavement, and the sound echoed along the gloom of the gallery, like thunder, every arch repeating the echo, and every nook and corner of the obscure passage taking up the sound, until, an indistinct murmur swelled from all sides, and the voices of the Invisible seemed whispering from the old and blood-stained walls.

"He dies at daybreak! Right, Hugo—the Goblet and the Ring, sent him to the doomsman!"

"And I—I—the Doomsman will have his blood! How looked he, good Balvardo, when the sentence of the Duke rang thro' the hall—"Death, Death to the Parricide?" Quailed he or begged for mercy!"

"Quail? 'Slife I've seen the eye of the dying war-horse, when the poisoned arrow was in his heart, and the death-cry of his master in his ears, but the mad glare of his eye never thrilled me, like the deep glance of this—murderer! Blood of the Turk, his eye burned like a coal!"

"Tell me, tell me, how was the murder fixed upon him? Who laid it to his hands?"

"Blood o' th' Turk! Must thou know everything. Then go ask the gossips, at the corners of the streets, and hear them tell in frightened murmurs, how the Poisoned Bowl was found on the beaufet, how the Signet-Ring was found in the bowl, how the Robe was thrown over the secret threshold, and—ha, ha, how one Balvardo swore to certain words uttered by the—Parricide, wishes for the old lord's death, hopes of hot-brained youth, and mysterious whispers about that Ring, and—"

"How one Hugo—ha, ha,—swore to his guilt in like manner. Faith did I— how I met the young Lord, in the southern corridor about high noon, how he turned pale when I told him, with every mark of respect, be sure, that he had forgotten his crimson robe, and—"

"So ye gave him to the DOOMSMAN?" shrieked the executioner, as his thick-set hump-backed figure was disclosed in the solitary light, hanging from the ceiling of the gallery—"So ye gave him—Lord Adrian—to me, to the pincers and the knife, to the hot lead, and the wheel of torture! You are brave fellows—ha, ha, he dies at daybreak—and the Doomsman thanks ye!"

The two sentinels watching in the Gaol of Florence, besides the gloomy door of the Doomed Cell, started with a sudden thrill of fear, as they looked upon the distorted form, and hideous face, of the wretch who stood laughing and chattering before their eyes.

Balvardo drew his stout form to its full height, and bent the darkness of his beetle-brows, upon the deformed Doomsman, and Hugo, clad in armor of shining steel, like his comrade, started nervously aside, as his squinting eyes were fixed upon the distorted face, the wide mouth, opening with a hideous grin, the retreating brow and the large, vacant, yet flashing eyes, that marked the visage of the Executioner of Florence. A dress made of coarsest serge, hung rather than fitted around his deformed figure, while a long-bladed knife, with handle of unshapen bone, glittered in the belt of dark leather that girdled his body.

"Sir Doomsman, thou art merry—" growled Balvardo—"Choose other scenes for thy merry humor—this dark corridor, with shadows of gloom in the distance, and the flickering light of yon smoking cresset, making the old walls yet more gloomy, around us, is no place for thy magpie laugh. No more such sounds of grave-yard merriment or—we quarrel, mark ye."

"We quarrel, mark ye!" echoed the sinister-eyed Hugo, gravely dropping the end of his pike on the pavement.

"St. Judas! My brave men of mettle are wondrous fiery, this quiet night! Ha—ha—pardon Sir Balvardo, I meant not to anger ye! Yet dost thou know that *it* makes my veins fill with new blood! and my heart warm with a strange fire."

"Thy veins fill with new blood! Ha—ha—ha!—Did'st ever hear of a withered vine, blackened by flame, bearing ripe grapes, or was ever a dead toad perfumed by the south wind? Hugo, his heart warms with a strange fire? Odor o' pitch and brimstone, what a fancy! Ha—ha—"

"Nay, nay, Balvardo. There is some life in the Doomsman's veins. Don't doubt it? Just fancy those talons, which he calls fingers, clutched round thy throat—W-h-e-w!"

"I say it makes my veins fill with new blood, my heart warm with a strange fire—this matchless picture! A gallant Lord, with the warm flush of youth on his cheek, strength in his limbs and fire in his heart, stretched out upon the wheel—here a hand is corded to the wheel, and there another, here a foot is bound to the spokes and there another. He looks like the cross of Saint Andrew—by St. Judas. A merry fancy—eh! Balvardo? Stretched out upon the wheel, he looks with his bloodshot eyes to the heavens. See's he any hope there? Laid on his back, he casts his last long glance aside over the multitude—the vile mob. See's he a face of pity there! Hears he a voice of mercy? None—none! Earth curses, heaven forsakes, hell yawns! And he is of noble blood, and on his brow there sits the frown of a lofty line. While the mob hoot, the victim holds his breath, and I—I the Doomsman approach!"

"God's death—he makes my blood chill!" muttered Hugo, glancing askance at his comrade, who stood silent biting his compressed lip.

"He writhes, for the hissing of the cauldron of hot lead falls on his ear, he feels his flesh creep, for the red hot glare of the blazing iron with its jagged point blinds his eyes as he gazes! He utters no moan—but he hears the beating of his own heart.

"He hears a step—a low and cat-like step—'tis mine, the Doomsman's step. The red-hot iron in one hand, the ladle filled with melted lead, hot and seething lead in the other, nay, start not, nor wince, good Balvardo—'tis no fancy picture."

"The Fiend take thy words—they burn my heart! Hold or by thy master, the devil, I'll strike ye to the floor!

"Hark—hear you that hissing sound? His muscular chest is bared to the light, these talon-hands guide the red-hot iron over the warm flesh, with the blood blackening as it oozes from the veins. He writhes—but utters no groan. Now lay down the iron and the lead; seize the knotted club, aloft it whirls, it descends! D'ye see the broken arm bone, protruding from the flesh? Hurl it aloft again, nor heed the sudden struggle and the quick convulsive agony, never heed them—all writhe and struggle so. It grows exciting, Balvardo, it warms me, Hugo."

Hugo muttered a half-forced syllable, but his parted lips and absent manner, attested his unwilling interest in the words of the Doomsman, while Balvardo, clutching his pike, strode hurriedly to and fro along the floor of stone.

"Again the Doomsman sweeps the club aloft! Crash—crash—crash, and then a sound, not a groan, not a groan, but a howl, a howl of agony!

"Look, Balvardo, look Hugo, you can count the bones as they stick out from each leg, from each arm, from the wrist and from the shoulder, from the ancle and the thigh, never mind the blood—it streams in a torrent from each limb, be sure, but the hot iron dries it up. Your melted lead is good for cautery—it heals—ha, ha, ha, let me laugh—it heals the wound, each blow the club had made. The picture grows—it deepens."

"Now, by the Heaven above, I see it all—" muttered Balvardo with a dilating eye, as his manner suddenly changed, and he leaned forward with unwilling yet absorbing interest. "This is no man, but a devil's body with a devil's soul!"

"His face is yet unscarred—unmoved save by the wrinkling contortions of pain. The mob hoot, and hiss, and yell—the play must deepen. Hand me the iron—red-hot—and hissing—give me the bowl of melted lead, dipped from the boiling cauldron. The Doomsman's step again!

"The victim's body creeps, and writhes in every sinew, his veins seem crawling thro' his carcass, his nerves, turned to things of incarnate pain, are drawn and stretched to the utmost."

"Look well upon the blue heavens, Parricide, for the red-hot iron is pointed, and—ha, ha, how he howls—it nears your eyes, it glares before them in their last glance. It must be done, why howl you so? Does it burn your eyes, tho' it touches them not? Ha, ha—I meant it thus."

"Balvardo, strike him down. He is not human—see his flashing eyes, his arms thrown wildly aside, with the talon-fingers, grasping the air!"

"H-i-s-s—it touches the eyeball, the eye is dark forever! H-i-s-s it licks up the blood, it turns round and round in the socket. Now fill the hollow socket with the lead, the hissing lead—and, ha, ha, now bring me another iron pointed like this, and heated to a white heat. Quick, quick, the victim groans, howls, writhes, and yells! Quick! Ah, ha, let the iron touch the skin of the eyeball, it shrivels like a burnt leaf, deeper sink the hissing point, turn it round and round, let it lap up the gushing blood. Now the lead, the thick and boiling lead, pour it from the ladle, fill the socket, it hardens, it grows cold—ha, ha, ha, behold the eyes of lead."

"I see them!" faltered Hugo, trembling in his iron armor.

"And I," echoed Balvardo—"I see them, oh, horrible, and ghastly, I—I—see the eyes of lead!"

"Quick, quick—why lag ye, man? Quick—quick, I say! The knife, the glittering knife. The Parricide howls not nor groans, but his soul is trampling on the fragments of clay. Quick, while his carcass is all palpitation, all alive with torture, all throe, all agony and pulsation, hand me the knife. I would cut his beating heart from the body."

"There, there—the flesh, severed to the bone, parts on either side—the ribs are bared—a blow with the jagged club, and they are broken. This hand is thrust within the aperture, I feel the hot blood, I feel his heart. It beats, it throbs, it writhes in my grasp, like a dying bird beneath the hunter's hand."

"Quick—the knife again—I hold the heart, cut it from the carcass, sever each nerve, snap each artery. A deep, low, trembling heave of the chest; a rattle in the throat.

"I raise the heart,—still quivering on high, it gleams in the light of day, and its warm blood-drops fall pattering on the face of the felon."

"The mob shout their curses and hoot their oaths of scorn."

"Quick, the pincers, the red-hot pincers—but hold—that shaking of the chest, that last heave of the trunk, that quivering in every splintered limb, with that quick tremor of the lip, ha, ha, that blanching of the cheek, with the blood oozing from every pore, that thick gurgling sound in the throat, he dies, the Felon dies, the Doomsman laughs, and from the shattered clod, creeps the Spirit of the Parricide!"

Hugo turned his face to the wall, and covered his eyes with his upraised hands. Balvardo stood still as death, gazing on the vacant air with a wild glance, as though he saw the Spirit of the dead. Neither moved nor said a word. The maniac wildness of the Doomsman awed and chilled them to the heart.

"This is the fate, to which ye have given him; this proud Lord now sleeping in the Chamber of the Doomed—to me, the Doomsman, to the wheel, to the knotted club, to the knife, the hot iron, and the melted lead, to the dishonor ye have given him! Ha—ha—ha—these hands itch for his blood. To-morrow's rising sun will gleam on the scene, this merry scene—THE DOOM OF THE POISONER."

The Sentinels heard a hurried footstep, followed by a closing door, the Doomsman had disappeared. They turned with looks of horror, of remorse, mingled with all the fear and torture that the human soul can feel, stamped in their faces, while from one to the other broke the whisper—

"He sleeps within yon cell—the Doomsman's cell, till the first glimpse of the morrow morn shall rouse him to this work—this work of horror and of—Doom."[1]

CHAPTER THE EIGHTH.

ADRIAN THE DOOMED.

THE wierd and mystic spirit that rules this chronicle, throws open to your view the cell of the Doomed.

It is a sad and gloomy place, where every dark stone has its tale of blood, every name, rudely scratched on the damp wall, its legend of despair.

All is silent; not a whisper, not a sob, not a sound. The silence is so breathless that you fear the spirits of the condemned, who passed from this chamber to the Wheel and the Block, may start into life—at the echo of a footstep from the dark corners of the room, and appal your eye with their shapes of horror.

The cresset of iron fixed to the rough wall, threw a dim light over the form of the Doomed, as seated upon a rough bench, with his head drooped between his clenched hands, his elbows resting on his knees, his golden hair faded to a dingy brown, falling over his shoulders and hiding his countenance, he mused with the secrets of his heart, and called up before his soul the mighty panorama of despair—the wheel, the block, the doomsman, and the multitude.

Adrian the Doomed raised his form from the oaken bench, and paced the dungeon floor. He was not shackled by manacles or clogged by chains.

It was the last night of his existence; escape came not within his thoughts, the walls were built of rock; hundreds of armed sentinels paced the long galleries of the prison, and a guard of two men-at-arms watched without the triple-locked and triple-bolted door of the Doomed chamber.

Suffering and endurance, anxiety of mind and torture of soul, had wrought fearful changes in the well knit and muscular form of the Lord of Albarone.

His countenance was pale and thin; his lips whitened, his cheeks hollow and his eyes sunken, while his faded locks of gold fell in tangled masses over his face and shoulders. His blue eye was sunken, yet it gleamed brighter than ever, and there was meaning in its quick, fiery glance.

"To die on the gibbet, with the taunt *and* the sneer of the idiot crowd ringing in my ears, my last look met with the vulgar grimaces and unmeaning laughter of ten thousand clownish faces—to die on the rack, each bone splintered by the instruments of ignominious torture, my scarred and mangled carcass mocking the face of day,—oh, God—is this the fate of Adrian, heir to the fame, the glory, and the fortunes of the house of Albarone?"

Pausing in his hurried walk, he stood for a moment silent and motionless as the sculptured marble, and then eagerly stretching forth his hands, cried—

"Father—father! noble father! I believe thy holy shade is now hovering unseen over the form of thy doomed son—by all the hopes men hold of bliss in an unknown state of being; by the faith which teaches the belief of a future world, I implore thee, appear and speak to me. Tell me of that eternity which I am about to face! Tell me of that awful world which is beyond the present! Father, I implore thee, speak!"

His imagination, almost excited to phrenzy by long and solitary thought, with glaring eyes, arms outstretched, and trembling hands, the agitated boy gazed at a dark corner of the cell, every instant expecting to behold the dim and ghostly form of his murdered sire slowly arise and become visible through the misty darkness. No answer came—no form arose. Adrian drew a dagger from his vest.

"Father, by the mysterious tie that binds the parent to the son, which neither time nor space can sever—death or eternity annihilate—I implore thee— *appear!*"

The tone in which he spoke was dread and solemn. Again he waited for a response to his adjuration, but no response came.

"This, then," cried Adrian, raising the dagger; "this, then, is the only resource left to me. Thus do I cheat the mob of their show; thus do I rescue the name of Albarone from foul dishonor!"

Tighter he clutched the dagger; his arms was thrown back and his breast was bared; and, as he thus nerved himself for the final blow, all the scenes of his life—the hopes of his boyhood—the dreams of his love, rose up before him like a picture.

And like a vast unbounded ocean, overhung with mists, and dark with clouds, was the idea of the DREAD UNKNOWN *to his mind.*

Amid all the memories of the past; the agonies of the present, or the anticipations of the future, did the face of the Ladye Annabel come like a dream to his soul, and the smile upon her lip was like the smile of a guardian spirit, beaming with hope and love.

"Oh, God—receive my soul!—Annabel, fare thee-well!"

The dagger descended, driven home with all the strength of his arm.

"*Adrian!*" exclaimed a hollow voice, and a strange hand thrown before the breast of the doomed felon struck his wrist, the instant the dagger's point had touched the flesh.

The weapon flew from the hand of Adrian and fell on the other side of the cell.

He turned and beheld the muffled form of a monk, who had entered through the massive door, which had been unbolted without Adrian's heeding the noise of locks and chains, so deep was his abstraction. The ruddy glare of torches streamed into the cell, and the sentinels who held them, in their endeavors to shake off their late terror and remorse, gave utterance to unfeeling and ribald jests.

"I say, Balvardo," cried the sinister-eyed soldier, "does not the springald bear himself right boldly? And yet at break of day he dies!"

"Marry, Hugo," returned the other, "he had better thought of making all these fine speeches ere he gave the—ha—ha—ha!—the physic to the old man."

Reproving the sentinels for their insolence, the muffled monk closed the door, and approaching Adrian, exclaimed—

"My son, prepare thee for thy fate! The shades of night behold thee erect in the pride of manhood; the light of morn shall see thee prostrate, bleeding, dead. Thy soul shall stand before the bar of eternity. Art thou prepared for death, my son?"

"Father," Adrian answered; "I have been ever a faithful son of the Holy Church, but its offices will avail me naught at this hour. Once, for all, I tell thee I will die without human prayers or human consolation. On the solemn thought of HIM who gave me being, I alone rely for support in the hour of a fearful death. Thy errand is a vain one, Sir Priest, if thou dost hope to gain shrift or confession from me. I would be alone!"

"Thou art but young to die," said the monk, in a quiet tone.

Adrian made no reply.

"Tell me, young sir," cried the monk, seizing Adrian by the wrist, "wouldst thou accept life, though it were passed within the walls of a convent?"

"The cowl of the monk was never worn by a descendant of Albarone. I would pass my days as my fathers have done before me—at the head of armies and in the din of battle!"

The monk threw back his cowl and discovered a striking and impressive face; bearing marks of premature age, induced by blighted hopes and fearful wrongs. His hair, as black as jet, gathered in short curls around a high and pallid forehead; his eyebrows arched over dark, sparkling eyes; his nose was short and Grecian; his lips thin and expressive, and his chin well rounded and prominent. And as the cowl fell back, Adrian with a start beheld the *monk of the ante-chamber.*

"Count Adrian Di Albarone, this morning thou wert tried before the Duke of Florence, and his peers, for the murder of thy sire. Thou, a descendant of Albarone, connected with the royal blood of Florence, wert condemned on the testimony of two of thy father's vassals, for this most accursed act. I ask thee, canst thou tell who it is that hath spirited up these perjured witnesses; and why it is that the Duke of Florence countenances the accusations!"

"In the name of God, kind priest, I thank thee for thy belief in my innocence. The author of this foul wrong, is, I shame to say it, my uncle, Aldarin, the Scholar. The reason why it is countenanced by the duke, is—" Adrian paused as if the words stuck in his throat; "is because he would wed my own fair cousin, the Ladye Annabel."

"Ha!" exclaimed the monk, "my suspicions were not false. Let Aldarin look to his fate; and, as for the duke—" thrusting his hand into his bosom, he drew from his gown a miniature—it was the miniature of a beautiful maiden.

"Behold!" cried the monk, "Adrian Di Albarone, behold this countenance, where youth, and health, and love, beaming from every feature, mingle with the deep expression of a mind rich in the treasure of thoughts, pure and virginal in their beauty. Mark well the forehead, calm and thoughtful; the ruby lips, parting with a smile; the full cheek blooming with the rose buds of youth—mark the tracery of the arching neck; the half-revealed beauty of the virgin bosom. Adrian, this was the maiden of my heart, the *one* beloved of my very soul. I was the private secretary of the duke, he won my confidence—he betrayed it. Guilietta was the victim; and I sought peace and oblivion within the walls of a convent. I am now in his favor—he loads me with honors; I accept his gifts—aye, aye, Albertine, the Monk, takes the gold of the proud duke, that he may effect the great object of his existence—"

"And that—" cried Adrian—"that is—"

The monk spoke not; a smile wreathed his compressed lips, and a glance sparkled in his eye. *Adrian was answered.*

In the breast of the man to whom God has given a soul, there also dwells at all times a demon; and that demon arises into fearful action from the ruins of betrayed confidence. The monk whispered something in the ear of the condemned noble, and then, waving his hand, retired.

CHAPTER THE NINTH.

THE FELON AND THE DUKE.

IN a few minutes the door again opened, and the stately form of the Countess of Albarone entered the traitor's cell.

Why need I tell of the warm embrace with which she enclosed her son? Why tell of her tears that came from her very soul—her deep expressions of detestation when the name of Aldarin, the scholar, was mentioned? Need I say that she was firmly assured of her son's innocence; that she saw through the mummery of his trial, and the trickery of his foes? Leaving all this to the fancy of the reader of this chronicle, I pass on with my history.

The kind discourse of mother and son was broken off by the clanging of chains and the drawing of locks. The light of many torches streamed through the opened door into the cell, and the gaily-bedizened form of the Duke was discovered.

With a last farewell, the Countess of Albarone retired; the door was closed, and Adrian was left alone with the Duke.

"Well, sir," exclaimed he; "I have condescended to visit you. Albertine, my confessor, told me it was due to a branch of the royal blood of Florence. It were best that you make a short story of what you have to say. My train wait without, and I am somewhat hurried." Here he opened his sleepy eyes, and, curling his bearded lip, tried to assume a look of dignity.

Adrian bowed down to the earth.

"The son of Count Di Albarone," said he, "feels highly honored by your condescension."

"Well, now, sir, what have you to say?" exclaimed the Duke. "Speak, ignoble son of an honored sire—inglorious descendant of a noble line. Speak! What would you say?"

"Merely this, most gracious Duke," answered Adrian, as he gazed sternly into the very eyes of the haughty prince, "merely this, that I have been doomed to death by thee and thy minions, in a manner that never was noble doomed before. Without form; on the proof of perjured caitiffs; without defence, have I been condemned for a crime, at the name of which hell itself would shudder."

The Duke sneered, as he spoke:

"Surely, I cannot help it, and a brainless boy takes it into his head to poison his sire."

"Pardon me, gracious Duke," said Adrian, as by a sudden movement he grasped him by the throat, and at the same time seizing his cloak of scarlet and gold, he thrust it into his gaping mouth.

Closer and yet more close he wound his grasp, and, scarce able to breathe, much less to speak, the Duke of Florence stood without power or motion. Adrian coolly tripped up his heels, and then placing his knee upon his breast by a dexterous movement, he tore away the scarlet cloak, and then cautiously placing one hand over the mouth of the prince, he gathered some straw with the other, and forced it down his throat.

Then unbuckling his own belt of rough doe skin, he wound it around the neck and over the mouth of the Duke, and having fastened it as tightly as might be, he proceeded to tie his hands behind his back; the cord he used being nothing less than the chain of knighthood suspended from the neck of his grace.

You may be sure this was not accomplished without a struggle. The Duke writhed and wrestled, but to no purpose. He could not speak, and the knee of Adrian placed on his breast, laid him silent and motionless.

And now behold Adrian, arrayed in the blazing cloak of the Duke, which descending to his knees, sweeps the tops of the fine boots of doe-skin, ornamented with spurs of gold. On his head is placed the slouching hat of the prince, surmounted by a group of nodding plumes, and beneath the folds of the cloak shines the richly embossed sheath of his sword.

Adrian surveyed his figure with a smile—that smile which arises from the recklessness of desperation—and then, without heeding the malignant glances of the Duke, he fixed him against the rough bench upon his knees, with his face to the wall, in an attitude of prayer and devotion—He threw his own sombre cloak over the back of his captive; and then, having slouched the hat over his face, after the manner of the Duke, he gathered up the cloak of crimson along his chin, and stood ready to depart.

He opened the door of the traitor's cell with a quickened pulse, and in an instant, found himself standing in the gallery where the muffled priest waited for the Duke. The soldiers bowed low to the wearer of the scarlet cloak, and the word was passed along the galleries—

"*Make way for the Duke—make way for his grace of Florence.*"

The monk now advanced, and locking the door of the doomed cell, he affixed to its panel a parchment signed by the Duke of Florence, and sealed with the seal of state. It declared that the prisoner, Adrian Di Albarone, was to be seen by no one until the morrow, when he was to suffer the doom of the law, by the terrors of the wheel.

This done, the monk fell meekly in the rear of Albarone, who paced along the gallery, saluted at the door of every cell by the lowered spears of the sentinels.

The gallery terminated in a staircase. This Adrian and the monk ascended, and at the top they found a company of gay cavaliers, who waited for his grace of Florence. The wearer of the scarlet cloak and slouching hat was greeted with a low bow. Adrian then traversed another gallery, and yet another; being all the while followed by the band of gallant courtiers.

"Urban," whispered one of these gallants to another, "methinks our lord is wondrous silent to-night."

"Why, Cesarini," replied his companion, "it may be that he is weeping for this young springald, Adrian. Marry, 'tis enough to make an older man than I am weep."

"Hist!" whispered the monk, "our lord would have you observe strict silence."

They had arrived at the lofty arching door of the castle leading into the court-yard, when Adrian was alarmed by a noise and shouting in the galleries which he had just traversed.

"All is lost!" thought Adrian, as his hand caught the hilt of his sword.

"Fear not," whispered the monk, "but push boldly onward."

They now descended into the court-yard, where a richly-attired page held a steed ready for his grace. Springing with one bound into the saddle, Aldarin passed under the raised portcullis, with the monk riding at his side, and the bridle reins of the courtiers ringing in the rear.

Thus far all was well. The monk leaned from his saddle, and whispered to Adrian:

"One effort more, brave boy. Nerve thyself for the trial at the palace gate."

Traversing one of the most spacious streets of the city of Florence, they soon arrived before the lofty gate of the palace of the Duke.

Here a crowd of men-at-arms, blazing in armor of gold, saluted the supposed Duke with every mark of respect.

And finally, innumerable dangers past, behold Adrian enter the palace, traverse innumerable chambers, hung with gorgeous tapestry, lighted by lamps of silver and of gold, and thronged with nobles and courtiers, who much wondered to behold their lord pass them by, without one mark of recognition or sign of respect.

At last Adrian arrived before folding doors ornamented with exquisite carving, and having the arms of the Duke emblazoned in glowing colors upon the panels.

"Push open the doors, and boldly enter," whispered the monk to Adrian, who immediately obeyed his directions.

The monk then turned to the gallant throng of courtiers, and said:

"My lords, his grace is unwell. He would dispense with your further attendance." The monk retired.

Never arose such a mingled crowd of exclamations of wonder as then burst from the lips of the cavaliers. One whispered their lord must certainly be woad; another that he must have been repulsed in some illicit amour; and a third seriously gave it as his opinion, that some devil or other had taken possession of the Duke of Florence. However, being well aware of the high regard in which the Duke held the monk Albertine, they all slowly trooped out of the ante-chamber, leaving it to the guards of the palace, who watched within its confines, as was their wont.

CHAPTER THE TENTH.

THE CHAMBER OF THE DULSE.

IN a lofty chamber, hung with tapestry of purple, embroidered with rare and pleasant designs, and lighted by lamps of gold, depending from the ceiling, Adrian and the Monk rested themselves after their arduous exploit.

In one corner of the apartment stood a gorgeous bed, with a canopy of silver and gold hangings, surmounted by a Ducal coronet. Around were strewn couches of the most inviting softness, and every thing in the chamber wore an appearance of luxury and ease.

Adrian reposed on a couch of velvet, and by his side was seated the monk. Before them was placed a small table, on which stood several flasks of rich wine, together with more substantial refreshments.

"Truly, sir monk," said Adrian, filling a goblet of wine, "I have heard of many unmannerly acts, but this deed of mine does seem to me to be the most unmannerly of all. I not only tied the brave duke, lashed him in the Cell of the Doomed, used his gallant steed, and worshipful name, but, forsooth! I must also repose me upon his couches, and refresh me with his wine!"

And Adrian laughed.

"Thou art merry, young sir. But an hour since—"

The monk was interrupted by a gentle knocking under the tapestry.

Adrian started up, and drew his sword, taking the precaution, however, to resume the scarlet cloak, and slouching hat.

The knocking grew louder. The monk removed the tapestry in the part from whence the sound proceeded, and having pressed a spring, a secret door in the wainscotting flew open, and a woman of beautiful countenance, and rich attire was discovered.

"Thou here, stern priest!" said the damsel, in a sweet voice, "I would speak with my lord."

"Mariamne, thou canst not see him to-night; he hath no time to trifle with such as thee. His thoughts are given to prayer."

The monk closed the door, and, turning to Adrian, said,

"Another of this miscreant's victims, Adrian. It was fortunate she did not see thee closely, for her eye would have detected where hundreds might look without suspicion. And now let us away; every moment increases thy danger; the duke may even now have freed himself, and set his minions in chase."

"To fly, I am willing, sir monk; but whither?"

"*Follow me*," said the monk, as he lighted a small lamp of silver. He then removed the tapestry, and discovered a secret door opposite the one afore-mentioned. This the monk entered, followed by Adrian, and a stairway of stone, some two feet in width, was revealed; it was cut into the wall and over-arched, and the distance between the steps and the arch not more than four feet.

With great care the monk led the way down the steps of stone, until they numbered thirty, when they terminated in a narrow platform, which, indeed, was nothing more than a step somewhat longer than the others. Here our adventurers descended another stairway, likewise ending in a platform, and then yet another stairway was terminated by another platform; and thus they descended stairway after stairway, and crossed platform after platform, until the increasing coldness and dampness of the atmosphere, warned them that they had penetrated far below the surface of the earth.

Suddenly the stairway ended in a large and gloomy vault, with walls and floor of the unhewn rock.

On the side nearest the stairway, a gate of iron was erected between the points of two large and irregular rocks.

Through a large crevice which time had worn into this gate, the monk and Adrian passed into a vault like the former, except that the dim light of the taper discovered the rough floor strewn with grinning skulls, and whitened bones.

Along this dreary place strode the monk, lighting the way, while, at his back followed Adrian Di Albarone. In about a quarter of an hour the vault narrowed into a confined passage, along which they crawled on hands and knees. This terminated in another vault, sloping upwards with a gradual ascent, which having traversed, our adventurers found themselves again between two narrowing walls, and finally, all further progress was stopped by a large stone thrown directly across the path. Adrian spoke for the first time in half an hour—

"And are we to be baulked after all the adventures of this night?"

The monk answered by pointing to the stone, to which he and his companion presently laid their shoulders, but their united strength was insufficient to remove it.

Again they tried, and again were they unsuccessful; they made a third attempt, and the stone was precipitated before them.

Seizing the light, Adrian threw himself into the breach, and discovered an extensive vault, hedged in by walls built of hewn stone, while the floor was covered by rows of coffins, with here and there a monument of marble. Throwing themselves into this place, they picked their way through the dreary line of coffins, when they came to a wide staircase which they ascended, until they found it suddenly terminated by the archway above.

The monk raised his hand, and drawing a bolt which Adrian had not perceived, he pushed with all his strength against the archway, and a trap-door rose above the heads of our adventurers.—Through this passage the monk ascended, followed by Adrian, who looked around with a gaze of wonder, and found himself standing in the aisle of the Grand Cathedral of Florence.

The moonbeams streaming through the lofty arched windows of stained glass, threw a dim light upon the high altar with its cross of gold, and faintly revealed the line of towering pillars which arose to the dome of the cathedral, as vast and magnificent it extended far above.

"My son," cried the monk, "give thanks to God for thy deliverance."

And there, in that lone aisle, as the deep toned bell of the cathedral tolled the third hour of the morning, did Adrian and the monk fall lowly on the marble pavement, and, prostrating themselves before the sublime symbol of our most holy faith, give thanks to God, the Virgin, and the Saints, for their most wonderful escape.

BOOK THE SECOND.

THE CAVERN OF ALBARONE.

CHAPTER THE FIRST.

THE PIT OF DARKNESS.

ONE moment in light, and the next in darkness—down through the gloom of the pit, plumb as a hurled rock, and swift as an arrow, the betrayed soldier fell, precipitated by the treachery of the scholar Aldarin.

The swiftness of his descent took from him all thought or sensation. His flight was suddenly terminated by a subterranean pool of water, into the depths of which he sunk for a moment, and then arose to the surface.

The coldness of the flood, together with an unconquerable stench that assailed his nostrils on all sides, restored the stout yeoman to sensation and feeling.

Spreading his arms instinctively outward, in an attitude of swimming, Rough Robin could neither guess where he was now, or with whom he had been conversing a moment since. His thoughts were wandering and confused, as are the thoughts of a man who dreams when half asleep and half awake.

Still swimming onward through the stagnant waters, Robin cast his eyes overhead, and discerned far, far above, a faintly twinkling light, somewhat of the size of a dim and distant star. He looked again, and it was gone. Around, above, and beneath was darkness: darkness which no eye could pierce, where all was shadow and vacuum—darkness that was almost tangible with its density. The cheek of the brave soldier was chilled by air that, heavy with dampness and mist, seemed as dead and stagnant as the waters in which he swam.

The light glimmering for an instant far above, brought dimly to his mind the person of Aldarin, and the incidents of a moment hence.

And then Robin thought that his fall of terror was only a dream, and, splashing and plunging in the dark waters, he sought to shake off the fearful night-mare that stiffened his sinews and froze his blood.

His extended hand touched a cold and slimy substance, and a small, bright speck shone like a coal of fire through the darkness. Robin grasped the slimy substance: it moved, and a noisome reptile wriggled in his hand.

Now it was that he became aware that the subterranean waters were filled by crawling serpents, who writhed around his legs, twined around his body, and struck his arms and hands at every movement. Their bright eyes sparkled in the waters, and their hissing broke upon the air, as they were thus disturbed by the presence of a strange visitor.

Robin was no coward, neither was he much given to strange fancies; but a feeling of intense terror chilled the very blood around his heart, as the thought came over him that he lay in that fearful place, of which so many legends were told by the vassals of Albarone. The peasantry had many stories of a vast, unearthly pit sunk far in the depths of the castle, where the fiends of darkness were wont to hold their revel and shake the bosom of the earth with the sounds of hellish wassail. Into this dark pit—so ran the legend— had many a shivering wretch been precipitated by the lords of Albarone; and here, unpitied and unknown, had the carcasses of the murdered lain rotting and festering in darkness and oblivion.

As the memory of these strange legends crept over the confused mind of Robin the Rough, he gave utterance to a faint shriek.

It was returned back to him in a thousand echoes, swelling one after the other; now like the sound of repeated claps of thunder, and again dying away fainter and yet fainter, as though many voices were engaged in a hushed and whispering conversation.

"Avaunt thee, fiend! avaunt thee!" cried the stout yeoman, as he still strove to keep himself upon the surface of the water. "Holy Mary, holy Paul, holy Peter!" continued he, between his struggles, "an' ye save me from these pestilent devils, I will—"

Here the yeoman plunged under the waters, and the sentence was unfinished.

"I will, by St. Withold, I will!" cried he, as he rose to the surface, "place at the altar of the first chapel at which I may arrive after my deliverance, a wax taper, in honor of all three of you."

The yeoman struck his arms boldly through the flood, as he continued:

"And, an' ye work out my deliverance, I'll never ask a boon of ye again."

Here he gave another bold push.

"I'll never ask a boon of ye more, but stick like a good christian to my own native saint—even the good St. Withold!"

Here, satisfied that his duty to heaven was done, the yeoman strove to gain some rock, or other object, upon which he might rest his body, much disjointed as it was by his fall of terror.

"It pains me—this wounded hand!" he cried—"But Aldarin my friend will reward me for the pain, some day or other."

A murmuring sound now met his ears; it was the sound of running waters. Onward and onward the bold yeoman dashed, and louder and yet louder grew the sweet sound of waters in motion.

In a moment he felt a sudden change, from the dull leaden stillness of a stagnated pool, to the quick flow and wild careering of waves in motion. And now he was carried onward with arrowy fleetness, while high above, the roaring of the subterranean stream was returned in a thousand echoes. Now tossed against the sharp, rough points of rocks; now plunged in whirling gullies; now borne on the crests of swelling waves, in darkness and in terror, bold Robin swept on in his career.

CHAPTER THE SECOND.

ROBIN ALONE IN THE EARTH-HIDDEN CAVERN.

THUS was he carried onward for the space of a quarter of an hour, when, bruised, shattered and bleeding, he was thrown by the swell of a wave, high out of the water upon a mass of rocks.

Here he lay for a long while, without sense or feeling. When he recovered from this swoon, it was with difficulty that he made the attempt to collect his thoughts; all was vague, indistinct, and like a dream.

"St. Withold!" at last he whispered, as if communing with himself; "St. Withold! but this Aldarin is, in good sooth, a most pestilent knave!"

He paused a moment, and then, as if to redouble his private assurance of Aldarin's villany, he resumed:

"Aye—a pestilent knave—ugh!"

This last interjection was a suppressed growl, which he forced through his fixed teeth, as, extending his arms, with the hands clenched, he made every demonstration of being engaged in shaking some imaginary Aldarin, with great danger to his victim's comfort and life.

"Ugh! Well, here am I, in this pit—this back-staircase to the devil's dining room—alone, wet, hungry, and in darkness. St. Withold save me from all fiends, and I'll take care of aught beside. Let me see. Mayhap I shall find some passage from this place. I am on solid rock that's well. Now for't."

Cautiously creeping along in the darkness, he followed the winding of the subterranean flood by its roaring, until he was suddenly stopped by an upright stone, which, to his astonishment, he found to be square in shape, and, feeling it carefully, he doubted not that it had been shapen by the chisel of the mason.

Over this stone Robin clambered, and alighted upon a large chisseled stone laid in a horizontal position, and over this was placed another stone of like form; and thus proceeding in his discoveries our stout yeoman found that a stairway arose in front of him.

With a shout of joy, bold Robin rushed up the steps of stone, which, wide and roomy, afforded his feet firm and substantial footing. Some forty steps, or more, now lay below him, when raising his foot to ascend yet higher, the yeoman found it fall beneath him, and in a moment he stood upon a floor, which to all likelihood was laid with slabs of chisseled stone.

Through this place he wandered, now stumbling against regularly-built walls, now falling over hidden objects, now passing through doorway after doorway, and again returning to the head of the stairway from which he started.

Hours passed. Sometimes Rough Robin would hear a faint booming sound far above, which he supposed was the bell of the castle, tolling for the death of the noble Count Di Albarone, known throughout Christendom, in a thousand lays, as the bravest of crusaders, and the gentlest of knights. The sound of this bell swung upon the breeze for miles around, whenever it was struck—so Robin remembered well; yet now, far down in the depths of the earth, a low moaning noise was all that reached the ears of the stout yeoman.

With every sinew stiffened, and with every vein chilled by the damp of subterranean vaults, scarce able to breathe in the putrid air which had never known light of sunbeam, his whole frame weakened by hunger, and his brain confused by his dream-like adventures, Robin, the stout yeoman, at last sank down upon a block of rough stone, where he remained for hours in a state of half unconsciousness, which finally deepened into a sound and wholesome slumber.

CHAPTER THE THIRD.

THE CHAPEL OF THE ROCKS.

THE MONKS OF THE ORDER OF THE HOLY STEEL HOLD SOLEMN COUNCIL IN THE WILD WOOD.

THE scene was a wild and solitary dell, buried in the depths of the forests, far away among the mountains; the time was high noon, and the characters of the scene were the members of a dark and mysterious Order, whose history is involved in shadow; whose names, embracing the highest titles and the wealthiest nobles in the Dukedom of Florence, are wrapt in mystery; whose deeds, performed in secret, and executed with the most appalling severity, are to this day known and celebrated as household words, in the legends of the valley of the Arno.

A level piece of sward, some twenty yards in length, and as many in width, extended greenly within the depths of the forest; its bounds described, and its verdure shadowed, by huge masses of perpendicular rock, which sprang upward from the very sod, towering in wild and rugged grandeur, amid the deep, rich foliage of forest oaks and with the clear summer sky seen far, far above, as from the depths of a well, forming the roof of this hidden temple of nature.

The rugged masses of perpendicular rock, piled upon each other in rude magnificence, surrounded the glade in the form of a square.

Viewed from the forest side, these rocks looked like one vast mound of massive stone, placed in the wild-wood valley by some freak of nature. A narrow, though deep and rapid stream, its waters shadowed to ebony blackness, laved one side of the steps of granite. It swept beneath an arching crevice, some three feet high, and as many thick, washed the sod of the hidden glade and rolled along its edge, foaming against the rugged walls; the waves plashing on high in showery drops, until it suddenly disappeared under the opposite wall, and was lost in the subterranean recesses of the earth.

The mid-day sun, shining over the rich foliage of the surrounding forests, where silence, vast and immense, seemed to live and feel; over the rough walls of the Temple of Rocks, scarce ever visited by human feet,—for strange legends scared the peasantry from the place, flung his beams down from the very zenith along the quiet of the level sward, with its encircling rocks, now animated by a scene of wild and peculiar interest.

Around a square table which arose from the centre of the sward, draped with folds of solemn black, sat a band of twenty-four men, each figure veiled in the thick folds of a monkish robe and cowl, each face concealed and each arm buried within the fold of the sable garment.

These were the priests of the Order of the Monks of the Steel.

At the head of the table, on a chair of rough and knotted oak, placed on a solitary rock, sate a tall and imposing figure, clad as the others, in the robe and cowl of velvet, with his face veiled from sight and sunbeam. His extended hand grasped a slender rod of iron, with a sculpturing of clearest ivory, fashioned into a strange shape fixed on the end—the solemn and revered Abacus of the Order.

This was the High Priest of the Order of the Monks of the Steel.

At the other end of the table was seated a figure, veiled and robed like the rest, yet with a taller and more muscular form, while his hand laid upon the velvet coverings of the table, grasped an axe of glittering steel.

He was the Doomsman of the Order.

His voice denounced, his voice consigned to death, his voice was like an echo from the grave, for it never spoke other words than the sentence of Judgment.

Grouped around the table, a circle of solemn figures, robed and veiled like the others, stood shoulder to shoulder, each form holding a torch on high with the left hand, while the right hand grasped a keen and slender-bladed dagger.

Silent and motionless they stood, the blue flame of the torch, held by the upraised arm, burning over each head; every right hand steadily grasping the dagger; while their robes scarce stirred into motion by the heaving of the breast, looked like the drapery of some monkish effigy, rather than the attire of living men. These were the Initiates, or Neophytes of the Order.

Their dagger it was that protruded from the breast of the victim, found by the affrighted peasantry in the lonely woods, or seen by the careless crowd thrown down, in all the ghastliness of murder, along the very streets of Florence; on the steps of her palaces, in the halls of her castles—even in the cloisters of her cathedral.

Whom the Order condemned, or the Doomsman doomed, they the neophytes of the Order, gave to the sudden death of the invisible steel.

Never had the sun looked down upon a scene as solemn and dread as this.

The chronicles of the olden time are rife with legends of secret orders, linked together in some foul work of crime, or joined in the holy task of vengeance on the wronger, or doom to the slayer; but these bands of men were wont to assemble in dark caverns, lighted by the glare of smoking torches, speaking their words of terror to the air of midnight, and celebrating their solemn ceremonies amid the corses of the dead.

The band assembled in the Chapel of Rocks were unlike all these, unlike any band that ever assembled on the face of the earth.

They met at noonday, raising their torches in the light of the sun, whispering their words of doom in the wild solitudes of the woods, with their faces and forms veiled from view, preserving the solemn unity of the Order, by a uniformity of costume, while the rugged rocks, golden with the mid-day beams, gave back, in sullen murmurs, the voice of the accuser, or the sentence of the doomsman, coupled with the low-muttered name of the doomed.

From their solemn noonday meeting in the Chapel of Rocks, they issued forth on their errands of death, leaving the reeking dagger in the heart of the tyrant, as he slept in the recesses of his castle; flinging their victims along the roadside of the mountain, or the streets of the city, while the faint murmurs of the multitude, gazing at the work of the *Invisible*, gave forth their name and mission: "Behold, behold the vengeance of the Monks of the Steel!"

As the sun towered in the very zenith, the high priest spoke, waving his solemn abacus from his oaken throne. His words were few and concise.

"Hail, brothers; met once again in the Chapel of Rocks. Hail, brothers, from the convent, from the castle, and the cottage, hail! Prince and peasant, lord and monk, met together in these solemn wilds, joined in the work of vengeance on the wronger, death to the slayer, I bid ye welcome. Herald arise; proclaim to the rising of the sun the meeting of our solemn Order."

And the veiled figure seated on the right of the high priest arose, and extending his hands on high looked to the east, chaunting with a low, deep-toned voice:

"Lo, people! lo, kings! lo, angels of heaven, and men of earth! The solemn Order of the Monks of the Steel, hold high council in the Chapel of the Rocks, beneath the light of the noonday sun. Vengeance on the wronger, death to the slayer!"

And rising with hands outspread and, solemn voices, three heralds successively made proclamation to the north, to the south, and to the setting sun, that the solemn Order of the Monks of the Steel, held high council in the Chapel of Rocks, beneath the light of the noonday sun, while thrice arose the wild denunciation—"*Vengeance to the wronger, death to the slayer!*"

"Priests of our solemn Order, ye have been abroad on your errands of secrecy. Speak; what have ye seen, whom do ye accuse, whom do ye give to the steel?"

"I come from the people," said a veiled figure, as he arose and spoke from the folds of his robe, "Yesternight, like a shadow, I glided along the streets of Florence, listening to the low-whispered murmurs of the scattered groups of people. Every tongue had some foul wrong to tell; every voice spoke of midnight murder, done at the bidding of a tyrant; every voice whispered a story of woman's innocence outraged, the gray hairs of age dabbled in blood, the poor robbed, the weak crushed; while the mighty raised their red hands to heaven, laughing with scorn, as if they would shake the blood-drops in the very face of God. Ask ye the name of the tyrant? Find it in the whispers of the people; the wronger and the slayer was the Duke—the Duke of Florence!"

"I come from the palace!" cried another robed priest, rising solemnly, and speaking from the folds of his robe. "Mingling with the nobles of Florence and the courtiers of the Duke, I heard low whispers of discontent, murmurs of rebellion, and dark threats of assassination. The Duke—the tyrant Duke— was on every lip, on every tongue. Florence is slumbering over the depths of a mighty volcano—a moment, and lo! the scathing fires ascend to the sky, the dark smoke blackens the face of day!"

"*I come from the scaffold!*" cried another dark robed figure, as he arose and spoke through his muffled garment. "Last night, a mighty crowd gathered around the gaol of Florence; every voice was fraught with a tale of horror, every cheek was pale, and every eye fixed upon a dark object, that rose in the centre of the multitude. Breasting my way through the throng, I rushed forward, I gained the place of execution, I beheld a dark scaffold rising like a thing of evil omen on the air. I beheld the wheel of torture, the cauldron, and the axe! 'For whom are these?' I cried. 'For a lord of the royal blood of Florence,' shrieked a bystander: 'for Adrian Di Albarone. To-morrow, at day-break, he dies; condemned by the Duke and his minions, on the foul accusation of the murder of his father!' I know the accusation to be false. At this hour, brothers of the Holy Steel, the ghost of the murdered shrieks for vengeance, before the throne of God!"

"Accusers of the Duke of Florence, do ye invoke upon your own souls the punishment accorded to the tyrant, should your words prove false?"

"We do!"

"Priests of the solemn Order of the Holy Steel what shall be the doom of the tyrant, the betrayer, the assassin?"

"Death!"

"Initiates of the Order, do ye accord this judgment?"

"Death, death, death!"

"Doomsman, arise and proclaim the judgment of the Order of the Monks of the Holy Steel?"

"Hear, oh heaven,—oh earth,—oh hell," arose the harsh tones of the doomsman, "Urbano, Duke of Florence, tyrant, assassin, and betrayer, is doomed! I give his body to the gibbet, to the axe, to the steel! Though he sleeps within the bridal chamber, there will the vengeance of the Order grasp him; though he wields the sceptre on his ducal throne, there will the death blow strike the sceptre from his hand, his carcass from the throne, though he kneels at the altar, there will the dagger seek his heart. Doomed, doomed, doomed!"

And then, in a voice of fierce denunciation, he gave forth to the noon-day air, the dark and fearful curse of the Order, whose sentences of woe may not be written down on this page; a curse so dark, so dread, and terrible, that the very priests of the Order drooped their heads down low on each bosom, as the sounds of the doomsman startled their ears.

"Let his name be written down in the book of judgment, as the Doomed!"

"Lo, it is written!"

And as the doomsman spoke, a level slab of gray stone, which varied the appearance of the green sward, some yards behind the chair of the High Priest, slowly arose from the sod, and, unperceived by the monks of the Order, two figures, robed in the cowl and monkish gown of the secret band, emerged silently from the bosom of the earth, and took their stations at the very backs of the torch bearers.

"Who will be the minister of this doom? Who will receive the consecrated steel, and strike it to the tyrant's heart?"

There was a low, deep murmur, a pause of hesitation, and then the priests communed with each other in muttered whispers.

"Who will minister this doom?" again echoed the High Priest, while the sound of footsteps startled the silence of the place. "Who will receive the consecrated steel, and strike it to the tyrant's heart?"

"Behold the minister!" cried a deep-toned voice as the strange figures strode toward the table. "*Give me the steel!*"

"It is Albertine!" echoed the members of the Order, and the wan face and flashing eyes of the monk were disclosed by the falling cowl.

"Behold the minister of this doom!" he shouted, advancing to the doomsman. "Death to the tyrant! Give me the steel!"

And as he spoke, the cowl fell from the face of the figure who stood beside the monk, and the torch bearers, the monks, and the High Priest, looked from their muffled robes in wonder and in awe, and beheld the face of—*Adrian Di Albarone.*

CHAPTER THE FOURTH.

THE CHAPEL OF ST. GEORGE OF ALBARONE.

THE SOLEMN FUNERAL RITES OF THE MIGHTY DEAD, CONVEYED TO THE TOMB, NOT AS THE VICTIM, BUT THE CONQUEROR.

THE beams of the midnight moon, streaming through the emblazoned panes of the lofty arching windows, mingled with the blaze of long lines of funeral torches, making the chapel of St. George of Albarone as light as day, when illumined by the glare of the thunder storm, and revealing a strange and solemn scene—the last rites of religion celebrated over the corse of the mighty dead.

The mingled light of moonbeam and glaring torch, revealed the roof of the chapel arching above, all intricately carved and fettered, the lines of towering columns, arabesque in outline and effect, the high altar of the church, with its cross of gold and diamonds, won by the lords of Albarone from the lands of Heathenesse, its rare painting of the dying God, its rich sculpturings and quaint ornaments; while along the mosaic floor, among the pillars, and around the altar, grouped the funeral crowd, marking their numbers by the upraised torch and spear.

An aged abbot, attired in the gorgeous robes of his holy office, with long locks of snow-white hair falling over his shoulders, stood at the foot of the altar, celebrating the midnight mass for the dead; while around the venerable man were grouped the brothers of his convent, their mingled robes of white and black giving a strange solemnity to the scene.

Beside the foot of the altar—resting in the ruddy glare of the funeral torches, robed in full armor, partly concealed by a pall of snow-white velvet, on a bier of green beechen wood, covered by skins of the wild leopard, in simple majesty,—lay the corse of the gallant lord of Albarone.

The raised vizor revealed his stern features set grimly in death, while his mail-clad arms were crossed on his muscular chest, robed in battle armor.

No coffin panels held his manly form; no death-shroud enveloped those sinewy limbs; neither did things of glitter and show glisten along his couch, heaping mockery on the dumb solemnity of the grave.

It was the custom of Albarone, that the knight who once reigned lord of its wide domains, should even in death meet the stern enemy of man, not as victim, but as conqueror.

Borne to the vaults of death, not with voices of wail and woe, but compassed by men-at-arms; environed by upraised swords, the silent corse seemed to smile in the face of the skeleton-god, and enter even the domains of the grave in triumph, while the battle shout of Albarone rose pealing above, and over the visage of the dead waved the broad banner of the warlike race.

Near the head of the corse, while along the aisles of the chapel gathered the men-at-arms and servitors of Albarone, were grouped two figures—an aged man and a youthful maiden.

With his head depressed, his arms folded meekly over his breast, his slender form clad in solemn folds of sable velvet, faced with costly furs, and relieved by ornaments of scattered gold, the Count Aldarin Di Albarone seemed absorbed in listening to the chaunt of the holy mass, when, in sooth, his keen eye flashed with impatience, and his lip curved with scorn, as he was forced to witness the ceremonies of a religion whose mandates he defied, whose awful God his very soul blasphemed.

The maiden, fair, and young, and gentle, her robes of white flowing loosely around her form of grace, her hands half clasped and half upraised, stood near the couch of the dead, her calm blue eyes fixed upon the visage of the corse, while the memory of the fearful scene in the Red Chamber swept over her soul, mingling with the thoughts of the felon now festering on the wheel of Florence.

The bosom of the Ladye Annabel rose and fell with a wild pulsation, and her rounded cheeks grew like the face of death, as thus waiting beside the dead, the thoughts of the past awoke such terrible memories in her soul.

Around, circling along the pavement, with stern visages and iron-clad forms gleaming in the light, were grouped the men-at-arms of Albarone, extending along the chapel aisles, in one rugged array of battle, while each warrior held aloft a blazing torch with his left arm, as his good right hand grasped the battle sword.

Here and there were scattered servitors of Albarone, clad in the rich livery of the ancient house, darkened by folds of crape, mingled with the humble peasant vassals, whose faces, stamped with sorrow, mingled with the general grief.

Every voice was hushed, and every foot-tramp stilled, as the last strains of the holy chaunt of the mass floated solemnly along the chapel aisles, while high overhead, above armed warrior and white-robed monk, floated the broad banner of Albarone, waving to and fro with the motion of the night air, its gorgeous folds bearing the emblazoning of the winged leopard, with the motto, in letters of gold.

As the last echoes of the holy ceremony of the mass died away along the chapel aisles, Count Aldarin glanced over the group of white-robed monks, with the venerable abbot of St. Peters of Florence in their midst, and along the files of the iron-robed soldiers, for a single moment, and then gazing upon the broad banner waving overhead, he spoke in a bold and deep-toned voice:

"Let the corse of Lord Julian Di Albarone be raised upon the shoulders of the ancient men who served as esquires of his body."

Four men-at-arms, whose heads were whitened by the frosts of seventy winters, advanced; and, raising the death-couch upon their shoulders, with the right leg thrown forward, stood ready to march.

At the same moment, the united strength of ten of the servitors threw open the huge oaken panels of a trap-door, which, cut into the floor of the middle aisle of the chapel, revealed a wide and spacious stairway, descending into the bosom of the earth.

The Count Aldarin seized the staff which bore the broad banner of Albarone, he flung the azure folds to the night wind, and his voice rung echoing along the chapel walls:

"Vassals of Albarone, form around the corse of your lord. Draw your swords, and raise the shout: 'Albarone, to the rescue! Strike for the Winged Leopard—strike for Albarone!'"

With the battle cry pealing, their swords flashing in the light, and their torches waving on high, the men-at-arms formed in files of four behind the bier, which now began to move slowly toward the subterranean stairway.

In the rear of the men-at-arms came the Ladye Annabel, followed by the venerable abbot, bearing aloft a crucifix of gold; while on either side walked rosy-cheeked children, clad in robes of white, and holding censers in their hands, which ever and anon they swung to and fro, filling the air with perfume of frankincense and myrrh.

Then came the monks, in their mingled robes of white and black, walking with slow and solemn tread, and holding in one hand a torch, while the other grasped a cross.

As the ancient esquires who bore the bier of beechen wood, arrived at the trap-door which discovered the subterranean stairway, the funeral train halted for an instant.

The sight was full of grandeur.

The light of a thousand torches threw a ruddy glow upon the folds of the broad banner—upon the glistening armor and bright swords of the men-at-arms—over the snow-white attire of the long array of monks, and along the cold face of the dead. The carvings that decorated the walls of the church—the altar, rich with a thousand offerings—the cross of gold, and the rare paintings—the arched and fretted roof, and the lofty pillars, were all shown in bold and strong relief.

"Ye ancient men who bear the corse of the Lord Di Albarone, ye who served your lord with a faithful service while living, prepare to descend into the vault of the dead, there to lay your sacred burden beside his fathers. Vassals of Albarone, grasp your swords yet tighter, and join, every man, in the battle song of our race. The house of Albarone enter the tomb, not with wail and lamentation, but with song and joy, as though they went to battle; with swords flashing, with armor clanking, and with the broad banner of the Winged Leopard waving above their heads."

Right full and loud sounded the voice of Count Aldarin, while his bent form straightened proudly erect, as though he were suddenly fired with the warlike spirit of his ancestors. His dark eye flashed as he shouted, waving the banner over the bier:

"Men of Albarone, to the rescue!"

"Strike for the Winged Leopard!—strike for Albarone!" responded, with one deep-toned voice the aged bearers of the bier, as they began to descend the stairway.

"Ha! an Albarone! an Albarone! Strike for the Winged Leopard! strike for Albarone!" shouted the men-at-arms, as, waving their torches on high, and brandishing their swords, they advanced with a hurried, yet measured tread, after the manner they were wont to advance to the storming of a besieged fortress.

The aged abbot of St. Peters suddenly forgot his sacred character, and stirred by the memory of the days when he had mingled in the din of battle, side by side with the noble Lord Julian, he caught up the war cry: "Albarone to the rescue!—a blow for the Winged Leopard!" and along the line of white-robed monks ran the shout: "An Albarone! Ha! for the Winged Leopard! Strike for Albarone!" and thus spreading from the men-at-arms to the abbot, from the abbot to the monks, the cry of battle resounded along the aisles of the chapel, and was echoed again and again from the fretted roof.

As the corse disappeared down the stairway, followed by the funeral train, the war song of Albarone was raised by the men-at-arms—wild and thrilling arose the notes of the chaunt, that had swelled in the van of a thousand battles.

The subterranean stairway seemed to be without end. At last, when some five score steps had been passed, the bearers of the corse found themselves in a long and narrow passage, which having slowly traversed, they stood at the head of a winding stairway.

This they descended, while louder, and yet more loud arose the chaunt of the battle song, mingling with the clash of swords and the clank of armor.

At the foot of this stairway lay another passage, narrower than the last, from which it differed in that it was hewn out of the solid rock, while the walls of the other were built of chisseled stone.

Along this passage the procession slowly proceeded, the walls approaching closer together at every step, until at last there was barely room for the bier to pass; when suddenly, as if by the wand of a magician, the scene was changed, and the funeral train found themselves in the vault of the dead.

CHAPTER THE FIFTH.

THE CAVERN OF ALBARONE.

THE FUNERAL TRAIN, BEARING THE CORSE ALONG
THROUGH THE GROUPS OF SPECTRAL-FORMS, ARE AWE
STRICKEN BY THE APPEARANCE OF A STRANGE KNIGHT.

ABOVE, the cavern roof spread vast and magnificent, like an earth-hidden
sky.

Around, on every side, in rugged grandeur, extended the rocky walls; and far
in the distance, the solid pavement seemed to grow larger and wider, as the
gazer looked upon its surface of substantial stone.

The light of the funeral torches flashing over the abrupt rocks, revealed the
level floor, and gave a faint glimpse of the vast arch extending far above. The
ruddy beams flashing on every side, disclosed a strange and bewildering
spectacle.

Around the walls of the cavern, and over the floor, were scattered figures of
gigantic stone, rising from the pavement, at irregular intervals, in various and
strangely contrasted attitudes, bearing the most singular resemblance to the
gestures of living men, yet with every face stamped with an expression that
chilled the heart of the gazer, as though he beheld a spirit of the unreal world.

A wild legend was written in the archieves of Albarone, concerning these
strange figures.

In the olden time, when eternal midnight brooded through these cavern halls,
a demon band shook the rugged arches with their sounds of hellish wassail,
startling the gloom of night and the brightness of noonday above, with the
echo of their shrieks and yells; while their foul blasphemies of the AWFUL
UNKNOWN infected the very air with a curse, and sent disease and death
abroad from the cavern over the land, until every lip grew pale, and every
heart was chilled, at the mention of the demon vault of Albarone.

It was when the impious revel swelled loudest; when the infernal goblet was
raised to every lip; when the glances of glaring eyes, burning with the curse
of Lucifer, were exchanged between the supernatural revellers; when the
sounds of mockery and yells of blasphemy, echoing and thundering around
the vault, realized a hell on earth, that the words of the Invisible broke over
the scene, and the figures of the demon band were suddenly transformed to
lifeless stone.

This wild tradition gained credence from the positions and attitudes of these strange statues.

The smallest of the figures was three times as large as the tallest and most robust of men; there were others whose heads of dark rock well nigh touched the cavern's roof, while their outstretched arms and writhing attitude filled the gazer with indefinable dread.

Some were springing in the festal dance, the smile, grim and ghost-like wreathing their lips of stone; some were circling in groups of wild revelry, their faces agitated by laughter; while others, with upturned countenances, bearing the impress of every dark and hellish passion, and arms thrown wildly aloft, seemed daring the vengeance of heaven, and mocking the power of God.

Among all these various and contrasted figures, there was not one form of beauty, not one shape of grace; but all were expressive of low, bestial revelry, servile terror, or else of sublime hatred and defiance.

Some were formed of the darkest, and some of the lightest stone. Here arose a form of dark rock, side by side with a shape of snow-white stone; yonder towered a figure of dusky red, and farther on, a form of dark blue, veined by streaks of crimson and purple, broke through the darkened air.

The ancient esquires who bore the corse, had faced the brunt of a hundred battles, and fought in the van of a thousand frays, yet it was not without a shiver of terror that they looked around upon this wild and unearthly scene, thronged with those dark and fiend-like figures.

As they advanced, a new wonder attracted the attention of the funeral train.

Far in the cavern, to all appearance near the centre, a vast mound, of a square form, arising from the level pavement, was hung with burning lamps, and overlooked by a figure of stone, which seemed to those of the funeral train to exceed all the others, both in the magnitude of its height, and the wildness of its attitude. The lamps burning above this mound, threw a strong light over the dark figure, and along the pavement, for some few yards around; while the space between the mound and the procession was lost in entire darkness.

The bearers of the corse, advancing towards the mound, led on the funeral train, who all, save the Count Aldarin, seemed seized with a sudden and indefinable dread. The battle song was still continued, the swords were still brandished, and the torches were still waved on high; but there was a tremor in the notes of the song, the swords were grasped with the nervous sensation that men ever feel when expecting to meet antagonists of the unknown world, and the waving of the torches was accompanied by the muttered exorcisms of the monks.

As for the Ladye Annabel, she leaned half swooning upon the arm of the venerable abbot, who, in good sooth, was as much frightened as the maiden.

The esquires who bore the remains of their gallant lord, had now gained near half the way over the pavement of stone, toward the mound; the last of the servitors had emerged from the narrow passage into the cavern and the whole train extending in one unbroken line, marked by the long array of torches flashing over the armor of the warriors, and the white robes of the monks, presented a striking and imposing spectacle.

Aldarin turned suddenly round, and exclaimed, with a wild gesture:

"How now, vassals? Why this tremor?—Whence this alarm? Do I not lead you? Raise the battle song of our race yet higher, and advance yet more boldly! The banner of the Winged Leopard waves above ye! Shout the war cry, and let your noble lord be borne to his rest as were his fathers before him. Shout the war cry—shout—"

Wheeling suddenly around in the warmth of his excitement, he turned from the men-at-arms, to the corse-bearers, and at the very instant, started a step backward with involuntary horror. The corse sate erect in the death-couch, the white pall falling back from the iron-clad shoulders while the light of the torches fell vividly upon its unclosed eyes as their cold, stony glare rested upon the face of Aldarin.

Aldarin felt his very heart leaping within his bosom, while big beaded drops of moisture, clammy as the death-sweat, stood out from his forehead.

"The Corse hath arisen in the death-couch"—he hurriedly whispered—"The eyes of the dead are unclosed, they are gazing around the vault of death."

"It is the custom of Albarone," exclaimed a white-haired Esquire,—"We have raised the corse erect, we have unclosed its eyes. The mighty dead of Albarone enter the vault of death, proudly and erect, with their unclosed eyes gazing fearlessly on the tomb—such is the custom of Albarone!"

"Thanks—brave Esquire—Thanks"—slowly and gaspingly exclaimed Aldarin, as he recovered his powers of mind. "Men of Albarone," he exclaimed in a loud and commanding tone, "Gaze ye upon the face of the unconquered Dead, gaze upon the erect form, the unclosed eyes, daring the terror of the tomb—and as ye gaze, let the battle-song of our race peal to the very cavern's roof! Shout the war-cry, shout—"

A figure clad from head to foot in azure armor of shining steel, leaped from behind a form of stone, arising from the cavern floor, at the head of the bier, and seizing the banner-staff from the hands of Aldarin, finished his sentence—

"Shout"—exclaimed the figure armed in azure steel—"Shout Albarone to the rescue! Death to the Murderer!"

The thunder-tones of that voice were known, along the line of men-at-arms, through the columns of the Monks. One wild shout arose from the warriors—

"Ha! For Albarone! Adrian, our Lord, comes from the dead to lead us! On— on! Strike for the Winged Leopard—strike for Albarone!"

Strange it was that the very men, who a moment before had trembled with undefined terror, now hailed with joy the presence of one whom they supposed to have risen from the dead.

In an instant all was confusion and uproar. The Esquires set down the corse, and together with the men-at-arms, clustered around the figure in azure armor, shouting and making the very cavern's roof re-echo with their exclamations of joy.

The tumult and out-cry, coupled with the name of Adrian, reached the ears of the fair Ladye Annabel, who already half swooning with terror, now felt her brain whirling in wild confusion, as she fell fainting in the arms of the Abbot of St. Peters.

"Brethren,"—cried the Abbot, addressing the monks—"Haste ye away to the upper air for aid, while I stay here with the maiden, and exorcise yon devil, if devil it may be, with solemn prayers and ceremonies. Away—away, the fair Ladye may die, ere ye can return with aid."

It needed no second word from the Abbot; the Monks gazed in each other's faces with affrighted looks, and then trooping hurriedly together, hastened across the floor of the cavern, followed by the Servitors, who but a moment past formed part of the procession. It was but an instant ere the white robes of the monks, and the gay livery of the servitors, were lost to view within the confines of the narrow passage.

The Abbot holding the fainting maiden in his arms, her white attire mingling with his sacerdotal robes, gazed around the cavern, and found to his astonishment that all around him was wrapt in darkness, while far ahead, he could discern the lights of the death mound, breaking through the gloom, with the glare of torches, held aloft by the men-at-arms, creating a brilliant space between his position and the mound of the dead.

"All is dark"—murmured the Abbot—"All is dark around me—yet far ahead, I behold the men-at-arms clustering round the Strange Figure—their swords rise aloft, and their distant shouts break on my ear! She lays in my arms, cold, cold and senseless. Save me, mother of Heaven, but I cannot feel the beating of her heart—I hear no sound of aid, no voice of assistance! The cavern is damp, and she may die ere they come with succor,—I will away and seek for aid myself. Lay there, gentle Ladye, at the foot of this strange Statue—thus I enfold thee in my robes of white—thus I defend thee from the cold and damp—in a moment I will be with thee again! God aid my steps!"

At the foot of a figure of stone, wrapping her form in his glittering robe of white and gold, which he doffed from his own trembling frame, the Abbot rested the Ladye Annabel, all cold and insensible, and then hastened from the Cavern in search of aid.

There was a long, long pause around the spot where lay the maiden, while fearful mysteries were enacting far beyond, on the summit of the Death-Mound.

When the Abbot again returned he was companioned by armed men, with glittering attire and flashing swords. He sought the resting-place of the maiden; he beheld nothing but the rough floor of the cavern. The Ladye Annabel had disappeared, and the grotesque figure rising from the pavement seemed to grin in mockery as the horror-stricken Abbot gazed upon the vacant stone, where he had laid the maiden down to rest, her form of beauty, sheltered by his sacred robes.

CHAPTER THE SIXTH.

THE ORDEAL.

WITHOUT much physical bravery, the Count Aldarin possessed a soul worthy of the noblest efforts of moral courage, yet now while the men-at-arms gathered with shouts and exclamations of joy, around the Azure Figure, he stood trembling like a reed shaken by the winter wind, his face at all times destitute of color, became lividly pale, and with quivering lips and chattering teeth, he remained for a moment silent and motionless.

Superstitious terror, he was wont to contemn, fear of the supernatural, he was known to despise, yet now when the voice of the dead rang in his ears, and the form which had been extended on the Wheel of the Doomsman, moved before his eyes, he thought the voice and form had sprung from the unknown recesses of the grave.

It was after the lapse of a few moments, that he summoned courage to advance through the crowd of men-at-arms, and fixing his keen eye on the form of the unknown knight, he spoke—

"Who Sir, art thou? What is thine errand in this lonely vault of the dead? Why disturb the funeral rites of the Lord Di Albarone?"

"I come to avenge his murder!"

"Ha!" shouted Aldarin—"His murderer is already doomed—even now he festers upon the wheel!"

"His murderer lives"—shouted the Figure, through the bars of his closed helmet,—"His murderer breathes, while the Corse asks in the speechless tongue of death—asks and prays to God, to man for vengeance! The Murderer walks the earth, walks in the calm sunshine, while the Murdered rots and crumbles in gloom and darkness. His murderer is here—aye among the brave soldiers, who followed Julian of Albarone to battle, stands the foul miscreant.—THOU ART THE MURDERER!"

A wild thrill of surprise and horror ran through the group. From heart to heart, like lightning leaping from cloud to cloud, darted the wild words of the accuser; from eye to eye flew the quick glance of vengeance, and from lip to lip swelled the shout of the avengers.

"Hew him down!" cried one—"For days have we all thought him guilty. Our suspicions are now confirmed—the corse pleads for his blood!"

"Down with the brother-murderer!"

"Lo! I whet my knife for his blood!"

"Our Lord"—exclaimed a tall and stalwart man-at-arms—"Our Lord Adrian doth rise from the dead to convict thee of the murder of thy brother! Miscreant, canst thou deny it?"

The four ancient Esquires said not a word, but each of them raised his dagger, they seized the Scholar Aldarin, with one firm grasp, their eyes were fixed upon his visage in one stern glare, their instruments of vengeance gleamed over his head, and with silent determination, they awaited the command to strike and kill.

The Azure Knight stayed their hands.

"Onward, brave soldiers"—he cried—"onward to the tomb of the race of Albarone. There will we administer the Ordeal to the old man, there, beneath the shadow of the Demon of our Race, shall he swear that he is guiltless. Onward—bearers of the corse—in the name of the Winged Leopard, onward!"

Raising the bier upon their shoulders, with the corse still sitting grimly erect, the ancient Esquires advanced toward the Mound, led onward by the Unknown Knight, while in the rear, surrounded by men-at-arms, walked the Scholar Aldarin, his head drooped low, and his arms folded across his breast.

He said no word, he uttered no sound of entreaty, but his keen gray eyes, half-buried by his contracting brows, seemed all aflame with the intensity of his thoughts.

The Mound, with all its ponderous outline, lighted by the lamps burning on the summit, now began to appear more clearly through the gloom.

At first it seemed like some vast pile of rocks, heaped on high by a giant-hand, and then, as the men-at-arms drew near and nearer, it gradually assumed a definite form, rising like a pyramid, its three sides fashioned into steps of living rock, while from the fourth, arose the dark figure of stone, towering far, far above, its arms wildly outspread, its face looking down upon the tomb, as its vacant eyes seemed fixing their weird and terrible glance upon the faces of the dead.

The strange procession reached the mound, they ascended twenty steps of stone, and the bearers of the corse found themselves standing upon the summit, from the centre of which arose a solid block of stone, some thirty feet in length and seven in width, while it was but four feet in height.

On the top of this rock, within the hollow of a cavity, hewn out of the living stone, lay the remains of the Lords of Albarone, placed there from age to age, from generation to generation, through the long lapse of six hundred years.

It was a strange scene.

The lamps of iron, curious in fashion and ponderous in size placed at intervals around the rock, cast their glaring light over the crumbling remains, each grisly skeleton attired in the warlike costume of the age that beheld his glory and owned his rule.

Here the thin and blackened arm-bones of a Gothic warrior were crossed upon his breast-plate of gold, which long years ago had covered the plain tunic, worn by these iron-men, who swept like an avalanche from the Alps of the North, over the fair plains of Italy.

The lamp-beams glimmering over the skeleton, revealed the bones below the breast-plate, mouldering into dust, while the fragments of the feet were encircled in the simple yet warlike sandals of iron once worn by the warriors from the land of the Goth.

Side by side with this relic, the bones of another skeleton gleamed grimly through the bars and armor-plates of a later age, wrapping the remains of the mighty dead, from the helmeted skull to the iron-booted feet.

And thus extending along the cavity in the surface of the rock, skull after skull and skeleton succeeding skeleton, reposed the Lords of the House of Albarone, types of contrasted ages, clad in strange and various costumes, or enwrapped in the stern iron armour, which had defended their living forms in the terror of battle.

The boast of the proud House—that the earth of the grave-yard should never soil a Lord of the race of Albarone—was fulfilled.

Over this singular tomb towered the dark figure of gigantic rock, its rude arms thrown wildly aloft, while its downcast eyes of stone were fixed upon the corses of the dead.

Many a legend, whispered beside the hearths of the peasantry, or told by the minstrel in the hall of the castle, inspiring its hearers with terror and awe, spoke in words of fear of the demon-form arising in the cavernous recesses of Albarone, its mighty power, and the strange sympathy it possessed for the race of the Winged Leopard.

Some traditions, dim and indistinct, yet fraught with wild mysteries, named the figure as the representation of the Northern-God ODIN, stating that in ages long gone by, it had been worshipped with infant sacrifice and midnight bloodshed, while the Lords of Albarone flung themselves in awe beneath its gloomy shadow.

Other legends named the rude creation of rocks as the Demon of the race of Albarone, brooding silently over the tomb of the Lords, while its heart of stone was sentient with a strange soul, its broad chest impassioned a conscious spirit, its giant limbs were instinct with a fearful life, and its eyes looked forth with an expression that froze the blood of the gazer to behold.

Such were the legends, differing in their style and incident, yet all uniting in throwing the veil of mystery and shadow over the dark, dread form of stone.

It was seen but once in the life time of a Lord of Albarone, when he celebrated the funeral rites of his predecessor, and the demon-form once seen, the cavern of the dead was never traversed by his living form again.

Thrice the funeral train passed round the tomb, the esquires bearing the upright corse, thrice they raised the wild chaunt of the battle-song of Albarone, while far and wide the depths of the cavern gave back the sound, swelling in a thousand echoes, like successive claps of August thunder.

The death-couch was then rested upon the platform of stone.

The ancient Esquires slowly raised the corse, again the battle-cry swelled through the cavern, the men-at-arms wildly clashed their swords together, while the banner streamed proudly in the torch-light.

"Men of Albarone!" spoke the solemn tones of the Azure-Knight; "The Count Julian of Albarone is laid beside his fathers!"

Louder clashed the swords, more proudly waved the banner, and higher and yet higher swelled the song as the mailed corse was placed in the cavity, side by side with its ancestors.

The figure in azure armor glanced round upon the group of men-at-arms, and exclaimed in a deep-toned voice, that thrilled to every heart—

"Fall back, vassals of Albarone. Let Aldarin, brother of the late Lord, advance!"

Aldarin advanced with a sneer upon his pale countenance.

"Ha—ha!" he muttered to himself, "they think to frighten me with their senseless mummery—their childish mockery! Frighten Aldarin with superstition—Aldarin, who believes not in their God! Ha—ha! I am here," he continued aloud—"What would ye with me?"

"Old man!" exclaimed the Stranger-knight, "look upon the corse of thy murdered brother.—Behold the features pale with death; the clammy brow, the sunken cheek, the livid lip—look upon that corse, and say you did not do the murder!"

The men-at-arms looked on with intense interest, their forms clad in iron armor, were crowded together, and every eye was fixed upon the Scholar.

The face of Aldarin was calm as innocence, as he replied—"*I did not do the murder!*"

"Give me thy hand—place thy fingers upon the livid lips of the corse."

Boldly did Aldarin reach forth his hand, and touch the compressed mouth of the mailed corse.

The lips slowly parted, and a thin stream of blood emerged from the mouth, and trickled over the lower lip and down the chin, staining the gray beard of the deceased warrior with its dark red hue.

The men-at-arms shrunk back with sudden horror, and each soldier could hear the gasping of his comrade's breath.

A tremor passed over the frame of Aldarin, and his face became pale as that of the corse beside which he stood.

"Wilt thou now say thou art innocent?" exclaimed the stranger-knight. "The corse—the lifeless form of thy murdered brother, shrinks at thy accursed touch."

"*I am innocent!*" cried Aldarin, recovering his determined tone of voice. "*By the God of heaven and earth, I swear it!*"

"What say ye, vassals of Albarone? Is this man innocent?"

Then arose one firm, determined cry from the men-at-arms—

"He is guilty—heaven and earth proclaim it! The dead witness it!"

And the depths of the cavern returned the hollow echo—"Guilty—guilty!"

They all advanced a step toward the accused. Each eye fired with one expression; the sinews of each hand were strained to bursting, as they grasped their well-tried swords.

"One trial more," exclaimed the figure in armor of azure steel. "Aldarin of Albarone, look upon that awful form which towers above us. Behold the arms outstretched, as if to hurl the red lightning bolt down upon thy guilty head. Mark well those eyes of stone—the fearful look of that dark countenance—the eyes are fixed upon thee; and the brow lowers at thee. Look, Aldarin of Albarone, look upon the Demon of our race. Call to mind the fearful legends of that demon's vengeance upon all who ever wronged the House of Albarone. Think of the time when those lips of stone have sent forth a voice to convict the guilty; when those arms of rock have been filled with life to crush the wretch whom the voice convicted. Old man, art thou ready for the ordeal?"

Aldarin cast one glance around. A dead silence reigned throughout the cavern. The torches cast a strong light upon the long line of robed skeletons, and upon the stern visage of the murdered Lord. The faces of the men-at-arms glared fiercely upon the accused: their eyes sparkled from under their woven brows, their lips were compressed, and their half-raised swords glowed in the ruddy light.

Aldarin looked above. The massive brow, the stone eye-balls, the sneering lip, of that dread dark face of stone, were all turned to glaring red by the strong light of many torches. Each sinew of the muscular arms; the clenched hands; the bold prominence of the gigantic chest; the strong outline of the towering figure, were all shown in bold and sublime relief.

Aldarin raised his hands on high.

"Dark form—Demon of our race—Before thee I swear—I am guiltless."

"*Murderer!*" a hollow voice exclaimed. The sound rung thro' the arches of the cavern like the voice of the dead.

"Ha!" shouted the men-at-arms, "behold—behold the Demon speaks; the lips of stone move; the eyes fire—behold!"

The voice again rung thro' the cavern—"*Murderer!*"

Aldarin started. The sneer upon his lip had fled. In a moment he lay prostrate upon the platform of stone, and a score of swords flashed over him.

"I confess—I confess!" shouted he, in hurried tones; "I ask but one moment to prepare me for death. Grant me this boon, and ye are Christians."

"Dog!" shouted one of the pall-bearers, "thy victim died without shrift—"

"So shalt thou die!" cried another.

"Lo! my knife is whetted for thy blood!"

"Hold!" exclaimed the strange knight, "let him have his request!"

Aldarin arose and drew from his vest a small missal, with clasps of gold, and covers that blazed with jewels.

"I would pray," he exclaimed meekly, as pressing the clasps of the missal, it flew open, discovering not the leaves of a book of prayer, but a hollow casket. Taking a small phial of silver from the bottom of this casket, he held it hurriedly to the flame of a torch, and then with as much haste, he applied the mouth of the phial to a bright stone that was fixed under the lid of the casket.

The stone emitted quick flashing sparks of fire, and a light misty smoke emerging from the mouth of the phial, spread like a cloud around Aldarin, and rolled through the vault in waving columns.

It was accompanied by a pungent odor, which, far sweeter than perfume of frankincense and myrrh, stole over the senses of the astonished spectators, gradually benumbing their limbs, and depriving them both of motion and consciousness.

The figure in azure armor rushed forward to seize the murderer, but his limbs refused their office, and he fell upon the platform of stone, his armor ringing as he fell. At the same moment, while the smoke grew thicker and the odor more pungent, the men-at-arms—both those who stood upon the platform and those who thronged the steps of stone—fell to the earth as one man. The ancient Esquires drew their daggers and advanced.

The Count Aldarin gave a derisive laugh.

"Dogs!" shouted he, "ye knew not of my last resort! I hold a power above your grasp—receive the reward of your insolence. Down, ye slaves!"

Flashes of fire played like lightning in the wreaths of smoke. The Esquires tottered and fell prostrate among their fellows.

CHAPTER THE SEVENTH.

THE BLOW FOR THE WINGED LEOPARD.

THE light of the lamps, burning along the tomb, fell over the steps of stone, and cast its crimson glow over the dread face of the Demon-Form, while the sands of the fourth part of an hour, sank in the glass of time. The knight in armor of azure steel, was the first to rise from the strange slumber which the chemical spell of the Scholar had flung around the senses of the avengers. He arose, he looked wildly over the steps of stone and along the cavern.— *Aldarin was gone.*

The azure knight gazed around the gloom and darkness of the vault of death, for some moments, while the utter silence of the place impressed his heart with a strange awe.

A sound struck his ear. It was the sound of men marching in order of battle. It grew louder, and was mingled with the clanking of armor and the clashing of swords. Listening intently for a few moments, the knight of the azure armor at last beheld a body of men-at-arms emerge from the narrow passage that led into the cavern, with long lines of torches shining upon a brilliant array of upraised swords, armor of gold, mingled with shining spears and waving pennons.

They advanced in regular order, being formed in two distinct columns, between which, at the head of the party, walked one distinguished from the others by the richness of his armor, while his voice of command showed him to be the leader of the company.

While they poured across the floor of the cavern, the knight of the azure armor scanned them with great attention, as he exclaimed, with a shout of joy.

"They come—the shallow-pated Duke and his minions. One blow—one good straight-forward blow, and I am Lord of the halls of my ancestors."

With his right hand he seized his sword, and with his left he waved the banner of the WINGED LEOPARD.

"Up—up!—Ye men Albarone. Up with your swords, and strike for the Winged Leopard, for your Lord and his rights!"

The men-at-arms awoke, like men awaking from troubled sleep and hideous dreams. They groped hastily for their swords over the steps of stone and along the platform, and in a few moments they stood erect and prepared for fight.

"Range yourselves, my brave men, on either side of the tomb, in the darkness. Ye number fifty in all; our enemies appear to count ten times our force. Behold!—they continue to pour into the cavern. But hist!—The watchword is—'Ha! for the Winged Leopard.'"

The men-at-arms of his Grace of Florence were now within one hundred yards of the mound.

"Well, by St. Paul," exclaimed the Duke, "this is certainly a very dreary looking place. Really one could imagine this cavern to be a very fit habitation for witches, devils, or any other unnecessary things. Where be these caitiff knaves, of which my Lord the Count Aldarin told us of? Advance, my brave men; find these villains. They have stolen the Ladye Annabel away—despatch them, and then we will have time to share the banquet of our lordly host!"

The broad banner of the Duke, of glaring red, having a lion rampant emblazoned on its folds, was now unfurled, and the company advanced in the same careless order, in which they had proceeded over the floor of the cavern.

"By the tomb of my ancestors, will I flesh my maiden sword. By the corse of my father, will I fight for my right."

The knight of the azure armor grasped his sword more firmly. In another moment the torches of the Duke's followers would flash upon the armor of his ambushed men, in another moment he would stand disclosed before the eyes of the Duke. With a flashing eye he measured the clear level space that lay between the mound and the advancing men-at-arms.

A whisper to his men—a firmer grasp of his sword, and a firmer grasp of the banner staff, and the knight in three good leaps, sprang down the twenty steps of stone, shouting as he sprang—"Ha! for the Winged Leopard! Ha! for Albarone!"

At his back, with swords drawn, and springing with all the litheness of youth, came the four ancient Esquires, and behind them, leaping from the opposite side of the mound, with swords likewise drawn, and with the war-cry pealing to the cavern's roof, came the two bodies of men-at-arms, numbering twenty-five in each company.

Another leap and another spring, and the azure knight stands within striking distance of the astonished Duke. Quick as thought he planted his banner in the cavern floor, and grasping his sword with both hands, he whirled it once round his head, and throwing all his strength in the blow, he brought it down full upon the golden crest of the tyrant, who was driven to the very earth by the vigor of the stroke.

In an instant the foot of the azure knight was upon the breast of the prostrate prince, and while the men-at-arms, on right and left, and the esquires at his back, were carrying on the strife right merrily, he prepared for another stroke. He shortened his grasp of the sword, and gazing sternly through the bars of his helmet, down into his fallen enemy's uncovered face, with all the strength of his stalwart arm, he essayed to send his weapon into his very throat.

The blow descended whizzing through the air, but its aim was foiled. One of the ancient esquires, with a stout stroke of his sword, sent a vassal reeling before the person of the Duke, and thus drove aside the blow of the azure knight, which sank deep into the lifeless corse thrown so suddenly before him.

And now the followers of the Duke gathered around the champions of the Winged Leopard, in vast numbers, hurrying forward without order, and dropping their torches in their haste.

The azure knight was driven back, and as he receded, the blood of the oldest of the gallant esquires stained his armor.

"On, my brave men!" shouted he. "A blow for Albarone!" At every exclamation a foe took the measure of his grave upon the cavern floor.

"Ha! for the Winged Leopard!" he shouted, as perceiving the head of the Duke among the throng, he essayed to greet him with one gallant blow. At the same moment, his men-at-arms sunk on one knee, and thus received the disorderly charge of their foes. It was in vain. On all sides thronged the followers of the Duke, and one after the other the brave champions of the Winged Leopard fell bleeding and dead upon the pavement of stone.

Onward and onward pressed the azure knight, gallantly breasting the flood before him, throwing his foes to the right and left, until he again fronted the Duke.

And at the very instant, with soft and noiseless footsteps, there glided along the steps of the mound of stone, a fair and lovely form, clad in a strange robe, of white and gold, soiled by the cavern earth, and floating abroad in the night air, in waving folds like spirit-wings. She gained the platform of the mound, and fixed one half-conscious glance upon the corse of the dead, while her large blue eyes warmed with a glance of holy affection.

"He sleeps, my uncle"—she murmured—"anon, I will give him the potion— and then—ah, then he will arise and smile upon me!"

She turned her wild glance to the scene passing in the cavern floor far below, she heard the distant shouts, she caught a vision of one well-known form, which her half-crazed brain deemed a visitant from the spirit world.

It was a picture of loveliness, rising amid gloom and death, the beautiful maiden raised to her full stature, one fair hand resting upon the dark mound, while with the other thrown wildly across her brow, she essayed to pierce the gloom of the cavern beyond. Her robes floated lightly round her form, revealing the delicate symmetry of that maiden shape, a glimpse of the snow-white bosom as it heaved in the light, the outlines of the neck, while the blooming loveliness of her countenance, half-shaded by the upraised hand, was varied by sudden and changing, yet dream-like expressions.

"I see his form"—she murmured—"and yet 'tis a dream—they seize him, they—O, heaven help me, they raise their swords above his head—"

"Maiden, fling thy robe!—fling the death-pall over the funeral lamps!"—a solemn voice broke on the air directly overhead.

She looked above, she shrieked with horror, for the cold strange eyes of the Demon-Figure met her gaze.

Meanwhile, breasting his way through the opposing crowd of foemen, the azure knight neared the person of the Duke, he stood before the tyrant face to face.

"Die, tyrant!" he shouted, as springing back to give effect to his blow, he threw his sword on high. It descended full upon the shoulder of the Duke, and severing his armor, snapped suddenly short, and the azure knight was left defenceless in the hands of his enemies.

"Up with the caitiff's vizor," shouted the Duke. "Let us see the bravo's face. Up with his vizor."

The captive knight cast a glance around, and beheld his followers—the dying and the dead—strewn over the floor of the cavern. The brave old Esquires lay side by side, their sinewy hands still grasping their broken swords, and their gray hair dabbled in blood.

"Sir Duke," exclaimed the captive, "behold the bravo!" He raised his vizor, and the features of Adrian Di Albarone, pale and sunken, were revealed. "Behold the bravo!"

"Now, by the body of God!" shouted the Duke, boiling with passion, "thou shalt not escape me this time.—Dog——"

"These hands itch for thy blood"—shrieked a shrill and ringing voice, and Adrian beheld the distorted form and mis-shapen features of the Doomsman, pressing forward from the throng of men-at-arms, with his talon-like fingers grasping the air, while his face wore the expression of a demon in human guise,—"These hands itch for thy blood! Ha!—ha! Once escaped—the second time, the hot iron, the melted lead and the wheel of torture, wait not for thee in vain! Ha, ha,—hark how the cavern roof joins in my laugh. Great Duke, the Doomsman claims his victim!"

"Duke—tyrant, I am in thy power!" shouted Adrian, gazing upon the circle of men-at-arms who surrounded him. "These thongs, they are for my wrists! Yon chains—they soon will fasten this body to the dungeon floor! Thou art sure of thy victim—Lo! I defy thee!"

And as he spoke, there came gliding from the darkness of the cavern, two forms, clad in robes of sable velvet, who advanced hastily along the floor, and stood between the victim and the Duke.

"Lo! I defy thee! Tremble for thine own head, tyrant and coward! Tremble and turn pale, for lo! even now, the axe glimmers high above thy head, whetted for the Wronger's blood—in a moment it descends—beware the blow!"

And as he spoke, while the Duke recoiled with a sudden start, and even the Doomsman trembled as he beheld the sable figures standing before his victim, silent and motionless, yet with the long curved dagger in their girdles, and the parchment scroll in their hands, all suddenly became dim and indistinct, and the cavern was wrapped in darkness.

The lights burning on the mound, were extinguished by an unknown hand, while every eye beheld a waving robe of white, fluttering in the air, the moment ere darkness came down upon the scene.

"Torches there!" shouted the Duke—"Look to the prisoner, vassals! Torches there, I say!"

Torches were presently seen hurrying from the farther end of the cavern, borne in the firm grasp of men-at-arms, and in a few moments a ruddy light was thrown around the spot where stood the Duke.

"Dog!" exclaimed the Duke, gazing hurriedly around—"Thou shalt bitterly rue this foul treason."

He looked around in vain. His prisoner was gone, and with him had disappeared the banner of the Winged Leopard.

The light of torches again gleamed around the Mound of the Dead. The figure of a maiden lay extended along the steps of stone, her white robes waving round her insensible form—it was the Ladye Annabel.

"Mighty Duke, behold the scroll!" shrieked the Doomsman, as he held aloft the parchment, which he had taken from the cavern floor—"Behold the scroll, it bears an inscription—read, read."

"*Tyrant thrice—warned, yet unrelenting, the Invisible for the last time bids thee prepare for the steel! Lo! Thy Death now walks abroad seeking thee with the upraised axe,—beware his path!*"

CHAPTER THE EIGHTH.

THE PAGE AND THE DAMSEL.

IN a richly furnished ante-room, adjoining the bower of the Ladye Annabel, on a couch of the most inviting softness, lay Guiseppo, well-known to all the castle as the favorite page of his grace of Florence.

A lamp of the most elaborate moulding, suspended from the ceiling, threw a brilliant light over the rose-colored tapestry that adorned the walls and relieved the eye, gaily embroidered with the history of the temptations of the blessed St. Anthony. Here forms of terror appalled, and there shapes of beauty cheered the venerable saint, who was distinguished by a nose of a very blooming hue, marking a face redolent with the kiss of the wine-god.

The floor of the apartment was carefully strewn with rushes, and here and there were placed couches rivalling, in downy softness, the one on which Guiseppo lay, while everything wore the appearance of ease and luxury.

The small, yet well-proportioned figure of the youth was arrayed in a doublet of fine blue velvet, embroidered with gold, and brilliant with jewelled chains, that hung depending from his neck. His well formed legs were shown to the best advantage by hose of doe-skin, fitting close to the person, and he wore boots of the same material, ornamented with spurs of gold. His doublet was gathered about his waist by a belt that shone with gold and jewels, and at his left side he wore a rare dagger, with handle of ivory and sheath of gold.

The features of Guiseppo were not formed after the regular line of manly beauty, yet every lineament was redolent of light-hearted mirth and gleesome mischief. His forehead was rather low, his eyebrows arching, and his hazel eyes somewhat protruding; his nose was a thought too large, his lips curving with a merry smile, his cheeks full and glowing, and his rich brown hair fell in clustering locks down upon his collar of rarest lace.

He laid upon the couch in an easy position, his hazel eyes sparkling yet more brightly, and his lip curving yet more merrily, as he gazed upon a billet which he held in his right hand over his head.

"To the fair Ladye Annabel," thus he murmured to himself: "to be delivered as soon as she recovers from her swoon—hum!"

Here the page sprang suddenly up into a sitting posture. It seemed as if some new thought had taken possession of his fancy. His eyes sparkled, his lip curved, his cheek rounded, and his whole frame shook with suppressed laughter.

"Oh!" he exclaimed, as the tears came into his eyes; "Oh! 'twas exquisite!" He gave his right leg an emphatic slap. "'Twas exquisite—exquisite—exquisite!" And laughing louder than ever, the page walked up and down the apartment, well nigh bursting with repeated fits of merriment.

"Oh! St. Guiseppo!" he cried, "an' I live to be an old man, I shall never recover it! Ha—ha—ha!"

Mayhap it was very fortunate for Guiseppo that the door leading into Ladye Annabel's apartment was opened, just at the moment when he seemed about dissolving in his merriment.

A lovely maiden, with dark eyes and jet black hair, entered the chamber, with an angry look, as if to reprove the author of this boisterous laughter; but no sooner did she behold Guiseppo than she rushed into his arms, pronouncing his name at the same time, to which he very quietly responded—"Rosalind!" accompanying the expression with a kiss.

Having seated themselves upon a couch, Rosalind began to recall the times of old, naming many a familiar scene, many a well-known spot, where they had rambled together, ere Guiseppo left the castle—within whose walls he had been reared—to be a page to his grace of Florence.

As Rosalind rattled on, Guiseppo sat in mute admiration, much wondering to behold the lively little child, whom he had left some two years since, grown up into a handsome and budding damsel. He gazed with peculiar admiration upon the boddice of green velvet, which fitted so nicely, revealing the shape of one of the finest busts in the world—so Guiseppo thought, at least. He also had some indefinite idea of the prettiness of the cross of ebony, which, strung around her arching neck by a chain of gold, rose and fell with the heavings of the maiden's bosom.

The dimple of the chin—thought Guiseppo—is very pretty; those lips are very tempting, but those beautiful, dancing, beaming black eyes—Guiseppo rounded the sentence with a sigh.

"I'faith, Guiseppo," continued Rosalind, "your merriment, but a moment ago, startled me with affright. You might have awaked my cousin, the Ladye Annabel. She is sleeping after her fright in that dreadful vault. Tell me, Guiseppo, what made you so merry?"

The mirthful idea—whatever it was—again danced before the fancy of the page, and he fell into a fit of laughter, interspersed with numerous exclamations of delight.

At last Rosalind wrung from him the cause of his mirth, which he told somewhat after the following fashion.

CHAPTER THE NINTH.

THE STORY OF GUISEPPO.

"ON the day my young Lord—so I must still call him—was doomed to die by the Duke and Lords of Florence, I felt very dull, and the brightest piece of gold in the wide world would not have hired me to smile. And as for laughing—St. Guiseppo, that came not with my thoughts!

(Rosalind very quietly asked if nothing could have made him smile? He pressed his lips to hers and did not dispute the matter any further.)

"Being in this melancholy mood, I requested permission of my gracious master the Duke, to visit Lord Adrian that night. My request was granted.

"It was but half an hour after midnight, that I stood at the door of the Doomed Cell, where I learned, to my great regret, that the Duke had just departed, leaving his commands that no one should see the prisoner until morrow. There was an order of state affixed to the door to that effect, having the private seal of the Duke impressed upon it.

"No sooner had I perused this paper of state—thou knowest, Rosalind, that I can both read and write—thanks to Count Aldarin, who taught me, with much care and not a little pains—no sooner had I perused this paper of state, then unslinging my cloak of blue velvet and silver embroidery, I assumed all the pertness of a page at court, as I cried—Stand aside, Sir Beetle-brow, and make room for my couch—and you, gallant sir, of the squinting orb, be pleased to shift your lazy carcass an inch or so, an' it suits you.

"The beetle-browed sentinel Balvardo, and his companion Hugo of the sinister eye, looked upon me with the most unfeigned astonishment, as throwing my cloak upon the stone pavement, I proceeded to lay my person upon its bedizened folds."

"Well, Sir Malapert," cried Balvardo, "thou art surely moonstruck. In the fiend's name what mean you by thus sprawling out upon the pavement, like a cat near the end of her ninth life, eh, Sir Page?"

Here Hugo chimed in with his say, consisting of a "by'r Lady!" expressed in tones of the most interesting wonder, which he finished with a "w-h-e-w!" given with twisted lips and great musical effect.

"Why, noble Sir, of the bull-head," I answered, "and right worthy Sir of the Squinting Orb, I intend to watch the coming forth of my Lord Adrian, an' it please your lordships—and, as I wish to sleep, I will thank thee Balvardo to turn thy ugly visage another way, for, an' I shut my eyes after looking at thee

I'll be certain to dream of half-a-dozen devils or so. Hugo *do* try and look straight ahead for only an instant, or the warriors in my dreams will all be cross-eyed—by St. Guiseppo!"

"'Hist! thou magpie,' exclaimed Hugo, 'hear'st thou not a noise, Balvardo?'"

"The sound that rivetted Hugo's ear, proceeded from the Doomed Cell, and was certainly the most curious of all sounds. It was not exactly like the mewing of a cat, neither did it altogether resemble the howling of a cur and it certainly did not sound like the bellowing of a bull, or the chattering of a magpie, yet in good sooth, it seemed as if all these noises had been caught and put in a sack, and having been shaken well together, produced the most infernal discord that ever saluted mortal ear.

"'The Saints preserve us!' shrieked Balvardo. 'Surely the devil has taken possession of the murderer—hark *how* he howls!'

"'*He* indeed!' cried Hugo, 'it's not only *he*; by'r Lady, there's a score of them. There it goes again. Beshrew thee but, 'tis like the howl of a whipped cur—'

"'Nay Hugo, nay Hugo, 'tis like the spitting and mewing of an hundred cats.'

"'Or the chattering of a score of magpies.'

"'Now it bellows like a bull.'

"'St. Peter be good to us!' exclaimed Balvardo, as the howling grew louder and louder. 'It is the yelling of devils, and naught else. Hark! Didst ever hear such a horrible noise, Sir Page?'

"I answered his question by repeated bursts of laughter; for although my heart was full heavy at the fate of Adrian Di Albarone, yet for my soul I could not hear such whimsical sounds without giving full rein to my laughing humor.

"Suddenly the noise ceased. In an instant a voice shouted from the inside of the Cell—'Ho! guards, without there! guards!'

"I was thunderstruck at the tones of this voice, which I at once knew could not belong to the Doomed Adrian.

"'Well!' exclaimed Balvardo, 'if the devil hasn't stolen the voice of our gracious Lord the Duke!'"

Hugo pursed up his lips and gave his musical "whew!" which intended to express astonishment itself astonished.

"'W-h-e-w!—By'r Lady, but the devil *does* speak in the voice of our Lord the Duke.'

"'*I am the Duke of Florence!*'—shouted the voice from the cell. 'Open the door, ye slaves!'

"'Avoid the Sathanas!' quoth Balvardo.

"'Be quiet, fiend!' cried Hugo.

"Exquisite sport—exquisite!" muttered I to myself, as a curious idea flitted through my brain, "Ho—ho—ho! The Duke of Florence locked up in one of his own prisons! Ha—ha—ha!"

"Louder rose the voice within the cell, and louder and fiercer swelled the exclamations of the sentinels; until having strained every bone in my body, with excessive laughter, I fell asleep thro' mere weariness.

"When I awoke, the first beams of morning were streaming along the prison galleries, and engaged in earnest converse with Hugo and Balvardo stood the ill-looking, wry-mouthed, and hump backed Doomsman of Florence.

"'The irons are hot, and the wheel is ready,' said the deformed caitiff, bring your prisoner forth. The cauldron of lead is hissing and seething while it awaits his coming. 'Tis long since I've tried my hand upon one of noble blood. Bring forth this noble boy, and let me see what mettle his flesh is made of. Thanks, Balvardo—thanks, Hugo, for 'twas ye that gave him to the Doomsman!'

"Here the villain performed several very graceful actions, such as tying an imaginary knot around his neck, with a 'chick', and then rehearsing in dumb show the whole process of punishment upon the wheel; concluding with an animated waving, pushing and thrusting of his hands, descriptive of the entire manner of disemboweling.

"And this, this was to be the fate of Adrian Lord of Albarone!

"Meanwhile Hugo had unlocked the door of the Doomed Cell, and, called the name of the prisoner without receiving an answer.

"'I'll wake him,' quoth the Doomsman, entering the cell; 'see! he lays flat upon his face. Get up, Sir Parricide; get up. There—there,' he concluded, bestowing a few kicks upon the prostrate occupant of the cell.

"The prisoner replied with a groan.

"'Ho! ho!—You will not stir, will you?' continued the Doomsman, as he dragged the prisoner from the cell into the gallery:—'See, Hugo, how the caitiff's hat is slouched over his face, and his hands are bound with his own belt. By St. Judas, this is a rare sight!'

"'His hands bound!' exclaimed Balvardo. 'This is not my work!'

"'Nor mine!' responded Hugo.

"'Remove his slouched hat, one of ye,' exclaimed the Doomsman, 'see ye not that both of my hands are employed in holding his carcass.'

"Hugo reached forth his hand and removed his slouched hat—'O! an' I live till fourscore, I'll never forget the scene that followed.'

"There, his arms ignominiously bound, resting in the embrace of the Doomsman, lay the Duke of Florence, his face pale with ire, his mouth frothing like a madman's, and his eyes bloodshot; and there stood the Doomsman, his gray eyes protruding with astonishment, until they seemed about to drop from their sockets, his mouth agape and his tongue lolling out upon his bearded chin; and there, likewise, stood Hugo and Balvardo, looking first at one another, then at the Duke, and then clasping their hands, they fall upon their knees and screaming for mercy—and there in the back-ground, his cloak muffled over his face, and his frame shaking with laughter while his eyes run over with tears of mirth, stands his grace's page, the trim Guiseppo. Was't not a rich scene, Rosalind?"

CHAPTER THE TENTH.

THE MEMORY OF GUILT.

ON the stately couch in the Red-Chamber, with the Count Aldarin bending over him, lay his Grace the Duke of Florence, attired in his boots and hose, with his under shirt thrown back, revealing the left shoulder of the Prince laid open in a deep gash.

As the Count Aldarin, holding a light in one hand peered earnestly at the wound, the Duke exclaimed—

"A horrid gash, Count? eh! Damnation! to be foiled by the villain twice— bound in my own dungeon like a criminal—struck down in that cursed cavern like a dog—damnation seize the—ah! Count, some wine; for the Saint's sake, some wine, I pray thee."

The Count turned hurriedly to the beaufet, and filling a goblet with wine that sparkled in the light with a ruddy glow, he hastened to give it to the wounded Duke, who raised it until it nearly touched his lips, when, as if struck by a strange fancy, he suddenly held it out at arm's length exclaiming as he gazed at Aldarin with a lack-lustre eye—

"I say Count, suppose there should be some *white dust* at the bottom of this goblet?—and—and—*a ring?* eh? Count?—Ugh!—Take it away—ugh!"

He flung the goblet from him, scattering the wine over the couch, while the vessel rolled clanging over the marble floor.

"How SIR?" cried the Count, speaking in a deep-toned voice that thrilled to the very heart of the Duke, "*what mean'st thou?*" The dark gray eyes of the Scholar flashed like living coals of fire, as he spoke.

"O, nothing," responded the Duke, "nothing—only I thought the murderer Adrian might—dost understand? A truce to all this. My Lord Count, what didst thou with those men-at-arms who raised their swords in the cause of the murderer?"

Right glad was the Count Aldarin to recover his usual calm demeanour as he answered this inquiry.

"Of the fifty treacherous caitiffs who raised their swords against the person of your grace, forty lie bleeding and dead upon the cavern floor.

"As for the others—" he finished the sentence by pointing to the arched window of the Red-Chamber.

The Duke looked over his shoulder and beheld through the opened window the black and gloomy timbers of a gibbet towering like an evil omen high over the walls of the castle, and backed by the soft azure of a cloudless summer night.

The beams of the moon fell upon ten ghastly and death-writhen faces and ten figures swung to and fro, while the groaning cords as they grated against the creaking timbers over their heads, seemed shaking their death wail.

"Curse the traitors—they have their deserts!" The Duke exclaimed with a meaning smile.

The Count said nothing, but bending over the form of the Prince proceeded to dress his wounded shoulder, after the manner prescribed by his scholarly studies.

And as the Scholar bent over the form of the Duke, the hangings of the couch, sweeping beside the Prince, waved to and fro, with a slight motion, as though the summer breeze disturbed their folds, and a dark form, robed in garments of sable, with a monkish cowl dropping over its face, glided noiselessly along the floor, and in a moment stood at the back of his Grace of Florence, holding aloft, above his very head, a slender-bladed and glittering dagger.

The Figure stood silent and immoveable, its face shrouded and its form robed from view, the dagger glittering above the head of the Duke, brilliant as a spiral flame, while the light of the lamp held by Aldarin, shone on the upraised hand, revealing the sinews, stretched to their utmost tension, while the clutched fingers prepared to strike the blow of death.

And at the very instant, as the Figure of Sable emerged from the hangings of the couch, at the back of the Prince, there silently strode from the folds of the tapestry on the other side of the bed, a veiled form, clad from head to foot, in a robe of ghostly white.

While the Figure in garments of sable, raised the dagger above the head of the Duke, the strange Form, arrayed in the sweeping robe of white, disappeared behind the hangings of the couch, on the side opposite the Scholar Aldarin.

"Curse the traitors—they have their deserts!" again exclaimed the Duke. "Count, how succeeds my suit with the Ladye Annabel? Dost think she affects me? Eh, Count?"

"Marry, does, my Lord Duke—this slight wound in thy shoulder will detain thee at the castle for a few days. Thou wilt have every opportunity to urge thy suit, and, and—the day of your nuptials shall be named whenever thou dost wish!"

And as Aldarin spoke, the knife rose glittering in the hands of the Sable Figure, and a pale face, marked by the glare of a wild and flashing eye, was thrust from the folds of the robe of black. It was the face of Albertine.

"Now, by St. Antonia, but that is pleasant to think of," exclaimed the Duke, as, complacently surveying his figure, he passed his hand over his bearded chin and whiskered lip—"as thou wishest me to name the day, my Lord Count, be assured, I shall not return to Florence without being accompanied by my fair bride—*Ladye Annabel Duchess of Florence*. It sounds well—eh, Count?"

A smile passed over the compressed lips of the Count, and a glance of wild joy lit up his piercing eyes, as he thought of the fulfillment of the dream of ambition that had haunted his soul for years.

"It does indeed sound well, my Lord Duke," he calmly replied, as he proceeded in his employment of dressing the wound. There was a pause for a moment, a strange, dread pause, while the hands of the Sable Figure trembled, as though Albertine, was nerving his soul for the work of death.

"My Lord Count, how curious it seems? eh? Count?" exclaimed the Duke in a tone of vacant wonder.

"To what does your Grace refer?" answered the Count.

"Why, Count, but three short days ago, upon this very couch lay your gallant brother; here he folded to his arms his Adrian. Now that very son is a—murderer—a parricide. I rest upon the very couch that supported the murdered remains of the late Count, and thou, Aldarin, his brother—"

"HIS MURDERER!" exclaimed a voice that thrilled to the very heart of Aldarin, and made the Duke start with terror.

And as he started the knife came hissing through the air, it grazed the robe of the Duke, it sank to the very hilt in the death couch.

The start of the Duke saved him from the steel.

"Eh! Count, what's that? Who spoke? eh?" The eyes of the Count distended, and his lips parted with affright as he spoke.

The Count looked up and beheld a sight that froze his very blood.

On the opposite side of the bed, among the crimson hangings, stood a figure robed in white, and there, two eyes, blazing like fire-coals, from beneath the deathly pallor of a half-veiled brow, looked steadily upon the trembling Aldarin.

The cheeks of that pale countenance were dug into fearful hollows, and the eyes were surrounded by circles of livid blue.

The Count gazed with intense horror at this apparition and the Sable Figure, who had hurriedly stooped, in the effort to wrench the dagger from the couch, with a noiseless grasp, looked up and started hastily backward as his eye rested upon the ghastly face, appearing amid the hangings in the opposite side of the bed.

"It is the face of the dead"—muttered Albertine, gliding hurriedly toward his place of concealment while the Duke was absorbed by the awe-stricken visage of Aldarin, whose very soul seemed starting from his eyes as he gazed upon the apparition—"It is the face of the dead—The time of the Betrayer hath not yet come!"

And as he spoke he disappeared, without being observed by either the Duke or Aldarin, while the Scholar, beheld the curtains on the opposite side of the couch rustling to and fro—he looked and the Spectre was gone.

"This is some vile trick!" cried Aldarin, grasping the sword of the Duke from the couch as he spoke. "Let the mummers, whoe'er they are, beware the vengeance of the Scholar!"

He rushed to the other side of the couch, he lifted the hangings, but discovered no one. With a hurried step, he turned to the tapestry that adorned the walls, and thrust aside the embroidered, folds. The secret door was closed, and he beheld neither sign nor mark, that might tell of aught concealed within its pannels.

And as Aldarin continued his hurried search, the Duke leaning back on the couch, felt some hard substance pressing against his side. Thrusting his hand along the couch, he felt the handle of a dagger, thrust from its resting place, and with a trembling arm, held the steel aloft in the light.

"It bears an inscription—Saints of Heaven, let me read—

'THE VENGEANCE OF THE MONKS OF THE HOLY STEEL.'"

And at the same moment, the Count Aldarin, leaned trembling against a pillar for support, and quaking in every nerve, one fearful thought possessed his soul as he murmured in a hollow whisper.

"Haunted, forever haunted—by thy gloomy shade, my murdered brother!"

BOOK THE THIRD.

THE LAST NIGHT OF THRICE SEVEN YEARS.

CHAPTER THE FIRST.

THE MAIDEN IN HER BOWER.

ALDARIN PICTURES TO THE LADYE ANNABEL THE GLORIES OF A LIVING-TOMB.

A LAMP of alabaster, placed upon a small table of ebony, beside which was seated the Ladye Annabel, threw its softened beams around the apartment, and leaving the hangings, the stately bed, and the luxurious couches, wrapt in twilight shadow, cast a lovelier tint upon a vase of flowers standing upon the table, and revealed the fair maiden's countenance and figure in soft and rosy light.

Her flaxen tresses, unrestrained by band or cincture, fell in a golden shower over her delicate neck and finely-turned shoulders; and streaming along the full and swelling bosom, but half concealed by the bodice of white, bordered by finest lace, they flowed soft and waving down to her very feet.

The figure of the Ladye Annabel realized an old saying, that nature shows all her art, and lavishes the richest of her beauties, upon her smallest creations.

In form slight and delicate, in stature somewhat below the usual size, the proportions of Annabel were of the most exquisite tracery of outline. Her arms, full and softly rounded, were terminated by hands small and white, with tapering fingers; her feet, thin and slender, and marked by an high instep, supported ancles as finely turned, as the movements of the maiden were light and graceful; the well-proportioned waist arose in lovely gradation into the bosom of rich and budding promise; the neck, gently arching, and graceful in every attitude, blended sweetly into the small and half dimpling chin, that harmonized with the face of loveliness and soul.

"Right beauteous shone those eyes of blue," says the chronicler of the ancient MS., "glancing pure thoughts and light-hearted fancies; and right lovely were those glowing cheeks, in which the snow-white of the fair countenance bloomed into a roseate hue; and lovely was the small mouth of parting lips, delicious in their maiden ripeness; and sweet, surpassing sweet, was the expression of that face, where love and innocence beaming from every feature, seemed like the golden fruit of fairy land, only waiting to be gathered."

Her face was a poem, written by the finger of God, in characters of youth and bloom.

A poem whose theme was ever beauty and love, speaking its meaning through the deep glance of a shadowy eye, sending forth its messages of sweetness from the smile of the wreathing lip, or preaching its lessons of thought and purity by the calm glory of the unclouded brow.

A face lovely as a dream, when dreams are loveliest, with an outline of youth and bloom, a brow clear, calm, and cloudless, over-arching the eyes of azure, whose brightness seemed unfathomable; with full and swelling cheeks, varying the snow-white of the maiden's countenance by the damask of the budding rose; a small mouth, with curving lips; a chin all roundness and dimple, receding with a waving outline into the neck, all lightness and grace; while all around, the luxuriance of her golden hair, unbound and uncinctured, fell sweeping and waving, with a soft, airy motion, through the sunbeams shimmered round the fairy countenance of the maiden.

Alone in her bower sate the Ladye Annabel, her lip curving with scorn while she glanced at the letter of his grace of Florence, as it was flung along the floor, unopened and unheeded.

Her soul was agitated by the fearful memory of the last three days of mystery and blood, and then came confused and wandering thoughts of the scenes she had witnessed but an hour since, in the cavern of the dead.

Her mind was lost in a maze of never-ending doubts, when she contemplated the fearful death of the late Count.

She had never for an instant believed that Adrian could be guilty of the accursed act, neither had she dreamed that it was her father's hand that dealt the blow.

The thought would have driven her mad.

Suddenly her thoughts were agitated by a fearful picture.

She saw Adrian stretched bleeding and dead upon the wheel—his limbs severed and torn, and his brow scarred by the instruments of torture, while the doomsman's laugh rang in her ears. As the picture grew upon her mind in all its horrible details:—the glazed eye and the writhen lip, the chest heaving with the convulsive sobs of death, and the throat straining with the death rattle,—the maiden covered her face with her hands, and shrieked:

"Save me, holy Mary, save me from these fearful fancies!"

And as she spoke, the maiden burst into a flood of tears.

"*Annabel!*" whispered a voice at once deep-toned and full of affection.

She looked up, and her father, the Count Aldarin, stood before her.

"My daughter," he continued, drawing a seat beside her, "how dost thou like these?"

He opened a casket which he held in his hand, and the light of the alabaster lamp flashed upon ornaments of gold and silver, such as might not shame a queen to wear.

There were bracelets for the wrists, there were chains for the arching neck, gems for the brow, pearls to be woven in the flowing hair; and as their bright and star-like blaze met the eye of the Ladye Annabel, she gave utterance to a cry of delight.

"I thank thee, father, I thank thee!" she exclaimed, as, clasping a bracelet of gold, bordered by pearls, around her fair and well-rounded wrist, she received it with a glance of admiration. "See, father, see! How beauteous are those pearls, how bright that gold, and the shape—how exquisite! O! father, this is kind of thee! 'Tis indeed a rich gift!"

"*It is a bridal gift!*" exclaimed the Count, in a low and quiet tone, and with his eyes fixed upon his daughter's countenance, as if to note each varying expression of the fair and lovely features.

Annabel started as if an adder had stung her.

"A bridal gift? Said you not so? A bridal gift? From whom is it, my father?"

"His grace, the Duke of Florence, sends thee this rare and costly present. He sends it with his ardent wishes for thy health. He sends these jewels with the hope that ere three days have run their sands, he may behold them shining on the brow of his fair bride—the Ladye Annabel, Duchess of Florence."

As in a calm and determined tone he spoke these words, a deadly paleness came over the damsel's face; her lips dropped apart, and her fair blue eyes distended with a vacant look, the slender fingers of each hand slowly straightened, unclasping their grasp of the casket, which fell heavily to the floor, as her arms dropped listlessly by her side.

The old man surveyed his child for an instant with a look which told of his deep, his yearning affection, combined with the strange fancies ruling his destiny through life. In an instant he again spoke, and his voice, as it came from the depths of his chest, sounded wild and thrilling to the maiden's ear.

"*My daughter!*" said he, taking her by the hand, "*thou shall wed this man!*"

Annabel replied not.

"Thou shalt, I say, wed the Lord of Florence. It must be so; therefore it were well that thou dost prepare thee for the bridal. I say it shall be so, my daughter. The word of Aldarin is passed!"

"Father," replied the Ladye Annabel, in tremulous tones; "father, O! look not so sternly at me, your eyes chill my very heart. I would do your bidding—the Virgin and all the saints witness me, I would—but, father—"

"Annabel," said the Count, in his deep tones of enthusiasm, "I have said it, and it shall be so. Wed the Duke of Florence, and behold thyself a—queen! All that heart can wish, or the wildest fancy desires, shalt thou possess, and claim as thine own. Wealth shall lavish its stores around thee, and honor shall bring the fairest and the noblest to bow low at the feet of the Ladye Annabel, Duchess of Florence.

"Lo! thou art in the ducal hall of Florence: behold thyself encircled by the gay and glittering throng; a thousand eyes are fixed upon thee in admiration, a thousand tongues speak their words of eloquence but to syllable that admiration, and a thousand swords, flashing in the light, are slaves to the slightest word of Ladye Annabel—the queen.

"The robes of a queen shall gird this lovely form, the stars of a coronet shall flash from that beauteous brow, and this fair hand, so beautiful in its alabaster whiteness, shall wave the sceptre over the heads of kneeling myriads! With a queenly port and a flashing eye, thou shalt look around thee, and behold the princely halls illumined by lamps, diffusing at once both light, soft as moonbeams, and fragrance sweeter than the breath of spring flowers. The lofty windows, with their rare carvings, shall give to view gardens rich with golden fruit, won from the far lands of the East, fragrant with shrubbery and gay with flowers, while ancient trees, in leafy magnificence, sweep their arching bows overhead. Fountains fling their columns of liquid diamonds up from the arbored paths, lulling waterfalls soothe the ear, distant music wakes delightful visions in the soul, solemn palaces, in all their grandeur of outline, break through the air of night! Palaces, gardens, unbounded wealth, rank, pride, place, honor—all, all shall be thine own!"

"All, my father, all—all—but love."

As Annabel spoke, her eyes filled with tears, and her voice was choked with the sobs that convulsed her bosom.

To say that the picture of the Count had no effect upon the maiden, would be uttering an absurd and unnatural fiction. In bright and glowing colors arose the gorgeous pageantry before the mind of Annabel: it was all saith the Chronicler of the ancient MSS.—it was all that a woman could wish, the fruition of a woman's most ardent aspiration. With Adrian, the companion of her childhood, the princely palace would have been like an abode of fairy land; with the Duke, it would have been a tomb—a golden sepulchre for the living-dead.

The answer of Aldarin was contemptuous and bitter.

"*Love!*—a dream—a phantom—a bubble!—*Love*, forsooth! the vision of warm-blooded youth, which all have felt, and none but fools obey, Girl," continued he, "I have said that thou shouldst wed the Duke, and—by my soul!—*thou shalt wed him*! My word—the word of Aldarin—is passed. Think not to deceive *me*. I know thy motive in thus setting the bidding of a father at defiance. It is because thou dost affect the murderer of my only brother,—of thy kind uncle,—the PARRICIDE, Adrian—"

"O! father, he cannot—cannot be the doer of so dread a crime."

"Who, then," exclaimed the Count, bitterly, "who then was the doer of so dread a crime? Speak, my fair daughter, *who* was't?"

"IT WAS THOU! THOU! ALDARIN THE SCHOLAR!" exclaimed a voice that sounded strange and hollow through the lonely apartment.

"Holy Mary, preserve us!" shrieked Annabel. "Father, whence came that fearful voice?"

The Count Aldarin replied not. The convulsive motion that heaved his breast, and strained the lineaments of his countenance, showed that he was making a desperate attempt to command his soul.

"'Tis naught, my daughter," he began; "'tis fancy—'tis—"

He finished the sentence by a howl of horror, that might have been uttered by a lost soul. Annabel beheld him gazing fixedly at some object behind her. She turned her head and saw a vision that drove the life current back from her heart.

A figure arrayed in the snow-white attire of the grave, looked with a pale and ghastly countenance, and hollow eyes, from among the folds of the crimson tapestry on the opposite side of the apartment.

With freezing blood, Annabel beheld the figure advance with a slow and measured step towards her. Her consciousness failed, and she fell insensible on the floor, at the same instant that Aldarin sank down with a yell of despair, while his mouth frothed, and his eyes glared like those of a maniac.

On toward the light advanced the figure in white.

In a moment it stood beside the prostrate forms of the father and child, and having gazed at them for an instant, it threw back the robe from its head, and the beams of the lamp flashed over the wan and ghastly face of the strange figure.

"Ha—ha—ha!" he laughed, in tones sepulchral with famine, "methinks I've frightened the old caitiff enow! O, St. Withold! but I do feel this fiend, Hunger, gnawing with its serpent teeth at my very heart! Nothing to eat for three days and as many nights! And this hand—half-severed at the finger joints—throbbing with pain all the while! Thanks to the hard lessons of a soldier's life, that taught me to wrap this rough bandage round the wound! Had it been my good right hand—St. Withold!—Robin had been a dead man three days ago! True, I did make out to crawl toward one of the dead soldiers in the cavern. How sweetly the wine in his flask gurgled down my parched throat! I am faint with lack of food. By a soldier's faith, I could eat a whole ox! St. Withold, an' I do not get some nourishment in the shortest time possible, I may as well wrap me up in this pall, so as to be ready for burial! Ugh! the priest shall not say his prayers over thee yet, my friend Robin; courage."

Having first divested himself of the funeral pall of the late lord, the famished soldier strode across the apartment, and opening the door that led into the ante chamber, he discovered Guiseppo and Rosalind seated upon one of the couches, apparently in the most amiable humor with each other.

"Look ye, sir page," exclaimed Robin, as he showed his wan and wasted features through the opened door, "an' ye stir not yourself right quickly, your master will be dead; and, fair damsel, the same may be said of your mistress, the Ladye Annabel."

Rosalind shrieked with affright at the hollow voice and shrunken figure of the bold yeoman, and Guiseppo sprang with one bound from the couch half way across the apartment.

"Fear not, Rosalind," he cried, drawing his dagger. "If it be a devil, I defy it in God's name; and if it be a man why I will try what this good steel can do."

"Tut, tut," exclaimed Robin, "put up your cheese-knife boy. Come hither. Know you me not?"

"No more than I do the devil."

"Mayhap then, fair Sir, you have heard of a *certain youth*, who on the night before he departed from the castle—the castle where his infancy had been passed—to be a page at court, took occasion to pour a sleeping potion into the wine of a *certain yeoman*; and then shaving one side of the yeoman's face; concluded by tying a dead cat around his neck, thus making an honest soldier a mock of laughter for all the castle. Did'st ever hear of such a page? Eh? Guiseppo?"

"Why the Virgin bless me," exclaimed Rosalind, "It's Rough Robin!"

"Eh?" cried the page with a stare of astonishment.

"If you value your life, Guiseppo," continued the yeoman; "Hie away, and bring me a dozen flasks of wine or so, and a round of beef. Speak not a word, but haste away. I am nigh starved to death, and the devil may tempt me to cut a slice from the trim figure of a certain page; away!"

As Guiseppo left the apartment, Rosalind asked the bold yeoman where he had been for the last three days, and wherefore he looked so much like a ghost risen from the dead merely for its own amusement.

"*My lord the Count Aldarin,*" replied Robin with a grim smile, "*despatched me— upon a long journey, to arrange matters of business entirely relating to himself.*"

Having thus spoken, he again entered the bower of the Ladye Annabel, and laying hold of the senseless body of Aldarin, he dragged him into the ante-chamber, and then returned to assist the damsel Rosalind in the recovery of her mistress.

CHAPTER THE SECOND.

THE LADY AND THE YEOMAN.

WHEN the Ladye Annabel opened her fair blue eyes, she gazed hurriedly around the apartment until her glance was met by that of the bold yeoman. She gave a faint scream, and her form trembled with affright.

"St. Withold!" exclaimed the yeoman—"but I do seem to frighten every one that looks at me, into fits. Fear me not, Ladye Annabel—'Tis I—Rough Robin—I would speak a few words to thee. The import of what I have to say is of a fearful nature."

"Ah!" said Annabel, "of what would you speak?"

Robin whispered a word in her ear.

The maiden gave a convulsive start. She clasped her hands and looked wildly in the yeoman's face, as she exclaimed—

"How was't done!—The doer of this deed—who was't?"

"Pardon me, Lady. For three long days and nights have I been without sustenance—I am faint—my brain burns, and mine hands tremble."

The Ladye Annabel made a sign to Rosalind, who was leaving the room, when she was met at the door by Guiseppo, bearing a wine flask in one hand, while the other supported a dish containing the fragments of a venison pasty.

"Bold Robin," said Guiseppo, "I contrived to abstract these from the wine cellar and the kitchen, without being noticed. I thought your business might require secrecy."

"Thanks, Sir Page, thanks—and now," continued the yeoman—"an' thou lovest thy Lord Adrian, wait in the ante-chamber, and see that no one enters. Fair Rosalind, I am waiting to close the door."

As he said this he gently pushed the damsel through the doorway, and carefully drawing the bolt he seated himself opposite Annabel. He then placed the pasty on his knee, and with a trembling hand filled a silver goblet to the very brim with wine. With all the nervous eagerness of famine, he lifted the capacious vessel to his lips, when he beheld a pale, cadaverous, spectre-like face dancing in the ruddy glow of the wine.

"St. Withold! 'Tis no wonder I have scared every body with my dried up visage!" He drained the goblet to the last drop. "S' death I'm frightened at that death's head myself."

He then plunged one hand into the pasty, and raising a piece of the rich crust, he devoured it in an instant; then lifting the flask to his mouth, he poured the luscious liquid down his throat, and his sinews and veins began to rise and swell, a ruddy glow ran over his ashy face, while the supernatural brightness of his eyes, gave place to a healthy, twinkling glance.

There was a pause of some ten minutes.

"St. Withold! but I thank thee!" cried the yeoman, as his eyes filled with a liquid which bore a strange resemblance to tears of joy—"Holy Mary, Holy Peter, and Holy Paul, ye shall have a wax candle apiece; instead of one to all of ye!"

The Ladye Annabel who had watched his movements with the greatest impatience, now exclaimed—

"For heaven's sake, good Robin, speak. What dost thou know of the fearful deed"—she looked hurriedly around the room—"*Of the murder?*"

"Ladye" replied the yeoman, "I'm a rough, blunt soldier—I know little of courtly manners, but so help me St. Withold, I would peril—I would sacrifice my life, to serve thee and—Lord Adrian—"

"Adrian? What knowest thou of Adrian? For heaven's sake speak." Her very soul glanced from her eyes as she continued.—"Oh, God! thou surely wilt not say that he—Adrian—is—is—THE MURDERER?"

"St. Withold!" muttered Robin, "but I have got myself into a nice predicament. Ladye I would say no such falsehood."

"It is a falsehood then?—Thanks—Holy Mary, from my soul, unfeigned thanks?"

"It is not Adrian: but Ladye—heaven help thee to bear it—the murderer is one who is mayhap as beloved of thee, as is Lord Adrian."

"*One as beloved?*" murmured Annabel—"surely there is no one as beloved as Adrian, no one save my father. Thou triflest with me, Robin."

"Nay Ladye I trifle not—again I say it is *the* one who is as dear to thee as Lord Adrian."

One word came from the maiden's lips.

"MY FATHER—" she shrieked, as if some awful thought had riven her brain.

She said never a word more, but her bosom which a moment past rose and fell convulsively, now became stilled; the excited flush of her cheeks died away into an ashy paleness, her lip lost its eager expression, her eyelids closed stiffly, and she fell heavily as a corse from her seat.

Robin sprang forward and extended his arms in time to prevent her from falling to the floor.

"I am a very fool," he said, bitterly reproaching himself—"a dolt, an idiot—a mere wearer of the motley doublet—a jingler of the belled cap would have known better. St. Withold, but *I am* an ass!"

Having his own reasons for not calling assistance from the ante-room, he used all kinds of expedients to restore the Ladye Annabel to consciousness. He chafed the fair and delicate hands, he deluged the brow as white as snow, with perfumed liquids contained in silver flagons standing upon the table; and after a lapse of a quarter of an hour he had the gratification of seeing her eyes unclose, and feeling her heart beat as he held her form in his arms.

The Ladye Annabel faintly spoke—"I have had a fearful—fearful dream. The Virgin save me from the dark spirits that inspire such fancies. I thought of *thee*—of *thee*, my father!"

She paused suddenly as she caught a view of the yeoman's face.

"*Thou* here!" she exclaimed in surprise, "wherefore is this?"

"St. Withold!" muttered the confused Robin, fearful of again referring to the late subject of horror. "Why Ladye, in truth I am here—because I am—not here—that is to say—s'death Ladye, I came here to serve ye."

"To serve *me*?" said Annabel wonderingly, "how wouldst thou serve *me*?"

"Ladye," cried the yeoman in utter despair of his ability to convey his ideas in a circuitous manner. "Ladye would you wed this Duke of Florence?"

"Sooner would I die!"

"How will you avoid the bridal?"

"God only knows," said Annabel, as she stood erect, "to his care do I confide myself. I have read legends of dames and damsels who have raised the dagger against their own lives when terrors such as threaten me, rose before their eyes,—but I cannot—cannot do it! All I can do"—and her head sunk low upon her bosom, and her arms drooped by her side—"all I can do is, to pray, earnestly pray; upon my bended knees *beseech* the Virgin that I may *die*!"

"Cheer thee up, fair ladye—cheer thee up," thus Robin spoke, "by the troth of an honest soldier, I swear that I will be near thee when the hour of thy peril draws nigh. I swear that my life shall be sacrificed to save thee!—And now I must be gone. This castle can no longer be Rough Robin's home. God be with ye!"

The Ladye Annabel placed a purse of gold in Robin's hand, and with many blessings on his head, she beheld him disappear into the ante-room.

Rosalind entered the room—Annabel exclaimed—

"Retire for a little while, fair coz: I would be alone."

As the black-eyed maiden retired, the Ladye Annabel sank down into a seat, and gave herself up to the wild and agitating thoughts that flashed through her brain.

The first beams of the coming morn shot through the tapestry that well nigh concealed the casement of the maiden's bower.

Annabel had fallen into a welcome slumber, and the soft beams of the lamp fell upon her calm and innocent face, revealing each feature in the mildest light, and softest shade.

A figure emerged from the tapestry, and advanced to the light, Adrian stood beside the sleeping maiden. His face was exceedingly pale and covered with blood, as also was the helmet, and the plates of the armor of azure steel. In one hand he grasped the furled banner of the Winged Leopard.

He turned and sought his place of concealment with a heavy heart; but ere he turned, he cast one deep, one agonizing look upon the lovely maiden.

"She is happy!—my wrongs shall not disturb her innocent soul—Farewell— my own loved—Annabel—farewell."

A kiss that told of heart-felt affection he impressed upon her ruby lips, and as he took a last fond, ardent gaze, a burning tear fell upon the unstained cheek of the Ladye Annabel.

CHAPTER THE THIRD.

THE VALLEY OF THE BOWL.

THE SCENE CHANGES TO THE MOUNTAIN LAKE, WHERE THE TRAGEDY OF THE HOUSE OF ALBARONE WILL AT LAST COME TO AN END.

FAR away among the mountains, the sunlight loves to linger, and the moonbeam is wont to dwell among the quiet recesses of a lovely valley, overshadowed by rugged steeps, that frown above and darken around a calm and silvery lake, embosomed amid the solitudes of the wild forest hills.

Around on every side, arise the hills, magnificent with the shade of the sombre pine, leafy with the branching oak, or verdant with the luxuriance of the green chestnut tree, while chasms yawn in the sunlight, ravines darken and fearful rocks, bear and rugged in their outline, tower far above the forest trees, away into the clear azure of the summer sky.

The hills sweep round the valley in a circular form, describing the outlines of the sides of a drinking goblet, while far below, the limpid waters of the lake, repose in the depths of this collossal vessel, giving a clue to the strange name of this place of solitude—THE VALLEY OF THE BOWL.

This quiet vale is situated some few miles from Florence, amid the same wild range of mountains that encircle the haunt of the members of the Holy Steel.

The light of the summer morning sun, was streaming gaily over the roofs of a mountain hamlet, clustered beside the shores of the lake, flinging its golden beams over the outline of each rugged hut, with tottering walls, or rustic tenement, with its ancient stones overgrown with leafy vines; when a group of peasants were gathered along the road-side, at some small distance from the village, in earnest and energetic conversation.

A short, thick-set and bow-legged youth, clad in the garish apparel of a Postillion[2] of the olden times, stood in the centre of the group, while around him were clustered a circle of the buxom mountain damsels, with their heads inclined towards each other, their arms and hands moving in animated gestures, as a boisterous chorus broke on the air, from the glib prattling of their busy tongues.

"Now, Dolabella," said the young man to a tall, black-eyed, dark-haired damsel, of a very swarthy skin; "now, Dolabella, it's in vain you try to make a fool of me. I don't believe any such thing—that's all."

Having thus spoken, he searched earnestly with his finger along his chin, and at last discovered a starved fragment of beard, which he pulled with great gravity, at the same time looking intently upwards, as if bent on discovering the evening star in broad day-light.

"Well! our Lady take care of your wits, good Signor Rattlebrain," thus answered the buxom Dolabella, "whether you believe it or not, makes not a whit of difference to me. But I tell you, Theresa, and you, Loretta, that last night, just about dark, as I was walking near yon cottage on the hill, with a beech tree on one side, and a chestnut on the other—"

"What!" interrupted the small, hazed-eyed Loretta, "mean you the cottage which the tall, strange old woman hired but yesterday?"

"The very same. Well, just as I was walking there, all alone, I heard a footstep!—"

"Our Lady!" exclaimed Theresa, who was distinguished by her hair of glowing red.

"Our Lady!—but you do not say so?" exclaimed the other.

"I heard a footstep, and stepping aside into the bushes, I saw a dark looking monk enter the cottage, and he was followed by a big, rough soldier; and *he* was followed by *such* a handsome cavalier, dressed in such a gay dress, and O! bless ye all—he wore *such* a fine, dancing feather in his cap! Upon my word, it waved like a sunbeam in the evening twilight!"

"What color were his eyes?" asked Loretta.

"Was he tall or short?" inquired Theresa.

"I suppose you will say next, that he had a *manly* figure? eh?" and the youth pulled his slouched hat fiercely over his right ear, and then halting on one leg, he threw the other forward, while with his arms placed akimbo, he seemed waiting for somebody or other to take his portrait.

"To be sure he had a *manly* figure," returned Dolabella, glancing contemptuously at the bow-legged youth; "he was none of your whipper-snapping, strutting, and boasting postillions; he was none of your conceited—"

"*Dolabella!*" exclaimed the youth in a pathetic tone.

"Well, Signor Francisco?"

"Dolabella, do you see the convent of St. Benedict yonder?"

He pointed to the dark and time-worn walls of the monastery, it stood among the forest-trees on the western side of the lake, upon the summit of a precipitous cliff, which towered in rugged grandeur from the bosom of the mountain waters.

The cheerful sunbeam was shining over the dark towers of the monastery over the surrounding forest-trees, and along the recesses of the gardens, that varied the appearance of the wild wood beyond the ancient walls, and the white cliff gave its broad surface to the light of day, yet there was an air of gloom resting upon the entire view, the dark towers, the white cliff, and the luxuriant gardens; while the reflection of the scene in the deep and mirror-like waters of the lake, was so calm, so clear, so perfect in the faintest outline, that it looked more like the creation of an artist's pencil, than a landscape of the living world.

As the pompous Francisco pointed to the dark walls of the monastery, an involuntary thrill ran around the group of peasant damsels, and there was a pause of strange silence for a single moment.

"The Monastery of St. Benedict!" murmured Dolabella, "Francisco, fear you not to make yon strange house the subject of your jest, even in broad daylight? The cheek of the boldest peasant of these mountains grows pale at the mention of yon gloomy fabric!"

"Tis said the ancient Dukes of Florence held strange festivals within those dark gray walls in the olden time."

"Even now, no one knows anything concerning the monks of this monastery. They give to the mountain poor with a free hand and a liberal blessing—yet, beshrew me, strange rumors are abroad, and muttered whispers speak of midnight orgies that it would shame an honest maiden to name, held within yon darksome house!"

"I jest not!" exclaimed the postillion; "I jest not. I am in earnest—by the True Cross, am I. Did you ever hear of the legend of yon whitened precipice? How a desperate youth threw himself from the rock, down into the ravine—and—and—mark me—if on some very bright and agreeable morning I should be found laying at the foot of the awful steep, scattered into a thousand fragments—then think of the victim of your perfidy, Dolabella. And you, Theresa, and you, Loretta, think of the miserable fate of Francisco—your victim—with remorse—with bitter remorse!"

Having thus given the damsels to understand that among them all, his heart was certainly broken, the little postillion strutted away with folded arms and a measured step. Indeed, by the immense strides he took with his inverted legs, it did really seem that he had been hired to measure the greatest possible quantity of ground, in the shortest possible number of steps.

The damsels replied to this pathetic appeal by a burst of laughter.

"I'll tell you what we shall do," said Dolabella. "This little whipper-snapper has been making love to all three of us, for nearly two years. Let us pretend to be desperately enamoured of this strange cavalier at the cottage."

"O yes—yes!" cried Theresa.

"Certainly! O certainly!" exclaimed Loretta.

"That will bring Signor Postillion to terms," continued the tall damsel, "and besides girls, we'll learn all about this strange old woman."

"This strange priest!" said Loretta.

"And this handsome cavalier!" cried Theresa.

And presently they separated; each determining to out-wit the other; both in regard to the strangers in the cottage on the hill, and to the securing of the gallant vagabond Francisco, who to do him justice, had those two important qualities necessary to winning the heart of a vain woman—saith the Chronicler of the Ancient MSS.—a glib tongue and a rare knack of making presents of all sorts of gairish finery.

CHAPTER THE FOURTH.

THE BRIDAL EVE.

THE HEBREW AND THE ARAB-MUTE ENTER THE COURT YARD OF ALBARONE, WHILE THE LADYE ANNABEL IS PASSING TO THE CHAPEL OF SAINT GEORGE.

THE azure sky was glowing with the mild warmth of the summer twilight, the zenith was mellowed with the light of the declining day, the western horizon was varied by alternate flashes of gold and crimson, when the ancient Castle of Albarone, thro' every hall and corridor, rang with the shouts of merriment, and the gay sounds of festival revelry.

From the various towers of the castle, pennons of strange colors and curious emblazonry, waved in the evening air, each flag, the trophy of some hard fought battle, while high over all, floating from the loftiest tower, the broad banner of the House of Albarone, gave its gorgeous folds, its rich armorial bearings, the motto in letters of gold, and the Winged Leopard, to the ruddy glare of the western sky.

The lowered drawbridge, and the raised portcullis, gave admittance to numerous bands of peasantry, wending from the various tenements that dotted the domains of Albarone, all clad in their holiday costume, while the air echoed with their light-hearted laughter, as the merry jest, or the gay carol, rang from side to side.

All along the hill, leading to the castle gate, and thro' the luxuriant wood circling round its base, hurried the peasant bands, their attire of picturesque beauty, giving variety and contrast to the scene, while now loitering in groups, now hastening one by one toward the castle, they peopled the highway, and thronged over the drawbridge into the court yard of the castle.

Walking amid these gay parties, yet alone and unaccompanied save by a solitary attendant, there strode wearily forward a personage who to all appearance ranked among a far-scattered people, at once the scorn and fear of Christendom.

Clad in a long coat of the coarsest serge, varied by numerous patches, with a piked staff in his hand, and a pack somewhat extensive in shape, strapped over his broad shoulders, the slouching hat which defended the head of the JEW, revealed a face, dark and tawny in hue, stern in expression, marked by a sharp and searching eye, whose glance seemed skilled in reading the hearts of men; a bold prominent nose, while the lower part of his cheeks, his chin and upper lip, were covered by a stout beard, which, black as jet, descended to his girdle, mingling with the long and curling locks of sable hue, that gave their impressive relief to the outline of the Hebrew's countenance.

By his side walked his slender-shaped attendant, to all appearance a youth of some twenty winters, yet his tawny face, marked by bold and regular features, half-concealed by masses of jet black hair, falling aside from his forehead, in elf-like curls, was marked by a deep wrinkle between the brows, a stern compression of the lip, and a wild and wandering eye, that glanced from side to side with a restless and nervous glance, that seemed to peruse the face of every man who came within its gaze, and read the characters and motives of all who journeyed onward to the castle.

Attired like his master, in garments of the coarsest serge, the Servitor of the Hebrew, bore on his shoulder, a voluminous pack, which seemed to oppress its bearer with an unusual weight, for he well-nigh tottered under the load.

Without heeding the sneer, and the jest which assailed him from every side, the Hebrew crossed the drawbridge, and passing under the portcullis he presently stood in the midst of the castle yard, where unstrapping his pack, he displayed his rich and gaudy stores to the eyes of the wondering multitude. His servitor also displayed his pack to their gaze, but stood silent and unmoveable, his arms folded, and his wild eyes glaring strangely over the faces of the crowd.

"Who'll buy—who'll buy?" cried the Hebrew, in the suppliant voice of trade, as casting his eyes around the court-yard, he surveyed the brilliant scene at a glance.

Around, all dark and time-worn, the walls of the castle—each casement blazing with torches—looked down upon various groups of the peasantry and servitors of Albarone, some engaged in light and gleesome gossip, while others were hurrying hither and thither, on errands pertaining to the feast which was to grace the castle hall on the morrow.

In front of the arching roof of the kitchen door stood the gray haired sharp featured, and sharp voiced Steward of the castle, engaged in superintending the operations of a number of hinds, who were severing the limbs of various fat bucks, and cutting up certain lusty beeves, and preparing various kinds of game, for the vast fire that blazed on the kitchen hearth.

Farther on, a minstrel was entertaining a circle of peasants, with the song of love, or the tale of knightly valor; at a short distance, the privileged fool, with his cap and bells, and fantastic dress, was uttering his merry quips and far-fetched jests, which ever and anon he varied by a nimble summersault, while the gaping crowd held their sides as their boisterous laughter broke upon the ear, with all its jovial discord and dissonance.

"Who'll buy! who'll buy!" shouted the Jew, "here's broaches for ye damsels fair—broaches and gauds, rings for your fingers, and crosses of ebony for your bosoms. Look ye how this heart of gold would sink and swell on a maiden's snow white breast! Here's plumes for the warriors' helmet; daggers for his belt, and trappings for his steed. Who'll buy! who'll buy!—Here's ornaments of gold and silver for the doublet of the page, essences for his flowing hair, and chains for his neck.—Who'll buy—who'll buy.—Broaches, gauds, rings, gems, plumes, belts, trappings, perfumes, chains, laces of gold! Who'll buy! Who'll buy! Gentles, list ye all! Chains, laces of gold, perfumes, trappings, belts, plumes, gems, rings, gauds, broaches. Who'll buy! who'll buy!"

"The Virgin save us all!" exclaimed Guiseppo who stood among the crowd that gathered round the Israelite, "the Virgin save us all, but *there's* a tongue for you, my good folks."

This was said with an attitude of mock astonishment, and corresponding grimace of the features.

"An' my tongue suits ye so well, gentle sir, may-hap you'll try some of my wares?"

"What have you, Sir Gripe-fist, that it would become *me* to buy?"

"Everything to suit a gallant page, everything. Except three wares with which the great merchant—*Nature*—must provide him, or else he'll make but a sorry page."

"And those wares—how do you style them?" asked the page.

"The first," replied the Jew with a demure look, "the first ware is somewhat dull and heavy, it is labelled—*Impudence*—may it please thee fair Page."

"Thou heathen hound, thou!" exclaimed Guiseppo, half amused and half angered. "How name you the second ware? Eh! Leatherface?"

"The second ware," the Jew replied meekly, "the second ware is light and feathery. It bears the name—*Self-conceit*. As for the third—"

"Aye the third," interrupted the page. "Go on my black bearded friend—go on—I'll borrow a good oaken towel to rub you down, when you have done."

"As for the third, it is the stuff of which the two others are made. It is heavier and duller than *Impudence*, and lighter and more feathery than *Self-conceit*, they style it *Ignorance*. And these three wares are the sole contents of the cob-web-hung storehouse of Sir Page's brain. An' it likes thee, fair sir?"

The Israelite bowed low as he spoke.

"Ha—ha—ha! fairly hit! Ho—ho—ho! The Jew turns Scholar, and preaches like a monk.—He—he—he! The trim Page is hit—fairly hit." Such were the exclamations that went around the laughing crowd.

"Now receive thy pay, thou son of Sathanas!" exclaimed Guiseppo, brandishing an oaken staff; "here's at thee!"

"Nay, nay!" exclaimed one of the spectators, "thou art fairly hit, sir Guiseppo."

"Aye, aye, fairly hit," cried another; and "The Jew has paid thee in thine own coin," a third shouted, throwing himself in the path of the page.

"Nay, nay, let him come!" cried the Jew, with a sneer. "Let him come. I'll tame his pageship."

"Dost thou mock me, thou dog!" As he spoke, the page raised his oaken staff, and whirling it around his head, he aimed with all his strength at the sconce of the Jew, who coolly turned aside the blow with his upraised arm, and in an instant he had Guiseppo by the throat.

He whispered a word in the ear of the page, and then, unloosing his hold, he began to gather up his wares.

The eyebrows of the page elevated with astonishment, and his lips parted. The bystanders gathered around Guiseppo with various expressions of their surprise at the sudden change that had passed over him.

"Why stare you so?" exclaimed a peasant maid.

"Art mad?" asked one of the yeoman of the guard.

"Perhaps moon-struck?" suggested another.

Guiseppo made no reply, but walked slowly away, while the Jew remained standing in the centre of the group, with his servitor waiting silently by his side.

"Look ye, son of Moses," cried one of the yeomen, advancing toward the Jew, "why stands this man of thine so silent and still? He moves not, nor does he speak; but his wild eye is glancing hither and thither like a fire-coal. Why does he stand thus mute and speechless?"

A grim smile passed over the bearded features of the Jew.

"Ask a post why it does not speak, or ask a war-horse to troll ye a merry song! You are a keen yeoman and a shrewd, yet did it ne'er strike ye that my servitor might be incapable of speech? A poor Arab boy, gentle sirs and damsels, whose dying father gave him to my care, when perishing on the field of battle, in the wilds of Palestine, some twenty years agone."

"A son of the paynim Mahound," muttered the yeoman, with a look of scorn.

"Nay he is of the faith of Christ," interrupted the Jew. "Behold, he wears the cross of Rome!"

"A sweet youth, and gentle-faced, though somewhat sad in look," murmured a peasant matron, gazing with a look of pity upon the tawny face of the Arab mute.

And while the group of peasant men and women clustered around the Jew and his Arab boy, a cry ran through the castle yard, echoed from lip to lip, and repeated by the crowd thronging the place, until the air seemed alive with the shout: "She comes, she comes! The fair Ladye Annabel is passing to the chapel of St. George! Make way for the betrothed! Make way for the Ladye Annabel! *Make way for the Duchess of Florence!*"

In a moment the court-yard was occupied by two files of men-at-arms, who extended from the great steps, ascending to the massive door of the castle hall, along the level space, making a lane for the passage of the Ladye Annabel and her train. The crowd came thronging to the backs of the warriors, gathering around the staircase, and blackening on every side, eager to behold the betrothed of his grace the Duke of Florence.

Foremost among the throng at the bottom of the stairway, his pack lashed to his back, and a small casket in his hands, the black-bearded Jew appeared to take great interest in the scene progressing before his eyes.

The Arab mute stood at his back, half concealed from view, and unseen or unnoticed by the survitors and vassals of Albarone.

In after times, some of the vassals remembered well that they observed the wild eyes of the Arabian glaring fiercely over the shoulder of the Jew, while his right hand was thrust within the folds of his coarse gaberdine, and his entire appearance denoted a mind agitated by some fierce resolve.

A low, solemn peal of music broke on the air, and a ruddy blaze of light was thrown from the recesses of the massive hall doors. In a moment a band of cavaliers, attired in all the glitter of spangled cloak and waving plume, came from the hall, and took their position on either side of the staircase, each gay cavalier holding a torch on high, while the gleaming light revealed each handsome face, wearing the polished smile, and the costumes varied with strange fancies of embroidery, and fashioned after every manner of device, were disclosed in all their luxuriance and splendor.

A murmur ran through the crowd, and the gaily-attired form of his grace of Florence issued from the hall door, followed by the slight figure of the Count Aldarin.

As they took their positions on either side of the hall door, the crowd below had time to notice the strange contrast between the Lord of Albarone and the Duke of Florence.

Aldarin, pale in face, slender in form, attired in his robes of solemn black, the cap of dark fur on his forehead, with the blaze of a single gem relieving its midnight darkness, standing silent and motionless on one side of the hall door, his keen gray eyes half hidden by his brows, as though he was absent with thoughts of more than mortal interest.

The Duke, the gallant Duke, all show, and glitter, and costume, a doublet of white satin encircling his well-proportioned form, a cloak of the most delicate crimson depending from his left shoulder, the hilt of his jeweled sword glittering in the light; while his dainty cap of pink velvet, with the snow-white plume thrown aside from its front, surmounted his vacant face, marked by the neatly circled hair, the carefully trimmed moustache and beard. His eyes glared vacantly to and fro, and it might easily be seen that his grace of Florence was on a mental excursion after his looking glass.

This flashing of torches, this gallant array, heralded the approach of the Ladye Annabel, who presently emerged from the hall door, followed by a long line of the bower maidens, arrayed, like their mistress, in flowing robes, white as the mountain snow untouched by the summer sun.

The face of the Ladye Annabel was pale as the attire that enveloped her slender form, and she leaned for support on the arm of her black-eyed cousin, the damsel Rosalind.

Pale and beautiful, the victim of the sacrifice of the morrow, neither returned the deep inclination of the head with which the Duke of Florence greeted her appearance, nor glanced upon the countenance of her father; but slowly moved down the steps of stone, her eyes downcast, and her face calm as the sculptured marble.

"She is pale," murmured Aldarin, "pale as death! She walks with the measured step of the victim walking to the living tomb!"

"I' faith, she is beautiful!" muttered the Duke. "My bride will hang like a pleasant costume on this royal arm!"

The black-bearded Hebrew gazed upon the Ladye Annabel with a keen and searching eye, while the Arab mute, standing at his back, bowed his head low on his breast, and veiled his face with one hand, as the other was thrust within the folds of his coarse doublet.

Slowly the procession ascended the steps of stone, one foot of the betrothed was upon the pavement of the castle yard, when a rushing sound was heard, a hurried footstep, and the Jew rushed through the men-at-arms—flinging himself at the maiden's feet, he threw open the casket which he held in his hand.

"Fair ladye," he cried, in a deep-toned voice, "It is the lace—the lace of price, which two days since I promised to procure thee. 'Tis worth its weight in gold—aye, an hundred times over! Look, ladye—'tis the best that gold or favor might procure."

The Ladye Annabel started at the uncouth appearance and bearded face of the Jew, while the bystanders seemed struck dumb with his audacity.

In an instant cries of execration arose on all sides. The Count Aldarin advanced hastily to his daughter's side, while the Duke of Florence muttered an involuntary oath, as two of the men-at-arms raised their swords to hew the Israelite to the earth.

It was a fearful moment, and the Jew seemed to feel that his fate was wavering like the sunbeam on the point of a brightened dagger.

He made a quick gesture to the Arab mute, he seized the wrist of the fair Rosalind, and looking her earnestly in the face, whispered a hurried word in the maiden's ear, deep and piercing in its import, yet inaudible to the group clustered around.

Rosalind turned pale, started quickly aside, but in a moment seemed chiding herself for this folly, as with a smile on her lip she spoke to the Ladye Annabel in a low and murmured tone. Annabel started, with the quick convulsive start that follows an overwhelming surprise.

She started, but in a moment recovering herself, she exclaimed with a firm voice, and extended arms—

"Touch him not—do the Jew no harm! It is by my command that he is here. Sir Merchant," she continued, with a smile of kindly meaning, "you will wait for me, in the hall of the castle—there will I look at your wares when the evening mass is done."

"This is wondrous strange," murmured Aldarin. "Some changing woman's fancy, I trow—"

"Certes, the lace must be rare in texture, and quaint in device!" half muttered the Duke. "Yet I never knew that there was magic in the mere mention of such costly gear, before this moment!"

The men-at-arms released the Jew, and the procession passed on towards the more distant precincts of the castle, where the light of many torches presently streamed from the arching windows of the chapel of St. George of Albarone, showing in full and beautiful relief the snow-white forms of the maidens, passing through the sacred door of the church followed by the Count Aldarin and the Duke, environed by a glittering throng of cavaliers.

Meanwhile, alone and in the darkness, deserted by the crowd, near the hall door, stood the Hebrew and his Mute Servitor, gazing ardently upon the receding procession, until the last cavalier disappeared within the walls of the chapel.

Then it was that a grim smile passed over the bearded face of the Jew, while the Arab boy started wildly aside clenching his hands with sudden agitation, as the strains of the Holy Mass, floating from the chapel, broke upon his ear.

An hour passed. The holy ceremonies of religion had ceased to echo through the walls of the chapel. The Ladye Annabel attended by her maidens had again passed into the castle hall. Beside one of the pillars of the lofty door, stood the gallant Guiseppo, his arms folded and his eyes fixed upon the heavens above.

Guiseppo was enrapt in the mysteries of a sombre study.

He was just wondering what the stars could be made of, whether they were veritable balls of fire, unstable meteors, or angel's eyes—how it chanced that they were lighted up so regularly every night, stormy ones of course excepted—where they went in day-time—and then he fell to thinking of angels, fairies, and other beings made all out of air—and from angels it was quite natural that his thoughts should pass to woman; and with the thought of woman came dim, floating visions of ancles well turned, black eyes beaming like living things, ruby lips wreathing in a smile, while they wooed the kiss of love. There is no knowing how far his musings might have gone, had he not been disturbed by the sound of a footstep breaking the silence of the castle yard. He looked in the direction from whence the sound proceeded, and beheld a strange figure, clad in solemn black, approaching from the gloom of the court-yard. It drew nearer and nearer, and Guiseppo beheld the form of the Scholar Aldarin.

He came slowly onward, toward the light burning over the hall door, and the Page remembered in after life that his face was most ghastly to behold, most fearful to look upon.

His head drooped upon his breast over his folded arms, his eyes dilated to their utmost, glaring vacantly on the earth, while his lips moved in broken murmurs, the Scholar ascended the steps of stone, as the Page observed him from the shadow of a massive pillar.

"It hastens, it hastens to perfection—THE MIGHTY SPELL! The marriage—ha, ha, Duchess of Florence!—HE shall live again—ha, ha! the world shall not say Aldarin toiled in vain! The secret—a few more days—ALDARIN LIVES FOREVER!"

And as the murmurs broke wildly from his lips, the Scholar disappeared within the shadow of the hall door, leaving the careless Guiseppo to the memory of that fearful face. It was an appalling memory. Guiseppo's cheek grew pale, and his whole frame trembled with an indefinable fear.

How long he remained in this state he knew not, but after a long lapse of dreamy reverie, he was startled by a slight tap on his shoulder.

Looking around, he beheld the beaming eyes of the fair Rosalind fixed upon him with a glance which for the moment banished the face of Aldarin from his mind, and made his heart knock sadly against his breast.

"What wouldst have, Rosalind?" *The maiden whispered in his ear.*

It was curious to see the change that came over the countenance of the page; the pallor vanished from his visage, which swelled out on either side as though he had an orange in each cheek, his lips were curiously pursed, while his eyes rolled about in his head after a strange fashion.

"Eh? Rosalind?" he cried, as if he had not understood her aright.

Again did the maiden whisper in his ear.

"By our Lady!" exclaimed Guiseppo, "but this does exceed everything that I ever did hear. Art not crazed, sweetheart?"

"Say, Guiseppo, wilt do it for my sake!"

The bewitching smile with which this was said, appeared to complete the conquest of the page.

"I'll obey thee," he cried, "but surely 'tis a strange request."

"*Strange?* nonsense! Never call the whim of woman—*strange*! Hie thee away and do 't immediately. I will tell thee more concerning this matter in the evening. Away! away!"

And as the lovely damsel tripped lightly down the steps and wended her way toward the castle gate, on an errand whose import may possibly be revealed in future pages of this history, the page Guiseppo entered the hall of the castle, while his frame shook with a pleasant fit of inward laughter.

CHAPTER THE FIFTH.

THE BRIDAL MORN.

THE WEDDING GUESTS CIRCLE ROUND THE HOLY ALTAR, WHILE THE SCHOLAR ALDARIN STRIKES HIS DAGGER AT THE INTANGIBLE AIR.

THE first flash of the morn that was to gild the fair brow of the Ladye Annabel with a ducal coronet, glowed faintly in the eastern sky, and the black-bearded Jew stood in the court-yard, casting his eyes earnestly about him, as if waiting the approach of one with whom he had made an appointment.

Not long did he wait, for presently emerging from a small door inserted in a wing of the castle, near the chapel of St. George, the page Guiseppo approached, with his form muffled up in his cloak of blue velvet and gold embroidery; while his slouching hat, drooping over his face, concealed his features entirely from the view.

By his side, at a respectful distance, walked the Arab mute, his head bowed low, and his face half concealed by his jet-black locks, while he tottered under the weight of his heavy burden.

As Guiseppo gained the side of the Jew, a sentinel was passing.

"Ho, sir page!" exclaimed the Hebrew, "thou seem'st fearful of the morning breeze. Hurry along—hurry along—or beshrew me, thou wilt not get the rare lace for the Ladye Annabel—the rare lace worth its weight in gold a hundred times told. Haste thee—haste thee!"

They crossed the court-yard, and presently stood before the pillars of the castle gate, which was guarded by four sentinels, attired in the livery of his grace of Florence.

"Fair sir," exclaimed the Jew, addressing one of the men-at-arms, "I would pass through the castle gate. I am bound for the village hard by the castle. Albarone, I think you call it?"

"Wherefore abroad so early?" asked the sentinel; "and why goes Guiseppo with you?"

"Yesternight, when I journeyed toward the castle, some of my most precious wares I left behind me at the hostel of the village below. The Ladye Annabel wishes to purchase some rare and costly laces. My business calls me and this poor dumb youth away to the north, and therefore is the page sent with me; he is sent to receive the wares purchased by the Ladye Annabel. Hast any thing further to ask, sir sentinel?"

And as he asked the question, the page Guiseppo and the Arabian drew nearer to the Jew, awaiting the answer with evident interest.

It was observable that the right hand of the mute was thrust within the folds of his doublet, while his blue eye, so strangely contrasting with his dark brows and darker hair, glared fiercely into the faces of the sentinels.

"I have nothing more to ask of thee, *now*," exclaimed another sentinel, advancing. "But had not the Duke sent me this pass for thee, thy servitor, and the page Guiseppo, the foul fiend take me, but I would have seen thy heathen carcass at the devil, ere a bolt should be drawn for thee to pass forth at this unseasonable hour. Thy way lies before thee, Jew!"

As he spoke, he applied a key to a small door which was cut into the massive timbers of the castle gate. The door flew open, and through the opened space the drawbridge was seen descending. One foot of the Jew was passed through the narrow entrance, when the sentinel who held the pass of the Duke, exclaimed:

"Why, Guiseppo, what aileth thee? Wherefore art muffled up in this fashion? Where are thy merry jests? Where is that magpie tongue of thine? Hast forgotten all thy mischievous pranks—eh, sir page?"

A low, moaning noise came from the mouth of the mute, as he seemed impatient of the delay.

"I have no time to trifle in idle converse," exclaimed the Jew. "Come on, fair sir, the morning breaks, and I must be on my way."

He took the page by the shoulder, and gently pulled him through the doorway, leaving the sentinels to their surprise at the strange silence of the mirthful Guiseppo, while the unfortunate mute slowly followed in the footsteps of the Jew, his right hand trembling with a scarce perceptible motion, as he buried it within the folds of his doublet.

With a hurried step, the Jew and his companion passed over the drawbridge, and in a moment standing upon the summit of the hill upon whose rocks and caverns the castle was founded, they viewed the winding road beneath.

The page turned his head—still concealed by his slouched hat—he turned his head for a moment toward the castle, and a slight tremor pervaded his frame.

Then his hand was extended, grasping the hand of the Arab mute, who returned the grasp with a firm pressure upon the white fingers of the dainty page.

"Let us onward! Let us onward!" whispered the Jew. "A long journey have we before us. Onward, I pray ye!"

They hurriedly wended down the hill, and ere an hundred could be told, their forms were lost to sight in the shades of the forest.

All bright and glorious came on the rising day, lighting up the cloudless azure with its kindly beams, shimmering over the waves of the broad, deep river, filling the wild-wood glade with glimpses of golden light; while the far-off mountains towered into the heavens, the white clouds crowning their rugged peaks, radiant with the changing hues of the morning sun.

And while the day wore slowly on, the paths leading through the valley toward the castle, the winding ways that passed through the recesses of the wild wood, and the great highway sweeping on toward Florence the Fair, were all alive with crowds of peasants, in their holiday attire, wrinkled age and red-lipped youth, mature manhood and careless boyhood, all hastening onward toward the castle of Albarone, anxious to behold the marriage of the Duke and the Ladye Annabel.

The day wore on, and the court-yard was thronged by strange and contrasted bands; the peasant in his gay costume, the vassal in his rich livery, side by side with the man-at-arms clad in glittering mail, while the servitors of the house ran hurriedly to and fro, passing with hasty steps from hall to hall, from gallery to gallery, as the confused sounds of preparation for the bridal feast awoke the echoes of the arching corridor or pillared hall.

The first quarter of the day had passed, and the shadow of the dial plate in the castle yard, was gliding over the path of high noon.

As gay a bridal party as ever the sun shone upon, waited within the walls of the chapel of St. George. They waited for the coming of the bridegroom and bride.

There were queenly ladies and beauteous damsels, gallant lords and gay cavaliers, blazing in gorgeous attire; there, mingling with the men-at-arms of Albarone, thronged the retainers of the Duke, robed in the royal livery of his house; and beside the altar stood the priest and the father, the venerable abbot of St. Peters, arrayed in his sacred robes, and the sage and thoughtful Aldarin, Count Di Albarone, attired, as was his wont, in the plain tunic of sable velvet, relieved by the sweeping robe of black, with his pale forehead surmounted by the cap of fur, glittering with a single gem.

Long will it be, by my troth, very long—thus runs the words of the ancient MSS.—ere the light of day will look down upon a scene so full of gaiety and grandeur.

The tall and swelling forms of the noble dames, arrayed in all the richest silks that the East might furnish, covered with gold and brilliant with jewels;—the noble figures of the cavaliers, their gay doublets hung with the symbols of the various orders of chivalry, their belts of every variety of ornament, and of every fancy of embroidery, their diamond-hilted swords, their jeweled caps, surmounted by nodding plumes and their cloaks of the finest velvet depending carelessly from the right shoulder, and falling in graceful folds over the arm,—combined with the glare of Milan steel worn by the men-at-arms, and the glitter of the rich liveries of the retainers of the Duke, formed a scene of vivid and contrasting interest.

The gallant party began to express their wonder at the long delayed approach of the Duke and his fair bride, and even the venerable abbot betrayed marks of impatience.

It was worthy of note, that for the space of ten minutes or more, the Count Aldarin had stood beside the priest, silent and motionless, with his eyebrows knit, and his lips compressed, while he gazed steadily at the slabs of the mosaic pavement in front of the altar, which, for the space of some half score paces or more, was left bare and unoccupied by the crowd.

At last, placing his lips to the ear of the abbot, and hurriedly glancing around, as if fearful of being observed, the Count whispered—

"*What doth* HE *here?*" he said, pointing to the pavement in front of the altar.

"To whom dost thou refer, my Lord Count?" inquired the Priest.

"S'life!" exclaimed the Count in a voice that trembled from some unknown cause; "S'life! I mean the *stranger*—he in the dark armor, with the raised vizor and that ghastly face. Dost not see him?"

"My Lord, there is no one before the altar attired in armor. Around us are the throng of Lords and Ladies—but all are arrayed in robes of peace. Mayhap you speak of one of the men-at-arms who stand yonder, near the door of the chapel?"

"Shaveling! I mean *the stranger* who stands in front of the altar. He with the plume as dark as death falling over that pale and lofty forehead. He who gazes so fixedly with those glassy eyes—gazes and looks, yet speaks no word. By Heavens, he means to mock me. I will strike him down even where he stands!"

He advanced hurriedly to the front of the altar, and in an instant the bystanders beheld him striking his dagger in the air, while his pale features were convulsed by a strange expression.

"Thou shalt not escape me!" he shouted.—"Elude me not—I'll have thee, coward! This to thy very heart! What, art thou dagger proof? Guards, I say, seize this traitor! Albarone to the rescue!"

It was with a feeling of indefinable awe, that the bridal throng beheld the Count Aldarin standing with his eyes strained from their very sockets, his brows woven together, and his whole face stamped with an expression which was neither terror nor hate, but seemed a mingling of terror, hate, and despair.

Two courtiers sprang at the same time from the group, crying as they drew their swords—

"My Lord, where is the traitor? Who is't?"

"Shall I be slain upon my own ground? Where is the traitor? Before your eyes he stands. *He!* I mean. Look—look! Behold! he leans upon the altar! He smiles in scorn—he mocks me!"

Aldarin stamped his foot with rage, and shrieked—

"By the Eternal God! but this is brave! Will ye see me murdered before your eyes! Seize—I say—seize the traitor!"

"Benedicite!" muttered the venerable abbot, gazing upon the wild face of Aldarin; "the fiend is among us!"

As he spoke, the Duke of Florence all daintily apparelled in his wedding dress, with surprise and vexation pictured in every lineament of his countenance, broke through the throng, exclaiming—

"My Lord Count, thy daughter is no where to be found. The Ladye Annabel hath gone: no one knoweth whither!"

"My Lord Duke," said Aldarin in a whisper, "can'st thou tell me who is the stranger?"

"Eh?" exclaimed the astonished Duke, gazing upon Aldarin with a vacant stare.

"*He* I mean who standeth by the altar. He in the sable armor—with the pale brow and the eyes of fire—with the dark plume overshadowing his helmet! By heavens, I behold under his plume the crest of the Winged Leopard!"

"By our Lady, but thou describest the late Count Di Albarone. Mayhap he comes from the grave to witness against his son, the vile parricide, he who hath fled with thy daughter. May the fiend curse him for't!"

"*Fled with my daughter? my daughter fled?*" shouted Aldarin, as he suddenly seemed to break the spell that bound him.

"Pardon me, my friends. Anxiety for my child—grief for my brother—have driven me mad.—My brain is fevered—I am ill. My daughter fled, say'st thou? How?—when? What meanest thou?"

The Duke hurriedly turned to Guiseppo, who stood among the throng of bower maidens, who had followed his Grace into the chapel.

"Guiseppo, advance. What said the Ladye Annabel when thou didst return this morning from thy errand beyond the castle walls in company with the Jewish merchant. Eh? Guiseppo?"

"My Lord Duke," replied the page, "I went not forth this morning from the castle walls—"

"Saving this presence," cried a man-at-arms pressing forward, "saving this presence, Sir Page, but there thou liest. Did I not see thee go forth this morning at daybreak?—the Jew with thee, and thy face muffled up as if thou wert ashamed of thy errand?"

"How say you?" cried Aldarin, whose native perception had returned, "His face muffled? Come hither, girl," he continued, addressing Rosalind, who stood among the throng of bower maidens. "Girl, when didst see thy mistress last?"

"My Lord Count," said the maiden, "I left the Ladye Annabel last night at twelve: I slept within the ante-chamber adjoining her bower. This morning on knocking at her door I found it fastened. I did not like to disturb her, so I waited—" here Rosalind seemed confused, while the blush deepened over her cheek. "I waited, my Lord Count, hour after hour, until my Lord the Duke came to lead the bride to church. Then—then—"

"By the body of God, but I see it all!" thus exclaimed the Count Aldarin. "I have been fooled—duped, and by thee, girl! Thou art my own sister's child, but think not to escape the vengeance of Aldarin! I see all—my daughter— the wanton!—has fled in the attire of this page, he too is a plotter, he who oweth life—fortune—everything—to me! Guards, seize the miscreant! Tremble—well thou may'st! Thou hast invoked the axe—beware its fall! To the lowest dungeon of the castle with him! away! To horse—to horse!" continued Aldarin, glancing round upon the astonished assemblage. "To horse—to horse!—mount every man! Scour every road, every path in the domains of Albarone! Sweep the highway to Florence! A thousand pieces of gold to him who brings the haggard back!"

CHAPTER THE SIXTH.

SIR GEOFFREY O' TH' LONGSWORD.

THE SPIRIT OF THE CHRONICLE THROWS BACK THE CURTAIN OF FATE, AND GIVES TO VIEW SOME GLIMPSES OF THE LAST SCENE, IN WHICH THE BARBS OF ARIMANES BECOME THE AVENGERS OF HEAVEN.

ALONG a mossy, winding path, that led through the sunlit glades and shady recesses of a green and bowery forest, two travellers, one a stripling and the other a man of some forty winters, were wending their way, while the dew was yet upon the turf, and while the morning carol of innumerable birds arose from the bosom of the rich foliage.

—Thus in his own enthusiastic way speaks the Chronicler of the Ancient MSS. His words, it is true are somewhat redundant, but yet there is heart in them after all.—

The cheeks of the youth were strangely puffed out, his lips were gathered like the mouth of a purse, while he whistled with an earnestness that was certainly wonderful. Presently he spoke—

"By'r Ladye, but that was the most exquisite thing of all. Eh? Good Robin? The idea of thy carcass being perched upon the back of the Demon Statue in that pestilent cavern. And frightening the old Count into fits, too! Ha! ha! ha! 'Twas rich! By the Saints it was! Oh, Robin, thou art certainly the very devil for mischief! That prank of gagging the old Israelite, and stealing his beard, coat, pack and all, was cruel, by my troth it was! Where didst thou leave the old gripefist?"

"As I told thee before, thou rattlebrained popinjay!" the other replied with a good natured smile. "With a heavy heart I wended along the highway, on the eve of the bridal, thinking of the fair Ladye Annabel, when who should I behold trudging before me, but this good son of Moses. I laid him upon the earth in a wink—gagged him, and concealed him in the cottage of a peasant, whose ears I filled with a terrible tale of the Jew's roguery; how he had stolen the plate of the castle, and so on. I then disguised myself in the Hebrew's attire; with what success you are already aware.—After I had effected the deliverance of the Ladye Annabel, I released the Jew who ran beardless and affrighted, as fast as his legs could carry him, out of the demesnes of Albarone!"

"Where didst leave the Ladye Annabel, Robin? Who was the Arab Mute? Where is he now?"

"I left her *in safety*, most sagacious Guiseppo. And as for the Mute—I'll tell thee anon. How didst feel when I came to release thee from the dungeon? eh?"

'O! St. Peter! By my troth it would make a picture. There I sat, upon the bench of stone; the taper flinging its beams around the dreary walls, my elbows resting upon my knees, and my face supported by my clenched hands; my mind full of dark and gloomy thoughts, and my fancy forming various pleasant pictures of the gibbet, which was to bear my figure on the morrow. Imagine this delicate form swinging on a gibbet—ugh! Thus was I employed, when I heard a noise like the drawing of bolts. I started, expecting to behold the Count Aldarin; he had *visited* the cell an hour or so past, and informed that I had the honor of being—mark ye, my soldier—*his son*. I started and beheld—thy welcome visage, my good Robin."

"Marry, it was well for thee that the secret passage was known to me. How sayst thou? Did the murderer aver that he was thy father?"

"Even so. The Count Aldarin, has ever been kind to me, yet I never thought I was connected with him by any ties of blood. I have always been known throughout the castle as *the foundling*. Pleasant name—eh, Robin? The tale runs that a peasant returning home, on an autumn night, discovered a child some three years old, crying in the forest. That child the Scholar Aldarin adopted, and called Guiseppo; which title was occasionally varied by the servitors of Albarone, to that of *Guiseppo Stray-Devil, Lost-Elf*, and others of like pleasing character. But whither are we wandering now, good Robin? This is the second day of our flight; whither are we bound?"

"Thou wilt know ere long. Didst ever hear of Sir Geoffrey O' Th' Longsword?"

"What, the stout Englisher! The brave knight who now commands the soldiers of our late Lord, in Palestine? He that is noted for the strength of his arms, and the daring of his spirit? Why all Christendom rings with his feats."

"Well, my bird of a page, I have lately heard by a wandering palmer, that a truce has been made, between that son of Mahound, Saladin, and the princes of Christendom. Further it is said, that a body of the crusaders have sailed from Cyprus, and are bound to Italy. Dost see aught in this, my popinjay?"

"The Saints help thy senses! Surely you do not mean to say that the soldiers of Albarone are returning home?"

"Marry but I do. I mean to wend towards the nearest seaport; I mean to—"

"By our Lady," interrupted Guiseppo, "I spy the dawning of our Lord Adrian's day. I do by heaven!"

And thus conversing they pursued their way along the forest path.

Higher and higher rose the sun in the Heavens, and its beams shone upon the armor of a gallant company which journeyed in brilliant array along a bye-road leading thro' a wide and shadowy forest.

Near the head of the company, on a stout black steed, rode a tall, stalwart man, full six feet high, broad shouldered, in form, with a stern, weather beaten countenance. His long white hair, escaping from beneath his helmet, the vizor of which was raised, fell upon his mail-clad shoulders, and his beard, frosted by time and battle toil, swept over the iron plate that defended his muscular chest.

On either side rode his Esquires, mounted on horses dark and stout, as that of their knight commander. They were brothers, and side by side had fought in a thousand battles.

Both tall, muscular, and dark featured; both having dark eyes, dark shaggy brows, stiff hair and beard of the same dark hue, they were known among the ranks of the crusaders as the twin brothers—the brave Esquire Damian, and the gallant Esquire Halbert.

Hard matter it were to tell one from the other, so much they looked alike, had it not been that the visage of Damian, was marked by a sword wound, which extending from the right eyebrow, passed over his swarthy forehead and terminated near the left temple; while a deep gash cut into the right cheek of Halbert, served to distinguish him from his brother.

In front of the knight, the standard-bearer, mounted on a cream colored steed, bore aloft a broad banner of azure. A winged leopard was pictured on its folds, and the inscription read thus—*Grasp boldly and bravely strike!*

In the rear of the gray haired warrior, a stout Englishman, riding on a dappled gray, held on high a crimson banner, bordered by white, on which was pictured a two-edged sword, having a long blade, and massy hilt. It bore the motto—

Hilt for Friend—Point for Foe.

Then, riding at their ease, came the men-at-arms arrayed from head to foot in their armor of Milan steel; their lances were in their hands; each shield hung at the saddle-bow, and each sword depended from the belt of buff.

The gallant band might number an hundred thrice told.

Behind these soldiers come the varlets of the train, riding beside the baggage wains, conveying the sick and wounded, who had endured the burning sun of Palestine, the toil and dangers of the seas, and were now returning to the land of their birth.

And there, riding before the baggage wains, four dark-skinned Moors, mounted on prancing nags, led each man of them, a steed black as night, at his bridle rein.

Untamed they were and wild; their eyes gave forth a gleam like the light of the fire-coal; their necks were proudly arched; their manes flung waving to the breeze. With a disdainful toss of their quivering nostrils and a light and springing step, the barbs trod the earth as gallantly as though they still swept over the desert plains of Araby.

Linked with the chain of this wierd chronicle, by a strange decree of Fate, these barbs, in the course of a few brief days, became the Instruments of the fearful vengeance of Heaven.

"Damian," said the stalwart knight, as glancing over the long line of men-at-arms, he gazed upon the Arab steeds,—"How the eye of Lord Julian will glisten when he gazes upon yonder mettled barbs! I' faith it makes an old warrior's heart beat, to look upon their arching crests, their eyes of fire, and their skins, black as death."

"A Paynim warrior gave these steeds in ransom for his freedom? Is that the story Sir Geoffrey?" asked Halbert, "Infidel though he was, he gave a most princely ransom."

"Hast ever heard the strange legend which the Arabs tell, concerning this race of steeds? They prize them, highly as their weight in gold, red gold. It is said that in the olden time, when Arimanes was hurled from his throne of Evil, by Ormaz, the Great Being of Good, the spirits of his followers, accursed and doomed, sought refuge in the bodies of a race of ebon-colored barbs, that scoured the plains of Araby with the fleetness of the wind, herding together in the vast solitudes of the desert, and untameable by man. At last, after a long lapse of centuries, the most daring of the Arab-chiefs, secured and subjugated to the control of man, two of these wild horses, from which sprung the race of the Barbs of Arimanes, or Demon-Steeds. Yonder horses, prancing and rearing in the grasp of the tawny Moors, are of this race. By my soul, their flashing eyes give them some title to the name they bear—the Barbs of Arimanes!"

"It joys a warrior's heart to look upon their sinewy forms," exclaimed the Esquire Halbert, with a flashing eye.

"They are slender and graceful as the wild gazelle," said Damian, "and yet your stout war-horse of the north bears not fatigue or toil with a better grace."

"Damian," said the stalwart knight, "Damian, art thou not sorrowed at the thought of leaving the Holy Land—the glorious scene of so many hard-fought frays? I trow we will all wish to be again in the midst of the gallant mellay; shall we not pine for the rugged encounter with the Paynim host— What sayst thou, Halbert?"

"He that leaves so brave a battle plain as is the land of the Holy Sepulchre, without a sigh of regret, is unworthy of the lay of minstrel, or love of ladye. For my part, I would all these truces were at the devil!"

"I say amen to thy prayer, good brother."

"Well, well, we shall soon reach the castle Di Albarone; we shall behold our brave leader, the gallant Count Julian. By the body of God, it stirs one's blood to think of his charge, that ever mowed down the Paynim ranks as though a thunderbolt had smote them! St. George! but I have seen glorious days."

"By'r Lady, but I have a sneaking fear that the wound of the Count may prove fatal."

"Fatal?" shouted Sir Geoffrey, in a voice of thunder. "Fatal? Say it not again, Halbert! Fatal, indeed! By my troth, Lord Julian Di Albarone, shall again lead *armies* to battle."

"I wonder," said Damian, "I wonder if that skulking half brother of the Count, still lives? I mean, he who accompanied the Lord Julian to the Holy Land, some score of years since. How was he styled? eh, Halbert?"

"ALDARIN, I think they called him. Sir Geoffrey, hadst not a quarrel with the bookworm? Didst not strike him before the Count at Jerusalem, in the presence of all the princes of Christendom?"

"Tush, a mere trifle! I mind it no more than I would the spurning of a peevish cur. But see! What have we here? Two wayfarers. Ha! one seems like a disbanded soldier! Spur forward, my merry men! They may tell us of our whereabouts: they may give us some news of Albarone. Spur forward!"

CHAPTER THE SEVENTH.

THE STUDENT AND THE FAIR STRANGER.[3]

THE bell of the convent of St. Benedict struck the hour of noon, when a young man, attired after the manner of a student, or Neophyte of the monastic order, was slowly wending his way along the path that led to the cottage on the hill, while on his arm, there hung a youth of a slender yet graceful figure and with calm, mild features, shaded by locks of golden hair.

Tall, sinewy, and well-proportioned in form, the face of the Student was marked by features bold and decisive in their expression; his blue eye was full of thought, and his forehead, high and massive, shaded by the cap of velvet, gave the idea of a mind powerful, energetic, and formed to rule.

His hair fell in clustering locks of gold over his neck and shoulders; his plain tunic of dark velvet descended to his knees, revealing a doublet of like material and color, worn underneath, fitting closely to his manly form; while his throat was enveloped by a simple collar of snow-white lace.

His companion wore a neat doublet of light blue, fitting close around the neck, scarce allowing the pretty ruffle that circled the fair throat to be seen, and reaching half way down the leg, it was gathered around the slender waist by a girdle of plain doe skin. His light hair was covered by a hat, with the rim drawn up to the crown on one side, and slouching upon the other, while it was topped by delicate white plumes, fastened by a diamond broach.

Winding amid the fragrant shrubbery that enclosed the path, the student and his companion attained the top of the hill, and passing through the small garden, they presently stood before the neat cottage, which, shadowed by a spreading beech on one side, meeting the foliage of a leafy chesnut on the other, was overrun in front by a fragrant vine, that clomb over the timbers of the doorway, and twined round the solitary casement; the broad green leaves quivering in the beams of the sun, and the trumpet-shaped flowers swinging to and fro in the wooing air.

The student tapped at the door. It was opened by a woman somewhat advanced in life, attired in the dress of a peasant, yet with a cross of ebony strung from her neck. Her look was somewhat severe and stern, her demeanor was commanding, and her figure still retained some remains of youthful beauty.

She started as she opened the door, and an unfinished word burst from her lips.

"Ah! Adr—tush! Leone, I mean—thou art early home to-day, my son."

"Mother," said the student, "this is my fellow scholar Florian, son to the Baron Diarmo of Florence. In yonder convent we pursue our studies in one apartment side by side. An hour since, as we strolled through the gardens adjoining the convent, my friend missed his footing, and severely bruised his ancle. Our home being nearer than the convent, I thought I could not do better then bring him hither. I need not commend him to thy care."

"Thou art welcome fair sir," the dame replied, with a kindly smile. "Enter our abode; 'tis humble, yet 'tis sacred, for the bounty of the convent bestows it upon my son and me, while he is preparing for the priesthood. Come in, gentle Florian."

They entered the cottage, and the door was closed.

No sooner had they disappeared than something rustled in the bushes and the bow-legged vagabond, Francisco, emerged into the light.

"Oh—ho!" he cried, "here's a mystery. The convent allow old Mistress Vinegar-face to reside on their land, in their cottage, while her son is preparing for the priesthood! A likely story, by'r lady! I see it all—'tis as I suppose—these two striplings, are those, for whom such an immense reward has been offered in the neighboring towns and villages. Will not gold line my pouch as well as any other wight's—eh? Via! Francisco! Vagabond no longer, but henceforth Signor Francisco! Via!"

Thus saying, he walked away with folded arms and a gigantic stride; and as he stalked away, the tall Dollabella, the red-haired Theresa, and black-eyed Loretta appeared from the bushes on the other side of the cot, and, bursting into a loud laugh, they tripped after the swelling "vagabond."

Meanwhile, within the cot, resting on a cushioned seat, the gentle Florian submitted his foot to the hands of the dame, who drew off the shoe and stocking, and applied ointment to the bruise; remarking, at the same time, that the foot was one of the smallest, and the ancle one of the prettiest in the wide world.

The student glanced at Florian, and smiled.

"Mother," said he, "I must away to the convent. Methinks it were better for gentle Florian to rest him here awhile. I will return anon, and accompany my fellow scholar along the shores of the lake to the monastery."

He kissed the cheek of the fair boy, and departed. Looking up into the rosy face, and catching the glance of the bright blue eye of the modest youth, the dame exclaimed, as she finished the dressing of the wound:

"Fair sir, if it please thee to grace our humble tenement with thy presence for the night, thou canst share the bed of my son. Methinks it were best for thee not to stir hence until the morrow."

"I thank thee, kind lady," the youth began, in a voice as sweet as infancy.

"*Lady*, say'st thou? I am but a peasant woman."

Florian blushed.

"Nay, pardon me—I meant no offence. Indeed, it seemed—"

The youth paused, while the blush deepened on his cheek.

"Never heed it, fair sir. This way is Leone's room. Mayhap thou wouldst like to repose thee awhile."

Florian followed her into a small apartment, with a window toward the east, a neat bed in one corner, a crucifix upon the wall, and a table, on which lay a missal of devotion.

The dame retired.

Florian stole noiselessly to the door, and drew the bolt. Then seating himself upon the bed, he covered his face with his hands, and the tears stole between the fair fingers, fast and bright, like drops of sunlit rain.

CHAPTER THE EIGHTH.

THE CASTLE GATE.

THE GROUP CLUSTERED BESIDE THE CASTLE GATE ARE STARTLED BY THE PEAL OF A STRANGE TRUMPET.[4]

"WELL-a-day! It's a sad thing to dwell in this lonely place, now that all of the ancient house are dead and gone!"

"'*Dead and gone,*' sir huntsman! Where didst learn to shape thy words? The Count Aldarin lives!"

"By my troth, he does, good Balvardo; and a right quiet time we peaceful folks have had for a day or so past. Here, have we no boisterous merriment; no sound of your squeaking pipe or tabret awakes the silence of these walls; no runlets of wine flow in the beaders of the banquet hall. All is quiet and still. Thanks to Our Lady for't!"

"Such quiet and such stillness, i' faith! Why, man, you cannot walk along the solitary corridors of the castle, without trembling at your own starved shadow. Didst ever see a place swept by the plague—all its living folk carried to the grave-yard, leaving old Death to take care of deserted chamber and lonely hall? Look around the court-yard of Albarone, and ask your heart—if heart you have—whether a plague has not swept this place? The saints defend me! it chills my soul to look upon these lonesome walls!"

"And I—look ye, gossips—I, Griseldea, tire-woman of my Ladye Annabel, have never damosel or dame, for two score long years—I am two score and six years, come next Mass o' Christ, not an hour more, i' faith—I have never, for two score long years, felt so dead in heart as I do now! In my Ladye's bower lie her garments of price; the tunic of blue and gold which she wore in her happy days; the white plume that once drooped over her fair brow, the snow-white bridal dress—all, all are there! But where is my Ladye Annabel? Grammercy, but these are doleful days!"

"Blood o' th' Turk! Tell me, good folk, are ye paid to howl in chorus? Hugo, didst ever hear such growling?"

"Faith, they do growl, somewhat like a herd of untamed bears! Yet, Balvardo, bethink thee—there's reason for't. W-h-e-w! When I think of the queer things that have chanced within these few days, I might wonder, I might growl; yes, Balvardo, I might growl, I might wonder!"

"Here, for three long days, since my lord of Florence left the castle, have we seen no sight of the Count Aldarin," exclaimed the huntsman.—"Mayhap he has buried himself alive—mayhap he has gone up to heaven, or more likely he has gone to—'s life, what a stitch in my side!"

"Softly, softly, sir huntsman, softly! Wise folk speak not lightly of the Count Aldarin. The rope on yonder gibbet swings loosely in the summer wind—thy neck may be the first to stretch its fibres!"

"Blood o' th' Turk, yet it does seem queer when one comes to think of it! Not three days ago, it was nothing but *'saddle me your horses, scour every road, bring back the traitor Guiseppo, and hew off his caitiff head! Now*—blood o' th' Turk, it puzzles me!'"

"*Now*, sir Balvardo, the word is: *'Pay all respect to Guiseppo; honor the youth as myself—he is dear to me in blood, dear to me in heart, honor Guiseppo, he rules the castle in my absence.'*"

"Sancta Maria!" cried the ancient tire-woman. "Tell me, gossip, tell me, sir huntsman, how came this about?"

"Not two nights agone, there enters the castle gate, a wandering palmer, clad in rags. Not satisfied with asking alms at the hall door, he must wander along the corridors of the castle, and prowl around the door of the cell where the damsel Rosalind is imprisoned. My Count Aldarin's suspicions are roused: he flings the beggar's robes from the palmer's face, and we all behold the—trim page Guiseppo!"

"Wonder of all wonders! Now, I'll never be astonished again in all my life!"

"Not even if any one should chance to believe the story of thy age, which thou art wont to tell! Hugo, look at gossip tire-woman, how her eyes are dropping from their sockets!"

"There stood the page Guiseppo—there stood the Count Aldarin! Nice group—eh! Axes and gibbets were the mildest things in our thoughts, when my lord takes the page by the hand, smiles kindly, and leads him away. An hour passes: the supper is spread in the banquet hall: my Lord Aldarin appears, and with him comes Guiseppo, clad in garments of cost—"

"And then comes the word: *'Pay Sir Guiseppo all respect—honor him as myself.'* Is't not so good gossip?"

"By my huntsman's word, it is even so! Now tell me, sir sentinels, waiting at the castle gate, while the Count Aldarin is buried in the depths of the earth, sir Hugo and Balvardo, sir steward and dame Griseldea, all of ye servitors of Albarone, is not this matter enough for a nine day's wonder? By'r Lady, I never heard the like!"

"Blood o' th' Turk, 'tis wonderful!"

"W-h-e-w! 'Tis passing strange!"

"Hist—Hugo! What sound is that? 'Tis like the tramp of war steeds!"

"Hark! The peal of a trumpet! This is wondrous."

And for a single moment the strangely contrasted group gathered at the castle gate, in the mild evening hour, stood motionless as statues, with the light of the setting sun falling over each face and figure.

There was Hugo, with his vacant face and sinister eye, clad like his comrade, Balvardo of the beetle brow, in glittering armor of Milan steel, each standing breast to breast, as, with pikes half raised, they listened to the trumpet peal swelling from the distance. There was the bluff huntsman of the castle, his rugged visage affording a striking contrast to the sharp features of the ancient steward, and the thin, withered countenance of the tire-woman, standing near him, while all around were clustered the servitors of Albarone, their gay liveries flashing in the light of the setting sun.

"Hark, Balvardo! The trumpet peal swells louder. I hear the trampling of an hundred steeds. Up, up to the tower of the castle gate, and tell us what is to be seen!"

Balvardo hastily disappeared, and while the group clustered round the lofty pillar awaited the result of his observations with the utmost suspense, ascended to the tower by a staircase built in the massive wall.

"What dost see, comrade?" shouted Hugo; "The trumpet peal grows louder, and I hear the tramp of war steeds pattering along the road to the castle gate. What dost see, Balvardo?"

"I see a strange sight, i'faith! Horsemen issue from the shadow of the wood toward Florence—horsemen arrayed in strange robes, black as night. I count one, two, three,—by my life, there's thirteen o' them, all mounted on cream-colored steeds!"

"Are they men-at-arms? Bear they a pennon at their head?"

"Blood o' th' Turk, I see no men-at-arms! They are clad in long robes, that fall sweeping almost to the very ground. Their robes are black as the death-pall, yet are they faced with a goodly border of glittering gold. Now the wind sweeps the robe of the foremost horseman aside. By my sword, he is clad in the attire of a paynim dog! Loose, flowing garments, with a belt of curious embroidery, while a dark turban surmounts his swarthy form."

"Ride they towards the castle?"

"They ride forward two abreast; the tall figure rides at their head. Tramp, tramp—God send they be not wizards in disguise! A new wonder, comrade; one of the party spurs his horse to the front—he is speeding toward the castle gate! Blood o' th' Turk, he holds a trumpet in his grasp."

"A trumpet, Balvardo? This should be the herald of the companie."

"He rides up the hill, he reins his steed on the very edge of the moat. Hark, how his trumpet peals!"

And while the shrill and piercing sound of the trumpet broke on the air, the group listening beside the castle gate were startled by the sound of a measured footstep.

With one start they turned in the direction of the sound, and beheld the person of the new comer.

He was a young cavalier, with a smooth face, unvisited by beard, yet stamped with the marks of premature and sudden experience, while his slender form, clad in a jewelled doublet, was half hidden by the folds of a sweeping robe of purple, that fell from his shoulders, varied by a border of snow-white ermine.

"It is *him*—the page Guiseppo," murmured the huntsman. "Mark ye, how changed he looks! His arms folded, and his merry face clad in a frown. Well-a-day! The world is all bewitched, or I'm no sinful man!"

"The page Guiseppo," whispered the shrill-voiced steward. "Know ye not his new title? 'My Lord Guiseppo, Baron of Masserio'—nephew of the Count Aldarin. Masserio is the name of one of the smaller baronies annexed by my lord of Florence, to the domains of Albarone. 'Tis said 'twas confiscated to the state, because its master meddled with the strange Order of the Steel, whose fame has been in our ear for these four months past."

"Sir sentinel, canst tell me what means this peal of trumpet, this clamor at the gates of Albarone?"

As Guiseppo advanced and spoke, every one in the group was impressed to the very heart with the change that had so lately passed over the appearance and manner of the page. A score of years could not have added more solemnity to his visage, or given a more deep-toned sternness to his voice.

In a moment the Lord Guiseppo—such is now his title—was possessed of the cause of the clamor at the castle-gate, and was about to speak, when the trumpet peal ceased, and the clear bold voice of the herald, broke upon the air.

"Peace to the Lord Julian of Albarone! My master salutes the gallant knight and craves entrance into the shelter of his goodly castle! Peace to the Lord Julian of Albarone!"

"Be thy master, the Paynim Mahound himself, or the Devil his father—" rang out the hoarse tones of Balvardo, from the tower above—"He is a few days behind old Death in his salutation. Lord Julian of Albarone sleeps in the Charnel-House."

"Then Sir Warder of the castle-gate, by thy soldierly courtesy, I pray thee inform me—doth his brother, the Scholar Aldarin yet live?"

"The *Count Aldarin* reigns *Lord of Albarone*."

"Then I pray thee, bear the salutations of my master to the Count Aldarin, and with his greeting bear this scroll!"

"S' life—here's a net for a man to tangle his feet with!" the group below heard the growling words break from Balvardo—"My Lord Guiseppo"—he exclaimed aloud, looking from the window of the tower—"What answer shall I make to this Wizard Herald of yon Paynim band!"

A sudden contortion passed over the features of Guiseppo, he raised his hand wildly to his brow, and trembled as he stood beside the castle-gate. The spasm-like expression that passed over his face, was scarce human in its meaning, and the spectators started back with a sudden fear. There are times, when the soul is shaken to its centre by the fierce war of contending emotions, when the heart struggles with the brain, while the reason totters, and the intellect reels on its throne. A contest wild as this; seemed warring between the heart and brain of Guiseppo, the new created Lord of Masserio.

"One moment, good Balvardo—Hugo, I am faint—some wine, I prithee!"

Hugo offered his arm to the tottering Guiseppo, and in a moment the Lord of Masserio, found himself sitting on a rough bench of stone, within the confines of the lower chamber of the Warder's Tower, while Hugo stood motionless before him, holding the brimming goblet of wine.

"Thanks, good Hugo—retire a moment, and I will be my own man again— let me think," he muttered in a half-whisper as the Sentinel retired—"Its like a dream—and yet the reality presses on my brain like a weight of lead. I feel no joy in my lordship. Three little days—Saints of Heaven—behold the change! Three days ago, a poor Page, journeyed with a band of gallant soldiers! He disappeared, no one save himself knew whither. He came to this castle in his Palmer's rags and perilled his life to rescue his Ladye-love. He was discovered—he already beheld the object of omen, held above his head—he expected the axe—and Sancta Maria! A coronet fell glittering at his feet. *His* son—*his* son! Great God how dark the mystery! My brain whirls— the wine, ha, ha—the wine."

"Sir Sentinel"—arose the voice of the Herald without—"Wilt thou bear this scroll to the Lord Aldarin?"

"And *she* is yet imprisoned! *He* my father! As God lives I'm bound to stand by him to the death! Robin's story—is it, is it true? The dark hints of the men-at-arms, with their leader Sir Geoffrey—might not this trumpet peal serve to unravel their meaning? The wine gives me nerve—my brain whirls no more. And Adrian and Annabel—must I desert their cause? Methinks I feel my heart strings crack, at the very word! And *he* is my father; *he* loads me with favors, burdens me with kindness—" the half crazed Guiseppo looked around the confined chamber with a fixed and steady eye—"*I will stand by my father Aldarin to the death*".

"Sir Warden, this delay is far from courteous—For the last time, wilt thou bear the scroll?"

"Let the men-at-arms be ranged, along the castle gate—"spoke the determined voice of Lord Guiseppo, as with a steady step and unfaltering manner he issued from the lower chamber of the Warden's Tower—"Call the men-at-arms of his Grace of Florence, now loitering in the halls of the castle, call the vassals of Albarone, silently yet hastily hither! Away Hugo—and thou Sir Huntsman! Let it be done without delay. Balvardo—mark ye, when I give the word let the drawbridge be lowered and the portcullis raised. We shall see what manner of men are these strangers—the Lord Aldarin shall judge them by their scroll!"

CHAPTER THE NINTH.

ALDARIN AND HIS FUTURE.

"IBRAHIM BEN MALAKIM SALUTES HIS BROTHER ALDARIN THE SCHOLAR."

THE beams of the declining day, glanced gaily thro' the arched windows of the Red-chamber, and the Count Aldarin paced with a hurried step across the marble floor, and his chest rose and fell, and his cheek flushed and paled, and now his voice was choked by rage, and again it was clear and deep-toned with hate.

"Baffled! and by whom? my own child. I have laid schemes—I have planned, I have plotted, and all for Annabel—my daughter. And she returns me—contempt and scorn. If, within the bowels of the earth, there is a place of torture, a boundless, illimitable and ever burning hell—if within the fire of the stars, there is written a Doom for the Damned, then to the very hell of hell, then to the very Doom of the Damned, have I sold myself, and all for thee, my daughter! What! a tear?—Shall I play the woman?—No—I will brace me up!—I will show the world the power of one who hates the whole accursed race. There was a time when I could weep, aye and talk of feeling and prate of the tenderness and humanity with any of them!—They gave me scorn, they heaped insult upon me!"

He looked around as tho' he would compass the whole human race with his glance, and an expression of demoniac hate came over his features while he whispered between his clenched teeth.

"*Have I paid the debt?* Ha! ha! Let those who wronged me answer. *Have I paid the debt?* The man never lived who struck the meek Scholar and saw another sun. Not one! not one!—Nay there was one. He scorned me before the Princes of Christendom—it was at Jerusalem—I gave him scorn for scorn—with his mailed hand he struck me to the floor! I swore revenge—the steel was false, the dagger failed, but on his life and heart have I wreaked vengeance, such as man never wreaked before! The revenge of Aldarin must not be fed with the blood of his foe? No—by the fiend—no! But with the very life drops of his soul! My victim fights for the glory of Albarone. Little does he dream who now doth rule the ancient house.—Miserable fool, he toils and wars far in Palestine—he toils—he wars for *me*! *Me*! his ancient, his sworn and unrelenting foe! *Ha! whence is that noise? Ha! ha! Surely it is not a groan from yon couch?*"

Pausing for a moment, he eagerly listened, and again he spoke.

"Let me gather my thoughts. Let me nerve my soul for the trial of this night. The stake I hold in my hand is a fearful one—the hand that would grasp the very secrets of the grave, the weird mysteries of Old Death, should never tremble."

He paced the floor yet more hurriedly, and was silent for a few moments.

"It is the very night!" he exclaimed, after a pause of intense thought. *"The grand problem upon which I have bestowed my youth—my mind—my soul—my all—will soon be solved. This very night completes the thrice seven years. For thrice seven years has the beechen flame burned beneath the alembic, in my laboratory; in war, in difficulty, in danger, and in death, has the azure flame still burned on with undying lustre. Unbounded wealth is mine!* IMMORTAL LIFE.

"In after-time, when long, long, centuries have passed away, men will speak of the glory, the mystery—and perchance the crime—that encircled the life of Aldarin the Scholar! And as the cheek of the listener grows pale, I—I—will be there, also a listener and to the story of my own fate! Aldarin will be there, but oh, how changed! Aldarin, no longer weak, trembling, bent with age—but Aldarin, young and glorious, with the signet of eternal youth and power stamped upon his unfading brow!

"Gold, gold, the talisman that rules the soul of man, gold that buys wisdom from the sage, Heaven from the priest, life from the leech, honor from the mighty, and virtue from woman, GOLD will be mine."

Turning aside, Aldarin drew forth from a recess in the walls, a parchment scroll richly illuminated, and covered with characters in the Arabic tongue. He drew near the casement, and unclosed this scroll to the light of the declining day, gazing upon the dark characters while a singular agitation pervaded the lineaments of his face.

It was the Book of his Belief—in which he had long ago written his ideas of God and Man. Shall we look into these wierd pages, even for a moment, and learn the nature of the Theology which gave shape and purpose to the life of Aldarin? We will glance at a single page of

THE BIBLE OF ALDARIN.

I. Who shall describe the incomprehensible Power, which gives life and motion to the Universe?

II. An Almighty Intellect, dwelling in the solitudes of infinite space, and yet pervading all Nature, guiding by his silent and overshadowing will, the courses of the stars, the fate of empires, and the destinies of men, living for ever, the commencement of his being, dated by a past eternity, the duration of his existence, bounded by a future eternity, He is the SOUL OF THE UNIVERSE.

III. Men have blasphemed this Universal Soul, with their vain titles. They have mocked Him with vainer creeds. They have enshrouded this simple Idea with a multitude of cumbrous falsehoods. They have buried it in the Charnel house of festering superstitions. Yet the Idea has survived, and lived, despite all these systems of error. It can never die. It is written on the heart of the new-born child, and cannot be erased, until you destroy the body and kill the Soul of that child. Whether adored in the shape of an obscene reptile—as in ancient Egypt—or in the form of a marble image—as in Greece and Rome—the Soul of the World is still worshipped, as the fountain of all life and motion; his Thoughts the deeds of the Universe.

IV. The Soul, from time to time, and at long intervals, has enshrined his Being in flesh, and walked the earth in the form of living man, and appeared among men,—the Incarnate Universe.

V. As the sun gives forth light, and is not deprived of a single ray, so the Universal Soul, sends abroad, beams of his existence, which are at once, portions of his glory and eternity. These beams of the Soul, are clad in forms of flesh, they walk the earth, they share in the temptations and disquietudes of mankind. Or, they are Spirits, invisible to the gross senses of clay, and yet dwelling on the earth and sharing in the destinies of its people. Are they clad in humanity? Then their knowledge of their Eternal Source is dim, undefined, and only felt by broken gleams. Sometimes that Knowledge comes upon them in all its power; they feel they know, that they are of the Almighty Intellect, beams of his brightness and pulsations of his heart. When this Consciousness bursts upon them, they are men no longer, but Leaders of the human race, and are known among men, as Prophets, Apostles and Redeemers.

VI. Even in their worst state, when most beclouded by the appetites and misfortunes of flesh, these Souls, born of the Universal Soul, retain a consciousness, however dim, of their origin, a glimpse, vague as it may be, of their destiny, and a portion, of the might of their Creator and Father.

VII. All men are not of the Almighty Soul, nor does every bosom throb with a pulsation of the Universal Heart.

VIII. Look abroad over the multitudes of mankind. Survey the Camp, the Court, the Cloister. Traverse the world of humanity from the kennel to the palace. What do you behold?

IX. Yonder, by a river shore, an army marches, its ten thousand spears flashing in the sunlight. Without a Leader, whose Soul is the Soul of these ten thousand men, this army is powerless; it is but ten thousand isolated links of a broken Chain. That Leader is a Ray from the Soul of the Universe; a Ray beclouded by the gory mist of carnage, yet still a Beam of the Eternal Sun.

X. Go to the Palace. There is a King there, who sits upon a golden throne, and drinks in the idolatry of cringing Courtiers, and arrays his form, in a garment, whose very tinsel has been purchased with the life blood of at least, a thousand men. This King rules an empire, levies taxes, makes war and peace, holds life and death in the hollow of his hand. He is only a Mock King after all; for as you gaze more attentively upon the source and machinery of his power, you will behold, far back in the shadows of his throne, some Monk with a tonsured forehead, or some Scholar with a withered face, and in the Monk or the Scholar, you in truth, recognize the Real King. For the Monk, and the Scholar are beams of the Almighty Intellect, darkened by sophistries or ferocious with superstition yet still Pulsations of the Universal Heart.

XI. One third of the world bows at the foot of the Cross. Another third worships a Crescent. The last third gives its adoration to images and creeds, as various as the faces of men.

XII. Dive into your heart and seek the Cause of all this. Do you find it in the magnificent temples; the armies of hired priests, the volumes of Cumbrous rituals? This is the manifestation of the Cause, or the corruption of the Cause, but not the Cause itself. Seek deeper. You will find that this Cross is adored, because ten Centuries and more ago, a Carpenter's Son, felt the full consciousness of his origin, even as he toiled in the workshop, beside his peasant father. The Soul of that Carpenter's Son, born of the Almighty Intellect, lives even yet, although its purity may be darkened by the Corruptions of earth-born Souls, and its power, manacled by ten thousand arms and appetites of flesh and blood. And thus, the Crescent is a symbol of the faith of millions, because some centuries ago, an Arabian camel-driver, even amid the sand and stars of a trackless desert, felt that he was a part of Eternity. Track the other religions, to their sources, and you will find that Beams of the Universal Soul, have appeared in forms of flesh, and passed away, leaving no record but their system or their creed.

XIII. Wherefore is there evil in the World? Wherefore does Good always entwine itself with evil? Wherefore does the Simple religion of the Carpenter's Son, which said, hundred of years ago, that all of truth was written in the words, Do unto others as you would have others do unto you, now hide and bury itself, under the feet of Popes, priests and monks, who say by their deeds, We do unto others as we would not have them do unto us?

XIV. It is a terrible question. Search your heart again. Question the Seers of immemorial time. Descend into the Charnel. Ask an answer from Death itself. Gather your soul within itself until the Spirits of the Other World speak to you.

XV. There is an answer to your question. Let us behold it. While the Universal Soul dwells Supreme, there lives another Power in the Universe. This Power is not eternal, and yet his existence appears like an Eternity when compared with the years of earth. He is not Omnipotent, and yet when compared with a mortal arm, HIS arm seems to be invested with Almighty Power. He lived before earth was born; he will live when earth and its creations are dead. He is at once the FOE and the INFERIOR of the SUPREME SOUL. He has been ever, at war with his Master he has defied his power, confounded his Almighty Good with Evil, and marred the beauty of his works. This inferior has been known by various names but a simple title, expresses at once, his name and his nature.

XVI. He is the SOUL OF EVIL.

XVII. Behold a wonderous truth.

When the UNIVERSAL SOUL, first imparted a portion of his being to living forms, or, forms of flesh and blood, the SOUL OF EVIL, marred his work, by creating other forms, unto whom he gave a part of his own malignant life, impulse and destiny.

XVIII. Do not hesitate. There is yet a more wonderous truth. These forms, in which the SOUL OF EVIL, embodied a portion of his being, resembled the forms, in which the UNIVERSAL SOUL, diffused beams of his light and eternity.

XIX. Through countless ages, the beings, born of Almighty Intellect, warred with the beings, created by the Soul of evil.

XX. At last, the children of eternity, clothed in flesh and blood, mingled their lives and lives, with the offspring of the evil Soul,—doomed to annihilation,—who were also clothed in flesh and blood.

XXI. The earth, on which we live was peopled by the generations of this mingled race; a race composed of Good and Evil, of Eternity and Death.

XXII. In these words, given above, all the mysteries of life, are explained.

XXIII. Wonder no longer at the perpetual paradox, presented in all ages by the human race. It is true that Good and Evil, fight an eternal battle, in the heart of man. It is true, that the basest have some consciousness of their Divine Origin; and that the best, have some throbbings, to remind them of an infernal paternity. Could it be otherwise? Man is made up, of two elements; he is the Child of two distinct races. One is the race of Light and Eternity; the other of Dark and Death.

XXIV. There have been men, whose entire nature, has been formed from the race of the Evil Soul. They have been called, Monsters, by their fellow men, and their name, has passed into a Curse.

XXV. There has also been men, whose entire nature, has been formed from the race of the UNIVERSAL SOUL. They are called, Angels, Demi-gods, by their fellow men, and their name is a Blessing.

XXVI. Search into your own heart. Ponder—reflect—look deeper. Digest these few plain truths, examine their proportions, as you would measure the exactness of a pyramid.

XXVII. Do you not discover the source of all the creeds, which have divided mankind?

XXVIII. Do you not discover the Key to the great mystery of the Universe?

And beneath all this was written——

"The Spirit of Jehovah is upon me to preach good tidings to the poor, sight to the blind, peace to them that are bruised——and to all men THE ACCEPTABLE YEAR OF THE LORD."

The last sentence, written not in Arabic but in Hebrew, and written by another hand then his own, filled Aldarin with inexplicable emotion.

"If these words spoken by the Nazarene are true, then is my whole life a lie," he said, and retired into the shadows of the Red-Chamber.

When he came toward the declining light once more, his brow was strangely troubled.

"How strange has been the course of my life! Let me gaze backward over the dark path I have trodden. This night thrice seven long years ago—amid the gloom of the Syrian battle plain, a dark-eyed Arabian gave me in ransom for his life, the book of his race, which he dared not read. And there, in that lone hour, as midnight gathered over the corses of the dead, did he sware by the Eternal Flame of the Fire-worshipper, that in body or in soul, he would be with my heart, and by my side this very night. THE BOOK spoke in words of fire of the secret, and—and—by my soul I have heard no message from the Arab Prince for three long years. He can not, will not fail me now!"

The door of the Red-Chamber was flung suddenly open, and the Lord Guiseppo hastily advanced, with an expression of deep gloom stamped on his brow. He held a scroll of parchment in his extended hand.

"Ha! My Lord Guiseppo, son of mine. I greet thee! Hast thou any message for me?"

"A strange man clad in Paynim costume, attended by a train of twelve, attired strangely as himself, wait at the castle gate. He sends his greeting and this simple scroll."

"A strange man clad in Paynim costume"—murmured Aldarin in a whispering tone—"A scroll! Give it me, Guiseppo—Ha! What words are these—*Ibrahim-Ben-Malakim salutes his brother, Aldarin the Scholar!*"

A warm flush like a sudden glow of sunshine passed over the face of Aldarin, his eye gleamed and brightened until it seemed burning its socket, and the Scholar stood for a moment agitated and motionless.

"Guiseppo!" he shouted in a voice of thunder as he turned towards the youthful Lord—"Away, away, to the castle gate and answer the giver of this scroll with the words—Aldarin greets his brother Ibrahim!"

"And then my Lord Aldarin"—

"Lead the stranger to my presence!"

And while Guiseppo turned to obey the behest of the Scholar, the Count Aldarin, strode with a hurried step along the floor of the Red Chamber, with his arms folded and his head drooped low upon his breast.

There was a long pause of absorbing thought.

"He comes—he comes, with the last scroll of THE BOOK! He comes with the Charm, which in the hands of Aldarin shall wake the dead! When the last scroll is read, when the last charm is spoken, then, then, Aldarin lives forever! And Ibrahim—ha, ha, 'twere but fair that the blood of the Priest, who first awoke this Idea within my bosom, should mingle with the blood of the victims, slain at the shrine of the awful Thought."

A dark and meaning smile passed over the lip of Aldarin, and again he communed with his own thoughts.

A footstep sounded through the ante-chamber; in a moment the stranger, tall and majestic, stood before the Scholar.

"Ibrahim gives peace and joy to Aldarin!"

"Peace and joy to Ibrahim-Ben-Malakim!"

As thus they saluted each other, in the Arabian tongue the native language of the one, and the familiar study of the other, Aldarin advanced and gazed upon the stranger.

His face was most impressive.

Regular in feature, dark and tawny in hue, the countenance of the stranger was marked by a high forehead, thick and bushy eye-brows white as snow, giving a strange effect to the glance of the full dark eyes, that looked forth from beneath their shadow: a compressed lip, half hidden by the venerable beard, that well-nigh covered his rounded chin and dark brown cheeks, and descended to his breast in waving locks, frosted by age and toil. A cap of sable fur surmounting his forehead, imparted a striking relief to the visage of the Arabian.

His attire was simple and majestic. A mantle or robe of black cloth, gathered around the throat, by a chain of gold, with a collar of snow-white fur, fell in long folds to his knees, bordered by lace of gold. As the robe waved suddenly aside from his commanding frame, it might be seen that the tunic which gathered around his form, was fashioned of the finest velvet glistening white in color, with a border of strange and mystic characters, his legs were encased in dark hose, and slouching boots of doe-skin, glittering with the knightly spur of gold.

"Thou art changed, Ibrahim!"

"And *thou* Aldarin!"

There was a long pause, while the Scholar and the Arab Prince perused each others features. When they again spoke it was in the rich Arabian tongue, each word a word of fire, each sentence a thought of wild enthusiasm.

"Twenty-one years, this very night, on the battle-plain amid the Syrian wilds, an Arab prince owed his life to the intercession of Aldarin the Scholar. He offered the Scholar gold for his ransom—the scholar refused the proffered dust. Speak I the truth, Aldarin?"

"Thou dost!"

"Struck by the noble nature of the thoughtful Italian, the Arab prince gave him a gift priceless in value, not to be bought with gold, or purchased with gems of price! A Book—a mighty book had descended to him, through a long line of gallant ancestors. The founder of the race of Ibrahim was a man of dark thoughts, and mysterious studies. Swept from the path of life in the midst of his mystic researches, he left THE BOOK to his children, with the last and most terrible Mystery, the final Charm, which gave importance to the whole volume, confided to their trust, in unwritten words—"

"These words thou wouldst speak to mine own ear and heart?"

"Even so, brother Aldarin! When I gave thee the Book, fraught with strange mysteries, a fearful oath, sworn by every son of the race of Ben-Malakim, bound me to keep the last words, which make the book complete, secret from thine ear, until I was assured thou hadst won the merit of the confidence."

"Thou didst swear by the Eternal Flame, that thou wouldst meet me this very night, in the soul or in the body, living or dead."

"I am here! The far-east rings with the fame of Aldarin the Scholar—the last secret is thine!"

"This night, at the hour of midnight, over the Altar of Marble, where the Heart of the Dead mingles its crimson-drops with the White Waters of the Alembic,—there,—will I crave the last Secret at thy hands!"

"There is one condition first."

"Name it!"

"Lo! it is written in the Scroll which contains the Priceless Secret. The Prince of Ben-Malakim must be a spectator in the lone chamber where the SECRET is carried into action; he must command in the Halls of the Scholar, who may receive the mystery, while the solemn ceremonies named by the Book, are in progress."

"The condition is strange—yet"—

"So read the words of THE BOOK!"

"Its behests shall be obeyed."

"Then Scholar, and friend, let the twelve warriors who follow in my train, take the place of the sentinels at the castle-gate; let them command in the castle-hall, and be obeyed as thyself until the morrow morn!"

"It shall be done. And now, my brother, draw near to the casement; let the warm glow of the setting sun fall over thy features I would look upon thy face, as was my wont in the ancient time. By my soul, thou art sadly changed—fearful wrinkles traverse thy countenance, thy hair and beard are gray; thine eyebrows white. A sad and fearful change!"

"The touch of time falls heaviest on the man of thought, good Aldarin. Thou too, art sadly, fearfully changed."

"And yet this night shall crown the toil of twenty-one years, with a boon almost beyond mortal hope. Yes—yes," he continued in a deep whisper, as the full glow of the setting sun fell over his face—"The sun sinks down in glory; his beams fall over the form of the mortal Scholar—Lo! his beams gild the sky on the morrow morn and—how my nerves fire, my heart is full to bursting—ALDARIN LIVES FOREVER."

CHAPTER THE TENTH.

THE SCHOLAR ALDARIN AND THE LORD GUISEPPO

THE LAST INTERVIEW BEFORE THE GRAND SCENE, FOR WHICH ALDARIN HAS TOILED, STRUGGLED AND ENDURED, FOR THRICE SEVEN YEARS.

"COME hither Guiseppo, son of mine, let me look upon thy face. Ah! I remember well—her countenance lives again in thine. Boy, walk by my side, along this solitary chamber; I would converse with thee. Hast thou not oftentimes thought me a dark and stern old man?"

"My Lord, I have. The story of the soldier,—Rough Robin——"

"Name not the slave! Name him not. Have I not scattered his fable of lies, to the winds? Art not satisfied with the guilt of this—Adrian? Speak Guiseppo—have I not told thee a fair and truthful story?"

"I fear me—oh! Saints of Heaven—I fear me—that thy story is true!"

"Thou *fearest* that my story is true! Is this well Guiseppo? Wouldst rather thy *father* had been guilty!"

"*My Lord*—"

"'*My father*' would sound as well."

"My father, then; an' I may speak the name; I thank God from my very heart that I know thee guiltless. Yet I had much rather—the Saints witness my truth—I had much rather, this spot of blood were washed from the garments of all who bear the name of Albarone."

"And do I not join in the wish! oh Guiseppo—Guiseppo Di Albarone, for I will call thee by thine own true name—look upon me, mark my face, gaze in mine eye! Thou hast known me for years, a man prematurely old, bent with age ere the sands of my manhood's prime had fallen in the glass. Thus hast thou known me Guiseppo."

"I have my Lord,—my father, and wondered at the cause."

"Yet hast thou ever noted the change, the fearful change, that has passed over this face within a few brief days? Dost mark the pallor of this cheek, the blaze of this eye? Dost see this forehead seamed by a single wrinkle between the brows; dost note these wan and wasted features?"

"Yes, yes my father, I do. What hath wrought this fearful change?"

"Canst thou ask? A mighty grief has been swelling the channels of my soul— grief for the *crime of Adrian*, grief that *his* hands, the hands of the son, should be red—dripping with his own father's blood."

He paused—covered his face—there was a moment of voiceless agony "and yet, even in this hour of agony, the resemblance, the sad resemblance, which has haunted me for years, comes back to my soul—"

"The resemblance, my father?"

"Boy, I tell thee, thy face is like the face of—Even now I see it!"

"Father?—"

"The face of thy mother!"

"I tremble my father; mine eyes are wet with burning tears. Tell me—oh, tell me of *her*—my mother."

"Twenty years ago, a nameless Scholar, who disdaining the din and battle of war, gave his soul to higher and purer thoughts, won the love of a proud and peerless Ladye. They might not wed, for she was the scion of a Royal line. It was evening, boy, calm and gorgeous evening—well do I remember the scene—when the proud Ladye gazed from the portico of a kingly palace, over the temples and the towers of Jerusalem. The glow of sunset was streaming over her face, and her full dark eyes, kindled with the grandeur of the scene, when, when—listen Guiseppo,—her boy, her bright eyed boy, lay prattling on her knee. The Scholar stood by her side—he was silent, for his heart was full—oh, God! methinks I see myself as *I was then*, even through the long lapse of years—"

"Thyself! The boy, who was't—the boy?"

"Listen; hear the sequel of this dark story. There, there, concealed by a column of that lofty portico, listening to the words of love that broke murmuringly from the lips of the Ladye, gazing upon the face of her bright-eyed boy, all smiles and laughter, there, unknown and unsuspected, stood the Fiend and the Destroyer. Guiseppo—pass thy hand over my brow—see, see, even after the lapse of twenty years, the cold, beaded drops, like death-sweat, stand out from my forehead at the memory."

"I am breathless, my father—the Destroyer who stood listening—he was— "

"Guiseppo, Guiseppo, let me whisper a world of horror to thine ear in a single word. The light of the setting sun, fell over thy—thy mother's face, proud, peerless and beautiful—her child prattling on her knee, her lover by her side—the first beams of the morrow's sun beheld her form, her form of grace and loveliness, flung prostrate over the marble floor of her chamber— *outraged, bleeding, dead.*"

"Oh, God! my brain whirls! And the Destroyer?"

"Was a knight, a leader among the Princes of the Christian Host who won Jerusalem from the Paynim legions. He had been scorned, rejected, despised by the Ladye—thy mother—and behold,—oh fiend of hell—behold his vengeance!"

"His name? Who—who—swept this devil from the earth?"

"He lives!"

"*Lives?* and thou couldst wield a dagger!"

"Boy, wouldst thou wreak full and terrible vengeance on the ravisher of thy mother?"

"Sate he upon the throne, slept he within the bridal chamber, knelt he at the altar, I would sacrifice the wretch, to the Ghost of the betrayed—"

"To thy knees, to thy knees, and take the oath of vengeance."

"I kneel, father, I kneel. The oath, the oath!"

"What manner of oath dost thou hold most sacred? Wilt swear by the Cross, by the Holy Trinity, by the Death of the Incarnate, or by the awful existence of God?"

"BY MY MOTHER'S NAME."

"Place the cross to thy lips, raise thy hands to heaven. Swear—by the Holy Cross, by the Awful Trinity, by the Incarnate God—by thy Mother's Name—that when thy eye first beholds the wronger and the ravisher, thy dagger shall seek his heart."

"I swear—I swear!"

"Though he sate on the throne, though he slept within the bridal chamber, though he knelt beside the altar!"

"I swear—I swear!"

And the hollow echoes of the Red-Chamber gave back the echo—"Swear— swear!"

It was in sooth, a strange and impressive scene.

The dim light afforded by the lamp of silver, pendent from the ceiling, glimmering over the hangings of the fatal bed, along the folds of the tapestry and around the massive furniture of the room—the figures of the scene, the aged man and the kneeling boy; Aldarin with his face agitated by contending passions, with his eye gathering a brightness that seemed supernatural, while Guiseppo half prostrate at his feet, raised his hands to Heaven and with every feature of his countenance darkened by revenge, looked above with flashing eyes as he uttered the response—"I swear—I swear!"

It was a strange and impressive scene—and the flitting shadows that fell over the hangings of the bed and along the floor, seemed to start into life at the deep earnest tones of the Avenger.

"The name of the Destroyer—my father—his name—his name!—"

The Count Aldarin stooped low, applied his lips to the ear of Guiseppo and whispered in a quick and hissing tone, the name of the Destroyer.

The kneeling Lord turned pale as death, as with a trembling voice he repeated the well known name.

He bowed his head on his breast, and clasped his hands in very agony.

"My fate," he shrieked, "is dark—oh Father of Heaven, most dark!——"

"Rise Guiseppo, my son," said the Count Aldarin in a commanding tone. "Rise Guiseppo, Lord of Albarone!"

"My father—your look is serious, and yet you utter but a merry jest. Methinks it ill becomes the hour."

"Guiseppo, Aldarin never deals in the jester's wares. No—no my son, I do not jest. Listen Guiseppo, and hear the solemn determination of my soul. The events of these few brief days; the fearful death of my brother, the knowledge that THE SON was the MURDERER; the flight of my—my daughter; all have conspired to confirm that determination. I have resolved to retire and retire forever from the world. Not within the gloom of the monastery, not within the shadow of the cloister, does Aldarin seek refuge from the sorrows of the world. No—no.

"Within the shadows of the most secret chamber of the Castle, (dead to the world, unseen by living man, save thee Guiseppo, and yet companioned by those Holy Men who this very night, arrived at Albarone, from the far eastern lands,) in penitence and in prayer will Aldarin seek to win favor from heaven for this—this—wretch, this father-murderer. Guiseppo—I charge thee—let men believe me dead, and when thy right to the Lordship of Albarone is questioned, speak boldly of the favor of his Grace of Florence. He will defend the castle from wrong and shelter thee from outrage."

"My Lord—my father, this is a strange determination! I beseech thee do not burden me with the rule of the Castle."

"It must be so Guiseppo! From this night henceforth, Aldarin is dead to the world. Whene'er thou wouldst say aught with me, a sealed parchment, placed within a secret drawer arranged in the side of the beaufet, will reach my hands.—And mark ye—let not a single day pass over thy head, without looking into the secret drawer of the beaufet."

"This is most wonderful! I ever thought thee a bold, ambitious man, and now I behold Aldarin whom all men name with fear, retire from the world, without a sigh."

"One word more, Guiseppo. When thou hast stricken the blow—when the Destroyer of thy mother's honor, lies low in death, then, then, hasten to the Round Room—thou hast heard of the chamber?—and within the solitudes of its silent walls, read this pacquet—it contains the fearful story of thy mother's wrongs."

"Forgive me, forgive me, my father—" shrieked Guiseppo, as if struck by some sudden thought—"Swayed by some alternate affection for thee as—my father—and regard for Adrian as—my friend, I have locked within the silence of my bosom an important secret—*Sir Geoffrey o' th' Longsword has returned from Palestine.*"

Had a thunderbolt fallen at the very feet of Aldarin, he could not have started more suddenly backward, or thrown his arms aloft with a wilder gesture.

"Sir Geoffrey o' th' Longsword, returned from Palestine!" he shouted—"where is he now? How far from the Castle? How many soldiers ride in his train? Was the murderer Adrian with him?"

"Father—it was his band I left, when disguised as a Palmer, I hastened toward the Castle. He lurks within the recesses of the mountains, some score of miles away—three hundred men ride in his train—Adrian, whom I believed guiltless, is with him."

"Did he speak aught of attacking the Castle Di Albarone?"

"After a lapse of seven days, it was resolved to attempt the surprisal of the Castle. From the vague hints I gathered, it seems that their plans were not well matured. Three days of the seven are now passed, and—"

"The attack will be made four days from this! By my Soul! it pleases me! Ha—ha—ha—Guiseppo, remember thy oath, the steel and the pacquet."

And as he spoke, the Count Aldarin strode toward the door, his face flushed by a wild glow of exultation, as he communed with himself in a low, murmured tone.

"Four days—ha—ha—ha! Four days glide by—and ALDARIN IS IMMORTAL."

Guiseppo was alone.

He gazed vacantly through the gloom of the Red Chamber and passed his hands over his eyes, as if in the effort to awake from some fearful dream.

All was solemn and silent around him, and he resigned his soul to dark memories, while the weary moments of that fearful night glided slowly on.

At last he sank down on the cold floor and slept.

A vision of his mother, his own beautiful and dark-eyed mother, rose smiling above the waves of sleep, and then the boy thought she stood beside him, holding a dagger in her fair white hand, while she beckoned him on to the work of vengeance.

He awoke.

His form was pinioned in the embrace of a woman's arms, and a woman's face hung over him, its large and lustrous eyes, mingling their light, with his own.

"Rosalind!" he shrieked as he sprang to his feet with surprise—"Rosalind here, in this lone chamber!"

"I am here—" she exclaimed as she fell weeping on his bosom—"'Tis a strange story Guiseppo, but—my heart feels chilled when I think of the fearful scene, which made this Red Chamber a place of death. An hour ago, I slept within the bower of the Ladye Annabel, which the Count allotted for my prison, when a strange figure, clad in robes of sable, strode into the chamber, and bade me enjoy my freedom, as he pointed to the open door! I hastened along the corridor, I descended the stairway, and sought refuge in this chamber, from two dark figures who seemed pursuing me, when I found thee, Guiseppo, flung prostrate along the cold floor, and—"

"Thou didst watch over me, when sleeping, love of mine? Thy prison hath not stolen the bloom from thy cheek or the fire from thine eye."

As he spoke the door of the Red Chamber was flung suddenly open, and the aged Steward of the Castle rushed to the side of Guiseppo, with hasty steps and a disordered manner, shouting as his gray hairs waved in the night wind—

"A message, Lord Guiseppo—a message of life and death! The Count Aldarin sends thee this—read, and read without delay—for I tell thee 'tis a scroll of life and death."

Guiseppo perused the scroll, and——

The spirit of the Chronicle beckons us on to the most dark and fearful scene of the Historie.[5]

CHAPTER THE ELEVENTH.

THE WHITE WATERS OF THE ALEMBIC.

ALDARIN AND IBRAHIM, GATHERED WITHIN THE CONFINES OF THE ROUND ROOM, HOLD THEIR SOLEMN WATCH, WHILE THE LAST SECONDS OF THE MYSTIC AGE ARE PASSING TO ETERNITY.

"TREAD lightly and with a softened footstep, Ibrahim, for the place in which you stand has been the home of the deathless Thought for twenty-one long years! Look—how the azure flame ascends in tongues of flame around the sides of the hanging alembic—it is the last night of its existence! On and on, through calm and cloud, through sunshine and shadow, for twenty-one long years has it silently burned—a little while, and the sands in yon glass will be spent—the Thought springs into birth, and the azure flame will be quenched forever."

With his slender form elevated to its full height, his arm extended, and his robe thrown back from his shoulder, Aldarin the Scholar glanced around the room, while his gray eye flashed and brightened as though his very soul looked forth in its glance.

His brow was calm, clear and unclouded; his compressed lip wore an expression of fixed determination; and a slight flush pervaded his pale countenance.

The light of the pendant lamp fell over the form of the venerable stranger, his dark-hued face, with the thick eyebrows, the waving hair, and the flowing beard, all snow white in hue, standing out boldly in the ruddy beams, while his dress of sable, relieved by the border of glittering gold, gave solemnity and dignity to his appearance.

He stood calm and erect, gazing with his eyes of midnight darkness, upon the strange altar, with its ever-burning flame of azure, or fixing his glance upon the wild and speaking features of Aldarin the Scholar.

"Advance, Ibrahim—advance to the altar of marble"—exclaimed the Scholar, with all the proud consciousness of the possession of a POWER beyond the reach of the mass of mankind—"Gaze within the alembic—what see'st thou?"

"I see a liquid clear as crystal, calm, motionless, and unruffled. The most gorgeous mirror might fail to rival its shadowless brightness. The alembic is heated to a white heat, yet the liquid bubbles not, nor seethes, nor wears any appearance of the effect of heat. It is beautiful—most beautiful."

"Every drop is worth a life. Within the recesses of this altar another flame, fanned by a subterranean current, burns beneath the Crucible, which at last will give forth the Secret of Gold.—Gaze upon yon hour glass, Ibrahim—the glass standing upon the corner of the altar—"

"The sands have fallen to within an half-hour of midnight—"

"When the last grain of sand falls in the glass, then will be complete the mystic age of toil. The waters of life will then be pure, the secret of gold will then be perfect. Twenty-one years will then have past since first, I set me down to watch yon never-ceasing flame. Twenty-one years—earth never beheld such years—each day an age, each year an eternity!"

"Thy toil hath been most difficult!" exclaimed Ibrahim, in his deep-toned voice—"the end draws nigh!"

"It was in that home of magnificent thoughts and mighty memories—the city of Jerusalem, that the Glorious Thought dawned upon my soul!—

"'To live forever,' I cried as I gazed upon the wide city, with its palaces and towers basking in the sunlight—'to pass beyond the years of mortal men, to exist while whole nations sink down to the slumber of the grave, while kings succeed kings and millions of the mass of men glide away on their inevitable march to the grave! To live forever—to feel life throbbing in my veins, health flooding my very heart, and youth, eternal youth crowning my brow, when Old Earth shall have been stamped with the footsteps of ten thousand years—oh glorious boon, oh guerdon worthy an age of toil!'

"I sought the boon when first I trod the Syrian soil, but my search was wild and vague—yon massive volume was placed in my hands—"

"And then, the search became clear and distinct?"

"Yes—yes! Truth after truth dawned upon me, ingredient after ingredient was added to the contents of the alembic,[6] and mad man that I was——but stay a moment, Ibrahim. Gaze again upon the liquid of the alembic, and tell me what thou see'st?"

"The same clear and undimmed liquid, resting calm and motionless within the depths of the vessel."

"Behold yon circular glass, resting beside the parchment scroll, on the corner of the altar. It will magnify an insect until it swells to the dimensions of the huge animal that haunts the forests of the far deserts of India—the elephant, methinks 'tis called. Apply the glass to thine eye, and gaze within the depths of the vessel."

"A strange and magnificent spectacle! The clear liquid spreads out into a magnificent lake, calm, unshadowed and rippleless. Yet stay—'tis shadowed by a small island floating in the centre, an island composed of some unknown substance, black as jet, yet scarcely perceptible even through the wondrous medium of this glass!"

"When that speck of jet shall have vanished, then will the charm be perfect!—I have said that I was rash and indiscreet—let my story witness. I disregarded the words of the Book, I thought twenty-one years too long and weary a time for me to sit in solemn silence while I watched the progress of the Secret. A few words in the volume hinted darkly and vaguely at a consummation of the Thought, attainable by one bold grasp—that grasp I made—yes, yes, though my very soul was shaken to the centre, and my brain reeled in the effort—I—I—*killed her*!"

"Killed her? Great God, what dark confession is this!"

"Yes—yes—I killed her, killed her as she slept in my arms and smiled in my face. I drove the steel to her heart—I dabbled her long dark locks in the warm blood that gushed from her bosom! Nay, start not man, nor turn aside with such sudden horror—hast not perused yon volume—know'st thou not the mystic words—"*The pure blood, warm from the heart of her thou lovest, more than aught in earth or heaven, poured into the liquid floating within the mystic vessel, will do the work of years in a single hour*—"

"And she—she was thy"—

"My wife, my wife! My own, my dark-eyed Ilmeriner. Her blood, the pure current of her very heart, purpled the White Waters of the Alembic—and—and, fool that I was, I would not even wait the hour of trial, I drank the liquid, greedily, and with loud exclamations of joy I drank, and paid the price of my rashness. I neglected to use the microscopic glass; the black speck had not vanished from the surface of the liquid. I lay for days insensible; when I awoke to reason I found this frame grown prematurely old. Had I but waited the little hour, the draught would have infused immortal life into my veins. I was rash—hasty—wild with the madness of my joy, and the draught proved poison."

"All thy efforts then were foiled."

"I was foiled, but I did not despair. Again I built the fire on the altar, again I added ingredient to ingredient; the corses of the dead I searched for the last and most powerful Charm; years passed, and the consummation of the Idea of my life approached, when—Fiend of Hell—I discovered that the price of my rashness was not yet paid! As I pored over the leaves of the mystic volume, a fearful thought, expressed in dim and shadowy words, sunk in my very soul"—

"Methinks I see some new horror, lowering over the cloud of guilt and blood that darkens the sky of thy life."

"Blood, there was, yes, yes, but no guilt. By the Awful Influence that has ruled my life, there was none! The Martyr of the Christian, strides to the stake, that is to cut short the brief thread of his puny life, with a few moments of pain, suffers, dies and is glorified. Is there no glory for Aldarin! Have I not also been a martyr? There there, ever before me, was the ONE GREAT IDEA, leading me on, and on, filling me with high hopes and grand thoughts, that all pointed to the final good of mankind—"

"Thou didst at first dream the Secret would benefit the mass of men? Ha—ha—thou wouldst have made the MOB, immortal!"

"It is past, the dream is past. Yes, yes, Ibrahim I join in thy laugh. I would have made the MOB immortal! Ha—ha! The multitude, what are they? Now the autumn leaf, blown to and fro by the wind; now the hurricane that a breath may raise; to-day all sunshine, to-morrow all storm and cloud! THE MOB! To-day, they strew palm-branches in the path of the Nazarene, and send their hozannas echoing to the sky,—'Hail, hail king of the Jews!' To-morrow, the Nazarene stands bound and pinioned in the halls of Pilate and their cry,—the cry of the Mob—comes shrieking through the casement *crucify, crucify him!*"

"This in truth is the many-headed mob."

"Have I not been a Martyr! Others have offered up their blood at the shrine of their Faith. I, I, have given the very blood of my soul! I have made a sacrifice of love; love such as man of thought alone can feel; I have rushed beyond the boundaries of thought, that confine the opinions of common men; I have dared the vengeance of the Faith beside whose altars I was reared; the arm of the God, whose existence was imprinted on my brain from infancy; I, I have dared the most terrible doom of all—the remorse of my own soul!"

"The words of the Scroll—what were they?"

"Hast thou ne'er perused yon volume of Fate?"

"A fear of the terrible mysteries inscribed on its pages, ever deterred the Princes of Ben-Malakim, from the perusal of the Mystic volume."

"A dark passage on the Scroll, vaguely hinted that in *case the* Seeker failed, in the first bold experiment, in case the life *drops* of *her* dearest to his heart, were spilt in vain, then, another sacrifice was to be offered, ere the Crystal Waters would be undimmed by the speck of jet—and, and—*Ibrahim, behold yon funeral urn.*"

"It stands upon the shelf, amid a heap of massive volumes, and time-eaten parchments. What means this funeral urn?"

"I cannot, cannot tell thee now. But Ibrahim listen—after long care and thought, care and thought such as never wrinkled the brow of mortal man before, I have arrived at certain, fixed principles of belief. These principles relate to the consummation of the Secret—the last Charm which will make it complete—the manner in which the Water of Life is to be tested, ere it is imbibed by mortal man. The Last Roll of the Mystic Volume, which thou hast borne from the far east, may confirm these principles or declare them *false*, but can teach Aldarin nothing. Look, Ibrahim, the sands have fallen to within the fourth part of an hour of midnight! Give me the last Scroll, I would read."

Ibrahim drew the scroll from his breast.

It was a massive roll of parchment, sealed at either end with an intricate seal of dark wax, stamped with strange characters.

Aldarin eagerly extended his hand, he seized the scroll, he tore the seals from either end, and unrolled the time-worn parchment.

And there, while with trembling hands and a flashing eye, the Scholar glanced over the strange Arabic characters, there noting his every glance, his every gesture, stood the solemn stranger, his eye dark as midnight, gazing with one fixed look upon the face of Aldarin, as though he would peruse the contents of the scroll, from the changing expression of the reader's countenance.

It was strange to note the contrasted gestures of the Scholar and the stranger, as the few last minutes of the mystic age wore slowly on.

While the Scholar eagerly perused the ancient manuscript, his eye gradually acquired a radiance and intensity of expression that seemed supernatural; his lip trembled; his quivering hands rattled the timeworn parchment; until the Round Room echoed with the sound. The Prince Ibrahim-Ben-Malakim started aside, and raised his hands to his brow with a sudden gesture as tho' he wished to stifle some bitter memory, or nerve his soul for the accomplishment of some fell purpose.

"AWFUL SOUL OF THE UNIVERSE!" shrieked Aldarin as he shook the parchment aloft, in the wildness of his joy—"I thank thee! I thank thee! All—all is written here—the principles of my belief are—true! Yes—yes! The last charm—the method of the trial of the Secret—the raising of the mighty dead—all, all are here! Ibrahim—Ibrahim, give me joy! Lo! I unveil to thy gaze the secret of the funeral urn!"

And with wild steps, and hasty manner, Aldarin strode across the oaken floor, he uncovered the funeral urn, he placed his trembling hands within its depths.

"Behold"—he shrieked—"Ibrahim behold the sacrifice!"

Ibrahim looked, he beheld the upraised hand of Aldarin, but he dared not look again.

Thrilled with horror at the sight, he, veiled his face in his hands, while Aldarin strode hurriedly toward the altar.

All was still as death in the Round Room.

"Listen, Ibrahim, listen!" exclaimed Aldarin—"Hark! how the red drops fall pattering into the white waters!"

Ibrahim listened in horror, but dared not look. In a moment, the funeral urn, again enclosed the object of horror, and the voice of Aldarin broke whispering on the air.

"Ibrahim, brother of mine, haste thee to the altar—seize the microscopic glass and gaze upon the white waters of the alembic! I dare not—I dare not gaze upon the working of the charm!"

And as Ibrahim raised the glass to his eye, Aldarin stood with his back to the altar and his face to the wall, his wild eye glaring on vacancy while he counted the last seconds of the mystic age by the motion of his trembling fingers.

"The sands of the glass have fallen to within ten minutes of midnight," exclaimed Ibrahim. "I gaze upon the white waters of the alembic! They spread before mine eyes in a calm and silver lake. The surface is crimsoned by waves of blood—the island of jet enlarges and widens!"

"Waves of blood—the island of jet widens!" shrieked Aldarin. "Two minutes of the ten are past! Oh, fiend of doom! can the charm prove false at last?"

"The waves of blood are dying away; the black substance diminishes in size!"

"Art sure, good Ibrahim? Gaze again upon the waters: do not, do not deceive me!"

"The waters are colored with a purple dye."

"It hastens—it hastens! Ha—ha! So read the words of the book! Why dost pause, Ibrahim? Four minutes of the ten are past!"

"The object of black still diminishes; and now the purple hue of the waters is fading away!"

"My heart—my heart is bursting; I cannot, cannot breathe! Ibrahim, Ibrahim, tell, oh! tell me, what hue do the waters assume? Thou art silent! I dare not turn and gaze with mine own eyes; do not mock me thus, Ibrahim!"

"A calm lake, cloudless, waveless, and beautiful opens to my gaze. The waters are clear as crystal. No shadow dims their unfathomable brilliancy, no object of blackness floats upon the surface. The sands have fallen in the glass—"

"Speak, speak, Ibrahim, or I will fall to the floor! Is there no shadow resting upon the surface of the white waters?"

"None, by my soul, none!"

"Then—then—Aldarin—is—immortal."

CHAPTER THE TWELFTH.

THE TRIAL OF THE WATERS OF LIFE.

"AS THE SANDS OF THE THIRD HOUR SINK IN THE GLASS—THE DEAD SHALL ARISE."

ARISING in tongues of flame from the floor of stone, a fire of crackling wood, cast its ruddy glare around the Cavern of the Dead; flinging glimpses of blood-red light along the earth-hidden roof, and imparting a strange appearance of warmth and life, to the hideous figures, scattered along the pavement of the vault.

Turned to burning red by the full glare of the flame, the gigantic Figure of Stone, which gloomed above the Mound of Death, seemed starting into life, as with arms thrown wildly aloft, and downcast eyes, it surveyed the strange spectacle extended beneath its stony gaze.

Ascending from the cavern floor, a square tent, for by that name alone it may be designated, formed of curtains of jet-black leather, gave three of its sides to the glare of the flame, while the fourth was wrapt in shadow.

The hangings of black leather were inscribed with strange and contrasted characters, fashioned in shapes of glittering gold, while from the aperture at the top, where the roof of the tent should have been placed, there arose, lurid folds, columns of smoke, winding upward to the far off ceiling of the cavern.

Near the tent of embroidered leather, arose a small, square and compact structure of ebony, in shape resembling a table, designed to serve the purposes of an altar.

On the top of the altar of ebony was laid an hour glass; a funeral urn, and a phial of glittering silver; a massive volume of time-eaten parchments; with an unbound scroll, falling to the very floor of the cavern.

Within the compass of a fathom's length from the tent of leather, was erected the fire of oaken wood which threw its ruddy glare around the spot, and flung vivid though flickering glimpses of light into the distant recesses of the cavern.

And there in the lone cavern, beneath the frown of the Demon-Form, with the blaze of the oaken fire, disclosing their faces and figures in bold and strong relief, there, while the hours of that fearful night, dragged heavily on, watched and waited Aldarin and Ibrahim the Son of the Kings[7].

Ibrahim, calm, solemn and erect, stood beside the Altar of Ebony, his sable attire, his dark hued face, with the gray hair, the white eye-brows and the flowing beard disclosed in the light, while he gazed in wonder and awe upon the immensity of that cavern, where the last and most terrible scene in the Mortal Life of Aldarin, was to add another legend of horror to the teeming Archives of Albarone.

With slow and measured steps, Aldarin paced the pavement of the cavern, in front of the sable tent. The light of the flame revealed his face, pale and colorless, stamped with an expression, calm and immovable it is true, yet fraught with strange and mysterious meaning.

"It is a dark and gloomy place—dost not think so Ibrahim?" exclaimed the Scholar advancing to the side of the Arab-Prince. "Look around! Behold the flashes of flame-light falling along the floor of the dread cavern, giving a lurid glare to the ceiling as it arises above our heads, like an earth-hidden sky, or casting their ruddy glare over the face and form of yon dark figure of giant rock. Is't not a dark and gloomy place, Ibrahim?"

"Here, along this gloomy cavern, might the warrior of a thousand battles walk and tremble as he walked, without the blush of shame for his coward fear. As I gaze around upon the dark mysteries of this funereal vault, methinks I behold the demons of the unreal world, clustering around me, laughing in my face, or mocking my very soul with their gestures of scorn!"

"Here will the last scene in the Mortal Life of Aldarin, startle the very gaze of yon dark dread face of stone. Tell me Ibrahim, how long hast thou waited in this solemn vault."

"Twice have I turned your hour glass since first we entered the cavern—it wanes toward the third hour after midnight."

"Thou hast not asked me any question concerning these dark hangings of embroidered leather. Thou hast not asked me why yon dark and lurid smoke winds upward from the confines of this sable tent. Nor hast thou spoken a word in relation to the secrets of this Tabernacle of Life—so the Book calls the sable tent."

"Ibrahim has waited the pleasure of Aldarin."

"Then listen, dark Arabian, when I tell thee—the dead, the mighty dead shall live again!"

"These words are mysteries to me!"

"Read yon mystic scroll, Ibrahim, and all shall be as the light of day to thee— read those words of fearful knowledge."

And with a faint and trembling voice, the Arabian gave to the air of the Cavern, the dim and mysterious words of the scroll:

"Lo! The Waters of Life are free from stain or pollution of earth. Wouldst thou prove them pure? Within the hollow of the coffin-like vessel of iron, place the remains of the Sacrificed and pile the fire of beechen wood around. When the iron pales from red to white, then warm the Heart of the Sacrificed with the white waters of the Alembic—when the heart throbs, then let it mingle with the Corse of the Coffin, and Lo! As the sands of the third hour sink in the glass—the dead shall arise!"

"There—there—within the Tabernacle of Life," shouted Aldarin, with an upraised arm and kindling eye—"There rests the Corse of the Sacrificed, there ascends the fire of beechen wood heating the coffin of iron to a white heat—within the confines of yon funeral urn, rests the Heart, and the phial of silver by its side, contains the priceless Waters of Life. Behold the sands of the third hour are falling in the glass—a little while and——how the thought stirs my very soul—the dead will live again!"

"The dead?" echoed Ibrahim with a gaze of wonder—"How meanest thou, Aldarin?"

"Must I then, unclose the darkest place in this seared bosom to thy gaze? Man, I tell thee—his form—the form of my brother shall live again!"

"Thy brother—Awful God!" whispered the Arabian in a tone, whose horror may not be described—"Thy brother then was thy last victim?"

"Pity me, Ibrahim, pity me!" shrieked Aldarin. "Swayed by two mingling and opposing motives—the one, ambition for the welfare of my child—the other, the all-absorbing desire for the Immortal Life on earth; but a few short days ago, I beheld approach the last moment of the Mystic Age of Toil. Then—then, I first learned the necessity of the fearful sacrifice, and—I drugged the bowl of death."

"This is too horrible for belief!" muttered Ibrahim; "Now—now my soul is firm for the work of the night!"

"Was I to falter when the hour of fear and doom drew nigh?" shrieked Aldarin, as his slender form rose proudly erect, and his impassioned face shone in the full light of the flame. "Was I, I, who had strode on to the guerdon of all my toil, unfearing and undismayed, though the dead body of my wife lay in my path, though the hopes of my heart fell withered and dead around me, while the spirit of my love for *her*, plead and plead in vain for pity; was I, ALDARIN, to spare the blow, when that blow would crown my earthly ambition, and complete my immortal toil? Ha—ha! The thought is vain!"

"Hadst thou no mercy?"

"In such a cause, I answer *none*. I tell thee man, had my brother pleaded for his life, and sprinkled my feet with his tears,—had he pleaded for his life in the calm, soft tones of childhood, the tones that brought back the memory of those days when our arms and hearts were interlocked—had he sprinkled my feet with such tears as wet this seared face, when I rescued him from the waters of the river that rolls without these walls, some thirty years ago—then even then, I could not have spared him! No, no, no! It was to be, and it was!"

"He shall rise from the dead, thou sayst? In what form shall he appear?"

"Fair, and young, and beautiful; youth shrined in his heart and power throned on his brow! His mind will be fresh with new-born vigor, yet Memory of the Past, shall never darken his bosom! The babe is not more unconscious of its pre-existence in another and a far-off world, than will be Julian my brother of the Past, with all its darkness and doom."

"How dost thou know, that he will arise in this form?"

"Spoke the Nazarine truth, when he said, 'Faith can remove mountains?' The Will of the Soul, armed with the consciousness of its immortal powers and infinite sympathies, can do more! THE WILL, determined and inflexible, can bend the invisible mysteries of the universe to its bidding, call up the fearful influences, ever at work within the bosom of Nature, and chain them, slaves of its power; bind the wild elements of man's heart in subjection, and awe the souls of the multitude, when aroused by passion, or maddened by revenge. THE WILL can sway the heart of man, to the windings of a path, dark as the way I have trodden, leading the Soul onward through mystery, and doom, and blood; teaching it to trample on Fear, laugh at the ghastly face of Remorse, and scorn the uplifted arm of God! 'Faith can remove mountains!' I cannot, may not, at this fearful hour, trace the operations of the Invisible Might. Suffice it to say—Aldarin wills that the Re-created shall walk forth in a form of youth and power, and it shall be so."

"Lo! The sands of the hour glass are well nigh spent. One-half of the last hour alone remains!"

"I will gaze within the Tabernacle of Life!"

Aldarin advanced, swept the sable hangings aside, and in a moment was lost to view.

Ibrahim also advanced to the front of the Tabernacle—as the mystic jargon of the Scholar named the tent—and listened with hushed breath and absorbing interest.

He could hear the subdued hissing of the flames within the Tabernacle; he could hear a low, scarce perceptible sound, like the seething of boiling lead;

and a penetrating perfume of mingled frankincense and myrrh, saluted his senses, mingled with the odor of decaying mortality.

A single moment passed while Ibrahim listened, and then he advanced to the verge of the vast fire, burning on the cavern floor, and stood for a moment wrapt in stern and solitary thought.

Clasping his hands across his chest, he drooped his head low upon his bosom, while the trembling lip and dilated eye attested the violence of the struggle at work within his inmost soul.

He raised his head and looked round.

Tall and erect—the ruddy glow of the fire, streaming over his majestic face, disclosing every outline of his imposing costume—the Arabian gazed around, and beheld the stern sublimity of the cavern of the dead.

Save the hissing of the flame, all was silent.

Not a word, not a whisper. Silence dwelt supreme, the Spirit and the Divinity of the place.

Far, far, above, the cavern roof, extending like a sky, received on each rugged projection, the ruddy glow of the flame. Long belts of flickering light were thrown along the pavement of stone, for a moment revealing the strange and fantastic forms scattered around the dim walls of the vault, in strong and startling relief; and then again the fire would suddenly subside, leaving everything, save the floor in its immediate vicinity, wrapt in thick darkness.

"A strange fancy," murmured Ibrahim, "Me-thought I saw yonder statues moving to and fro,—a wild delirium of my fancy."

"It throbs—it throbs—it palpitates."—a deep-toned, yet wild and thrilling voice broke the silence of the cavern—"Look, Ibrahim, how the Waters of Life, hasten the completion of the Mighty Labour!"

Ibrahim hurriedly turned and beheld Aldarin, standing beside the Altar of Ebony, grasping the phial of silver in one hand, while with the other he raised on high the Secret of the Funeral Urn, that may not be named by man, or written down on this page, lest incredulity should smile in ignorant scorn, and shallow unbelief, make a mock of the Dark Fanaticism of the Past.

"It throbs—it throbs—it warms with life!" again shrieked Aldarin, as he rushed within the confines of the hangings of sable—"Lo! The coffin of iron is heated to a white heat; the charm hastens to perfection!"

"Mine eyes are cheated by vain delusions!" muttered Ibrahim, "But a moment agone, and methought the arabesque figures were flitting to and fro, and now—as I live, there 'tis again—I behold dim shadows gliding round yon funeral pile?"

As he spoke the fire waned, and a sudden darkness, only relieved by faint flashes of light came down like midnight upon the cavern.

Ibrahim looked around and beheld Aldarin standing near his side, holding an open missal in his hand, which disclosed a hollow casket—instead of the emblazoned leaves of a book of devotion,—glittering with a gem that shone through the gathering darkness like a star.

And as the Arabian looked he beheld Aldarin apply the mouth of a small silver phial which he held in his hand, to the surface of the gem, while a meaning smile stole over his face.

The fire blazing on the cavern floor, lighted up with sudden vigor, and white columns of smoke, rolling from the silver phial, gathered in waving folds above the head of Aldarin, and swept far away, like the wings of a mighty bird, until they encircled the giant outline of the Demon Form, towering far, far overhead.

"Ibrahim, my brother," cried the voice of Aldarin, "I would welcome the Arisen-Dead with sweet perfumes and fragrant incense. 'Tis thus the Book commands!"

He looked forth from the cloud of smoke that enveloped his form, and started in surprise as he beheld the erect form of the Arabian.

The chemical spell, from whose influence the Scholar had defended himself, took no effect on the form of the Arabian Prince.

"The all-penetrating essence of the dead pervading the cavern and imbuing the atmosphere, renders the spell powerless!" he murmured with a frown of impatience. "And yet Aldarin and his new-risen brother must have no witness of their mighty mysteries! Though he had a thousand lives, still must he carry my secret where 'twill be safe—to—ha, ha, to the grave!"

"The sands of the glass are falling," cried Ibrahim advancing, "one-fourth of the last hour alone remains!"

"And while that fragment of time is gathered to eternity, the Water of Life is darting like lightning through the body of the dead—and—and—yet hold a moment, good Ibrahim! Dost thou not envy my immortal career? Dost desire to drink the Water of Life? Lo, the flagon is at thy command—drink, Ibrahim, and become immortal!"

"Drink I will!" exclaimed Ibrahim with a meaning smile, as he took the flagon in his grasp which the Scholar had substituted for the phial containing the Water of Life—"Drink I will, but first I will give thee a proof of my power!"

"Thy power? I am all amazement—"

"Learn, mighty Scholar, that the children of the race of Ben-Malakim, hold the power of calling up from the silence of the grave the spirits of the dead or, summoning from the uttermost parts of the earth the spectres of the living."

"These are idle words. Ibrahim, thou triflest with me!"

"Aldarin gaze around thee—all is dark and indistinct, the fire has burned to its embers, and the cavern beyond is wrapt in shadow. Aldarin, cast thy memory backward over the scenes of thy life, and tell me—which of thine enemies wouldst thou summon before thee in this scene of gloom?"

"He will drink the flagon at last," muttered Aldarin; "I'll even humor his whim. I would behold the forms of two slaves, whom I hate as darkly as my soul can hate. I would behold"—he whispered the names between his clenched teeth—"summon the slaves before me, if thou can'st!"

"Lo! it is done,"—shouted the Arabian—"Spirits of Ben-Malakim, appear— in the name of God, appear!"

"I hear a hushed sound like the tread of armies," murmured Aldarin—"Yet all is dark around me."

Scarce had the words passed from his lips when a dim yet lurid light, issuing from an invisible source, streamed around the cavern, and the face of Aldarin, tinted by the ghastly radiance, was stamped with an expression of wonder and awe.

Around, on every side, gathered along the rude pavement, shoulder to shoulder, a shadowy multitude stood dimly revealed in the lurid light, with dusky and immovable faces looking from beneath the shadow of sable helmets, ponderous with waving plumes.

And as Aldarin looked, the cavern was for a single moment wrapt in the darkness of midnight.

The gloom was again succeeded by the lurid light, and before the very eyes of the Scholar, gazing him sternly and fixedly in the face, stood two warrior forms, motionless as statues.

One was a stern old knight, clad in glittering armor, with long waving locks of snow-white hue falling far beneath his helmet, along his venerable countenance and over his iron-robed chest.

The other wore the appearance of a bluff soldier, next in rank to an Esquire, for he was clad in attire of substantial buff, with the rugged outline of his unplumed cap, surmounting a massive forehead, seamed by wrinkles and hardened by battle-toil.

There was something intensely horrible in the wild glow of triumph with which Aldarin regarded the spectres.

"Ha—ha! The vulgar hind, whom this hand consigned to darkness, arises to swell the triumph of the Scholar! But the other form—'tis the form of my mortal foe! He comes in spirit to look upon the glory of Aldarin! A few brief days and over his heart and brain will blacken the vengeance of the Scholar—vengeance such as never shadowed earth or darkened hell. Away with these phantoms, Ibrahim—my brain is 'wildered with too much joy—away!"

Through the gloom, he advanced toward the figures, he reached forth his hand, expecting to grasp the intangible air, when it rattled against the rugged plates of iron defending the breast of the venerable warrior.

The echo of the rattling armor was returned by a clanking sound that rang to the very cavern's roof, a sound like the clashing of a thousand swords. There was a brief yet fearful pause. Aldarin held his breath and his hands clutched convulsively at his throat.

"Behold," shouted the voice of Ibrahim, "behold the spectres by the light of a thousand torches!"

And at the magic word, the Cavern of Albarone was all alive with light, the light of a thousand torches, grasped by the mailed hands of warriors, while the stalwart forms of the men-at-arms, gathered in one dense and sombre multitude along the pavement of stone, rose clear and distinctly in the ruddy beams, and their sable plumes waved like a forest in the air.

Aldarin looked from side to side—he passed his hand wildly over his forehead, he strove to arouse his soul from this fearful dream.

It was no dream, Great God of Truth and Vengeance! it was no dream.

On every side the gleam of arms broke on the eye of Aldarin; on every side the frown of warlike visages met his gaze; and his glance was returned by the ominous glare of a thousand eyes.

The spell broke—the reality sank down upon the soul of Aldarin.

His face was stamped with an expression that brought to the minds of the gazers the horror of a soul plunged into eternal torment from the very battlements of heaven. He extended his right arm with a wild gesture, and clenched the hand until the sinews seemed bursting from the skin: his lips parted; his jaw sank to his very breast, while his full gray eye glared like the eye of the tiger at bay, rolling its glance from side to side, dilating every moment, and flashing like a meteor.

"Ibrahim—Ibrahim—I am betrayed!" he shrieked, turning to the Arabian. "Albarone to the rescue!"

He turned to the Arabian, he beheld him standing calm and erect beside the altar of ebony. He advanced to his side, and as he raised his hand to grasp the robe of the stranger, he started backward with a howl of despair whose emphasis of horror may not be described in words.

The snow-white beard, the gray hair, the white eye-brows, fell from the tawny face of Ben-Malakim, and Aldarin beheld the visage of—*Albertine, the Monk.*

Then it was that the soul of the old man sank within him, then it was that he raised his trembling hands aloft, shaking them madly in the air, while a wild yell of execration burst from the Phantom Band.

"Men of Albarone!" arose the shout of the gray-haired knight; "Behold the murderer of your Lord!"

"Behold the brother-murderer!" shrieked the stout yeoman, standing at the side of Sir Geoffrey. "These eyes beheld him hug his brother in the foul embrace of murder!"

And as he spoke the band of men-at-arms came pressing slowly and solemnly on, glittering swords flashed in the light, and low muttered cries of vengeance broke on the air. Closer and more close they gathered, while Albertine stood silent and motionless regarding the scene.

"The sands have fallen to within five minutes of the time!" madly shrieked Aldarin. "The charm may yet be complete!"

He wildly turned from the advancing knights and yeoman, he turned towards the Tabernacle, he heeded not the cries of execration that arose on every side, he trembled not at the frown of the Demon-Form towering far, far above.

He turned towards the Tabernacle, he was about to rush within the folds of the sable hangings, when he started back to the very breast of Sir Geoffrey o' th' Long-sword, with a wild exclamation of joy.

There, before his very eyes, in front of the sable tent, stood a youthful form, clad in a dress of glittering white, his arms folded on his breast, while with his face drooped on his bosom he gazed fixedly at the visage of Aldarin, and as he gazed the night-wind played with the floating locks of his golden hair.

"Behold, behold, men of Albarone," shouted Aldarin, with a wild laugh of joy, "your lord hath arisen from the dead! Before your eyes he stands, calm and mighty; youth in his heart, and power on his brow! Ha—ha—ha! I did— I did slay him! But I have raised him from the sleep of death! Behold—ha, ha, ha!—behold!"

A breathless stillness followed his words.

"Slave of thine own wild delusion," exclaimed Sir Geoffrey o' th' Longsword, as he advanced, "thou art gazing upon the form of Adrian Di Albarone."

"The avenger of his father's blood!" shouted the form, advancing to the light. "Murderer, behold thy doomsman."

Aldarin bowed his face low on his breast, and veiled his eyes in his hands, while a sound like the death groan rattled in his throat. His was no common agony. His was no mortal sorrow. His bosom trembled not with the throes of grief for the wife stolen by death, or the child torn from his embrace by unknown hands; the tears he wept were not visible tears, pouring from his eyes along the furrowed cheek. No, no.

His soul wept within him, tears such as giant souls alone can weep, when a mighty THOUGHT is slain, when the IDEA of a life is crushed.

"Avengers of your lord, advance," shrieked Sir Geoffrey o' th' Longsword; "advance, and seize the murderer!"

Aldarin turned; a thought flashed over his soul.

Three minutes of the last hour yet remained. The sands of the glass had not yet fallen. That little shred of time gained, he might yet complete the charm; the mystic age of toil might yet be rewarded by the immortal boon.

He flung himself at the feet of Sir Geoffrey o' th' Longsword; yes, yes, the proud and unrelenting Aldarin threw his form prostrate on the cavern floor, and, with upturned gaze, clutched the knees of the knight.

"Give me, give me but three minutes of life—three minutes alone, and then ye may lead me to the death."

The knight trembled: he had been prepared for scorn and defiance, but not for tears.

For a moment he hesitated.

"Away with his magical pranks, away with his works of hell!" arose the shout of the stout yeoman, as, with one rude grasp, he tore the tented hanging of the Tabernacle from the poles which supported their folds. "St. Withold! what infernal cookery have we here? Thus, thus I scatter the magical fire— thus I overturn this coffin of iron! Gather around, ye men of Albarone: scatter the works of this demon along the floor of the cavern!"

It was the work of an instant.

While Sir Geoffrey trembled: while the monk Albertine stood beside the altar of ebony, veiling his face in his hands; while even Adrian, the son of the murdered, hesitated and paused, ere the request of Aldarin was refused, the men-at-arms, led on by Rough Robin, overturned the coffin of iron, heated as it was to a white heat, and scattered the embers of the fire over the floor. The nameless secret of the coffin he concluded beneath the dark hangings of the Tabernacle.

Aldarin slowly arose to his feet. All emotion had vanished from his face. Stern, calm, and fearless, he gazed around. He looked over the vast expanse of the cavern roof, he marked the dread face of the DEMON FORM towering far above, he gazed upon the hurrying forms and agitated faces of the men-at-arms.

"Lead me, lead me to my death—" spoke the fierce tones of Aldarin the scholar. "I scorn and defy ye all."

Albertine, the monk, still clad in the dark robe and majestic attire of Ibrahim Ben Malakim, strode suddenly to the side of the scholar, and thrust a parchment roll in his hands.

"Man, I betrayed thee," he whispered, in tones that attested his agony; "Man, I betrayed thee, though my heart smote me in the act. Yet I will not scorn thee in this thy final hour. The parchment, the parchment—grasp it with a grasp like death; the phial, the phial!"

He turned, and continued in a loud voice, audible to the avengers: "Sinner, receive this book of prayer; it may comfort thy final hour."

Aldarin took the parchment, and calmly folded it to his bosom.

"I scorn ye all," he shrieked. "I defy your vengeance, I dare the doom ye would inflict. Aldarin fears not death."

"To the gibbet with the murderer," shouted Sir Geoffrey o' th' Longsword. "Aye, upon the same gibbet where blacken the forms of the brave soldiers of Lord Julian, there let the miscreant expiate his crimes."

And the men-at-arms echoed the shout, until the vast cavern roof resounded with the words of doom: "To the gibbet—to the gibbet with the fratricide."

In a moment the cavern was left to silence and eternal night.

Never since that fearful hour has human foot trode the funeral vaults of Albarone.

Along dark passages, through subterranean corridors, and up tortuous stairways, poured the flood of men-at-arms, bearing with them the scholar and fratricide.

At last winding through the same passages traversed three hours agone by Aldarin and Ibrahim, passing through the chemical laboratory, which has never been disclosed to the eye of the reader, the crowd of avengers reached the Round Room.

The altar was overturned, the books and parchments torn from the shelves, yet the scholar quailed not, nor uttered word of lamentation.

Gloomy corridors were then traversed, massive stairways ascended, the hall of the castle passed, and at last Aldarin emerged from the castle door, and stood upon the slab of stone surmounting the flight of steps.

He gazed around, while the avengers came thronging at his back; and as he gazed, the court-yard of the castle became the scene of a strange spectacle.

CHAPTER THE THIRTEENTH.

THE OATH.

THE VENGEANCE OF ALDARIN, THE SCHOLAR.

"IT is a fair day, and the sun shines brightly. Ha—ha! The sky above is clear, and the earth seems laughing with joy in the very face of day!"

Aldarin smiled as he spoke, and gazed above. It was the hour of early dawn. The first beams of the sun shone over the eastern battlements of the castle, mellowing the azure sky with their radiance, while the fresh and balmy air of the summer morn fanned the burning forehead of the Scholar. It was the last time he would behold the beams of the dawning day; it was the last time his burning brow should be freshened by the kiss of the morning breeze, and yet he smiled. Aldarin gazed around.

A yell of horror broke upon the summer air, and far along the court-yard extended the living sea of men-at-arms, arrayed in their sable armor, mingling with the vast crowds of the peasant vassals, all fired by the same instinct of bloodshed. The beams of the rising sun shone over a thousand maddened faces, as every voice swelled the shout of vengeance, and every hand shook in the light some weapon of death and vengeance.

Look where he might, on every side, the gleam of flashing eyes met the gaze of Aldarin; all along the court-yard the blackened mass swayed to and fro, like the waves of the ocean in a storm; and again heaven gave back to earth the combined yells of innumerable voices, mingling together in that fearful sound—the shout of a vast body of men, maddened and crazed by the impulse of carnage. "To the gibbet!" arose that shout of doom. "To the gibbet with the brother-murderer!"

With one glance Aldarin surveyed the scene around him.

There, grouped along the steps of stone, stood the stout yeoman, his brow wearing a steady frown, as, with his sword half drawn from the scabbard, he gazed upon the face of Aldarin; there stood two figures veiled in robes of sweeping sable, while—near his side—the erect form and venerable face of the knight o' th' Longsword confronted the Scholar.

"Sir knight," exclaimed Aldarin, with a smile wreathing his pinched lip "though ye are somewhat hurried in your work of doom, I would make one brief request, ere I am borne hence. Is there no one in all this crowd who will bear a message from me to my son, the Lord Guiseppo?"

"That will I," exclaimed the sharp-featured steward of the castle, advancing from the crowd. "Guilty thou mayst be, and thy hands stained with a brother's blood, yet the request of a dying man may not be refused."

"Give me the scroll."

Aldarin bared the withered flesh of his left arm: he drew a poignard, small and delicate in shape, from his girdle, and while the crowd looked on in wonder and in fear, he stained the point of the stilletto with his blood. Another moment passed, and with the dagger's point, hurriedly traced certain characters on a small slip of parchment which he also drew from his girdle.

"Bear this away," he shouted, "bear this away to the Lord Guiseppo, and tell him that his father is on his way to the gibbet."

"Man of blood and crime," exclaimed Sir Geoffrey o' th' Longsword, as he advanced to the side of Aldarin, "thy life has been full of dark and fearful mystery; hast thou no dying words of repentance to speak, ere the cord tightens round thy neck? It is not well to dare the presence of God, with so much blood upon thy soul."

Aldarin bowed his head low on his breast, and the bystanders whispered one to the other that the dreaded old man was wrapt in thought.

"A confession I have to make—dying words of repentance I have to speak," exclaimed Aldarin, as he gazed upon the crowded castle yard.

"Thou dost remember, Sir Geoffrey, that twenty years ago we saw each others faces in the wilds of Palestine?"

"I do, I do!" exclaimed the knight, as a mingled expression of bitter memory and deep feeling passed over his wrinkled visage. "Twenty years agone, we saw each other's faces within the walls of Jerusalem."

The sound of a hurried and uneven footstep broke upon the air, then a wild shout echoed from the castle hall, and in an instant, the Lord Guiseppo rushed from the hall door and confronted the Scholar Aldarin, his face pale as death, his eyes rolling madly to and fro, while his trembling right hand shook the parchment scroll above his head.

"This scroll, my father: what means its words of omen? Yon blackning crowd—their looks of vengeance—what means it all, my father?"

Aldarin advanced, and flung his arms around the form of his son, gathering him to his heart in the embrace of a father.

And as he gathered him to his heart, he whispered a few brief words in the ear of the Lord Guiseppo, those words thrilled the youth to the very soul; for his eye flashed brighter than ever, and his cheek grew more deathly pale.

"Thy oath—thy oath!" hissed the hollow whisper of Aldarin.

Guiseppo turned suddenly round, he flung himself at the feet of Sir Geoffrey, and looked up into his face with a voice of anguish, as he shrieked.

"Spare my father—spare, oh! spare the weak old man!"

"Though the angels of God plead for his life, still must he die!"

"Then die, wronger and betrayer! Then die, midnight assassin and ravisher! The spirit of my mother nerves my arm and points the steel!"

And as the words fell from his lips, ere an arm could be raised, or a word of horror spoken, Guiseppo sprang to the very throat of the knight, grasping his long gray hair with one hand, while with the other he inserted the glittering dagger between the armor plates of his victim, and drove the steel down from the left shoulder to the very heart.

It was the work of a moment; the lightning flash might not be swifter, nor the thunderbolt more sudden.

One instant the spectators beheld the kneeling youth, and the warrior waving his hand with stern determination, as he turned from the prayer of mercy; the next moment their eyes were startled by the upraised dagger, and the blow of vengeance.

The knight tottered heavily to and fro, looked vacantly around, and then sank into the arms of Robin the Rough, with the haft of the dagger protruding from the armor plates of his left shoulder.

"Father!" shrieked Guiseppo, shaking wildly above his head, the right hand, the hand that winged the dagger. "Father, my mother is avenged; behold the doom of the ravisher!"

"Thou hast done well!" spoke Aldarin, in a quiet, yet trembling tone, while his lips wore an even smile. "Boy, thou hast done well! Now, Guiseppo, read, read the pacquet—the pacquet in thy bosom."

And while the horror-stricken spectators—Robin the Rough, the figures in sable robes, the peasant-vassals, and the men-at-arms—remained awed into a fearful silence by the scene,—the silence that ever precedes the march of death,—Guiseppo thrust his hand within his bosom, drew the pacquet from its resting place, and with his trembling fingers broke the seal.

"Man of guilt and bloodshed," exclaimed the dying knight, as he convulsively placed his hands on the wound near his heart. "I am dying—my heart grows cold, and mine eyes are dim—thy vengeance is gratified; now, now, tell me—"

"Hadst thou ever a child, Sir Geoffrey," interrupted Aldarin, advancing to the side of the knight: "a fair-haired and soft-voiced boy, whose smile was thy joy, whose presence was thy sunshine?"

"Speak, speak—what knowest thou of my boy?" gasped the dying knight, as a look of agony passed over his face. "'Tis sixteen years since I beheld his face in the land of his birth, the city of Jerusalem. He was torn from my embrace by an unknown hand."

Aldarin looked around over the sea of faces, and smiled as he beheld a peasant whetting his knife on the very stone on which he stood.

That smile of incarnate scorn seemed to break the spell of horror that bound the multitude.

"To the gibbet, to the gibbet with the fratricide!" again rose the fierce yell of vengeance, and the men-at-arms came crowding up the steps, while a score of upraised daggers were about to drink the blood of the doomed murderer, when Robin the Rough threw himself before the object of their vengeance.

"Stain not your steel," he shouted; "stain not your steel with traitor's blood; away to the castle gate with him! Let the dog die a dog's death!"

And at the word, the Esquires Halbert and his gallant brother Damian advanced from the crowd, and seizing Aldarin by the arms, they dragged him down the steps of stone, while the multitude gave way on either side, shrinking from the touch of a murderer, as one would shrink from the garments of the plague-smitten.

"There is fire in my heart, there is hell in my brain!" arose a tremulous voice, that was heard far along the castle yard, thrilling the bystanders to the very soul. "God of mercy, it is, it is not true! The parchment is a lie—a falsehood written by the very fiend of hell! I did not—no, no, I did not—wing the *blow* to *his* heart! God of heaven witness me, I raised not the steel for *his* blood!"

And as the multitude, bearing Aldarin to his doom, heard that shrieking voice, they looked back, and beheld the Lord Guiseppo standing over the prostrate form of his victim, his face pale and colorless, his lip livid as with the touch of death, while his eyes rolled their ghastly glance over the faces of the crowd, and his arms hung palsied by his side, with the fatal parchment quivering in the grasp of his trembling hand.

"FATHER, FATHER!" his shriek again arose on the air, as he knelt by the side of his victim; "FATHER, THE MURDERER IS THY SON."

The old man raised himself on one hand, grasped the hand of the maddened boy, as he gazed silently into his face, while his very soul seemed absorbed into some unreal dream of horror.

"My son," he whispered with a mournful smile, "*and the dagger in my heart—*"

"Thy son!—ha, ha?—I could laugh till the very heavens echoed my voice!" and as he spoke, Aldarin, the Scholar, looked backward toward the castle steps, where the boy knelt beside the dying knight. "Thy son—ha, ha, ha!—and the dagger in thy heart! Yes, yes, it thy son? Sir Geoffrey, a parting word: dost thou remember a blow—aye, a blow from the mailed hand of a warrior, a blow which struck the Scholar to the floor while the princess of Christendom stood laughing round the scene? Dost thou remember the insult, the contumely, the scorn. Then look upon the face of thy boy, whom I stole and reared to be thy murderer, look upon his youthful face, peruse each feature, and—a smile stole over his face—*think of the vengeance of Aldarin, the Scholar.*"

With cries of execration, with yells of vengeance, the men-at-arms gathered around the fratricide, and as their brandished swords shone in the light, they bore him towards the castle gate, leaving the slab of stone before the pillars of the castle door to the solitary companionship of the father and son.

It was true—darkly and fearfully true—Guiseppo was the son of Sir Geoffrey o' th' Longsword.

Guiseppo was kneeling upon the stone; his arms were gathered around the form of his father, and his eyes were fixed in one long gaze upon the face of the dying man.

He marked the hue of that venerable countenance as it grew paler every moment: the lip white and colorless, the eyes wild and wavering in their glance, the livid circles gathering like the taint of corruption beneath each eye; he beheld the signs and heralds of coming death; he heard the quick gasping struggle for breath, and yet he spoke no word, he uttered no sound of agony.

"I see her face in thine," murmured the old man, as he gazed upwards upon the countenance of his son. "It is no dream,—and—and—thy dagger is resting in my heart!"

Guiseppo was silent.

"Boy, look not upon me with such fearful agony—thou art forgiven!" gasped the old man. "Raise the hilt of my sword to my lips; I would kiss the cross ere I die. And now thy hand is firm, seize the haft of the dagger, and draw the blade from my heart."

Guiseppo gazed upon the face of his father with a vacant look, yet still he uttered no word.

"Draw the dagger from my heart!" gasped the dying man.

Guiseppo seized the haft of the dagger, and slowly drew the blade from the heart of the murdered man.

CHAPTER THE FOURTEENTH.

THE FATE OF THE FRATRICIDE.

THE ELEMENTS ARISE IN BATTLE, DARKENING THE EARTH WITH THEIR STRIFE, AS THE WIND SHRIEKS THE DEATH-WAIL OF ALDARIN THE SCHOLAR.

ONWARD toward the castle gate, walking to his death, and *yet receding from the grave at every step*, with the fierce faces of the avengers frowning around him, with cries of execration and deep muttered oaths of vengeance deafening his ear, onward toward the castle gate, with an even step and an erect form, strode the Scholar Aldarin an icy smile on his lip, and a sombre light in his eye.

He knew not why they bore him onward—fearless of death, come in what form it might, he cared not.

The castle gate was reached. A dark-robed monk rushed from the shadow of the massive pillars, and while his white hairs waved in the morning breeze, he raised a cross of iron aloft in the sunbeams—

"Sinner—there is mercy above—even for thee! Behold the symbol of that mercy!"

"Ha—ha—curses on thee and thy symbol of—mercy! thou shaveling! Were not my hands stayed by these cowards I would strike ye down in my very path! I curse ye all!" he shrieked, gazing around the crowd—"I blaspheme your religion, I mock your * * *! Will ye not strike? Aldarin laughs at your steel! Are ye afraid of a weak and trembling old man? Fear ye the Scholar, even in his last hour? Lo! my breast is bare—I defy the blow!"

"Thou wilt have striking enough presently," cried Robin the Rough— "Throw open the castle gate there. Let the portcullis be raised and the drawbridge lowered."

The gate was passed, and the drawbridge crossed. Aldarin stood upon the platform of turf surmounting the summit of the hill; beneath him descended the road into the valley; on either side yawned chasms dark and deep; while the rocks upon whose massive piles the castle was founded, threw their fantastic forms from amid clumps of brushwood, and here and there colossal stones rose brightly into the sunshine from the depths of the gloomy void.

Aldarin looked around, and beheld the face of nature clad in the smile of sunshine; waves of foliage rising in the light; the bosom of the Arno calm and beautiful as a silver mirror, seen through the intervals of undulating hills; the Apenines frowning in the far distance, and the calm blue sky, glowing with the first kiss of morn, arching above.

Aldarin looked around upon the face of nature, but another spectacle fixed his attention and excited his wonder.

Not far from where he stood, four dark steeds were rearing and springing on the sod, while their grooms, four swarthy Moors, whose distorted faces scarce resembled the visages of humanity, were forced to exert all their giant-strength in the effort to hold the wild horses of the desert.

Wildly with their hoofs the barbs tore the sod, scattering the loosened earth in the very face of Aldarin; their eyes flashed like coals of flame, their sinews seemed to creep under the smooth and glossy skin, black as midnight; their crests proudly arching, gave their manes, long and dark, to the breeze; while with quivering nostrils and a shrill piercing neigh they seemed panting to break loose from all restraint and dart like lightning down the steep.

"What would ye with me now?" exclaimed Aldarin, as a strange wonder and a darker fear gathered around his heart. "Cowards that ye are, ye still delay your work of murder. I would this merry mysterie were finished—"

"To the gibbet with the brother-murderer!" arose the thunder shout of the multitude. "To the gibbet with the wizard and sorcerer!"

"To the Doom, to the Doom!" shouted the stout yeoman. "*To the Doom*, but not to the gibbet!"

Robin the Rough smiled and waved his hand to the Moors who led the barbs of Arimanes down the steep, while Damian and Halbert followed at their heels, bearing the Fratricide to his doom.—

Meanwhile the multitude thronging from the castle-gate, in one dense crowd, began to darken over the rocks that hedged in the moat, as the men-at-arms followed Aldarin down the hilly road, their upraised swords glittering in the first beams of the morning sun.

At the foot of the hill there lay a piece of level earth, some hundred paces square, sloping toward the east into a green meadow, backed by a wood; on the west it was hedged in by the forest trees, on the north arose the road leading to the castle, while towards the south the highway to Florence wound upwards along the brow of a precipitous hill.

Arrived at this level space—the theatre of the last and most fearful scene in his life—Aldarin beheld the stout yeoman ranging the men-at-arms along the foot of the hill, shoulder to shoulder, presenting one firm compact front, their upraised swords glittering over their sable plumes, their armor of steel shining in the morning sun. At his very side, in the centre of the level space, the wild horses of the desert were rearing and plunging in the hold of their grooms, as their shrill and piercing neigh broke on the air.

Aldarin cast his gaze above.

There crowding along the rocks, that confined the moat, form after form face after face, thronged the vassals of Albarone, gazing with silence and awe, upon the strange scenes passing in the valley below. For the moment every voice was stilled, every cry was silenced; with hushed breath and fixed brows, the men of Albarone, awaited the last scene of this tragedy.

And as Aldarin gazed around, he beheld two soldiers advance, holding thongs in their hands twisted out of the hide of the wild bull, while the tawny Moors, at a sign from Robin the Rough, placed their steeds haunch to haunch, the heads of two of the barbs looking towards the east, while the others were turned towards the west.

Robin the Rough advanced.

He gazed for a moment around the scene, and then approaching the side of Aldarin, spoke in a calm and even tone, as though the dignity of his solemn office, the avenger of the dead, imbued and elevated his soul.

"Thou hast invoked the blow, thou hast defied the steel, blasphemed our religion, and mocked our God."

"Traitor and Fratricide—turn thee and behold the vengeance of that God."

"Behold the manner of thy death—Murderer, look at these barbs of the desert; see how they paw the earth, how their quivering nostrils snuff the air—mark those forms of strength, those sinews of iron!"

"Ere an hundred can be told, lashed to the limbs of these horses, thine accursed carcass shall be scattered to the winds of heaven, while thy blood-stained soul, goes trembling to its last account! Thou art a brave man—we would listen to thee, while thou makest a merry mock of death, and of such a death as this!"

Aldarin turned, he looked at the wild horses, placed haunch to haunch; a deformed Moor holding each steed; he marked their forms of strength, their sinews of iron; and a slight tremor, scarce perceptible, passed over his frame.

"I am ready—" he slowly and distinctly spoke, with a calm smile—"I am ready even for this death. Cowards and slaves I defy ye!"

"Thou art a wise man—" again spoke Robin the Rough in his mocking tone—"and yet mere fools have deceived and duped thee! Yesternight, within the confines of the Red-Chamber, thou didst wait the coming of a Brother-wizard who was to journey from the far wilds of the east. Thy brother-wizard twenty-four hours agone, rode from the very walls of Florence, secured by the favor of this tyrant-duke—Ha! dost thou tremble?"

"This—this—is false!" gasped Aldarin—"Ibrahim journeyed not from the wilds of the east."

"He came from the east attended by a train of twelve Arab knights and a band of Christian warriors, whom the courtesy of the Crusades, gave to the service of the friend of Saladin. He arrived at Florence, he beheld the tyrant duke, and at high noon yesterday rode from the walls of the city, bound for the Castle of Albarone. He was a venerable man and a mighty, this Ibrahim—for his long beard—ha,—ha—trailed down to his very breast! Who was it that made captives of his companie, and confined his own royal person in bonds, while the men of Sir Geoffrey wended to the castle clad in the garments of the Arabian retinue? Old man breathe the question in a murmured voice for it was the work of—THE INVISIBLE."

Aldarin veiled his face in his hands, and pressed his lips between his teeth, until the blood trickled down to his very chin.

"Off with the murderer's attire!" shrieked Robin the Rough—"Off with tunic and hose, belt and boots! Strip him to the very skin! Demon, thy magical pranks shall not avail thee, now! We will lead thee to thy death, unarmed with magic casket or wizard phial! Advance comrades and disrobe the murderer!"

Aldarin raised his head as the soldiers with the thongs advanced, while the men-at-arms noted that his face was ghastly white in hue, yet calm as the Summer Morn then dawning in the eastern sky.

"Is there not one man in all this crowd, who will bear a message from a father to his daughter!" he slowly exclaimed—"The Ladye Annabel, she is my child, and—by the fiend ye dare not refuse a father's request!"

There was a pause, while two figures clad and veiled in sweeping robes of sable, stole silently thro' the throng of the men-at-arms, and stood beside Robin the Rough.

"Will no man hear the last words of a—father to his child?"

"I—I—will bear the message—" exclaimed one of the sable figures, speaking from the folds of his robe—"I will bear thy dying words to the Ladye Annabel!"

Aldarin trembled. He knew the voice; and strange memories came crowding around him, as he fancied the tones of his murdered brother living again in that husky sound.

"Bear the parchment scroll to the Ladye Annabel. Tell her—tell her—it came from the hands of *one* who loved her thro' life, and gave his lost thoughts to *her*, in the hour of a fearful death. And look ye man—" he continued in quick and gasping tones—"ye need not tell her, how her father died—ye need not speak of his doom—say to her, that Aldarin died in his bed."

"I will—I will—as God lives I will!"

"Tell her that Aldarin with his last words, blessed her with the blessing of the God in whom she believes!"

"It shall be done!" exclaimed the voice, and the hand of the veiled Figure grasped the parchment scroll—"It shall be done!"

Robin turned from the scene, and gazed above. "How say ye men of Albarone—" he shouted pointing to the Barbs of Arimanes—"shall the Wild Horses, rend the body of the murderer into atoms? Is our sentence just?"

There arose from rock, from hill, from valley one shout—"It is the judgment of Heaven—the judgment of Heaven!"

Slowly and silently the soldiers disrobed the Scholar, and at last he stood disclosed in the light, with the folds of his under tunic floating around his slender form.

"Lead him to his doom?" shouted Robin the Rough.

"Ye shall not lead the old man to this fearful death!" arose the shriek of the Figure who had received the parchment from the hands of the Scholar—"I forbid this work of doom!"

The robe fell from the form of the stranger, and Adrian Di Albarone confronted the stout yeoman, his hands upraised, and his blue eye gleaming with a wild light, as he shrieked forth the words, "I forbid this work of doom!"

"Adrian Di Albarone," exclaimed the deep-toned voice of Robin the Rough, as he seemed inspired with an awful feeling of the duty which he owed the dead; "to-morrow, these gallant men, the vassals clustering round yon heights, and thy poor servitor, who stands before thee, will joy to call thee— Lord!—This day is sacred to another master, to another Lord—this day is sacred to the God of vengeance. This day we own no earthly rule, we stand apart from all human things; we have sworn not to eat, nor drink, nor sleep until we have fulfilled the work of doom!"

"Thou will not scorn my prayer for mercy;—Adrian Di Albarone asks the old man's life of thee! He is stained with my father's blood, but I would not have him die this fearful death—spare the old man's life!"

"I am the avenger of Lord Julian of Albarone! Ask the God above to spare the fratricide—for I cannot, cannot stay HIS judgment!"

Adrian turned away, for the stern faces of the men-at-arms told him that his pleadings were all in vain. And as he glided from the place of death, the robes were thrust aside from the face of the other figure, and every eye beheld the visage of Albertine the monk.

"Old man," exclaimed the voice of Albertine, from the shrouded folds of his robe, "hast thou no prayer to offer, no words of penitence to speak ere thou art led to thy doom?"

"I am ready for my death;" exclaimed Aldarin, extending his arms—

"I scorn your whining prayers, and as for words of penitence—look ye—is there aught of repentance written on this cheek or brow?"

"To whom dost thou resign thy soul!"

"To the AWFUL SOUL OF THE UNIVERSE!"

Thus exclaimed the fated man, as his slender form rose proudly erect while his extended hands were raised in the act of solemn appeal.

"Ye may tear this body into fragments, ye may rend this carcass into atoms, doom me to the death of fire, or consign this form to the decay of the charnel-house, *yet ye cannot destroy Aldarin*! His soul will live and live forever! It may float on the unseen winds, it may glare in the lightning's flash, or strike in the thunderbolt; it may come back to the earth, in the storm, the horror and the doom: or it may wander far, far in the solitudes of the VAST UNKNOWN, where eternal fires lash the shores of desolated worlds—still will it live and live forever! A beam of the AWFUL SOUL can never die!"

Albertine gazed upon the erect form and flashing eye of the Scholar and saw that his labour was in vain. With a look which mingled bitter and contrasted feelings, he turned away from the scene, gathering the folds of his robe over his face as he disappeared.

"Lead me to the death," cried Aldarin in a tone of bitter scorn. "Or are ye afraid of a weak and withered old man? Ha—ha! ye are brave men!"

"Lead him to his death!" echoed Robin the Rough.

Attired in his under tunic, Aldarin was led forward. Damian seized him by the shoulders and Halbert his feet. They raised him upon the haunches of the steeds, with his head to the east.

Robin the Rough advanced, and grasping a thong, twisted out of the wild bull's hide, from the hands of one of the men-at-arms, slowly wound the cord around the body of one of the wild horses, and looping it in a firm knot, secured the right arm of Aldarin to the back of the restless steed; while Damian bound the left to the other steed, Halbert, assisted by the men-at-arms, bound his legs to the backs of the opposite horses, winding the thongs again and again, around the bodies of the impatient Arabs, until his blood spouted from the withered flesh of the fratricide.

"Wind your thongs yet tighter friends of mine!" the sneer broke gaspingly from the lips of the doomed. "I defy your malice and laugh at your doom!"

The interest now was most absorbing and intense.

Along the whole extent of blackened rocks, frowning above the level space, gathered the multitude gazing on the scene with gasping breath and woven brows; while the men-at-arms, circling along the base of the hill, stood silent and motionless, their upraised swords still glittering in the first beams of the morning sun.

And there, in the centre of the space of highway earth, placed haunch to haunch, stood the barbs of Arimanes, their eyes flashing as though a demon-soul lived and moved within each sinewy form; there were gathered the deformed Moors, each sable groom holding an ebon steed by the nostrils, for the bridles were now cast aside; there, standing at the side of each wild horse, the avengers of the dead, with the right leg advanced and dagger drawn, awaited the word of vengeance; and there, with his face turned upward to heaven, helpless and motionless, intense pain shooting through every vein, and quivering along every sinew, filling his brain with fire, his heart with ice, Aldarin the fratricide smiled in scorn, as the moment of his doom came hurrying on.

"Avengers of your Lord," shouted Robin the Rough, "raise your daggers, and as the word falls from my lips, bury them to the hilt in the flank of each steed!"

"A word—a single word," whispered Aldarin, in a subdued voice. "Draw near—I would say my last farewell—"

"What would'st thou have?" exclaimed one of the men-at-arms, advancing.

"When I am dying, ere the heart is cold, or the brow chill, approach and gaze upon my countenance, and as you gaze, take to your very soul."

"Speak—man of blood—thy moments are well nigh spent."

"Take to your very soul," whispered the fratricide, as he slowly, and with difficulty, brought his head round to his right shoulder—"THE CURSE OF ALDARIN!"

"Avengers of your Lord," exclaimed the stout yeoman—"strike deep, every man into the flanks of his steed!"

"*The curse*," shrieked a hollow voice, "*The Curse of Aldarin!*"

"Strike,—I say—strike!"

The daggers sunk into the flanks of the horses, buried to the hilts; the Moors leaped back; the maddened steeds sprang forward, with one wild bound, straining every sinew in the effort to free themselves from their accursed burden.

It was in vain.

They sank back, with a maddening howl, each steed upon his haunches, the accursed fratricide uttered a yell of intense and overwhelming agony—it died on his lips!

With eyes of fire with streaming manes, their nostrils extended, and all their vigour gathered for the effort, the steeds again leaped forward, springing madly from each other, and darting into the air, with one terrible impulse—

The scene swam for an instant before the vision of the spectators.

They looked again. A limbless trunk lay in the dust of the highway, spouting streams of blood—along the green meadow careered two black steeds—through the dense forest thundered the others.

One of the men-at-arms, approaching the carcass, gazed for a moment at the dread face. His eye glanced over expressions of the features, convulsed by the throes of the parting soul; the eye yet fired with hate, the lip curved with scorn; the sunken jaw oozing blood from every pore; the quivering flesh and changing hues of the visage. All the ghastliness and fear of this countenance, met his vision at a glance; he uttered a howl of horror, and fell stiffened upon the earth, as the last spark of life fled from the remains of the fratricide. When the soldier awoke, his eye was vacant, and his reason gone. He was a maniac! He had received the last words of the Doomed, and the Curse was on him forever.

Another moment passed, and the crowd came rushing from the rocky steeps, filling the air with fierce shouts, and wild yells of execration, while the men-at-arms, circled round the bleeding trunk, gazing upon the wild and unearthly countenance of the Scholar, in wonder and in awe, each man whispering to his comrade, a word of fear, as he marked the expression of blasphemous and fiend-like scorn, stamped upon the visage of the FRATRICIDE.

And while they circled round, struck dumb with a nameless awe, two Figures, arrayed in robes of sable, rushed through the throng and confronted Robin the Rough, as he stood stern, silent and awe-stricken, they gazed upon the Dead.

"It is—" exclaimed the solemn voice of Adrian Di Albarone—"It is the judgment of Heaven!"

From rock, from hill, from valley, from forest and from castle-wall, arose the stern echo,—

"The Judgment of Heaven—the Judgment of Heaven!"

On, on, like lightning, darted the ebon steeds, bearing the torn and shattered limbs, reeking with the life blood, yet warm and smoking. On, on as tho' the spirit of the lost, had entered their maddened forms. On, on, they flew!

Onward! and onward! sped the wild horses, tracking their course with blood, and rushing past the cottages of the affrighted peasantry, like beings of the unreal world, fired with the soul of Arimanes, cursed with the Spirit of the *Evil One*! Onward and Onward!

One brave barb, came plunging from the depths of a wood, and a precipice mighty and steep, was before him, but he heeded it not. Down an hundred fathoms into the boiling water he fell.

Another black steed sank into the calm waters of a placid river; another reached the sea, and plunging in its depths, swam far, far, into the wide expanse of the waters and was heard of no more.

The last—swept like the wind, by hamlet and tower and town. The live-long day he urged on his career. The blood streaming from his nostrils, his limbs weakened, and his sinews unstrung, he entered the confines of a long valley, where a calm lake, gave its bosom to the evening sun.

His pace was unsteady and he staggered to and fro, yet still the bloody fragment hung at his back. At last he fell and died, and the scene of his death was before a pleasant cottage on the green hill side. Much wondered the solitary Student of the cot, as he surveyed the carcass of the gallant steed. Little did he wot from whence he sped or the cause of his flight.

Meanwhile gathering around the shapeless trunk, the men of Albarone built a pile of the branches of oaks, that had lain mouldering for years in the forest, and soon a broad bright flame arose, and it burned till the setting of the sun, when a storm gathered in the west, and heralded by thunder, and armed with lightning, it swept over the earth, and the ashes of the *fratricide*, mingling with the whirlwind, never more polluted the green bosom of the earth.

Thus runs the legend of the Doom of the Poisoner, thus runs the legend of the death that befel.

ALDARIN THE FRATRICIDE.

BOOK THE FOURTH.

THE QUEEN OF FLORENCE.

CHAPTER THE FIRST.

A SILVERY MOON AND A CLOUDLESS SKY.

THE AGED DAME OF THE COT ON THE HILLSIDE LEARNS THE MYSTERY OF AN UNFASTENED DOUBLET.

"NIGHT among the mountains—oh, glorious and beautiful!" arose the voice of the Wanderer, as with one bold grasp he attained the topmost rock of the hoary steep, rising far above forest and stream—"Night among the mountains—the calm moonbeams sleeping on the lake—the boundless azure arching above—the rolling sweep of forest and the rugged outline of precipice and steep—the far-off convent, its towers looming through the distance, like a cloud of evil omen—Night among the mountains, glorious and grand and beautiful!

"Thank God for the breeze, the cool and freshening breeze! It sweeps over my forehead, burning as with the ravages of hidden flame, it bears the fever from my cheek, and the madness from my brain. And yet I must on, and on—afar I behold the peaceful cot, appearing amid the luxuriance of the hill-side vines—my steed lays bleeding and dead in the vale below, still must I on, and on!

"God of Heaven, will that face never depart from my soul, the brow darkened by superhuman hate, the eyes all aflame with the Curse of the Fratricide, the white lips, and the sunken jaws; with the blood oozing from every pore! Even now I behold the face! And to her ear—help me Saints of Light—to *her* ear must I bear the manner of his doom!

"The moon shines in the heavens, calm and beautiful—when the mild radiance of her beams pales before the glory of the uprising sun—then, then, will the angels of fate, write in the books of the Unknown, the Doom of Adrian, the last of the race of Albarone!"

And as the words broke murmuring from his lips, he flung his form from the summit of the steep, and grasping with eager hands the point of each projecting rock, at last descended to the bed of the valley, and sped onward on his errand of woe, while higher in the heavens up rose the moon.

High in the heavens arose the full orbed moon, and calm and lovely was the sight, as enthroned in the very zenith of the boundless azure, this thing of beauty and of beams, shed a shower of silver radiance down on the silent bosom of the quiet vale, mirroring her rounded glory in the deep waters of the mountain lake, giving a ghastly lustre to the white precipice, from whose foundations arose the walls of the lonely convent, mossy with age and darkened by time.

In this wide world of ours—so runs the wild rhapsody of the Chronicler of the ancient MSS.—in this wide world of ours, there are, I ween, many things sublime and beautiful and grand, yet what sight may compare with a cloudless heaven, a silvery moon and a lovely extent of woody hills and grassy vales? Never minstrel struck harp—never romancer spoke the fancies of his brain, that did not hymn thy praise, O! beauteous thing of brilliance and of beams! For ages and for ages thou hast held thy way of glory through the arching heavens—thou hast looked down upon warriors marching in all their pomp, and thou hast beheld their withered forms strewn over the battle plain;—lovers have poured forth their love beneath thy light, and again thou hast looked down upon their quiet graves;—nations have risen and fallen;—monuments that gave promise of eternal duration, have crumbled in the dust;—cities have towered in deserts, and deserts have won the place of gorgeous cities, yet still kind nurturer of holy thoughts, inspirer of heavenly fancies, yet still thou passest on in thy course of light, and thus, with brilliance unpaling and unpaled, glorious as when God first bade thee roll through the azure expanse, thou shalt urge thy way until the final trump of doom.

Arising in the calm moonbeams, the roof of the lonely cottage gave its wreathing vines, all gay with flowers, to the motion of the night air, while the gleam of a taper, shooting from a crevice of the closed lattice, varied the shadows which darkened over one side of the tenement, by a single thread of light.

Meanwhile the beams of the taper gave light to the principal chamber of the cottage, where the stately mother of Leone the student, sate wrapt in deep meditation.

"Strange!"—thus she murmured—"Strange! Scarce seven days since we first concealed ourselves in this lonely vale, and Adrian—ha! I may be overheard—Leone has won the friendship of this noble youth of Florence. Not that he acquires honor thereby—by my troth, no!—the youth is a good youth, and a fair, but the friendship of Emperors cannot add glory to the heir of Albarone—fool that I am!—ever repeating the name of our race! Strange it is, very strange, that the gentle Florian should take up his abode in our cot! He is ever with Leone!—They walk, they eat, they drink together, and together they pursue their studies! The fair stranger shall in time become the leader of armies—but my son—the last of an honored race, shall become a—*monk*. The thought is maddening!"

The dame arose and hurriedly paced the room. As she strode to and fro she perceived the door of Leone's apartment slightly ajar, and impelled by mere restlessness, she took a mother's privilege, and softly entered the room.

No sooner had she opened the door, than a sight met her gaze, that caused her to start back to the very threshold with astonishment.

Seated beside the table, on which a taper cast its dim light, over the opened volume, the chairs of the students were drawn close together, their backs were turned to the dame, the arm of Leone was around the slender waist of the gentle Florian, and with their heads laid one against the other, the rich golden locks of Leone mingled with a shower of flaxen tresses that fell over the shoulders and down the back of the fair stranger.

Treading on tip-toe and much wondering at the unusual length of Florian's hair, the dame approached.

"Thou art weary, my love"—the whisper broke from Florian's lips—"thy dress is soiled with dust and torn by travel—thy face is wan and haggard, and—the Virgin save me—thine eyes are bloodshot! Thou hast been absent two long and weary days. Hast journeyed far to-day, Adrian?"

"A score of miles, since the sunset hour."

"And thou didst see the old castle yet again?"

Adrian replied in a whisper, and then as they conversed in low murmurs, the dame observed the form of her son agitated by a slight trembling motion, while ever and anon he turned his head aside veiling his face in his hands.

Nearer drew the dame, and looking over the heads of the students, a tremor of surprise ran over her frame, her hands were involuntarily raised, her thin lips parted, her gray eyes expanded, and her eyebrows arose to the very roots of her hair. Silent she stood and motionless as stone.

The evening being somewhat warm, the broach that fastened Florian's doublet at the neck, was unloosed, and the opening garment gave to view a neck of the most surpassing whiteness, spreading into shoulders of flowing outline, and budding into a bosom of virgin tracery of form, all glowing with the warm blood of youth, and heaving with the pulsations of passion.

CHAPTER THE SECOND.

THE CLOUD GATHERS AND THE SKY DARKENS.

THE dame essayed to speak. Her voice died away in an unmeaning rattle of the throat. One hand she extended, and seizing Leone by the shoulder, with the other she tore the maiden from his embrace—

"Apostate!" she began in tones that trembled with rage, "is it thus thou honorest the race whose name thou bearest. Away!—I will never look upon thee more! Away!—and with thee take thy——, I will not speak the title of shame;—Away!"

As she spoke she raised her hand to strike the shrinking maiden, who, with head drooped on her bosom, and quick blushes coursing over her face, strove hurriedly to fasten the broach of her doublet.

"Strike her not, mother!" cried Leone, throwing himself before the damsel, "Assail her not with words of shame!"

He took the hand of the blushing maiden and continued—"Fear not, love, there is none to harm thee. Mother, behold my bride!"

"Annabel!—Thy bride? Wherefore this concealment? Why this unmaidenly disguise? How is't, my son—how is't?"

"As for the disguise it was assumed to aid her escape, and then,"—he whispered into his mother's ear—"and then I thought thou wouldst not affect the niece of the—the—s'life, mother, I cannot speak the word of any one connected with Annabel!"

"My son, my son! what hast thou done? Answer me—befits such doings with thy profession? Art thou not intended for a minister of Heaven?"

While the dame spoke, the figure of a monk darkened the opened doorway, advancing to Leone he threw back his cowl, and discovered the dark brow, the wan face, the flashing eyes of Albertine, the monk.

"Lord Adrian," whispered the Monk, "at the hour of sunset, when the dark storm arose, howling its requiem over the remains of the Fratricide, thou didst hasten from the castle of Albarone, bound for this lonely valley. Thou hadst not gone an hour's journey from the castle walls, when I tracked thy footsteps, bearing news of fearful import. Thy haunt hath been betrayed to the tyrant, by a traitor from the lonely valley. Even now, the Duke spurs his steed toward the valley of the mountain lake, attended by a band of minions; even now the voices of his bravoes startle the air, shrieking for thy blood!"

"And the INVISIBLE?" whispered Adrian—"where is their dagger of vengeance, while the tyrant rides abroad on his errands of wrong?"

"Listen, Lord Adrian! This very night, while the Duke is absent from the walls of Florence, will Lord and Monk, Prince and Peasant, joined in the solemn oath of the holy steel, arise in the might of men who have sworn at the very Altar of God to be free, and ere the morrow's sun, Florence the Fair and Beautiful, will own another Sovereign! The Invisible work in secret, as doth the earthquake—man alone beholds the bursting of the storm!"

"Hark! I hear the sound of horses' hoofs, mingled with the clatter of arms!"

"God of Heaven! The Duke approaches!" shouted the Monk—"I must be gone—all thought of escape for thee and thy bride is vain! Adrian, Adrian, bear a firm heart through the perils of this night, and in the morrow's dawn will blaze the star of thy Mighty Fortune! Hath the Duke any issue, or is he the last of his line?"

"He is the last of his race," answered Adrian, "why dost thou ask?"

"Thou wilt learn anon!" exclaimed the Monk.

He turned and sought the door, but as if struck by a sudden thought, he again approached Adrian, and whispered in tones that seemed to come from his very soul—"Fare-thee-well, Adrian, fare-thee-well! I have loved thee much, very much. There was a time when my heart was as young as thine, my soul as pure. But now—Ha! *now* I would have my revenge, although the chasm of hell yawned beneath me—nay, although between me and the object of my hate yawned the gulf of perdition, I would leap the abyss and drag him down, down to the eternal flames that now hunger for his accursed soul—Fare-thee-well, Adrian—I'll never see thee more!"

The Monk was gone. The fearful look that fired his countenance, and the awful tones in which he spoke, haunted Adrian Di Albarone until his dying hour.

Scarcely had Albertine disappeared, when there was the sound of trampling feet in the outer apartment, and presently the figure of his Grace of Florence occupied the doorway, while the heads of his followers were seen looking over his shoulders.

He looked around the apartment with a curious eye, as if he sought the wanderers. At last his glance rested upon the form of the disguised Annabel, and advancing toward the damsel, he flung himself at her feet, exclaiming with all the grace of attitude and expression at his command.

"Fair Ladye, it is with joy beyond the power of words to tell, that I hail thee by the title of the—Fair Ladye Annabel, Countess Di Albarone!"

"How sayst thou?" exclaimed Annabel, forgetting her boyish disguise in her eagerness, "How sayst thou? Ladye of Albarone?"

"Aye, fair Ladye. Thou art *now* the Countess Di Albarone, soon shalt thou be my own loved Annabel, Duchess of Florence."

The Duke leaned earnestly forward, trying to look as much like a lover as might be—his face wore an expression of deep solemnity, his protruding eyes made an effort to sparkle, and his attempt to soften his voice, gave one the idea of a magpie trying to sing.

Annabel cast an agonized look at the Duke—

"Sayst thou nought of my father?" she exclaimed. "Is he sick?—is he ill?—Tell me that I may hurry to him!—For heaven's sake tell me!—my father is—"

"DEAD!" cried the Duke.

"Dead!" echoed the dame, starting with surprise.

Annabel heard no more.

"Coward and tyrant," shouted Lord Adrian, as he caught the sinking maiden in his arms, "away with thee from this humble tenement. Defile not my bride with the pollution of thy touch—By the honor of my race! I would give the brightest jewel in the coronet of Albarone, for one good blow at the carcass of this craven hound!"

"Ho! art thou here my gay springald?—*Thy bride*, indeed?—Guards advance, seize the miscreant!—I will teach him to raise his unholy hand against his liege Lord!—away with him to the lowest dungeon of yon convent. On the morrow he shall be carried to Florence, there to answer for his treason!"

Unarmed and weaponless Adrian beheld himself at the mercy of the tyrant. The soldiers advanced,—in vain was his defence—in an instant he found himself in the hands of his foes, and as the minions bound his hands behind his back, he heard the beetle-browed Balvardo—for he was among the throng—whisper in the ear of the Duke—

"At what hour my Lord?"

"'Slife canst not do it without my bidding?—When all in the convent is still—at midnight let it be done!—See to't!"

"Aye, aye, my Lord, at midnight it shall be done!"

"And the Bridal," cried the Duke, turning to the Ladye Annabel, as she rested in the arms of the Countess. "The hour after midnight shall witness the joyous scene—the marriage of the Duke and his betrothed!"

CHAPTER THE THIRD.

THE DEATH BOWL.

THE FOOTSTEPS OF THE RAVISHER STARTLE THE SILENCE OF THE MAIDEN'S CELL, WHILE ADRIAN PREPARES FOR HIS DOOM IN THE VAULTS BELOW.

IT was in a lone chamber, where the dark walls, unrelieved by tapestry or wainscotting, were rendered yet more sad and gloomy by the fitful flashes of a taper, placed upon a small table of blackened oak.

The sable hangings of the couch standing in one corner, the floor of stone, wearing the same dead and leaden hue, the massive furniture of the room, and the grotesque carvings ornamenting the heavy pillars, all were in unison with the grave-like silence of the air, which seemed heavy with doom and burdened with death.

In the centre of the apartment, her white robes loosely flowing around her peerless form, her fair and rounded arms upraised, her head slightly inclined to one side, her cheek, now warm with hope, now pale with fear, stood the Ladye Annabel. Her hair of sunshine luxuriance was swept back over her neck and shoulders, while her bosom rose in the light, and her breath came thick and fast, the convulsive gasps, breaking the death-like silence of the apartment, with an echo of strange emphasis.

Sleep had fled from her eyelids. She arose and watched, she knew not why, but still she watched and trembled as she listened to the slightest sound.

"I listen, I tremble, and my heart is chilled with a nameless fear," murmured the Ladye Annabel, pacing the dark floor of the apartment with indecisive and hurried steps. "The hour wears slowly on, the fatal hour after midnight, when this unrelenting Duke will claim my hand, this hand already given to another, by the minister of Heaven! Holy Mary! behold the bridal—a lonely cell, hidden in the depths of this fearful monastery, the altar of black, the dark-robed monk, the tyrant-Duke and the victim; the time, the hour after the bell has tolled midnight, no hope, no aid, afar from human consolation, or the voice of human friend—such will be the second bridal of Annabel, wife of Adrian Di Albarone!"

She paused with an involuntary thrill of fear, as the vivid details of the picture rose before her mental vision, and then came another thought of horror— *the bride must be widowed ere she weds a second time.*

While dark and fearful imaginings haunted her soul, and well nigh crazed her brain, the fair and gentle Ladye Annabel felt a strange and deadening sleep stealing over her frame, and with a half-muttered prayer to the Virgin, she sank slumbering on the couch, the hangings of sable closing over her form, and concealing her from the sight.

All is silent within the cell. Low, suppressed sounds break from distant parts of the monastery, half-heard shrieks, and deep-muttered groans. For a dreary half hour, the cell is left to silence and solitude; when a distant footstep is heard, then a strange echo runs along the corridors of the Convent, and the small door of the lonely room, grating on its hinges slowly opens, and a Figure, buried in the folds of a sweeping robe of black, and bearing a small lamp of iron in an extended hand, stalks cautiously along the floor of stone.

The Figure paused with a trembling and indecisive movement in the centre of the floor, and then a face flushed by wine, and ruddy with excitement, was thrust from the folds of the robe of black.

"All silent and still," exclaimed a voice, indistinct with wine. "An half hour of midnight—the sleeping potion has taken effect! It has, by St. Antonia!"

He approached the bedside, and with the trembling hand of a coward, flung back the sable hangings of the couch. The light of his lamp, fell vividly upon the form of the sleeping maiden, as she reclined on the sable furs covering the couch, while her flowing robes, white as the undriven snow, gave a strange contrast to the ebony darkness of the bed.

"I' faith she is beautiful—*eh, Aldarin? Faugh! I forgot—the man is dead!* That bloom upon her cheek—'tis like the opening rose. How soft that heave of the bosom as it rises from the folds of the white robe—*torn to pieces by wild horses*—that arm, with the dress falling softly around its outlines, the small hand, the tapering fingers—*a most accursed fate*—and the attitude, the cheek reclining on the arm, the form laid so carelessly along the couch, the feet, small, delicate—*torn into a thousand fragments, an arm here, a leg there, and*—By the Saints I must e'en crave a kiss of this sleeping beauty—"

And stooping slowly over the bed, with the lamp extended in one hand, the Duke glanced nervously around the room, and then with a rude grasp of the flaxen tresses, he wound the other around the maiden's neck, his unholy hands touched her virgin bosom, with its globes of beauty heaving and throbbing as his fingers pressed the snow-white skin, while his sensual lips, steaming with wine, were pressed upon her unstained cheek, his grasp growing closer, and his eyes gloating over the Ladye's face and form, as that kiss of pollution rested on her cheek.

"Ha—ha!—the sleeping potion,—she is mine—she is mine. The braggart Adrian hugs his death in the vaults below—I gather his bride to my arm in the cell above. Ha—ha—the sleeping potion!"

No thought of mercy, no whispering of pity, no silent pleading of right, for a moment restrained the purpose of the ravisher.

He gathered her form closer to that breast which had never been the home of one ennobling thought, he wound his hand around her neck; again was her bosom and cheek polluted by the plague-spot of his touch.

"She is mine!" chuckled the ravisher. "Mine, and none other than mine!"

The Ladye Annabel murmured in that fatal sleep, she tossed her rounded arms wildly to and fro; the potion was in her veins, and around her heart, and the nightmare on her soul.

Another start, and she awoke.

She slowly unclosed her large blue eyes, she fixed their glance upon the flushed countenance of the ravisher, with a look that went to his very soul, and caused the arm that encircled her form to tremble like a leaf tossed to and fro by the wind.

"Murderer!"

The solitary word broke from her lips, and her look of wild gaze was again fixed upon his face. He trembled before her glance—he quailed like a whipped hound—he unloosed his hold.

"I am not," he muttered, springing backward from the couch. "It was not me. He is not dead; he lives—"

"Murderer!" she again murmured, in that low, deep-toned voice, while her face of calm and dreamy beauty was stamped with a weird expression that awed the ravisher to the very soul.

"Even now thy evil angel writes thee liar, in the book of thy misdeeds. Even now thy victim writhes in the throes of death within the vaults below; ay, ay, beneath thy very feet he dies. Why stand ye over the corse? Doth not the pale face and the cold brow fright ye? On whom is fixed the glare of those stony eyes—on whom? On thee, murderer, on thee; on thee they glare with the accusing glance of death!"

"She is crazed! Save me, all good saints—she is crazed! She sweeps toward me with a measured stride! Great God! she walks not—she glides slowly on; she moves like a spirit—a thing of air!"

He shrunk back, cringing before the glance of those eyes from which all reason had fled; he shrunk back step by step as she advanced, awed by the upraised arms, with the robes of white waving slowly to and fro; awed by the supernatural look visible in every line of the face of the Ladye Annabel, and in a moment found himself leaning for support against a dark stone pillar of the cell.

"Murderer!" she murmured, looking him full in the face. "I hear thy victim groan, I hear him writhe. Look ye, good angels, he denies it, and look, look how the red blood drops from his trembling hands!"

With that look which filled him with involuntary horror, she glided backward step by step, she reached the small door of the cell, and flung it open with her outspread hands.

"He denies it, he denies it; and the blood—ha, ha, ha!—hark how it patters on the floor!"

With that low, muttered laugh which chilled his very blood, for it was the laugh of madness, the Ladye Annabel again awed the Duke of Florence—the ravisher in heart—with her gaze, and then springing through the cell door, her form, with its waving robes of snow, was lost to his sight.

He saw her form no more, but a low muttered laugh came whispering along the galleries of the monastery, and half-formed words broke on his ear.

"Where is now the ravisher, flushed with wine and maddened with lust; where is now the proud Duke, haughtily attired in robes of price, with dishonor on his heart, and the foul purpose on his soul?"

Crouching against the wall, trembling in every limb, his eyes vacant with terror, his whiskered jaw half dropped upon his heart, his hand still nervously grasping the iron lamp, he listens to the low, muttered laugh creeping to his ear from the far distant corridors; he listens and shakes with fear, but says no word.

Along the dark galleries she flees, filling the old arches with echoes of that low muttered laugh; through the midnight passages she winds, stairways she ascends, and her delicate feet descend the dampened steps of stone; alone, in darkness, and in nameless fear, she glides on her flight of terror.

The cool air sweeps over her fevered brow, the dampness of the atmosphere chills her bosom, and by slow degrees the flight of madness, caused by the drugged potion, passed from her soul, and the Ladye Annabel is restored to reason and to thought.

Oh! fearful reason, oh! terrible thought, to which madness were joy, insanity, in its wildest flight, happiness the most intense.

"The bride must be widowed, ere she weds a second time!"

She rushed on, never heeding the darkness; she rushed on, never heeding the cold. She might save him yet; oh! even yet she might save him.

And through the dark passages of that deserted part of the monastery she wound, until her hands, extended on either side, touched the opposite walls, wet with moisture, and crawling with vermin; when the echo of the arches, succeeded by a dead, deafening murmur, told Annabel that she strode along a confined corridor, far under ground, growing narrow and yet narrower at every step.

A moment passed, and her extended hands were met by waving folds of tapestry, that swept across her path, and terminated the narrow corridor. Thrusting her hands eagerly among the hangings, she turned them suddenly aside, and started back with surprise, as a broad belt of light was thrown along the gloomy passage. With hushed breath and a throbbing heart, she gazed beyond the hangings of dark leather, and while her blue eyes dilated with wonder and fear, she beheld a strange and startling scene.

Two figures were kneeling upon the floor of an apartment, narrow and confined, as regards dimensions, and square in shape, hung with gorgeous folds of embroidered tapestry, dark-green in hue, with matting of strange pattern and curious device, brought from the far Eastern lands, strewn over the pavement of the room. The only object that broke the uniformity of the place, was a dark robe flung over some massive body in an obscure corner.

The light, clear and brilliant in its flame, placed on the matting between the kneeling men, threw its vivid beams on each face and form, over every line of their features, over every point of their apparel.

The Ladye Annabel stifled an expression of surprise which rose to her lips at the vision of this luxuriously furnished cell, in the midst of gloom and damp, and then with a writhing heart took in the details of this strange picture.

One of the kneeling figures was a soldier, the other was a monk.

The soldier, with his muscular hand laid on his bent knee, grasped a massive sword; his beetle brow surmounted by stiff and matted hair, giving a darker expression to his small and ferret-like eyes; while his companion, robed in the dark attire of a monk, with a pale, solemn face, lighted by the glare of an eye that seemed to dilate and burn, looked upon the man-at-arms with a glance meant to read more than the rugged visage—meant to read his very soul.

The Ladye Annabel listened to their low and muttered conversation with her very heart mounting to her throat.

"Thou wilt do it—eh, Albertine? Thou knowest my orders, sir monk?"

"The steel or the bowl?"

"The same, by the fiend! The hour—when the clock of the tower strikes twelve. He said so—thou knowest whom I mean. Why that dark and bitter smile? Blood o' th' Turk, monk, that smile shows thy white teeth—I like it not!"

"Nay, good Balvardo, be not angered with me. I was but painting a quiet picture to my fancy. Our victim, his eyes rolling in the death-struggle, his blue lips whitened with foam, his arms outstretched with the last convulsive spasm, and then—ha, ha!—the music of the death rattle! 'Tis excellent, i'faith, the picture—ha, ha, ha!"

"Look ye, monk or devil, whate'er ye be, I'm your man, when a good deed of cut-and-thrust is to be done, and the wretch is despatched with a blow. But as for this merry-making over the dead, I like it not. Blood o' Mahound, not a whit of it! I can wet my sword in a man's blood as nicely as your next man, but it likes me not to wet my tusks with the vile puddle, and grin while the red drops fall from my lips. No more o' your death grins, monk, or—'s death!—we quarrel!"

"Ho—ho—ho! so the humor suits ye not, *honest* Balvardo. Dost know the depth of the sea, or the number of the millions slain by old Death? Then know the hate I bear *my* victim; then count the lives I would crush in my revenge, had he as many as the millions trampled under the feet of Death! Is't not cause for merriment, *good* Balvardo?"

"Look ye, sir monk, thou hast ever been known as the prime tool of his grace,—'s life! I should mention no names,—and therefore do I resign my part in this night's work to thy hands. When 'tis done, thou knowest—"

"Where shall I place the body?"

"Here!" cried the hoarse voice of the soldier, and the Ladye Annabel saw him rise; she beheld him striding across the matted floor, toward an obscure corner of the apartment; she beheld him as he placed his rough hand upon the dark robe flung over the rising object.

"Here let him rest," he cried, raising the robe, "and rest forever!"

The Ladye Annabel beheld a sight that gathered the big drops of sweat thick as the death dew on her forehead. Her heart was swelled to bursting, and she turned away from the sight for a single moment, with the impulse of overpowering horror.

When she looked again, the black cloth was again resting on that object of terror, while Balvardo was advancing toward the monk with his usual heavy and measured stride.

"Hast aught to hold the wine, *good* Balvardo?"

"In yonder closet thou wilt find the wine. Here is—curse this cloak, how its folds tangle about my body!—here is the goblet."

The Ladye Annabel felt the death-like feeling of ice creeping around her heart; and as she looked, she thought she beheld the monk Albertine grow pale with horror, while his compressed lip seemed to tell a story of fearful yet hushed emotion.

The goblet held forth in the hand of the Sworder, was the goblet of gold with which the poisoner of the Red Chamber had administered death to the lips of Julian, Lord of Albarone.

"Man!" exclaimed Albertine, with a blazing eye and livid lip, "how came this goblet—this death-bowl—in thy possession?"

"'Slife! Dost not know the story? One of the witnesses who gave testimony against that—that—I mean *he* who sleeps in yonder chamber—received this goblet as a mark of the accuser's gratitude. I was that witness. Blood o' th' Turk, there goes the clock—one, two, three. Sir monk, to thy duty."

"Father of mercy, he is false at last!"

And as the words broke from the Ladye Annabel's lips, she beheld the monk take the goblet in his hands; she beheld him empty a paper filled with white powder into its depths.

She could look no more; a cold, icy feeling seemed to freeze the very blood around her heart; her limbs refused their support; she sank slowly down upon the damp floor, and yet the words spoken in the adjoining room came to her ear like the echo of far-off shouts.

"Four, five, six. Monk, wilt delay all night? To thy victim!"

The monk strode across the cell, holding the goblet under his robe; he approached a spot where the tapestried hangings, slightly swept aside, disclosed the entrance into another room.

"Adrian," whispered the monk, "dost sleep?"

"Sleep!" echoed a hollow voice from the inner cell. "Sleep, when there is fever in my brain, and fire in my heart! Dost jest, good Albertine?"

"Nay nay, Adrian, I jest not. I have a sleeping potion which will give thee rest."

"The rest of the grave, in the arms of the skeleton-god," muttered Balvardo, with a low chuckle.

"Would that thy potion could minister sleep eternal," spoke the hollow voice, and a hasty footstep was heard. "And yet I would not die yet—no, no! She still lives. I would not die, save in her arms, and by her side!"

And as the voice sounded strange and hollow through the cell, the tapestry rustled, and Adrian Di Albarone stood before the monk.

Adrian Di Albarone it was, but the manly form was bent with chains, the black velvet attire of the student was soiled and torn; while the faded countenance, the sunken cheek, the lips compressed, the hollow eye-sockets, and the quick and fiery eye, all told a tale of the agony of years endured within the compass of a single hour.

He stood before the monk, and his chains clanked as he stood, while his wild eye drank in each line of Albertine's visage.

"You spoke of a soothing potion, good Albertine."

"Seven, eight, nine," muttered Balvardo.

The monk spoke not a word; he strode to the closet—he seized the flask of wine—he filled the goblet to the brim.

"Drink, Adrian," he cried, "drink, and be refreshed!"

Adrian raised the goblet to his mouth with his chained right hand—he wet his lips with the ruddy wine; and then, as if seized by some fearful spell, he stood motionless as death, while his right arm straightened slowly out from his body, with the hand convulsively clutching the bowl of death.

"It is, it is!" he shrieked. "It is the goblet of the Red Chamber! God of Heaven, what means this mystery? Speak, Albertine. Wouldst thou betray me?"

"Ten!" meanwhile continued Balvardo, in the background.

"Adrian!" cried the monk, starting back with a solemn gesture, "I stand upon the verge of the cliff of Time; beneath me roll the surges of that shoreless ocean which men name ETERNITY! Ere the morrow's dawn, I leap from the cliff; the surges of that awful sea will bear me on—on to the vast Unknown! Thinkest thou I would betray thee? Drink, and be refreshed."

"Eleven, twelve! the time is up!" soliloquized the sworder.

"I drink," cried Adrian, with a wild gesture, "I drink; for thy words are truth, and thine eye bears no falsehood in its glance! I drink the goblet of the Red Chamber to the dregs!"

A shriek that might never be forgotten rang through the corridor and chamber, and a slight form, arrayed in robes of white came rushing from the folds of the tapestry.

Adrian beheld the dreamy face of the Ladye Annabel, her cheek pale as the robes she wore, while, with glaring eye and voice of horror, she shrieked:

"Drink not—in God's name do not drink—the bowl is drugged with death!"

He flung the bowl aside, but ere it left his hand it was received in the quick grasp of the monk; he raised his chained hands on high, and ere they were lowered, his Bride lay panting on his breast!

Oh, where is the magic of human words that may picture the deep and fearful interest of that meeting, the gush of contending feelings, the rapture sparkling in the eye and beaming from the lip, the heart all pulsation, the blood all fire, the arms flung convulsively round each other's neck, the look of the Doomed, the long, last, lingering look upon the face of the beloved, her upturned eyes, her cheek now crimson and now snow, her tresses of gold waving over her robes of white, and her form of beauty flung over his bosom, with every vein swelling with delight, every nerve quivering with joy!

They meet as lovers meet, when, standing on the opposing rocks of Time and Destiny, they fling their arms across the chasm, nor heed the vast eternity that yawns below, ready to engulf and destroy.

"Drink not, oh, Adrian, drink not—the bowl is drugged with death!"

"The time is up," muttered the hoarse voice of Balvardo—"The guards are within call, good monk, an' he refuses the dose."

"Adrian Di Albarone," cried the monk, fixing his full and solemn eyes upon the chained knight, "drink the bowl, I implore thee! By the memory of the Cell of the Doomed, by the memory of the Chapel of the Rocks, by the memory of the perils we have shared, the deaths we dared together, in the name of thy father, whose ghost now looks down upon thee, in His name, most solemn and most dread, I adjure thee—drain the goblet to the dregs!"

"Dark and mysterious man," cried Adrian, sharing the wild glance of Albertine, "give me the bowl, I drink——"

"Adrian, for my sake touch it not—poison nestles like a snake within its depths!"

"Hold me not, Annabel—grasp not my arm——"

"For the sake of God, oh, do not, do not drink!"

"I must, I must! It is not thy hand, Albertine, that gives the bowl—it is the hand of Fate, thrust from yon blackening cloud, which all my life has thrown its shadow over my path! Give me the bowl—though ten thousand deaths were darting from each sparkle of the wine, still—I drink, and drain the goblet to the dregs!"

In vain the upraised arm of the Ladye Annabel, in vain her look of fear, her voice of horror!

As she clung to his chained arms, he raised the goblet to his lips, he drained it to the dregs.

"He smiles," muttered Balvardo, "the monk smiles as he gives the death-bowl! I see not his cloven foot, nor do I see his horns—not a whit o' 'em. Else might I suspect the devil were lurking in yon monkish robe."

Adrian handed the goblet to the monk.

Albertine received it with a deep and meaning smile.

Scarce had the hand of Adrian been extended in the act, than his arm fell like a weight of lead to his side, and Annabel felt her lover leaning heavily upon her shoulder, while her fair arms might scarce stay him in his fall to the floor.

"Monk," cried Adrian, as, sinking upon one knee, he fixed his ghastly eyes upon the face of Albertine; "monk I trusted thee, and thou art false!"

"His brow is cold," murmured the Ladye Annabel, as, sinking on her knees by his side, she supported Adrian's head upon her virgin bosom. "See! the big drops of the death-dew stands out from his forehead—and this, monk, this is thy work!"

As the terrible look of the dying man met his eye, Albertine seemed struggling with some terrible pang, but when the words of Annabel and her look of intense agony came like a death-bolt to his heart, he hurriedly advanced, he looked at the group, he spoke in a voice tremulous with agitation, yet deep and solemn in its every accent—

"Ye scorn me now, fair Ladye, and raise your hands in a gesture of reproach most terrible to bear; yet the day will come, when the voice of scorn will be changed to the sound of pity, when those very hands will strew fresh flowers over my grave!"

"Has —— given up its model of devils!" muttered Balvardo, in the background. "'Slife, I can murder a man in hot blood or cold blood, but as for this heaping taunt on taunt—I like it not—by the Blood o' th' Turk!"

"He is dead—cold and dead," murmured the Ladye Annabel, as she gazed upon the pallid face of Adrian. "He does not breathe; Mother of Heaven, I cannot feel the beating of his heart!"

Ere the words had passed her lips, the dying man sprang with one bound to his feet; and while his bloodshot eyes rolled ghastlily from face to face, he flung his arms aloft, and tottered across the chamber, laughing wildly and with maniac glee, as he pointed to the dark object rising from the floor, covered with the folds of the dark robe, that swept over its surface like a pall of death.

"Monk, behold—behold the doom of Adrian of Albarone!" he shouted with a wild and husky voice, as he stooped, with a sudden movement, and tore the robe from the object which it concealed. "There, there stands the assassin, here the victim, and—ha, ha, ha!—*behold the coffin!*"

He swayed heavily from side to side; he flung his arms hurriedly aloft in the vain effort to preserve his balance, and then, with a fixed and staring eye, he gazed upon the face of Albertine with a look that froze his blood.

"Monk, I trusted thee, and thou art false!"

The sound of a falling body echoed around the room, and the lifeless form of Adrian Di Albarone lay extended across the coffin, while the out-spread hands clutched the dark panels with the convulsive grasp of death.

"Wait one hour," muttered the monk to Balvardo; "wait one hour, ere thou bearest the corse to the grave. 'Tis now the midnight hour: an hour from this time, the Duke—ha, ha!—will wed his bride; an hour from this time, and thou mayst bear the corse to the grave!"

"Be it so," growled Balvardo. "Then this pestilent Adrian will trouble me no more! Blood o' Mahound, the grave is a wondrous sure prison; it needs nor bolt nor bar; old Death stands jailor at its door!"

"Ladye!" cried the monk, as he advanced to the side of the Ladye Annabel, raising the maiden, whose senses seemed stupified with horror, from the floor, "behold the corse of thy love! Advance, Ladye—rest thee by its side—gather the head of the corse to thy bosom! Watch beside the corse one hour—a single hour—and let nor man nor devil wrest the lifeless body from thy grasp!"

The Ladye Annabel opened her large blue eyes with a stare of vacant wander, and smiled as she gathered the head of the corpse to her bosom, twining her fair and delicate lingers in the golden hair of the dead.

CHAPTER THE FOURTH.

THE CELL OF ST. ARELINE.

A LAMP of iron, all rusted and time-eaten, suspended from the arched ceiling of a small apartment of the convent of St. Benedict, reserved in especial for strangers, threw a dim light over the figure of his grace of Florence, reposing on a velvet couch, and upon the blazing armor of the attending men-at-arms, who waited beside their lord.

A smile, full of self-satisfaction, rested upon the lip of the Duke, and a glance full of agreeable fancies lit up his eye, as he contemplated the fulfillment of all his schemes.

"The forward boy punished for his insolence,"—thus ran his musings— "done to death for the treasonable act of lifting his hand against his liege lord—this accomplished, the fair Annabel is mine, and with her I acquire the rich domains of Albarone. A servitor but a moment since bears me intelligence that she has recovered from her madness. By'r Ladye, my exhausted coffers shall be replenished to the brim! Ha—ha ha! Then I shall war and conquer. Why not *I* as well as others of my rank and power? I shall war—I shall conquer—I shall—"

"My Lord Duke," exclaimed a sentinel, thrusting his head from between the folds of a sable curtain that hung across the apartment, dividing it from an adjoining chamber, within whose walls were the followers of his grace. "My Lord Duke, a monk of the convent craves audience with your grace—shall I admit him?"

"Aye, let him enter."

And in a moment, there stood before the Duke a monk attired in the dark robe of his order: his hood was drawn over his face, and, with depressed head and folded arms, he seemed to wait the commands of his grace of Florence.

"Thy errand, sir monk?"

"I come by the bidding of the Father Abbot, to lead thee to the cell of the blessed St. Areline."

"Ah! I remember me. As I dismounted at the gate of the Monastery, the reverend abbot told me that it had been a custom, from time past memory, for all strangers visiting the holy house of St. Benedict, to pass an hour in the cell of this saint—St. Areline, methinks she is styled. Further, he told me the saint has the power of revealing future events. Is't so, holy father?"

"Even so, my Lord Duke. When besought, on bended knee, in the silence of midnight, the form of the blessed saint appears fired with supernatural life: her eyes flash and her lips move, and the doom of the suppliant—whether for good or for evil—is revealed."

"At midnight, say'st thou? 'Tis a lone hour. By'r our Ladye, but the evil one may have something to do with the matter."

"That may not be, my Lord Duke. The holy Areline died in the odor of sanctity. The scorner and the outcast of heaven alone doubt her holiness and power. For three centuries hath the fame of St. Areline been sounded abroad, and now it were sin unpardonable to say aught against her sacred name."

"Lead on, holy father; in God's name, lead on: I'll follow thee. Hugo! I say, Hugo!"

The face of the ill-looking sentinel with the squinting eye, appeared among the folds of the sable curtain.

"Hugo, where is Balvardo, thy comrade—eh? Speak quickly—where is Balvardo?"

The sinister eye of the sentinel squinted yet more fearfully; he looked confusedly round, and stammered forth:

"My Lord Duke, he is—he is—"

He paused suddenly, and finished the sentence by pointing downward with the forefinger of the right hand, with a sort of diving motion.

"Ah! I had forgotten *that*, good Hugo! Thou wilt attend me, vassals; and ye, sirs, shall also accompany me to this midnight ceremony."

While he thus spoke, the monk threw open a door at the end of the apartment opposite the sable curtain, and, followed by the Duke, attended by Hugo and the two men-at-arms, with torches in their hands, he presently was traversing a long gallery, with his head still depressed and his arms still folded on his breast.

"By'r our Lady, but thou art wondrous chary of thy good looks!—eh, sir monk?"

"It becomes not a sinner like me to be otherwise than humble. It becomes not a poor brother of St. Benedict to assume an erect port and a bold countenance before—*his grace of Florence!*"

"Well said, by my troth! Whither art leading me, holy father? Ha! a stairway; it extends above us as though it had no end. Ugh! how those torches glare—how gloomy these arches seem! Lead on, sir monk!"

Ascending the stairway, they found themselves in a winding gallery, with floor of stone, low arching roof, and narrow walls. Through the mazes of this passage they swiftly wound, and presently they stood at the foot of another stairway.

"By St. Peter!" exclaimed the Duke, "but these passages are like the windings of a witch's den. How runs the night, holy father?"

"When I left the halls of the convent, the sands of the hour glass had fallen to within an half hour of midnight."

"Ah! we shall be just in time for the trial of St. Areline's power. Another gallery! By'r Ladye, but this is wondrous! In the name of thy patron, St. Benedict, I adjure thee, monk, tell me are we not near our journey's end?"

"See'st thou yon oaken door that terminates the gallery? The oaken door with large panels, and topped by arches of dark stone? There an' it please thee, my Lord Duke, must thou leave thy attendants, and alone, and in the dark, we will enter the cell of the blessed St. Areline."

"How? Leave my attendants? 'Alone,' sayst thou? 'In the dark'? Beshrew me, sir monk, but this saint of thine is somewhat difficult of audience!"

"The reward she offereth is beyond price. A knowledge of the future—the dim and shadowy future! Thou shall behold thy coming deeds written in characters of light; thy future conquests shall spread themselves before thee like the varying beauties of a lovely landscape. Thou shall—"

"'Slife! thou talkest well! Enough: we stand before the oaken door. Enter—I'll follow thee!"

The monk passed his hand over one of the panels of the huge door, and pressing a secret spring, a narrow passage was opened, through which the brother of St. Benedict disappeared, followed by his grace of Florence.

"There they go," Hugo exclaimed as the panel closed. "There they go upon their madcap adventure. The saints save me from all such folly!"

"And me, comrade," cried the tallest of the men-at-arms, letting the sheath of his sword fall heavily upon the pavement of stone.

"I say amen to your prayers," exclaimed the other, looking very wise in the torchlight.

"Ha! what noise is that?" cried Hugo, as he gave a sudden start.

"'Tis down in the court-yard," exclaimed the tall man-at-arms. "Hark! 'tis the clashing of swords—the rattling of spears—the clashing of armor."

"Shouts, too!" cried the other soldier, "Ha! war cries! 'Slife! it sounds as if they were battering down the gates! Hark! again! and again!"

And thus, while the sounds waxed louder, and the cries grew fiercer in the court-yard below, the men-at-arms, and their companion, Hugo, waited, with the utmost impatience the coming of their lord.

An hour passed.

The Duke had not appeared. The tall man-at arms fixed his eyes upon the massive door, and struck the secret panel with his spear, urged by all the vigor of his stalwart arm. Another and another blow. The wood yielded, and the open space gave passage to the man-at-arms, who forced his way through, followed by his comrade and Hugo of the sinister eye.

Their torches flashed upon the walls of a square apartment, with floor and roof of stone. No living creature was there. A small, narrow door gave entrance to another apartment. Three pillars of time-worn stone supported the arched roof, and divided the place into three sides, with floor of variegated stone. One side of the apartment, was concealed by a curtain of sable velvet.

This Hugo hurriedly drew, and in an instant his ungainly figure was reflected in a vast mirror of dazzling steel, which, reaching to the arched ceiling above, twice the height of a man, extended on either side as wide as it was high. Around the apartment was no sign of passage way or secret door; all was bare and rugged stone, and the place was without bench, stool, couch, or furniture of any kind.

"By'r Ladye!" shouted Hugo, "that monk was the—devil, and he has run away with our lord! W-h-e-w!"

And the three fairly shook with mingled surprise and terror, which was presently increased to alarm and horror by the clashing of arms in the outer apartment.

CHAPTER THE FIFTH.

THE WONDERS OF ST. ARELINE.

NO sooner had the oaken panel closed behind him, than the Duke found himself cautiously groping his way in utter darkness, being guided by the sound of the footsteps of the Monk.

Presently the Monk laid hand upon the Duke's shoulder.

"Kneel, mortal, kneel," he exclaimed in a voice which the Duke thought wondrously changed of a sudden, "kneel and behold the wonders of St. Areline! Speak not upon the peril of thy immortal soul!"

Upon the pavement of stone the Duke sank down, and the Monk began to murmur certain mysterious words, in a low, yet deep tone, and thus he continued for the space of the fourth part of an hour, when a light was seen dimly gleaming at one end of the place, and presently another and another, and gradually increasing in radiance they soon appeared to the wondering eyes of the Duke, dancing within the surface of a vast mirror of dazzling steel.

Strange it was that although the meteors,—for such they seemed—grew more brilliant every moment, and shed a more intense brightness along the surface of the mirror in which they shone, yet not a ray of light escaped to illumine the apartment, and the figures of the Duke and the Monk were wrapt in mid-night shadow.

And now soft clouds of feathery mist began to roll within the surface of the mirror, and the meteors gradually faded away into an universal brightness, which like the mellow beams that herald the coming day, poured a flood of rosy light over the tumultuous chaos within the dazzling steel.

"Behold!" cried the Monk, "behold the blessed St. Areline!"

A dim and ghastly form arose from amid the rolling clouds, far in the distance; nearer it drew and nearer, and presently the outlines of a nun, attired in the solemn hood, and sweeping robes of white, became clear and perceptible.

Advancing to the front of the mirror with a gliding motion, the hands of the spectre were folded upon its breast, and the hood of white, hung drooping over its face.

The Duke trembled with terror, and his brow was wet with large drops of moisture that oozed from his shivering skin.

"*Mortal!*" exclaimed a voice, soft as the tones of a spirit of light,—"*mortal, what wouldst thou know?*" The voice came from the shrouded face of the spectre.

With tremulous voice, and as if urged by some invisible power, the Duke shrieked forth—

"I would know my doom—I would know my fate!"

The hood fell back from the head of the Spectre, and its arms slowly extended!

"O Jesu!" shrieked the Duke,—"Look, look! the skeleton hands, the fleshless skull, the hollow eyes! One hand grasps a cross, and one a grinning skull.—Look, look!"

"Speak not!" whispered the Monk, "speak not upon pain of eternal doom!"

The voice again sounded through the cell.

"Dost thou seek in the name of the Holy One? Dost thou ask trusting in his Saints?"

"I do!"

"Thou art answered!" and the bare and hideous bones of the spectre head were covered, quick as a flash of light, with ruddy and healthy flesh, the hollow sockets gleamed with dark and brilliant orbs, and the skeleton hands glowed with life, as a skin of rosy loveliness shrouded the disjointed bones.

"Thou art answered!" and as the spectre whispered the words, a skeleton form came gliding along the mirror, holding an hour-glass in its fleshless hand.

"*Behold!*" exclaimed the vision pointing to the things of graves, "*behold thy doom?*"

A shriek of horror came from the lips of the Duke.

"O, horror of horrors!" he shouted, "It is the form of Death!—Look! look! Behold! He turns, he turns with a ghastly smile—he points to the hour glass!" The tyrant, assassin and betrayer started forward with every nerve quivering with the intensity of his terror. "O God of Heaven! *The Sands of the glass are run!*"

"Ha!" shrieked the Monk, with a wild yell, that sounded like the howl of a dying war-horse. "Heaven wills it, thy sands are run, thy doom is fixed!"

A stream of light poured around the cell, brighter than the blaze of the noon-day sun, and a clap of thunder shook the pillars to their very centre.

With his eyes rolling with affright, the Duke glanced upward, and beheld the Monk standing erect, his arms outstretched, and his hood cast backward from his face.

"O God! *Thou* here! Albertine—thou here!"

"Ha! It is *I!*—Thy fate—thy curse—thy doom!"

The Duke felt himself seized in a grasp of iron, and hurriedly dragged along the pavement of stone.

In a moment he heard the sharp spring of a door closing behind him, and brushing his hand over his eyes, to restore his fading vision, he looked around.

A spur of the whitened steep on which the convent was founded, arising some twenty feet above the body of the mass of rock, was imbedded in the darkened wall of the tower, with its summit extending in a platform some three feet square, toppling over the dark abyss below.

Level as the sun-dial and smooth as polished steel, the summit of the rock, projecting from the tower, might scarce afford a resting place for footstep of human thing. In silence and in awe the Duke gazed around.

Above was the moonlit sky, below far, far below, a hundred fathoms down sunk the dark and shadowy abyss, separated from the waters of the lake by a ridge of rocks, that arose along the shores of the mountain tarn, overlooking the sullen blackness of the impenetrable void, on one side, while on the other towered and frowned above the walls of the gloomy convent.

Gazing hurriedly around, the Duke beheld the walls of the Monastery, extending on either side of the tower, in whose stones the platform-rock was imbedded, all smooth, even and moss-grown; at his back leading into the cell of St. Areline, was the secret door, fashioned in complete resemblance to the wall around, fast closed and secured, while high overhead arose the dark and frowning fabric of the tower, its rugged outline, rising like a thing of omen into the dim blue of the midnight sky.

This platform of rock was never looked upon by the peasantry of the valley, save with wonder and with awe—a thousand dark traditions, named the tower as the scene of many a deed of murder, and a thousand legends dyed the platform stone with the crimson drops of innocent blood.

"Where am I," shrieked the Duke with a low, murmured whisper. "It is a dream, a dream of horror!"

"Thou art in the temple of my vengeance!" the response came hissing between the clenched teeth of the monk. "Behold its roof, yon sky, the walls, the boundless horizon, the floor, the wide earth; and the place of sacrifice, yon bottomless abyss!"

CHAPTER THE SIXTH.

THE WATCH BESIDE THE DEAD.

"ALL—all is dark!" the voice broke wild and whisperingly through the midnight gloom of the place—"I have been dreaming—ah, me—a sad and darksome dream! Methought Adrian lay cold and dead in my arms, while my hand was entwined in the locks of his clustering hair, as they fell over his lifeless face. It was a dream, a fearful dream—yet—mother of heaven—do I still dream, or is this darkness real?"

She extended her hands, she passed them hurriedly along the floor, where her form lay prostrate, and as she thus wildly sought to grasp the form so lately reposing in her arms, she exclaimed with a murmured shriek—

"It flashes on me! All is real—The coffin and the corse, the assassin and the bowl of death—all is dark and terrible reality!"

Passing her cold and stiffened hands, slowly along her forehead, the Ladye Annabel endeavored to recall the tragedy of that fearful night, in all its details of horror, and as scene after scene, action after action, word succeeding word, came back to her memory, another fearful mystery passed like a shadow over her brain.

"The corse reposed in these arms—where is it now? Who hath stolen the body of the dead from my embrace? And the coffin—it is gone! They have borne him to the grave!"

And as the low whispers broke from her lips, this fair and gentle creature, whose nature was soft and yielding, as is ever the nature of a *true woman*, in moments of calm and sunshine, yet susceptible of deeds of the highest courage and noblest determination, in the hour of storm and cloud arose from the floor, her frame all chilled and stiffened by the hard repose of that fearful watch, and extending her hands she wandered slowly around the chamber, seeking with hushed breath, for the coffin and the corse.

All was darkness, thick and intense darkness.

Slowly and with cautious steps she paced around the room, passing her hands along the folds of the tapestry, or extending her small and delicate foot in the effort to touch the coffin, but her search was all in vain. She wandered around the chamber, until her recollection of the particular features of the room became vague and indistinct, and at last with trembling hands and a bewildered brain, she stood erect and motionless.

"All—all is vain!" she cried—"corse and coffin are all gone. They have borne him to the grave!"

While the weary moments dragged heavily on, she stood silent and unmovable, endeavoring to catch the faintest echo of a sound, or hear the slightest whisper of a voice, but all was silent as death.

At last a distant and moaning murmur reached her ears.

Gradually though slowly it deepened into a booming sound, and at last the subterranean arches of the old convent seemed alive with gathering echoes, and the long corridors gave back the tramp of footsteps and the hum of human voices.

"They come—they come"—whispered the Ladye Annabel—"They come to bear me to the bridal!"

The bell of the convent, deep-toned and booming, rang out the hour of— one—the fatal hour after midnight.

"Strike for the Winged Leopard—strike for Albarone!" the shout came echoing along the corridors.

"Strike for Albarone and Florence!" the mingling war-cry reached the ears of the maiden. And in a moment, the tapestry, concealing the entrance to the room from which Adrian had issued ere he drank the bowl, was hurriedly thrust aside, and amid the blaze of torches, the Ladye Annabel, beheld the glare of armor and the flash of upraised swords, while the stern visage of the warrior-band were gazing upon her pale countenance and trembling form.

"Saved, by St. Withold!" shouted a soldier, springing from the crowd— "Ladye tell us, in God's name, where is the Lord Adrian?"

"They have borne him to the grave!" was the whispered and ghastly response.

The bluff soldier turned aside, and it might be noted that his blue eyes were wet with tears. In a moment he again faced the crowd of warriors.

"Behold the Queen!" he shouted, and the men-at-arms sank kneeling to the floor—"all hail the fair Ladye Annabel, Duchess of Florence!"

And the solitary chamber rung with the echo of the thunder shout—

"All hail the Fair Ladye Annabel, Duchess of Florence!"

CHAPTER THE SEVENTH.

THE COFFIN AND THE CORSE.

THE CLOCK STRIKES ONE, AND THE SWORDER SEALS HIS FATE BY A TOUCH OF THE FATAL SPRING.

FAR beneath the Convent, down in the very bosom of the earth, far beneath the chamber of the death-bowl, alone and in darkness, rested the coffin and the corse for the space of an hour, awaiting the spade and the Sexton, the priest with his prayers, and the grave with its silence.

The sound of trampling feet, broke along the silence of the earth hidden passage, and presently, through the crevices of the dungeon door, thin rays of light streamed along the cell.

Then there was drawing of bolts, and rattling of chains, and in an instant the ruddy glare of torches, revealed the ill-looking form of Balvardo, standing in the doorway, and beside him stood a short, thin old man, with slight locks of gray hair, falling upon his coarse doublet.

There was a vacant and wandering expression in his eye, while his parched lips, hanging apart, gave an idiotic appearance to his countenance. The long, talon-like fingers of his withered right hand, grasped a spade covered with rust, and eaten by time.

"Ha—ha!" laughed Balvardo. "The potion which I gave *her*, some hours ago, wrapt her in a sleep, like the slumber of old death. Blood o' the Turk, how her hands clutched the body o' the dead, when I first tried to tear it from her arms—even in her sleep she clutched it! I have him at last—sound and sure! He escaped me in the cell of the Doomed, escaped this sword in the Cavern of the Dead, and—and—now, by the fiend I have him at last!"

The Sworder advanced to the Coffin, he gazed upon the pale face of the dead, with a long and anxious look.

"He, he, he," chuckled the old man. "Why did thou hate him, noble Captain?"

"I know not," muttered Balvardo, with an absent air, "yet I always had a sneaking suspicion that one day or other, this man, now a corse, would work my death! A queer feeling always haunted me, that made me feel like the felon walking to his doom, so long as this—father-murderer remained alive! Now he is dead, but I fear him yet, and will fear him till he is safely buried i' the earth!"

"Thou wouldst cover his face with this rich, yellow earth?" sneered the ancient man,—"He, he, he! The grave hides all secrets!"

"To thy duty, Old Gibber-jabber," exclaimed Balvardo, "Here's thy man. Lay hold of him, and help me to drag the coffin to the other side of the dungeon. Pull him along—there—there!"

Throwing the coffin upon the damp earth, the old man placed a smoking lamp near the prostrate head of the corse, and then intently watched the motions of Balvardo, who was drawing the point of his sword along the surface of the earth.

"Let me do't, let me do't, most noble captain," exclaimed the old man, pushing Balvardo aside,—"for years, and years, and years, man and boy, have I wielded this good spade, here in these nice, cozy, comfortable chambers! He—he—he! To think a fellow like thee, with that miserable tool, that is unworthy to be called a—spade—to think that a stranger like thee, should think to excel me—Old Glow-worm—in laying out a grave!—He—he—he!"

"Old Glow-worm!—Ha, ha, ha!—a choice name by my soul!"

"A very good name; *they* call me so—they who bring me food every day—they poke it through the big door through which thou didst pass, most noble captain. A merry time we've had of it here—a merry time!"

"*We!*—who dost thou mean?"

"Well! Thou art a fool, beshrew me!—*we*, I and my comrades, who always receive our food at the big iron door. Here, long, long, very long, we have lived in these nice cozy chambers.—Sometimes *they* fight and kill one another—then I dig their graves! See! how nicely the rich earth turns up! This is a spade!"

Prattling after this fashion, the poor old idiot turned up the earth till he stood in a square hole about a foot in depth, when a glance at the pale visage of Adrian arrested his attention.

"He, he, he! *They always look so!*—Queer,—eh, noble captain!"

"What! hast ever had any other business of this sort?"

"Why, bless ye, most noble captain, I've put scores and scores of them under the rich, yellow earth. *They* bring 'em to me—*they* at the big iron door. This is earth for ye! Look! how the spade sinks into the mould!—He, he, he!"

"What an old devil!" muttered Balvardo to himself. "How canst thou be merry in these gloomy pits! eh, Old One!"

"Merry?—He, he, he! *Merry* didst say, why bless ye, when I and my comrades gather round our food, I am as merry as is the sound of this spade, driving into the earth! Merry! why I sing, most noble captain, I sing!"

"*Thou* sing! Ha, ha, ha! Thou, indeed!"

"Why not I, eh? Beshrew me but thou art a fool! I can sing such a right mirthful song—but they never like it—they my comrades!"

"By Saint Peter, I'll wager a stoup of wine, that thou didst never see the light of day—eh, old rat?"

"*Day!* what is that?—But for my song—here goes!"

And then busily plying the spade, in a cracked voice he sang the following words, in a sort of wild chaunt, which he occasionally varied by sounds that resembled the yell of a screech-owl.

THE SONG OF THE ANCIENT MAN.[8]

DIG THE GRAVE AND DIG IT DEEP.

Dig the grave and dig it deep—
Straight with the mattock dig each side,
Dig it low, and dig it steep—
Dig it long and dig it wide!

As he sang, the old man plunged the spade lustily into the earth, and throwing aside the large lumps of clay, he continued with great glee—

Here while nations rise and fall,
Here while ages glide,
Here wrapt within its earthy pall,
Must the crumbling corse abide!
Then raise the chaunt,
Then swell the stave,
Here's to death, all grim and gaunt,
And to his home—the grave!

He wound this up with an unnatural noise, half shriek, and half yell, and the hollow and dread dungeon arches gave back the strain.

"He, he, he!—I know a merrier catch than that! List ye, my noble captain."

He then made a motion with his hand, as if in the act of drinking, and then a shout of wild laughter sounded through the cell.

Ha, ha! Ha, ha!—Drink to the full,
Drink to the sound of the clanking bone;
Fill high with wine the fleshless skull,
And swell the toast without a moan—

Hurra! for Death with his bony hands,
Hurra! for Death with his skeleton form,
He holds the thunderbolt.—On high he stands,
He mows them down in calm or storm—

He swept his spade around with maniac glee, and then in a voice louder and shriller, while his shrunken breast heaved with the wildness of his emotion, he sang,

Then raise the chaunt,
Then swell the stave,
Here's to Death, all grim and gaunt,
And to his home—the grave.

"A brave song! Ha, ha, ha! By my faith a brave song! Where didst pick it up, Old Screech-Owl, eh?"

"Glow-worm is my name," replied the other demurely,—"Glow-worm—ah! but this is rich earth! Look! what big, lusty clumps. He, he, he! How cold and pale he looks—he that I am to bury—See!"

"He doth look cold and pale!" muttered Balvardo. "Is the grave deep enough, Devil-darkness? Let's house him in' th' earth without delay."

"The grave scarce reaches to my middle—deeper let us dig it, noble captain—deeper!"

"I tell thee, Devil-darkness, I cannot look upon the cold and stony face of the dead! Deeper thou mayest dig the grave—but the body must be hidden from sight in the meanwhile. 'Slife—I left my cloak in the vaults above, and I have no robe to throw over the coffin!"

"He—he—he, thou'rt a brave man, yet poor old Glow-worm knows more than thee! Look around the cell, most noble captain, and tell me what thou see'st!"

"I see the rough walls of stone, the roof of rock, the floor of clay. Not a whit more, by the Fiend!"

"Look again—pass thine eyes along the wall opposite yon oaken door. What see'st thou now, most noble captain?"

"I see a bolt of iron, rusted and time-eaten, projecting from the wall—"

"Wouldst know how to open a passage into the stone room, next to this cell? Move the bolt quickly to and fro, and yon massy stone will roll back into the stone-room! Thou canst lay the coffin within its walls, until the grave is deep enow."

"The bolt moves—ha! The stone, the massive stone glides from the wall—another push at the bolt! There—blood o' Mahound, I behold a dark passage into this dismal room! 'Slife! there is a current of air rushing from this open space—what may it mean?"

"Dost wish to hide the corse? Eh—most noble captain? Lay hold of t'other end o' th' coffin, and I will raise this end. We'll bear it to the stone-room!"

In a moment they raised the coffin, and bearing it toward the open space, Balvardo retreated backwards, through the passage, and in another instant was lost to view, while the foot of the coffin still projected into the dungeon-cell.

"Bear it through the passage, Glow-worm!" cried Balvardo. "In a moment we will have it laid along the floor of this dreary place!"

"It is heavy," cried the old man; "my strength fails me. Thou wilt have to bear the burden thyself, most noble captain! Glow-worm lifts no heavy burden!"

"Be it so," growled Balvardo. "Slife I like not to be alone with the dead! Slowly, slowly, drag the coffin along the floor of stone, there—it rests against the wall! Now for the grave."

"What dreary sound is that, thundering far above? Oft have I heard it, yet ne'er could tell what it might mean?"

"The Convent clock strikes—one!" muttered Balvardo. "A few moments and my reward is sure!"

"Beware the secret spring!" shrieked the old man, as though his crazed mind had been fixed by some sudden thought. "Beware the secret spring! It sticks from the floor near the very wall, where thou hast laid the coffin. An' thy foot presses the spring the stone rolls back, and—he, he, he—*thou art buried alive!*"

It was too late! Even as the old man spoke, Balvardo stumbled along the floor of the stone-room, his foot pressed the point of iron projecting from the floor, and the massive rock rolled back to its place, in the masonry of the substantial wall.

"I fear, I fear," murmured the old man, gazing around with an affrighted look; "I fear *they*," pointing above, "*they* will lash me for this! He, he, he! I bade him beware of the spring within the stone-room, and he would not. I cannot turn this bolt, the old man is not strong enough. Ha, ha, here is a torch; Glow-worm has not had a torch in his hand for years! Ho, ho, ho, the noble captain came here to bury the dead, and, ho, ho, ho, he *is buried alive!*"

CHAPTER THE EIGHTH.

THE FATE OF THE BETRAYER.

SWEETER THAN THE LOVE OF WOMAN, DEARER THAN
GLORY TO THE WARRIOR, POWER TO THE PRINCE, OR
HEAVEN TO THE DEVOTEE, IS THE CONSUMMATION OF A
LONG SOUGHT AND SILENTLY TREASURED REVENGE.

"WHERE am I?" shrieked the Duke, as he stood upon the platform of the convent tower. "'Tis a hideous dream, 'tis a fearful nightmare! Ha! my brain reels. I'll gaze no longer down the fearful abyss! Is there none to awake me, none? Horror of horrors! This demon hand will strangle me, closer and tighter it winds around my throat, ah!"

A wild laugh of intense joy came from the chest of the Monk. "I feast upon thy misery," he cried, "wretch, I banquet upon thy agony! Ha, ha, ha! *The glory of this moment I would not barter for all the joys of heaven!* Dost thou shiver, dost thou tremble, well thou mayst! Look down, far, far below! Dost see any hope there, what says the whitened precipice? Hath the dark abyss no voice? Look above, canst glean naught from the frown of the tower that is over thy doomed and devoted head? Or mayhap the secret door may afford thee consolation? Speak—thou for whose crime earth hath no word, hell no name, speak that I may feast upon the music of thy quailing voice!"

Tighter he wound his grasp around the throat of the trembling wretch, and with his dark eye flashing with all the frenzy of supernatural revenge, he shook the form of the Duke over the awful abyss.

"Is't thou, good Albertine? Hold, hold, or I shall fall. 'Tis a fearful steep! Behold, a flock of snow-white sheep are grazing in yon distant vale, they seem but as mice at this fearful height. Thou, thou wilt not harm me, good Albertine?"

"Look, look!—Behold her pale form is floating in the moonlight, her face is wan, and her look is that of despair! Ha! her glazing eyes are fixed upon thee—*thee*—her BETRAYER! She beckons me over the steep!—I come—I come!"

"Nay, good Albertine, grasp me not so tight!—Bring to mind the days when we were sworn friends—"

"*Friends?* Doomed man, the memory of former days shall but hurl accumulated torture upon thy head!—FRIENDS?—Ah! like a dream it comes over my mind! I was a peasant boy—thou didst raise me to rank and power, and I have loved ye as brother loves brother. Could my life have served thee, it would have been laid at thy feet. My life thou did'st not take. No! no! But the treasured hope of years, the glowing fancies of a musing boy, the anticipations of happiness that haunted my dreams by night, and lived in my thoughts by day; these—at one fell remorseless blow, thou did'st sweep away. It was upon *her* grave; the grave of thy victim, that one thought possessed my soul. For years and years have I planned, have I schemed, nay wept, *prayed* for the fulfilment of that thought. And now it is fulfilled. I have thee in my grasp! Think'st thou a thousand worlds would buy thy craven life? That heaven or hell would tear thee from my hand?"

Again he gave utterance to the frenzied joy of his soul in a loud wild laugh, that burst fearfully upon the midnight air.

"Albertine spare me, spare me! Take not my life."

"Spare thee? and yon pale form waving me onward? spare thee? wretch, I tell thee all nature is celebrating thy doom! The moon is sinking below the horizon, and the stars gleam through the gathering pall of darkness like funeral fires! *Spare thee?*"

"Ha! whence come those shouts! I may yet be saved!"

"Thou mayst be saved—ha—ha—ha! It gives me joy to drag thee o'er this steep, craving and hoping for life, to thy latest grasp! Look around Urbano, Duke of Florence, look around and behold the fair and beautiful earth, scene of thy crimes—nay, nay THY CRIME—behold the earth for the last time!"

It was a weird and awful scene.

The dizzy height of the platform rock, the vast azure with its boundless horizon, all beaming with the grandeur of the stars, the massive hills sweeping around the mountain-lake, darkening the clear waters with their midnight shadow, the pile of rocks uprising beyond the darkness of the unfathomable abyss, the silence and the awe that rested upon the hour, broken by the sound of far-off shouts, while on the very verge of the eastern sky, bloody and red, the full-orbed moon was sinking slowly down, casting a dim and lurid light over mountain and stream, convent and plain—all formed a scene of dark and fearful interest.

The Universe, awful and vast, seemed to hold a strange sympathy with the Revenge of Albertine the Monk, the stars gave their solemn light to the scene, and the blood-red moon lit up the funeral pile of the Doomed.

"I gaze around, 'tis an awful scene. And thou, thou wilt spare me, good Albertine?"

"As thou didst spare thy victim, when her voice rung in thy ears of stone, shrieking for pity!" The response came hissing through the clenched teeth of

Albertine! "Betrayer, I again tell thee all nature is celebrating thy doom! The moon is sinking below the horizon, and the stars gleam through the gathering pall of darkness like funeral fires!"

Thrilled with terror and appalled to the very soul, by the erect form and flashing eye of the Monk, the Duke stood trembling and quivering like a reed, on the verge of the platform rock.

"Choose the manner of thy death! Leap from the rock, or behold, I raise before thy very eyes this dagger; the dagger of the Holy Steel!"

"Thou wilt not slay me thus, good Albertine," shrieked the Duke. "Mercy—for the sake of God—mercy!"

"Thine own *mercy* I give back to thee! Leap from the rock, or this dagger seeks thy heart. Ha! that pale form, that dim and shadowy face, floating in the midnight air, with the eyes of speechless woe! She beckons me onward. He comes, pale spirit—thy betrayer comes! An instant, and lo! before the bar of eternity he shall tremble at the frown of the Unknown!"

It was a scene of sickening horror, yet dignified and consecrated by the mighty revenge of the monk.

His face pale as death, his lips livid with fear, his eyes rolling and vacant in their glance, the Duke stepped tremblingly backward, while the monk strode one step forward, raising the keen steel aloft, with a slow movement, yet with a quick eye and a determined arm.

"Leap—leap—or the dagger seeks thy heart!"

The Duke looked wildly around, and, shaking his hands aloft, gnashed his teeth in very despair.

Another moment!

The monk alone stood on the platform, while a rushing sound swept through the air, far, far below, as though a weight of iron had been toppled from the rock.

Albertine slowly advanced to the edge of the platform, and gazed into the void below.

With a fixed and glaring eye, with the dagger raised aloft in his right hand, he gazed below, and beheld the folds of a garment waving through the darkened air, while a yell most fearful and maddening to hear, came shrieking from the darkness of the void, resounding to the very heavens above, until the air grew animate with the sound of despair—unutterable despair.

Then came a crashing sound, as though a heavy body had fallen against the projecting points of the rugged rocks, and then all became silent.

Silence gathered over the universe, like one vast brooding shadow of omen and doom.

The wild flush of excitement vanished from the face of the monk.

With a calm brow, a compressed lip, a cheek pale as death, and a full dark eye, that seemed blazing forth from the shadow of the brow, he folded his arms silently on his breast, and looked up to the midnight heavens.

"She beckons me over the steep, she beckons me; and, with her burning eyes fixed upon my face, she waves her hands, and bids me—on, on! She points to the scenes of the past: God of my soul, how real, how vivid, how like the pictures of memory! The cottage in the vale; the sunshine sleeping on the roof sheltered by vines; the lordly hall and the friend—*the friend*—the outrage, the lifeless form, and then comes the spirit of my desolation, laughing with scorn as he points to the shadow blackening o'er the dial plate of destiny!

"Nay, nay, wave not thy hands with that slow and solemn motion—glide not so ghastly to and fro—thine eyes burn in my very soul! I come, I come! Albertine glides onward to his bride!"

With folded arms, with calm and immovable countenance, fixing his glance upon the vacant air, without a fear, a sorrow, or a sigh, the avenger stepped from the platform rock, and with the speed of an arrow driven home by the strong arm of the archer, he sank into the darkness of the abyss.

There was a low moaning exclamation of joy, and the setting moon looked on the falling form no more.

CHAPTER THE NINTH.

THREE DAYS ELAPSE.

JOY COMES AND POWER, BUT DEATH HAS GRASPED THE VICTIM.

THE morning sunshine, streaming through the deep silled casement of the convent cell, filled the lonely chamber with light.

The arching roof and the pavement of stone, the dark gray walls, thronged with monkish effigies, and the distant corner of the room, all glowed with warm glimpses of the daybeams, while a solitary soldier strode slowly along the floor, his brow darkening with a frown, as, with his clear blue eyes fixed on vacancy his mind was absorbed in painful thought.

"St. Withold! and all the Saints in heaven or earth save me now!" he absently muttered, as his right hand grasped the hilt of his good sword.—"Here's a new wonder, a fresh mystery! Three—three days agone—we were all fighting and slashing, leading murderers to death, and pulling Dukes from their thrones, daring death in as many shapes as swords are fashioned, and all for my Lord Adrian, and lo! we bend all things to our will, dethrone the tyrant, and fill the people's throats with an outcry for the new duke, and what comes next? Answer my good Robin—answer my old friend—where is the new duke? God knows, and the Saints might tell, an' we knew how to ask them, but not a whit does Rough Robin know about the matter. The old priest was wont to tell me that the ways of HIM above—off with thy cap, Robin—were full of mysterie. I never knew what he meant till now—"

The small door of the cell slowly grated on its hinges, and as the yeoman turned to discover the cause, he beheld standing before him a cavalier whose form was attired in glossy purple and bright gold, yet all soiled and tarnished with dust, while his young face, pale and careworn, bore traces of the fearful struggle that had shaken his soul within the past few days.

"Ah—Guiseppo! Pale and careworn—thine attire covered with dust—thy broken plume sweeping o'er thy brow——whence came ye boy, in such attire and in such a ghastly trim?"

"I greet thee, good Robin. Yesternight I left the Castle of Albarone—this morn I journeyed from the walls of Florence!"

"Thou dost bear a message?"

"I come from the nobles and the people of Florence! Three nights agone the old walls of the fair city rang with the clash of arms and the peal of trumpet, while the tramp of contending foemen shook the floor of the ducal palace, and the glimmer of their swords was reflected in the very mirrors of the Tyrant-Duke. The morning dawned at last, and dawned on Florence, no longer oppressed by the tyrant, or awed by the vassals of his power. Then it was that the nobles of Florence named their new Duke, then it was that the people confirmed their choice, while the solemn HIGH PRIEST OF THE INVISIBLE, by a parchment scroll affixed to a pillar of the grand cathedral, pronounced his blessing on the fortune of Adrian, Count of Albarone and Duke of Florence—"

"Thus far all was well. Then ye learned the mysterious disappearance of Lord Adrian? Speak I the truth, Guiseppo? The dark scenes which three nights agone gave new legends of horror to the walls of this convent of darkness? The death-bowl administered by the hands of Albertine—the watch of the Ladye Annabel beside the corse—the disappearance of the body, and what troubles me but little, the disappearance of the tyrant-duke? A thousand such dukes might disappear, and we could tell, without a doubt, what became of them all, 'the devil takes care of his own' saith the adage—"

"Hast thou no word of the Lord Adrian?"

"Ask the tombs in the aisles of the convent chapel, which yesternoon we ransacked in search of his body, and let their yawning mouths tell the story of our fruitless labor. St. Withold! scarce a foot of earth in the convent garden that we did not turn to the sun in our search—not a cell in the earth-hidden recesses of this foul den, that we failed to illumine with the glare of our torches, not a wizard nook or a blood-stained corner in this devil's hall, but was laid open to the light, in our strange chase after the body of the dead! And it was all in vain, Guiseppo, all in vain!"

"The Ladye Annabel—hast thou no word of her, Rough Robin?"

"St. Withold, I see her now! Traversed we the dark walls in search of the corse? She went with us, though her feet sunk ankle-deep in the dust of the dead, at every step. She led us on to the fatal room, where the corse had been stolen from her grasp, while bewitched by the drugged potion; she pointed the way to the dark cavern beneath the convent, and when every heart failed, awed with supernatural fear, she, even the fair and gentle Ladye Annabel, still cried on, and on! An' the saints shower not their blessings on her head, I'll turn Paynim-hound, and kiss the crescent!"

"Dwelleth the Ladye still within the Convent walls?"

"Since the hour of our search yesternight, she hath shrouded herself within the recesses of the apartments furnished for her use by the vassals of

Albarone, when they hastened hither, two days agone. Hast thou a message for the Ladye?"

"I bear a message for the Ladye, and a parchment scroll for the INVISIBLE! Robin come hither—a word in thy ear!"

With the mystic sign of a Neophyte of the Holy Steel, he asked the way to the solemn place, where the order assembled holding their secret yet mighty councils.

"Even now they hold their solemn council, within these convent walls," answered Robin the Rough.—"In a moment I'll lead thee to the secret chamber. Yet stay a single moment, Guiseppo. Thou knowest I left the castle on that fearful day, when, when, od's death I cannot name the deed—"

"That blow, Saints of Heaven! will the *memory* never pass from my brain! Thou wouldst speak of—of my father?"

"Does the old man live?"

"When thou didst leave the castle, I stood watching silently beside the door of the chamber where lay my father, my own father, stricken down by the hand—the hand of his own son."

"You watched beside the door, while the leech who had been hurried from the City of Florence disrobed your father, and probed the dagger wound?"

"And I—I, stood trembling beside the door waiting the appearance of the leech, every moment expecting to hear the words—'Thy father is dead! *Dead*—murdered by his *son!*' I stood beside the chamber door, all alive with horror, my fancy picturing the dagger, which but a few hours agone, I had drawn from his heart, the point crimsoned with one fearful stain of blood, there I stood, fire in my brain, and hell in my heart, when—"

"Ha, ha, ha—Ho, ho, ho! I have the brand, the flaming brand," a wild and maddened voice awoke the echoes of the corridor leading to the cell, with its tones of maniac yell. "Ho, ho, ho! I have the brand, the flaming brand! Look ye how it flashes on high, 'tis a serpent, a merry serpent with tongue of fire! Ha, ha, for the brand, the flaming brand!"

The small door of the cell grated on its hinges, and in the very centre of the pavement, brandishing a fire-brand over his head, there stood, a weak and trembling old man, his thin face, with the vacant eye and hanging lip, flushed with madness, while his voice half shriek and half yell, rang echoing round the room.

The brand, ha, ha, the flaming brand! Ha, ha, ye brought the old man no food! Ho, ho, ho, Old Glow-worm and his comrades starve, yet there is a merry blaze in the vault below, I trow! Rafters are all aflame, massy bolts are red with fire, and my comrades go shouting merrily through the long vaults, waving their brands on high, and singing a joyous song as they go—

"Then raise the chaunt,
Then swell the stave—
Here's to Death, all grim and gaunt,
And to his home, the grave!"

CHAPTER THE TENTH.

THE MYSTERIES OF THE CHRONICLE.

TO BE READ BY ALL WHO WOULD LOOK BEHIND THE
CURTAIN OF FATE, AND GAZE UPON THE SECRET SPRINGS
THAT MOVE MEN TO DEEDS OF WOE AND WAR AND DEATH.

"FLORENCE is free!"

"Florence is free!" echoed the Monks of the Holy Steel, and the shout
resounded through the circular room of the tower, repeated by the
Neophytes of the Order, with one wild acclaim, "Florence the fair and
beautiful is free!"

Slowly the High Priest of the Order arose.

From the dome of the tower the light fell dimly over the scene.

The Monks of the Holy Steel were seated around the square table, their faces
veiled, their forms muffled in sable robes.

The figures of the Neophytes, (or Initiates) were grouped around the
Superiors of the Order. They stood shoulder to shoulder, along the walls of
the Tower-Room, every one with a dagger in his right hand, a torch in his
left.

The torches were extinguished, for the work of the Order was accomplished.

Stately and erect, in the midst of this scene, towered the tall figure of the
High Priest, veiled and muffled like the others, his hands extended over the
heads of the brethren in a gesture of benediction.

And at the other end of the table sate the veiled Doomsman, his rough hand
appearing from the folds of the black robe, laid upon the handle of the axe,
whose steel was crusted with the rust of blood.

"Three years ago," thus spoke the High Priest, "the cry of blood, day and
night, unceasingly and forever, went up to the throne of God calling for
vengeance.

"From the walls of the fair city it shrieked, from the plain it echoed, from the
mountain side that low moaning voice rose up to the blue sky, pleading for
the doom of the assassin, the death of the tyrant.

"Then it was in times of blood-shed and slaughter, in the day of foul misrule
and galling wrong, when the grim bravo whetted his knife on the stones of
the altar, and the corses of the murdered crowded the sanctuary of God, then
it was, that a few brave and determined men, evoked from the shadows of

the past, a POWER, mighty yet secret, blasting as the thunder-stroke, yet invisible as the grave!

"The POWER of the STEEL—winged by the hands of those twin-sisters of vengeance, SECRECY and MYSTERY.

"Three years past, and on the lips of men, there grew a mighty word—the Steel, the Holy Steel!

"The bravo still smote his victim in the silence of the night, but ere the morrow's sun, the corse of the assassin lay prostrate beside the murdered.

"The wronger still pursued his work of violence, but it was by stealth and in secrecy; the tyrant still filled the air with shrieks of death and cries of despair, but the trembling tones of his own guilty voice mingled with the last words of the slain.

"The secret band were abroad—the invisible struck their keen dagger suddenly and without mercy, from the cloud that enclosed their existence, and more terrible on the lips of men grew that sound of fear—*The vengeance of the Holy Steel.*

"Not many days agone, the work which the Order had sworn to fulfill, was hastened by a new crime of the tyrant. The last baron of the race of Albarone, whom the brethren of the steel had resolved to raise to the Ducal throne, awaited within the walls of a dungeon the coming of the morrow, which was to bring to his head the woe and the doom, the axe, the wheel, the scaffold, and the stake. Doomed on a false accusation, doomed on the testimony of forsworn tools of power, Adrian of Albarone had laid him down to die, when the Messenger of the Steel appeared, the rescue was planned, and the morrow morn beheld the prisoner free.

"The march of fate strode swiftly on. All men named our brother—may God receive his soul—as the tool and minion of the Duke, while—it gives me joy to say it—he walked abroad the messenger of the steel."

"All hail the spirit of Albertine!" arose the solemn exclamation of the brethren—"all hail the incarnate spirit of our order!"

The last scene came hastening on. And the hand of fate pointed to this lonely Convent of the Mountain Lake, as the place where the wrongs of years should be avenged, where the Tyrant should meet his secret and fearful doom.

"For long years these halls had been peopled by a monkish band, who wore their sacred robes as a cloak for blasphemies too horrible to name; while the Dukes, the Tyrant-Dukes of Florence, startled these ancient walls with the noonday debauch, and midnight orgie, the sunshine murder, or the torch-light massacre!

"Here not many days agone, came Albertine the Monk. Still in the confidence of the Duke—for a specious tale blinded the eyes of the Tyrant with regard to the part our brother bore in the escape of the Doomed—still in the confidence of the Duke, the convent doors flew open at his word. Lord Adrian found a home within these walls, and day by day, secretly and surely, Albertine made converts of the Abbott and the Brethren of this Monastery of crime.

"A few days past, the tools and minions of the Duke, they now became the sworn Neophytes of the Order of the Holy Steel. It was the purpose of Albertine, to lure the Duke to the lonely Convent, and while the sound of his midnight wassail, awoke the echoes of the old walls, the Avenger would strike the dagger to his heart. The treachery of a peasant of the lonely valley hastened his schemes to their completion.

"The last night came. The Duke, flushed with pride, and made reckless by revenge, rode through the convent gates, companioned by his bravoes, who held their knives on high, shouting for the blood of Adrian, the Traitor.

"And while they prepared the doom of Lord Adrian, in the lonely valley, the INVISIBLE bestrode the mighty storm of vengeance that darkened over the night in Florence. The morning dawned on Florence the Free!

"The morning dawned over the lonely valley, and the blood-stained Convent. Along the halls, and through the vaults of the ancient fabric were heaped the corses of the bravoes, while the Brethren of our Order, ran from hall to hall, from vault to vault, lifting the red steel on high, as they sought for new victims, while the shout of vengeance rang pealing from roof to floor, until the air seemed animate with the cry of death.

"The Monks of the Steel came hurrying to the convent, two hours after midnight, but they came too late.

"The Duke, Albertine and Lord Adrian, all had disappeared.

"The morning dawned on Florence, unshackled and free, but the Duke, chosen of God, was gone.

"Brethren, ye have all heard the fearful story of that night of terror—the farewell of Albertine, uttered in the hillside cot, his sudden re-appearance before the eyes of Adrian, when awaiting his doom in the earth-hidden vault—ye have heard how the bowl of death was given to the Duke-elect by the monk—the singular disappearance of Albertine and the Duke when they entered the Chamber of St. Areline—all has reached your ears, and all is wrapt in mystery—"

"The dark story of the bowl of death, hath been darkening o'er my soul since that night of terror and joy," exclaimed a veiled Monk of the Order through the folds of his robe as he slowly rose from his seat. "A light breaks over the chaos of doubt and mystery—a sad and fearful light. Albertine crazed by revenge, maddened by his thirst for the blood of the Tyrant Duke, beheld the midnight hour approach, while the Brothers of the Invisible still delayed their coming. The Duke bade him perform this work of doom. Albertine must either refuse, or excite the suspicion of the tyrant. 'Twas a terrible thing—oh, most terrible to poison the young Lord at the bidding of this changeling Duke, but Albertine had no alternative. The plans of revenge were not yet altogether ripe, an hour would warm them into life. He was forced to slay Adrian to retain the confidence of the Tyrant—sooner would Albertine make the Fair City itself a desert of whitened bones, than the Duke, against whom his very soul had sworn vengeance, should live. He slew Lord Adrian, though his heart wept blood-drops in the act—and then came his strange and mysterious vengeance on the Tyrant."

A low deep murmur ran round the walls of the Tower-room.

Every heart was impressed with the terrible truth shadowed in the words of the Brother of the Steel, and in a pause of intense silence, each heart solemnly mused on the dark story of Albertine, his last crime, and his last revenge.

"Adrian sleeps with his murdered father," again spoke the High Priest. "Brothers of the Holy Steel, prince and peasant, lord and monk, joined in the work of vengeance on the Wronger, death to the slayer, ye who won for the Fair City, peace and freedom, ye who rule her destinies, guide her fate, your High Priest asks you the solemn question—Who shall wear the Ducal Coronet of Florence?"

The bold words were yet ringing on his lips when a shout from the stairway leading to the tower, rang through the circular room—

"Ha—ha—ha! I bear the brand—the flaming brand! See—how it whirls on high—look how it blazes! Ye sought well and ye sought long, but ye could not find old Glow-worm and his comrades!"

The small door of the tower-room was flung suddenly open, and rushing through the aperture, the slender form of the weak and trembling maniac stood disclosed before the vision of the secret brothers; the blazing torch he grasped in his right hand flinging a blood-red light over the veiled figures of monk and neophyte, while the walls of the room were illumined with fitful glimpses of the ruddy beams.

"Ha—ha—ha! The brand, the flaming brand! Ye sought well and ye sought long—but ye might not find the nest of old Glow-worm and his brothers! Merry was the fire they built—merry, oh, merry! Cheerily the flame arose—

oh cheerily! And now—ha, ha, stone burns, roof burns, floor burns, all is fire—and ha, ha, I bear the brand, the flaming brand!"

And as the maniac swung the burning brand, whirling and hissing round his head, there came hastening through the narrow doorway a gaily attired cavalier, bearing the trembling form of a young and lovely woman in his arms, followed by a stout and bluff soldier, whose face was stamped with an expression of alarm most strange to see on his determined features, while he aided the youth and maiden onward in their flight from the smoke and flame below.

"Health to the Holy Steel!" cried the cavalier rushing forward; "I bear a message from the Lords and People of Florence!"

"Ye will have to be wondrous hasty with your messages, I tell ye!" exclaimed the bluff soldier. "For d'ye see—all below us is flame and death—the convent is on fire, by St. Withold!"

"Brethren of the Holy Steel," exclaimed the High Priest, as opening the pacquet he gazed calmly round over the erect forms of the uprisen monks and neophytes of the order—"who shall wear the ducal crown of Florence?"

"The Ladye Annabel!" echoed the Brethren of the Holy Steel, with one unanimous shout. "Live the Ladye Annabel, Queen of Florence!"

A moment passes—behold the spectacle!

A fair and lovely form, clad in robes of fluttering white, stands trembling in the midst of the group of black-robed men who cluster round, kneeling on the pavement, as they raise their hands in one hurried movement, and shout with wild acclaim—

"Live the Queen—live the Ladye Annabel, Duchess of Florence!"

And as the Secret Brethren sank kneeling round, priest and neophyte, all with heads bent low, before the form of the Ladye Annabel, who gazed around with a vague and wandering look, there standing erect with a flushed cheek and a rolling eye, the ancient man of the vault flinging the brand aloft, whirling the flame round and round again, as he shouted—

"'Tis merry, 'tis merry, ha, ha! 'Tis merry, 'tis merry—hurrah! Old Glow-worm is a demon—these all are demons! Ha, ha! Fire above, and fire below—old Glow-worm is king! On—on—brothers—on—light up the cozy nooks with the red flame—fire the timbers, heat the old rocks, scare old Death with the light! Ha—ha—ha! The stone rolled back, and he—*was buried alive!*"

"Up, up—an' ye bear the hearts of men—up and save yourselves and save the Queen!" shouted Robin the Rough. "The fire has chased us through the long galleries of the convent, from chamber to chamber, from room to room, has it followed roaring at our heels! Up, and save the Queen! Her attendants have escaped or fallen in the flames. Yonder by the window of the stairway is our only hope! A staircase of massive stone, built outside the walls of this tower, leads downward to the southern wing of the convent, yet untouched by flame! Up, and save the Queen!"

"Listen, Brothers of the Invisible, listen to the last words ye shall ever hear from your High Priest. Our oath is fulfilled, the Tyrant is dead, Florence is free! And here in this lofty tower, environed by flame, with the roaring of the fire in our ears, and the lurid smoke rolling up to the heavens, with flame and death all round, here in this dark and blood-stained House of St. Benedict, do I, your High Priest and Sire, dissolve the Order of the Monks of the Holy Steel!"

"When Wrong arises, then shall ye again spring into life, when Murder walks abroad in the sunshine, laughing in the face of God, then shall His ministers again raise the Invisible steel! Till then I dissolve your band, give back your oath."

"Prince and peasant, lord and monk—off with your sacred garments, off with the vestments in which ye have been robed as the avengers of God, off with hood and cowl—stand forth as ye are and raise the shout—Live the Ladye Annabel. Live the Queen!"

"Live the Ladye Annabel—" the shout rang pealing to the tower-roof— "Live the Queen!"

It was like magic!

Down fell hood and cowl, down fell sable vestments and midnight robes, and there disclosed in the light of the flaming brand, stood the prince in his jewelled robes, the knight in the surcoat of glittering velvet, the lord in his gay doublet, the merchant in his silken tunic, the peasant in coat of serge, the priest arrayed in sacerdotal white, glittering with the sacred insignia of gold, the scholar in his flowing gown of sable, all stood there, rising stately erect in the light, proud representatives of their various classes, types of the GOTHIC MAN,[9] however named, or styled, all joined in the holiest cause on earth, the freedom of their native land, lifting up their hands and voices in one wild burst of enthusiasm, as they hailed the Ladye Annabel, Queen of Florence, chosen by the people, chosen by the lords, chosen by the priests, chosen by God!

A strange smile of delight stole over the lovely face of the Ladye Annabel, as standing calm and erect, her blue eyes was fixed on the vacant air, with the gaze of one entranced by some vision of far-off bliss.

"We shall meet again,—" she said and smiled—"Oh joy, we shall meet again!"

"Buried alive—ho, ho!" shrieked the ancient man, in a low chaunting voice—"Ha—ha! The stone rolls back—I have the brand, and then—ho, ho, hurrah! *Buried alive!*"

CHAPTER THE ELEVENTH.

THE BURIED ALIVE.

THE SPIRIT OF THE CHRONICLE, LEADING THE WAY
THROUGH THE CHAMBERS OF SLEEP, AND TRANCE, AND
DEATH, SOLVES THE MYSTERIE OF THE LIFE OF ADRIAN DI
ALBARONE.

AFAR through the gloom and twilight that hangs between the visible and the
unreal world, we behold the Spirit of the Chronicle, leading us onward to a
dim and shadowy land peopled by Dreams and thronged with Thoughts,
robed in forms of light or clad in shapes of doom.

It is the land of Death—the land of the Grave.

The awful region, where the soul, parted from its house of clay, looks over
the wide expanse of shadow, and beholds every thought that ever visited its
mortal form, spring up into tangible being and life, now gladdening its eternal
vision with images of loveliness and beauty, and again affrighting the pale
Spirit with shapes of ghastliness and woe.

Thus, as his dread Record draws near its close, thus speaks the Chronicler of
the Ancient MSS.——

DEATH—mighty and irresistible, look down upon the cold corse, and tell us,
when does thy hand first unveil the Eternal to the eye of the Soul.—

LIFE—thou mockery and blasphemy, gaze upon the form of the Mortal
Thing, and give us to know, when does thy power cease, when does thy
victim pass from thy grasp?

Ye each dispute the possession of the Soul, upon a shadowy battle-field, and
now the victory sways to the skeleton, and now to the thing of Flesh. Men
know this battle-field by various names, they call it SLEEP, they call it
TRANCE, they call it DEATH.

First the body sleeps, then it is entranced, then it dies. First the Soul gazes
with a dim eye upon the Eternal World, then its vision is enwrapt and
absorbed, and at last, as the clay dies, it is all Spirit, and Thought, and Dream.

Come with us, reader, with hushed breath and a solemn footstep come with
us, while we tread the halls of Old Death, tracing the Soul through the
chambers of Sleep and Trance, into the full light of the AWFUL
UNKNOWN!

Adrian Di Albarone drank the Bowl, and drained it to the dregs, and as he drank, the lovely face of Annabel swam round him in wild confusion, mingling with the dark countenance of Albertine, and the bronzed visage of the Sworder, while his heart seemed turning to fire, and his brain to molten lead.

He drained the bowl to the dregs, and then fell prostrate over the coffin, and then came a cold and unconscious pause, when his heart, and his brain, were wrapt in forgetfulness, covering his soul like a thick mist, or the deep darkness of midnight.

Awaking slowly from this oblivion of soul, he beheld looking him calmly, yet fixedly in the face, the countenance of his father, Lord Julian of Albarone, pale as death, and livid with the hues of corruption yet lighted by the deep glance of those shadowy eyes, that seemed to burn in their very sockets, like meteors seen through the dimness of the day-break mist.

As this face so wild, so lofty and so ghastly in its supernatural expression, faded slowly away from the vision of Adrian, his soul became the prisoner of mighty Dreams, the Spirits of the Grave, who called up before his eye, this dark and startling Mysterie.

THE MYSTERIE OF LIFE.

He stood in the court-yard of an ancient castle, with the frown of the old walls glooming over his head, while the blaze of the festal lights thrown from the lofty windows gave a ruddy light to the scene.

Gladsome strains of music, the light-hearted laugh of the reveller, the gay carol of the minstrel came echoing to his ear.

He looked around the courtyard, and beheld ranged under the shadow of the ancient wall the chariots of the great and proud, extending in long and brilliant array, as far as eye could see, each chariot with its panels blazing with heraldic emblazonings boasting its gallant attendance of four noble steeds, decorated with gay housings and waving plumes, red, azure and snow-white in hue, while numerous servitors, attired in liveries of every color and gaudy device, ran to and fro, their shouts of boisterous merriment, mingling with the voices of their Lords, joining in the glee song of the banquet hall.

Ascending a massive stairway, with snow-white marble steps, and rare paintings adorning the wall, Adrian made his way through the crowds of feasters, passing to and fro, through the stream of servitors bearing dainty viands to the revellers above, and in a single moment stood within the glare and glitter of the Festival Hall.

It was in sooth, a grand and magnificent scene.

The pillars of a lofty hall swept away from the spot where he stood, in grand perspective, each lofty column bearing its burden of wild flowers, quaintly wreathed around sculptured frieze and capital, hanging in long festoons to the floor, or borne to and fro by the summer breeze.

The glare of ten thousand lamps, arranged amid the intricate ornaments of the ceiling, hung along the towering columns or pendant in the night air, gave a dazzling light to the scene.

The dancers went merrily over the bounding floor, each eye gleaming with revelry, each cheek glowing with the merriment of the hour, and the Spirit of the Dance giving life to every step, animation to every motion of the revellers.

Placed on the balcony above his head, the band of minstrels filled the air with music; pillar and column, ceiling-arch and obscure nook, gave the strains with redoubled echoes, until the air seemed animated with melody, and instinct with the life of joy.

Floating on the waves of sound, the forms of dame and damsel, lord and cavalier, seemed swimming in the atmosphere, their eyes flashing light, their hands gaily upraised, their voices mingling in a festal song, as they undulated to and fro, now circling here, now grouping there, now clustering in a crowd, and again darting away over the floor, like a flock of frightened birds scared by the swoop of the falcon.

Adrian gazed over the scene, until his eye grew sick with loveliness, his ears deafened by the sound of mirth, revelry and music, he gazed around and marked the forms of beauty swaying in the dance, here the blooming form of mature womanhood, bounding amid the dancers, there the blushing cheek of girlhood, receiving the warm blaze of the festal lights o'er the velvet skin, here soft lips and azure eyes, mingling their messages of love, there delicate hands pressed thrillingly together, on every side the form of a queenly dame revealed in the light, or the soft bosom of a princely damsel, heaving from the folds of her vestment—on all sides beauty and grace, music and motion, commingling their fascinations, while the heart filled with melody, and the pulse throbbed with joy.

And as Adrian looked, with a wild thrill of delight, he beheld one lovely form, standing apart from the dancers, while her face of dreamy beauty was gazing sadly over the scene, the deep blue eye gleaming with thought, and the swelling cheek paled by melancholy, as the strains of festival music came to her ear.

It was the Ladye Annabel!

With a wild cry of delight, Adrian sprang forward, and as he sprang, his bride turned, beheld his face, and came swimming into his arms.

Another moment and they joined the throng of dancers speeding gayly over the floor, their hands interlocked while their glances mingled, and the soft whispers of each voice, spoke of the dear memories of the olden time.

It was when the dance swelled gayest, when the minstrels gave forth their most joyous notes, when all around was life and music and the waters of joy came bubbling to the brim of every heart, that a strange voice, deep, and whispering in its tones, broke over the very heart of Adrian.

"Man, thou art full of joy, and around thee every cheek glows with health, every eye sparkles with life. Behold, I show thee the Mysterie of Life and Death! Thou art doomed to return to this Festal Hall, one hundred years from this night, when thou shalt behold the Festal Scene, which death will open to thy gaze!"

And at the very word, Adrian lost his bride in the throng of dancers, and all grew dark as midnight.

The music and the dancers, the forms and beauty and the pillared hall, all, all were gone, and a strange consciousness was impressed upon the brain of Adrian, that one hundred years from the festal night had passed away, and that he had been wrapt in slumber for a long and dreary century of time.

THE MYSTERIE OF DEATH.

He stood in the court-yard of the ancient castle yet again.

A broad blaze of light poured from the windows of the festal hall, while the peals of strange and unknown music broke murmuringly on the air.

Adrian gazed around the court-yard, with a feeling of awe, gathering heavy and dark around his heart.

There was the castle yard, the same as in the olden time, yet not altogether the same.

Gleams of moonlight stole through the chinks in the tottering walls of the court-yard, wild vines threw their long branches from among the age-worn stones, and the owl, like a thing of evil omen disturbed the air with its sullen murmur.

Gazing along the court-yard, Adrian beheld a strange and ghastly spectacle.

Beneath the shadow of the dark gray walls, along the very space occupied by the array of chariots, one hundred years before, there extended a long line of death-cars, hearse succeeding hearse, all draped in folds of black, with four dark steeds, heavy with hangings of dark velvet, attached to each chariot of the grave, while the coachman's seat was tenanted by a grisly skeleton, attired in the gay livery of the noble lord whom he served in life.

With maddened steps, Adrian hastened along the whole line of hearses, he beheld each death-car, with its four black steeds, their heads decorated with sable plumes, their bodies concealed by folds of black velvet, he beheld the skeleton driver seated on every hearse.

He saw the paraphernalia of death and the grave, and as the horror grew darker at his heart, he shouted aloud, asking in tones of wild amazement, the cause of this fearful panorama of woe and gloom.

There came no answer to his shout.

All was silent, save the murmur of the owl and the peals of strange music floating from the windows of the Festal Hall.

"What means this fearful scene?" whispered Adrian, as he seized the skeleton servitor of a gloomy hearse by the arm—"What means the long array of death cars?"

The skeleton extended his fleshless jaws, in a hideous grin, and with his skeleton hand, brushed the dust of the grave from his gay doublet of blue and silver, and arranged the tasteful knot of his silken sash.

Still no voice came from his bared teeth, no answer came from his fleshless visage.

"Fiend of hell," shouted Adrian, "this sight will drive me mad."

"Nay, nay, good youth," exclaimed a soft and whispered voice at his very shoulder. "Be not alarmed, 'tis but a festal scene. One hundred years from this night we all thronged yonder dancing hall, 'tis our pleasure, or mayhap our doom to return to the scene of our former gaiety. I was master of ceremonies an hundred years ago, I am master of ceremonies, ha, ha, yet once again. Will it please ye to choose a partner?"

With a feeling of involuntary horror, Adrian turned and beheld a Figure, clad in a gay robe of purple, faced with snow-white ermine, holding the rod of office in his hand, while a group of rainbow-hued plumes, hung drooping over his brow.

Adrian dashed the plumes aside, he beheld, oh sight of mockery, the fleshless skull, the hollow eye sockets, the cavity of the nose, the grinning teeth, and the hanging jaw, while the hand grasping the wand of office, was a grisly skeleton hand.

He turned from the bowing skeleton, and was rushing away with horror, when a new wonder fixed his attention.

The master of ceremonies waved his wand, and each skeleton driver leaped from his hearse.

Another signal and the long line of skeletons, each attired in gay and contrasted livery, extended their skeleton hands, and lifting the pall on high disclosed the gloomy burden of each death car, the coffin draped in black, with the heraldic plate of gold, affixed to each coffin lid.

A third wave of the wand from the master of ceremonies, and the skeleton drivers, unscrewed each coffin lid, and Adrian beheld the occupant of every tenement of death, slowly rise from their last resting place, gazing beneath the shadow of the uplifted funeral pall, around upon the court-yard.

As they gazed, Adrian beheld each fleshless skull, wearing the horrible grimace of death, looking forth from beneath their gaudy head-gear, the plumed cap, or the jeweled coronet, while their skeleton hands, arranged the folds of their attire, brushing the coffin dust from the gay robe, or fixing the tarnished ruffle around the neck with a yet more dainty grace, while the skeleton drivers, slowly let down the steps of each hearse fashioned in its sable side. The last signal was given by the master of ceremonies.

And with a low bow, each skeleton servitor extended his hand, to receive his fair lord or ladye, his fair young mistress or his gallant young master, as arising from their coffin, they placed their feet on the steps of the hearse, and slowly descended into the court-yard of the ancient castle.

"Great God, they are thronging around me," shouted Adrian, "skeleton after skeleton, clad in the gay costume of life, descend from the funeral hearse wending in one ghastly throng toward the hall door, on their way to the festal scene. Oh, ghastly mockery! here are the forms of those who died when young, and the trembling skeletons of those whom death summoned when bending with the weight of years. Here are the skeletons of warrior and courtier, knight and minstrel. All wear glittering costumes, all mimic the actions of life. Cavalier takes the hand of Damosel, and Lord supports the form of Ladye, while the fleshless jaws, extend and grimace but speak no word. They utter a low moaning sound like the deaf mute when he essays to speak. 'Tis horrible, most horrible, this ghastly array of mockery, and hark— strange peals of music, are floating from yon lofty windows of the banquet hall!"

And as he spoke, the spectral train disappeared within the shadow of the hall door, and he was left alone with the long line of hearses and the skeleton servitors.

"So please ye, gentle sir, wilt thou not trip a measure in the joyous dance?" spoke a voice at his shoulder, "Lo! the peals of merry music, lo! the hum of the dancers feet, moving merrily over the floor. Wilt please thee to take my arm?"

Adrian turned and beheld the bowing Skeleton-Master of Ceremonies.

"I'll e'en secure thee a fair partner!" whispered the skeleton as he led Adrian through the hall door and along the massive stairway. "Look, good youth, the paintings are somewhat tarnished, very little tarnished since we beheld them last, and, ha, ha, well, well, such things will come to pass, the marble steps of the staircase are cracked by the footstep of time. This way, this way, my good youth. Lo! we are in the festal hall!"

With a gaze of horror, Adrian beheld the hall, whose floor he had trodden some hundred years agone. He beheld the lofty pillars, the magnificent arch, the balcony for the minstrels, all illumined by the glare of pendent lamps, all, all the same, yet still all sadly and fearfully changed.

The lofty columns were decorated with evergreens, but flowers gathered by the hand of beauty from the wild wood glade no more adorned capital and frieze.

The ivy, green companion of old time, clomb round the towering pillars, and swept its canopy of leaves along the arching ceiling, while the night-wind rustling through the worm-eaten tapestries agitated the long tendrils of the trailing vine with a gentle yet solemn motion.

"Lo! the dancers—ha, ha, the dancers!"

Circling and whirling, grouping and clustering, the skeleton-band went swaying over the floor, their gay dresses fluttering in the light, while the ruddy lamp-beams fell quivering over each bared brow, tinting the hollow sockets with a crimson glow, and giving a more ghastly grimace to the array of whitened teeth.

"Lo! the minstrels—a skeleton-band, whose fleshless skulls appear above the lattice-work of yon balcony. Merry music they make—clank, clank, clank! They beat the hollow skull with the cross-bone—clank, clank, clank! Each skeleton minstrel waves on high a human bone, striking it on the hollow skull—clank, clank. Clank, clank. Clank, clank, clank!"

And as the grinning skeleton, master of ceremonies, pointed above to the spectral minstrels, Adrian listened to the music that echoed round the hall.

A wild clanking sound assailed his ears, with a hollow mockery of music, while a deep, booming, rolling sound like the echo of a distant battle-drum broke on the air, maddening the skeleton-dancers with its weird melody.

The revel swelled fiercer, and the mirth grew louder, awaking the echoes of the ancient hall with one deafening murmur.

"Lo! the dancers divide—behold the spectacle! On yonder side extend the lords and cavaliers, on this the dames and damozels. They prepare for a merry dance—will it please thee chose a partner?"

And as the skeleton spoke, he pointed to the form of a maiden, clad in snow-white robes, who with her face turned from Adrian, seemed absorbed in watching the motions of the dancers. Adrian gazed upon this maidenly form with a beating heart, and advanced to her side.

"Behold thy partner!" cried the master of ceremonies.

The maiden turned her face to Adrian, and he stood spell-bound to the spot with sudden horror.

Looking from beneath a dropping plume, snow-white in hue, a skull stared him in the face, with the orbless sockets, the cavity of the nose, and the grinning teeth turned to glowing red by the light of the pendent lamps.

Adrian stood spell-bound but the form advanced, flinging her skeleton hands on high—

"Adrian, Adrian," whispered a soft woman's voice issuing from the fleshless skull; "Joy to me now, for I behold thee once again!"

"I know thee not" shrieked Adrian with a voice of fear—"I know thee not, thou thing of death! Wherefore whisper my name with the voice of her whom this heart loved a hundred years ago, and will love forever? Off—off—thou mockery, nor clutch thy skeleton arms around my neck, nor gather me in thy foul embrace!"

"And thou lovest me not!" spoke the sad and complaining voice of the skeleton—"Adrian, Adrian, gaze upon me, I am thine own, thine now and thine forever!"

"And this," whispered Adrian, as the fearful consciousness gradually stole over his soul—"And this is my love—my Annabel! Death, oh ghastly and invisible Death, couldst thou not spare even—her!"

"Advance dames and damosels!" rung out the words of the master of ceremonies.

And at the word, the long line of skeleton-dames and damosels, arrayed in rarest silks, blazing with jewels and glittering with ornaments of gold, came swaying quickly forward, extending their skeleton hands to their partners, who half advanced from the opposite side of the hall, and then they all swept back to their places, with one sudden movement rattling their skeleton fingers with a gesture of boundless joy, as they stood beneath the glare of the dazzling lights.

"Advance lords and cavaliers!"

Quickly and with lightsome steps the skeletons arrayed in costly robe and glittering doublet advanced to the sound of the unearthly music, and gaining the centre of the hall, sprang nimbly in the air, performing the evolutions of the dance with the celerity of lightning, and having greeted their fair partners again retired to the opposite side of the hall, uttering a low and moaning sound of laughter as they regained their places.

"Minstrels strike up a merrier peal! Clank, clank. Clank, clank. Clank, clank—clank!—Merrier, merrier—louder, louder—let the old roof echo with your peals of melody! Now gentles advance, seize your fair partners and whirl them in the dance!"

With one wild bound the skeletons sprang forward from opposite sides of the hall, pairing off, two by two, lord and ladye, cavalier and damosel, and in a moment the whole array of revellers swept circling round the hall, moving forward to a merry measure, clanking their skeleton hands on high and uttering low peals of laughter as they whirled around the bounding floor.

Adrian gazed upon the scene in wild amazement, while the skeleton arms of *her he loved*, gathered closer round his neck, and as he gazed he became inspired with the wild excitement of the scene, he clapped his hands on high, he joined in the low muttered laughter, he mingled in the mad whirl of the spectral dance.

Faster and faster, whirling two by two, their fleshless skulls turned to glowing red by the glare of a thousand lights, their hands of bone clanking wildly above their heads, while the low moaning chorus of unreal laughter echoed around the hall, faster and faster circled the skeleton dancers, gay doublets glittering in the lamp-beams, robes of silk flung wavingly to the breeze.

On and on with the speed of wind they swept, these merry denizens of the grave, pacing their march of mockery, their dance of woe, with a ghastly mimicry of life, reality and joy.

And as Adrian flung his arms around the skeleton-form of his bride, gathering her to his bosom, while their voices joined in the moaning chaunt of unreal laughter, the voice which he had heard an hundred years before, again came whispering to his ear.

"Behold the Mysterie of Life and Death! To-day the children of men live and love, hate and destroy. Where are their lives, their loves, their hatreds, and their wars, in an hundred years? Behold—ha, ha, ha! *Behold the Mysterie of their life and their death!*"

CHAPTER THE TWELFTH.

THE REAL MORE TERRIBLE THAN THE UNREAL.

ALL was dark. Not a ray of light, not even the gleaming of a distant star, but deep and utter darkness.

Adrian awoke from his dream. Did he awake to another dream, or to a reality yet more terrible?

He lay prostrate, and he felt his limbs confined as though they were bound with cords. He extended his hand, and it touched a smooth panel of wood, extending along his right side. A strange horror, to which the horrors of his late dream were joy and peace, gathered like a deadening weight around his heart. He threw forth his left hand, and felt a like panel of smooth wood extending along his other side. Raising himself slowly from his prostrate position, with every nerve and fibre of his frame stiffened and cramped by his hard resting place, he passed his quivering hands along the panels of wood, and with that insupportable horror deadening over his heart, he felt and examined the shape of his—COFFIN.

Bowing his head between his hands, the wretched man essayed to weep, but the fountain of his tears was exhausted.

He could not weep.

And then, as with trembling hands he examined his emaciated face, with the cheek-bones pressing hard against the parched skin, he beheld rising before his soul, one ghastly idea, which would pale the cheek of the bravest man that ever went to battle, or chill with horror and despair, the heart of the holiest Priest that ever offered prayers to God, an idea to which all other horrors were as nothing, all terrors, all fears, all deaths trifling and insignificant.

And the nameless thought, his husky voice gave to the air in a hollow whisper.

"BURIED-ALIVE!"

And a hollow echo returned the word "*alive, alive!*"

"It comes back to my soul," he slowly murmured, "the scene in the chamber of the convent—the Monk—oh, curses on the traitor—the potion, all, all come back to me! Buried Alive! Devil in human shape—he did not drug the bowl with death, but with—sleep! This, this is the revenge of the Duke, and, and Albertine was the tool of the triple murderer! Buried Alive!"

He tried to arise from the coffin, but for a long time his efforts were in vain.

His frame was stiffened in every sinew, and his limbs were benumbed by his long repose.

At last he stood erect upon the floor of stone, and extending his hands, grasped the massive walls.

"There is yet one hope," he murmured, "there may be some outlet from the funeral vault!"

With slow and leaden footsteps he passed along the wall, measuring its length. It was five paces long. The stones were all solid, massive, and firm. His upraised hand touched the ceiling, as it extended some three inches higher than his head.

Clutching the massive stones, he paced along the other walls or sides of the room, with weary and difficult footsteps, and at last traversed the three sides, and leaning against the wall, he endeavored to impress his wandering mind with some definite idea of the shape and dimensions of the vault.

"I stand in a small room, with floor and walls of massive stone," he slowly muttered, "it is square in shape, and each side of the cell is five paces in length, and somewhat more than the stature of a man in height. The stones are solid, and to all appearance are some three feet thick. There is no outlet, no passage from the vault. I am indeed—Buried, and buried alive!"

He passed with difficult steps along the fourth wall of the vault, determined to repose his shattered frame awhile, even though his resting place was his coffin. In a moment measuring three paces, he arrived at the spot where he supposed he had left the coffin. Extending his foot to and fro, in search of his late tenement, he was struck with a new horror:

"It is gone—the coffin is gone!"

Words cannot picture the utter horror with which this was spoken.

All the despair that an Angel of God might feel, when toppled from the battlements of Heaven into the infernal abyss, then visited the breast of Adrian Di Albarone.

"It is a mere phantasy," he exclaimed, "I have chanced upon the wrong side of the room."

Again the sides of the vault were paced, and yet the coffin was not within his reach.

It was gone from its position near the wall, and his physical strength did not suffice to advance toward the centre of the room.

What invisible hand was it, that removed the Coffin?

As the question was asked by the heart of the wretched man, it found its answer in one fearful doubt.

"And am I, in truth, within the bounds of that fearful place, which wild Poets have fancied, and dark-robed Monks have preached? Am I in sooth lost, and lost forever? Is death a dream? or an eternal succession of realities that seem but dreams—horrors too fearful for even the damned to believe? And this, this is—hell! I could bear the tortures of the eternal fire, the lash of the fiends I might defy, the lightnings of wrath would inspire with me with some portion of the Awful Spirit who winged their bolts of vengeance—but this narrow cell, this eternal confinement in a place visited only by Dreams, while hunger tortures and thirst burns, hope animates, and despair holds but half the human heart—this, this is too horrible. God of vengeance, give me, oh give, the punishment of the undying worm, the torture of the eternal frame, but spare, oh spare me—*this*!"

He fell on his knees, and kissed the cold floor as he bent his forehead against his clenched hands, making the narrow cell all alive with his shriek—

"Spare; oh spare me—*this*!"

As he bowed low on the floor, a singular sound—most singular in such a place—met his ear. It was but a low sound, yet it was a fearful one.

He heard the deep breathing of a living creature.

It might be the echo of his own broken gasps, the thought flashed over the mind of Adrian, and for a moment he held his breath, and listened with all his soul absorbed in the result. Again the deep breathing of a human creature met his ear—

"Is it man or devil?" thus ran the thoughts of Adrian—"Mayhap he may give me water to quench my thirst, or mayhap he will—ha, ha,—take my accursed life. Could I but speak—for my voice does nought but murmur—I'd even ask him to plunge his poignard in my heart."

A whizzing sound disturbed the air, and at the very instant the blow of a sword descended on the left arm of Adrian Di Albarone, while a heavy body fell to the floor, within two paces of the spot where he knelt.

"The blood flows from the wound," the glad thought darted over the mind of the Buried-Alive, "Would I had strength to tear the doublet-sleeve from the arm, then I might drink my own blood. Yet hold—the blood oozes through the gash in the sleeve, and, and Great * * *! I may drink my own blood!"

He raised the wounded arm to his mouth and greedily drank the blood.

In a moment he felt the influence of the draught.

His veins seemed fired with new life, his brain became for the moment calm and clear, his heart regained its vigor, and gifted with temporary strength he arose on his feet, grasping the sword of the unknown in his good right hand.

Another moment passed, and with his right hand he wound a bandage of linen, torn from his bosom, around the wounded arm, securing it by a knot tied with the teeth and hand.

Meanwhile he heard the sound of panting breath, not two paces distant from the spot where he stood, and as he listened a deep-muttered groan broke on his ear.

Calling all his powers of mental and physical vigor to his aid he spoke in a faint yet determined voice—

"Who art thou?" he exclaimed.

"Thy murderer!" was the gasping response.

"How long hast thou been in this place of death?"

"Long—enough—to starve! Hell and devils! I burn—thirst—starve!"

"What wouldst thou have?"

"Bread, bread! Water—I'd sell my soul for water!"

"Wherefore didst thou strike me?"

"I thought ye a spirit—and—and—I wanted to test your quality. Kill me, an' thou art a man of flesh and blood—kill me, kill me!"

"Thy voice is strange and hollow, yet methinks I remember your tones. Thy name is—Balvardo!"

"'Twas I that swore thy life away, 'twas I that brought thee to these vaults to bury thy corse beneath the earth—kill me, kill me!"

"Is there no opening to this vault?"

"A secret door—a passage—the spring, that opens on the other side—the spring that shuts—on this side. I—ha, ha, may hell seize my soul, I buried myself alive—and kill me!"

Adrian shuddered—and grew cold. He could hear the gasping of the poor wretch as he struggled for breath, he could hear the groans of his unseen assassin; well he knew that long absence from nourishment from food alone could lay the sworder helpless as an infant along the floor.

And as his mind struggled with the mighty horrors that gathered round him, his attention was arrested by a singular circumstance.

While the hushed and whispered conversation had been in progress between Adrian and Balvardo, the room had been gradually growing warmer and warmer, and at last the walls became heated, the ceiling emitting a warmth almost insupportable, while the confined air of the cell grew like the atmosphere of a furnace.

"What new horror is this!" faltered Adrian. "Tell me, how hast thou existed thus long in this vault of death, without air?"

"A well," gasped the wretch, "centre of the stone-room—current of air from under the earth."

Impressed by these incoherent words, Adrian advanced slowly along the floor, avoiding the prostrate body, and in a moment stood near the centre of the room.

He extended his foot—it touched a substance that gave back a slight sound; it was his coffin.

Another extension of his foot, and a whizzing sound assailed his ears, ploughing the air far, far below his feet, then the rebound of wood splintered to pieces on a pointed rock came welling up from earth-hidden depths and echoed around the room.

He listened with hushed breath for a long and weary moment.

The sound of a pebble falling in water, far, far below, came dimly and faintly to his ear, like the pattering of the water-drop upon the age-worn rock.

"Ha! A well, deep as the fathomless abyss, sinks down from the centre of the room. Let me measure its width—two good paces. The coffin has whirled down into its bottomless depths—I hear the splintered pieces falling in the water far, far below. A slight current of air issues from the well—and the heat of this vault of death grows fiercer every moment—"

"Kill me, and then thank God thou hast strength left to hurl thee down the dark abyss—— I burn, oh, fiend of hell, with thirst and flame I burn!"

Adrian sate him down on the edge of the well, with his feet dangling in the abyss, and gave his very soul to one long and painful effort of thought.

Death clutched him with a thousand arms, death was in the heated air, death came gibbering and laughing in the form of famine, and from the very depths of the abyss the doomed lord could fancy he beheld the form of the Skeleton-God, with arms outstretched to grasp his victim as he fell.

There was no hope.

He must die. He must die afar from the voice of friend, afar from the sight of earth, or the vision of the blue sky, he must die by the slow gnawings of famine, the gradual withering of fire, or by one sudden plunge into the abyss below.

He sate him down to die—his arms were folded, and yet with an eager gesture he held his face over the darkness of the abyss in the nervous effort to inhale each breath of air.

He strove to compose his mind to prayer, but the gasping of the wretch lying near his side diverted his attention from thoughts of God and the better world.

"Why didst thou hate me?" he slowly asked.

"I was afraid—thou—wouldst—live to do me wrong. Thou art revenged—I die by inches!"

The wretch groaned in very agony, and Adrian could hear his fingers clutching convulsively along the floor of stone.

"My God, my God," cried the doomed lord, as his very soul was wrung by the woe of the forsaken wretch; "would I had one cup of water to cool his burning tongue—"

"Ha—ha—ha! He mocks me with the name of water! Tell me, thou fiend, is *he* not revenged?"

"The heat grows fiercer—the air of this vault is turning to fire! He gasps for breath. Man give me thy hand. Let me drag thee near the well—the freshening air may cool the fire in thy heart and veins."

And extending his hands through the darkness, with his body inclined to a level with the pavement, he sought the form of the famine stricken sworder.

He grasped the hands of the wretch; the fingers were thin and wasted, resembling the bones of a skeleton rather than the hands of a living man.

Slowly and with a careful motion Adrian dragged the dying man along the pavement, he laid his head on his knee, as he sat on the verge of the well, and passed his hand over the massive brow of his assassin.

He shuddered in the very act. Clear and distinct, the harsh outline of the withered brow, pressed against his hand, and he could feel the eye sunken far in its socket, and the cheeks hollowed by the touch of famine. It was more like a skull than the face of a living man.

"I feel the fresh air on my brow," gasped Balvardo; "my feet are withering with heat, and mine hands burn! Oh fiend of hell—I see a fountain, a cool and showery fountain—the clear waters are streaming over pebbled stones, and the green moss is wet with the sparkling drops. Hist! I will crawl to the fountain side, I will bury my face in the waters—ha, ha, ha, I will drink, I will drink! Fiend, fiend—curses on thee, thou hast changed the waters to *blood*!"

He uttered a wild yell of horror, and the vault of the dead gave back the echo—"Blood, blood!" while Adrian passed his hands over the beetle-brow of the murderer, and parting the matted hair aside, held the famine-eaten face in the full current of the subterranean air.

All was dark as chaos ere the fiat of God spoke worlds into being, yet here was a spectacle that the angels of His throne, veiling their awful faces before the Presence, might gaze upon even through the darkness, and gaze with tears of joy. Here was the assassin, the sworder, the false-witness, and the sworn foe, resting in the arms of the man whose body his oath had given to the doomsman and the wheel; whose footsteps he had tracked like the bloodhound snuffing the footprints of his victim, fierce, unrelenting, and hungering after blood; here was the wretch who had borne him to this vault, placed his body in the house of death, consigned him to the famine and the fire, the nameless horror and the agony that the cheek grows livid to name; here was the man who had buried him alive, and yet he held him in his arms, fanned his withered face, and brought the fresh air to his parched lips and burning brow.

It was as the sworder had gaspingly uttered a fierce revenge, and yet such vengeance as the Man of the Cross, the God shrined in flesh, would have taken on his most blood-thirsty foe.

The end drew nigh.

The moments, those moments of horror, which seemed lengthened to years, dragged on with steps of lead, and the room grew like a furnace, the walls gave forth an intolerable heat. The ceiling rapidly became a canopy of invisible fire, as the air itself changed to unseen fire, began to burn into the flesh of Adrian, as the wretch in his arms writhed and writhed in helpless agony.

"Water—water—water!" gasped the Sworder.

A thought flashed over the mind of Adrian.

"There may be water in this well—a fountain may spring bubbling from its depths, while we perish on the brink! The way is deep and dark—a single misplaced grasp or foothold, and my body goes whirling to the abyss below; yet I am urged on by a power I cannot name—I will descend the well!"

A moment and the head of Balvardo lay on the pavement of the stone-room, while the body of Adrian hung swinging in the abyss, as, with his hands grasping the projecting stones, he began that fearful descent.

"I go to bring thee water!" he shouted in the ear of the famished wretch—"I go to bring thee water for thy burning tongue and brow."

"Then, take this—*this*—" was the gasping response, and Adrian felt a substance of metal pressed against his brow by an extended hand; "'twill hold the—the water, or, ha, ha,—the blood!"

Hanging over the abyss by the grasp of one trembling hand, Adrian seized the metal substance with the other.

It was a goblet, a goblet of gold, embossed with strangely shapen flowers, and heraldic insignia, and as Adrian placed the vessel within the confines of his doublet, a shudder of horror caused his frame to quiver over the unknown void.

It was the goblet of the Red Chamber.

First grasping a pointed stone with one hand, then inserting his foot in a crevice of the masonry, then clutching another stone with the other hand, while his remaining foot rested in another crevice, he slowly began the fearful descent of the well.

"This then is the foul den of torture, built by the tyrants of Florence, long, long ago!" The thought crossed his brain. "The well hath been fashioned by the tools of the mason, yet the damp has worn deep hollows between the rugged stones. Hark!" he uttered the involuntary exclamation, "a stone has fallen from my grasp—I hear no sound—none, none! The abyss may be without bottom or depth. Hist! a hollow murmur breaks the silence of the air, far, far, below—the stone has sounded the depth of the well!"

"Water, water—men or devils, give me water!" the shrieking tones of the wretch in the stone-room came faintly to his ear. "Ha, ha! Thanks, thanks—they hand me a cup, a cup of good, clear water, and I drink—oh, horror, horror,—it turns to blood!"

With every nerve quivering, his hand trembling as he grasped the stones, his foot shaking with a nervous tremor as it sought the crevice which might give it momentary support, Adrian continued his terrible descent, until some twenty yards of the subterranean well rose above his head, while the low moans, the piercing shrieks, and the hollow laughter of the Sworder came fainter, and yet more faint to his ear.

Extending his foot in search of a crevice, he was astonished to find it resting on a solid rock, that hung jutting over the abyss, at a point where the well, diverging from its perpendicular course, made a slight inclination to the opposite side.

Grasping the rugged stones with the eager clutch of his trembling hands, Adrian hung swinging over the abyss, as with extended feet, he examined the formation of the well at this particular point, and tested the extent of the jutting rock.

He looked over his shoulder, and a wild thrill of surprise ran over his frame.

"Mine eyes burn with famine," he slowly murmured; "they deceive me! Great God they mock me with a wild dream—I fancy the well grows lighter and lighter—but 'tis a dream, a mocking dream!"

As he spoke, a cold substance pressed against the palm of his right hand as it grasped the stone—it moved and writhed, while a hissing sound broke on the ear. Two points of flame, like minute yet intensely brilliant fire coals, glared before the very eyes of Adrian, and as the hissing grew louder, he found that a vile serpent wriggled between the fingers of his right hand.

With a sensation of unutterable disgust, he suspended his body by the left hand, and dashed the monster down the abyss with one quick motion of his hand.

The impulse with which he flung the serpent from his grasp, caused his body to quiver and tremble over the abyss, while the sinews of the left hand seemed bursting from the skin, as with the nervous grasp of despair, the doomed lord strove to recover the stone lately clutched by the other hand.

With one wild sweep he regained his grasp, springing heavily on the jutting rock in the action, while a deep rumbling sound disturbed the silence of the well. Another moment passed. Well was it for Adrian that he had refrained from trusting to the rock for support. The massive stone slowly swung to and fro, trembling over the depths of the well, and then with a crash like thunder, went whizzing down the abyss.

Up, up, from the fathomless depths, thundering and shrieking, arose the deafening echoes, yelling like spirit-voices in the ear of the trembling man, as he swayed to and fro over the blackness of the void.

It was a moment ere Adrian might recall his wandering thoughts.

He looked over his shoulder, he gazed upon the opposite side of the well. God of Mercy, was it a dream, a phantasmal creation of fancy, a mocking delusion of his crazed brain? There, before his very eyes, gilding the opposite side of the wall, a golden space, large as the human hand, shone in his very face.

"It is the light of day!" muttered Adrian, as his heart rose to his very throat; "it is, it is the light of day!"

"Ha, ha, ha! water!" the shriek came yelling from the room far, far, far above—"water, water!"

Grasping the stones below, Adrian descended another yard, when a ray of light shone on his face from a crevice in the wall to which he hung, trembling with a new joy, quivering in every nerve with a new life.

He thrust his right hand into the hollow of the crevice, and as a large flat stone fell echoing before him, a gush of light streamed through the wide aperture into the darkness of the abyss.

"I stand within a rock-bound passage!" exclaimed Adrian, "'tis narrow as the grave, narrow as a coffin, yet twenty yards beyond I see the light of day! Great God give me strength; do not, do not fail me now! Strength, a little strength, and I may yet be saved!"

Prostrate upon the floor of the narrow passage, which the falling stone had disclosed, he turned his body, and, thrusting his face into the gloom of the well, once more gazed far, far above.

"Murderer that he is, I will not desert him!" he cried; "he has been my comrade in the living tomb—he shall be my comrade in the light of God's own day!"

No sooner did the words pass his lips, than a shriek of intense horror, came pealing down the abyss, a mass of red fire crowned the summit of the well, and hot cinders, and burning coals swept through the darkness of the void, hissing by the very face of Adrian, and marking their flight with long lines of streaming flame.

Adrian withdrew his head from the well and listened.

A low moan, a choking groan, and then a succession of yells, resounded through the void. Then the crackling of flames, then the falling of age-cemented masonry; then a wild shriek, and then a voice of horror—

"I burn, I burn! oh fiend of hell, I burn!"

The air was cloven by the rushing of a falling body, and thundering down the well, with arms outspread, with his face all crushed and blackened, stamped with a look of agony that might never be forgotten, Balvardo was for a moment disclosed by the light shining through the aperture, before the very eye of Adrian, and then there was a hissing noise, followed by a sullen rebound, and then all was still.

The soul of Balvardo, the Sworder, stood beside the soul of his master in the judgment halls of the Unknown.

"Away, away!" shouted Adrian, maddened by the memory of that despair-stricken face; "away from this earth-hidden hell! Strength, my God, oh give me strength, and I may yet be saved!"

Creeping on hands and knees, he advanced along the subterranean passage, the light growing brighter at every step, and at last the twenty paces were left behind, he crawled from the rock, he stood in the open air.

His voice failed him, he gazed around.

Far, far above him, ascended the gray steep on which the Convent was reared, far, far above him, he beheld the blue sky, tinted with the glow of the dying day, he beheld the platform rock and the frowning tower, wrapt in clouds of lurid smoke, while tongues of forked flame, swept up to the very azure, turning the glow of the setting sun to bloody red.

He stood on the side of a ravine, with the darkness of the abyss yawning beneath him, while the rugged ascent of rocks on the opposite side rose towering before his eye, veiling the mountain lake from his sight, and giving a faint glimpse of the eastern sky.

Dark and dreary, tangled with gnarled shrubs, rough with rifted rocks, a score of fathoms down, sunk the wild abyss, with the hills, or rather the overhanging cliff gathering around its blackness, like the sides of one vast death-bowl of ebony.

In truth it looked like the crater of an extinct volcano.

With a glance Adrian beheld the smoke and flame, the Convent and the blue sky above, the glimpse of the eastern horizon, the rocks ascending on the opposite side of the ravine, and the blackness of the abyss below, and then his soul was riveted to a spectacle of horror extended at his very feet.

There before his very eyes, a mangled carcass was thrown along the surface of a rugged rock, the trunk, the limbs, the arms, the garments and draperies of gold, all mingled in one foul mass of corruption, while the face was buried amid a cluster of stunted shrubs of laurel.

Adrian reached forth his hand, he raised the face, he beheld the blue tint of corruption, the eyes lolling from their sockets, the blackened tongue hanging from the mouth!—

"The Duke," he shrieked, "the Duke of Florence!"

He turned from the sight with intolerable disgust, and as he turned, he beheld appearing from amid the shrubs, on the other side of the small platform of sand on which he stood, a bared arm laid along the earth grasping a keen and slender-bladed dagger, with a grasp that death and corruption could not unclose.

Adrian sprang forward, he unwound the dagger from the grasp of the hand, he beheld a parchment scroll secured around the haft of the glittering steel. He tore the scroll from the dagger, he flung it open to the light, and beheld these words written in a fair unwavering hand—

"Brothers of the Invisible! When this hand that writes these words is cold in death, the scroll of Albertine the Monk, will tell the story of his vengeance on the Tyrant-Duke.

"The midnight hour is now past—I go to plunge the dagger of the Holy Steel in the Heart of the Doomed. Ask ye for the Heir of Albarone! Three hours ago, ere the Duke arrived in the valley, I bade him farewell forever. Midnight came, and I learned that the Son of Lord Julian was about to meet his death in the vaults of the Convent.

"One way of rescue alone remained. Protected by my supposed love for the Duke, I blinded the eyes of the assassin, and offered to do his work of death. Then mingling a potion, which would minister sleep,—not death,—I gave it to Lord Adrian—even now his bride gathers his slumbering form to her embrace in the vaults of the Convent—even now the assassin waits to bear the body to the grave.

"One hour from this ye will arrive in the valley, and your eyes will behold the slumbering form of your Prince—the lifeless corse of the Tyrant! I go to finish—"

The scroll broke off abruptly, yet there was enough written to fill the heart of Adrian with an emotion of joy he had never felt before.

He sprang among the bushes, he dashed the laurel leaves aside, he turned the blackening face of the mangled corse to the light. He clasped his hands on high in silent prayer, while his burning tears fell streaming over the face of Albertine the Monk.

Meanwhile gathered along the green sward of a level meadow, extending from the Convent gates, to the south of the mountain lake, a band of gallant warriors, reined their war-steeds upon the turf, their upraised spears marking their numbers by long lines of glittering light.

A thousand banners waved in the sunset air, and the peal of bugle, and the stirring notes of the trumpet went echoing upward among the old convent walls wrapt in smoke, lighted by giant-pillars of blood red flame.

In front of the band of warriors, a group of noble lords and high-born dames, plumed cavaliers and gay-robed damsels,—all mounted on prancing steeds, swept circling around the figure of a fair and beautiful Ladye, whose jet-black barb, with its watchful groom, stood reined in their midst.

Every tongue was silent, and every eye was fixed upon the death-like paleness of the maiden's countenance, contrasting strangely with the gorgeous robes of purple and gold that drooped round her young and lovely form.

Her head bowed slowly on the neck of her steed, and the tears of a never-dying grief came gushing between the fair and delicate fingers that strove to veil her face.

She wept, the fair Ladye Annabel, whose steed was about to spring forward in the triumphal procession, that would soon give Florence its lovely queen; the coronet was on her brow, the swords of a thousand warriors were at her beck, and yet she wept.

Suddenly a wild murmur ran through the warrior-throng.

Uprising in the light of the burning Convent—that dark haunt of blood and awe, now toppling to its foundation, a gray rock, its base concealed by stunted shrubs, while its brow was turned to the flame-beams, attracted the gaze of every eye, as a strange spectacle hushed the whispers of every voice.

A hand, white as marble, was thrust from behind the rock, lifting a goblet of gold in the light of the setting sun.

Deep muttered whispers broke along the warrior-throng, every voice spoke of some new omen crowning the horrors of the convent during the last hour of its existence, and the murmurs of the lords and ladies clustering at her side, attracted the attention of the Ladye Annabel.

She slowly turned, she gazed upon the uplifted hand with the goblet of gold rising above the verge of the gray rock—not more than twenty paces from her side—she gazed in wonder and in awe.

And as she gazed, a wan and haggard face appeared above the rock, and a wasted and trembling form, clad in garments of price all soiled and torn, stood on the verge of the massive stone, flinging the goblet wildly aloft, as a peal of maniac laughter came thrilling to the maiden's ear.

It was a solemn and impressive scene!

There swept the knightly host along the green meadow, their spears gleaming on high, there darkened the smoke and lightened the blaze of the burning convent, there the calm lake extending ripples along its mountain-shores, gave its still bosom to the crimson glare of the flame, and there standing erect upon the brow of the gray rock, his slender form boldly and clearly relieved by the background of the convent walls, the light of the flame, the beams of the setting sun; Adrian Di Albarone, crazed by famine, and maddened with new-born joy, shook wildly aloft the Goblet of Gold, while his maniac laugh broke echoing on the evening air.

CHAPTER THE LAST.

THE CATHEDRAL OF FLORENCE.

THE TASK OF THE WEIRD SPIRIT IS DONE—THE CURTAIN OF FATE FALLS OVER THE TRAGEDY OF THE HOUSE OF ALBARONE.

JOY to Florence now, oh joy to the fair city in her streets and through her lordly halls, joy to the prince of the palace and the peasant of the cot, joy to the mountain and the dell, joy to the hill and the valley, joy to the silvery river, joy to the homes of men, joy to the shrines of God, joy, joy, forever joy!

The Duke, the people's Duke is come to reign! Baptized by trial, chosen by the People, crowned by the Invisible, anointed by God, he comes to reign!

—So, after many pages of varied and peculiar interest writes the Chronicle of the Ancient MSS. in his extravagant way.

There are light voices filling the air, there are soft steps tripping through the lordly halls, there are costly draperies sweeping over marble floors, there are strains of music awaking the echoes of ancient domes, there are processions thronging the streets in all the pomp of crucifix and banner, gallant knights ride to and fro, shaking the glitter of their snowy plumes aloft, the poor creep from their dens of want, the mighty pour from their homes of pride, the sordid miser forgets his money bags, the merchant his wares of cost, the scholar his musty book, the bravo his knife, the children of misery their care, and all, aye all, come thronging to the high Cathedral of Florence, when the solemn priest will, ere an hour, amid the glad shouts of thousands, anoint Adrian Di Albarone, Lord Duke of Florence, and crown his fair bride, the Ladye Annabel, with the coronet for which Aldarin gave his soul.

It is morning, glad and joyous morning, the calm azure arches over the fair city, gorgeous with temple-dome and palace tower, while the gay people hasten to the grand Cathedral, anxious to behold the Duke and his fair bride.

THE POSTILLION AND THE BUXOM DAMSELS.

And there tripping merrily along were three peasant damsels, arrayed in their holiday attire, and with them a bow-legged youth attired as a postillion, strutted on his way with extended stride and lofty air, which seemed to say, that all this parade and show, was made for his sole benefit and especial amusement.

"Sancta Maria! How he trips it along!" thus spoke the tallest of the damsels "beshrew, but Sir Francisco is wondrous proud, since he was knighted by the Duke!"

"How! knighted?" cried the damsel of the merry black eye.

"What mean you?" cried the red-haired maiden, and the bow-legged postillion looked over his shoulder with a vacant stare.

"Was he not honored with the collar, the hempen collar?" cried the tall maiden. "Did not that rough soldier of the Count Di Albarone that was, the Duke of Florence that is now, did not Rough Robin knight Sir Francisco with his own hands? How dull you are!"

"Ugh!" exclaimed the postillion shrugging his shoulders. "What unpleasant things you do remember! And yet the Duke said something very flattering, when he directed the rope to be taken from my neck. He said, says he, he said, I tell you—that I—

"Was a little impertinent, insignificant, busy-body," exclaimed Theresa, laughing. "But Francisco what mean you to do with the reward, you received from the Duke that was murdered, eh? Francisco?"

"Yes, yes, what are you going to do with all that gold?" cried Dollabella, and the three gathered around the youth with evident interest, expressed in each face in the glittering eyes and the parted lips.

"Why Theresa, Dollabella, and Loretta," answered the postillion, looking slowly round, with an expression of the deepest solemnity, "I mean to—that is, I intend—by'r Ladye the Cathedral bell is ringing. Come along, girls!"

"Ha, ha, ha! 'Tis a fair day and a bright," laughed a shrill voice at the elbow of Francisco, "Florence is full of joy and e'en I, I am glad."

A tremor of fear ran round the group as they beheld the form of the speaker, the distorted face, the wide mouth, the large rolling eyes, and the deformed figure with the unsightly hump on the shoulders, giving a half-brutal appearance to the stranger, while from lip to lip, ran the whisper—

"The Doomsman, the Doomsman!"

"Aye, aye, the Doomsman! And why not pray? Dare not the Doomsman laugh? Ha, ha, ha! What a fine neck thou hast for the axe, good youth; or now that I think o't it would stretch a rope passing well. 'Tis a fine day, good folk, and I'm hastening to the Cathedral, to behold the crowning of one of my children, that is Children of the Axe."

"Thy children?" echoed Francisco, aghast with fear. "Can a shadow like thee, have children?"

"Children o' th' axe, boy. I' faith if all the world had their own, I'd have thy neck—a merry jest, nothing more boy, ho, ho, ho! Do'st see these fingers."

"Vulture's talons rather!"

"These, these were round his royal throat, while the lead, the seething lead waited for his princely body, and the wheel of torture was arrayed for his lordly repose. Ha, ha, ha! I would see him crowned, by the fiend would I! But come boy, thou knowest somewhat of city gossip, tell me, does this Sir Geoffrey O' Th' Longsword, stabbed by his own son, a good boy, he, he, he, does he yet live?"

"Have not prayers been offered in all the Cathedrals for the miracle?"

"The miracle? Enlighten me, good youth!"

"Hast thou not heard, how the force of the blow was swayed aside, by a piece of the true wood o' th' cross, which the old soldier had worn over his heart for years? A miracle, old shadow, a miracle!"

"Nay, nay, call me not shadow, I'll never darken thy way to the gallows. But tell me, fair sir, did not the dagger pierce the old man's heart?"

"It grazed the heart, but did not pierce it. Any city gossip might tell thee this, old thunder cloud!"

"And so the old man lives?"

"He doth! Thou art wondrous sorry that he still breathes the air, I warrant me?"

"Nay, nay, good youth. I bear Sir Geoffrey no harm, but dost see—the wheel, the axe and the boiling lead, all were ready for the boy Guiseppo, and, and, but 'tis the will of heaven! I can bear disappointment, he, he, he, in all matters, save in one. Thy neck boy, ha, ha, ha, the Doomsman's fingers itch for thy neck!"

And while the peasant-group, the three buxom damsels, and the light-brained postillion, shrunk back from the touch of the distorted being with disgust, and stood thrilled with the fear of his words of omen, the Doomsman glided away, mingling with the vast crowd who thronged the streets of the wide city.

Standing upon the throne of gold, attired in the purple robes of a prince, Adrian Di Albarone, glanced with a brightening eye, and a swelling heart, upon the gorgeous scene around him, and then his glance was fixed upon the fair and lovely maiden by his side, whose eyes of dreamy beauty were downward cast, while a soft flush deepened the hue of her cheek, as she seemed to shrink from the gaze of the vast multitude, extending over the pavement, and along the aisles of the cathedral.

Adrian cast his eyes upon the throng around the throne.

There stood bold Robin, the stout Yeoman, attired in a garish appareling, which he seemed to like not half so well as his plain suit of buff, defended by armor plates of steel; and there his locks of gray, falling on his knightly surcoat, emblazoned on the breast with the red cross of the crusaders, stood the brave Sir Geoffrey O' Th' Longsword, attended on either side by the gallant esquires Damian and Halbert, each with a grim smile on his scarred face, as he surveyed the pomp and show glittering along the cathedral aisles.

Standing at the back of his father, his eye downcast, and his thoughts, Guiseppo seemed musing on the fearful blow, which had well nigh burdened his soul with the nameless crime. He said nothing, nor spoke of the pomp around him, but with folded arms stood silent and apart.

Standing beside her queenly cousin, with a group of bower maidens clustering around, the damosel Rosalind glanced from side to side with a merry twinkle of her eye, and look of maidenly wonder, as the glare and the glitter, the pomp and the show of the scene broke on her vision, and came thundering on her ear.

Amid the throng of noble dames, towered the stately form of the Lady Di Albarone, with a proud smile on her lip, and a haughty glance in her eye, as she looked with all a mother's pride upon her son's advancement to his right of birth and honor.

And higher grew the sound of pipe and cymbal, mingling with the roll of drum, and the peal of trumpet, and deeply booming along the arches of the cathedral, came the voice of the swelling organ, seeming as though some spirit of light had trained the mountain thunder to the strains of harmony, now soft and gentle, now awful, now sublime, and ever filling the soul with high and glowing thoughts.

And now the bright sunbeams came flaunting through the arched windows of the cathedral, and every eye was fixed upon the throne, and every voice was hushed in expectation, as the moment of the approaching ceremony drew nigh.

A murmur ran along the aisles of the cathedral, and it deepened into a cry—

"He comes, the holy abbot of St. Peter's of Florence!"

And every sound was hushed, as the venerable man of heaven raised the golden coronet, set with rarest jewels, and the sceptre of ivory from the altar of the cathedral, and ascending the steps of the throne he was received by Adrian Di Albarone with lowered head, and bended knee.

"Sound heralds, sound!"

And then the heralds, standing one on either side of the throne, gave a blast loud and long to the air, and proclaiming to the lineage, the title, and the birth of Lord Adrian Count Di Albarone, they flung each man, his glove upon the marble floor, challenging all the world to say aught against the right of descent claimed by the duke elect. There came no answer to the challenge.

"Lord Adrian Count Di Albarone," thus spoke the abbot; "in the name of God, in the name of Christ and St. Peter, and by the blessing of the Holy Vicar of Christ upon earth, I proclaim thee Sovereign Lord of Florence, the city and the field, the mountain and the stream! I bestow upon thee the golden coronet—wear it with glory and honor. I place this sceptre of ivory in thy grasp—wield it with justice and truth. Arise Adrian, LORD DUKE OF FLORENCE!"

As thus he spoke, with his mind glowing with the memory of the day when he had mingled in the battle fray, side by side, with the sire of the gallant youth who knelt at his feet, the tones of the abbot's voice rose high and clear, and with eyes upraised to heaven, and outspread hands, he seemed to implore a benizen upon the bridal pair.

One shout, long and deep, ascended from the multitude. Adrian arose upon his feet, and lifted the gorgeous coronet from his brow. He took the fair Ladye Annabel by the hand, and as the blushes grew deeper on her cheek, he impressed upon her brow a kiss that told at once of the love of the youth for his mistress, and the admiration of the knight for his fair ladye.

He extended his hand, and in an instant the coronet rested upon the brow of the lovely bride.

The vast cathedral roof echoed with the thunder shout of the myriad voices, the strains of the swelling music filled the air, at each pause of the deafening cries of joy; the warriors flung their swords in the air, the fair dames and damosels waved their snow-white hands on high, and one universal gush of joy hailed the fair Ladye Annabel Duchess of Florence!

"My own fair bride," Adrian whispered, "the night has passed, and our morning cometh."

While her heart yet throbbed with indefinable emotion, Adrian led his gentle bride to the ducal chair, and side by side, they awaited the homage of the noble throng of lords and ladies, knights and damosels.

Many a noble lord, and many a haughty dame, advancing to the throne, bowed low at the feet of the Duke Adrian, and kissed the fair hand of the Duchess Annabel.

At last a man of lofty stature, and commanding port, with locks of gray hair falling back from a stern, determined face, paled by disease, and wan with thought, and ascending the steps of the throne, sank on one knee before the duke.

"Rise, brave knight," exclaimed Adrian; "rise brave Sir Geoffrey O' Th' Longsword; rise lord keeper of our castle Di Albarone. Thy youth has been wasted fighting for the cause of the late venerated lord; thy age shall be rendered calm and peaceful within the walls of the castle, with whose brave soldiers thou hast so often gone forth to the ranks of battle."

And placing the baton of command within the hand of the brave knight, he raised him from his kneeling position. Sir Geoffrey o' th' Longsword replied not to the Duke with words of flattery.—One glance of the eye, and one grasp of the hand, was all the answer that greeted the Duke Adrian.

Then came Robin the Rough, ascending the throne with a half-solemn air, as though he were afraid of soiling the steps of gold. With a true soldier's salute he dropped on one knee, awaiting the command of the Duke to rise.

"Arise, bold Robin," said Adrian, unsheathing the sword that hung at his side—"Arise—no longer Robin the stout yeoman, but Sir Roberto Di Capello, Lord of the Lands of Capello!"

No sooner did bold Robin feel the sword of the Duke slightly pressed upon his shoulder conferring knighthood, than he sprang upon his feet, and looked around with surprise and wonder expressed in his distended eyes and parted lips.

"Hast any boon to ask, Sir Roberto?" exclaimed the Duke.

"Why, an' it please thee, my Lord Duke," answered Robin, recovering from his surprise—"Why an' it please thee, I have a boon to ask. I had much rather follow thee to battle in my old attire, in my coat of buff and my armor of steel. I like not this dainty trim."

With a smile the Duke granted his characteristic request, and as the bold soldier retired, Adrian waved his hand to one who stood in the throng around the throne. From the ancient chronicle we gather these words concerning

"THE ROMANCER."

A man attired in a tunic of dark velvet reaching to his knee, and with long locks of dark brown hair falling beneath the velvet cap of the scholar, now came forward and ascended the throne. In stature he was of the middle height, slim and well formed, with a face marked by irregular features, full cheeks, a mouth with large lips, while his hazel eyes, looking from beneath dark eyebrows, warmed with the inward soul.

"Most famed Romancer"—thus spoke the Duke to the person who knelt before him. "Most famed Romancer of the North, wear this signet for my sake. Men shall long keep in memory the wondrous Histories which thy pen, full of fancy, hath pictured. Add now to the number the Historie of the House Di Albarone. Take this ring as an earnest of future bounty. Thou shalt away with me to the Holy Land, thou shall chronicle the wars of the Christian and the Paynim. ERICCI IL NORMANI arise!"

Thus spoke the flattery of the Duke to the humble Romancer, thus he bade me indite my poor Historie, which, should it ever outlive this century, will serve at least to give some small glimpses of the crimes, the glory and the fame of the House Di Albarone.

And now, with his beaming eye no longer glowing with gaiety, but dark and thoughtful, came the Page Guiseppo; and side by side with the damsel Rosalind he knelt and did homage to his Lord. But why tell of Guiseppo and Rosalind—Is not the story of their fortunes found in the Historie of the Page and the Damsel?

The Duke turned to the vast multitude. He raised his sword on high.

"Witness, ye gallant knights, witness, ye fair dames, I now swear upon the hilt of my sword, that the morrow's sun shall behold me and my followers bound for Palestine, there to fight for the Holy Sepulchre. And so help me God and St. George!"

And there stood Adrian, with his ducal robe of purple thrown back from his shoulders, his right hand pressing his sword hilt to his lip, his left arm raised to the heavens, while his eyes flashed with all the enthusiasm of his soul.

The cry ran like a lightning flash through the temple, every voice was for Palestine, every tongue shouted—"on—on to the rescue—God for the Holy Sepulchre!"

Sir Geoffrey o' th' Long-sword raised his sword on high, the Ladye Annabel, fired by the holy feeling of the moment, lifted the cross of ebony depending from her neck to her lips, as a thunder-shout arose from the multitude, and while all was exultation and joy, bold Robin the stout yeoman flung the broad banner of the Duke to the air, and the bright sunbeams shining upon the azure folds gilded with dazzling light the blazonry of gold, and every eye beheld the armorial bearings of the Lord of Florence, with the words in letters of gold—

"GRASP BOLDLY, AND BRAVELY STRIKE!"

"It is past, the dark and fearful night," again repeated Adrian, as he gazed over this scene of wild enthusiasm; "Lo! the morning cometh!"

As he spoke the cathedral was suddenly darkened, a thick mist filled the Church, and one man could scarce distinguish the form of another by his side.

A wild, hollow laugh sounded to the very roof of the cathedral, it rung upon the senses of the vast multitude, and was echoed from every aisle of the solemn temple.

"What means the darkness?" Adrian shouted, drawing his sword; "Hist! I hear a footstep. It passes over the throne. It passes between me and thee Annabel; yet I see no form, I hear no voice."

"Ha, ha, ha!" The wild laugh again rose upon the dark and twilight air.

"He stands by my side!" shrieked the Ladye Annabel; "It is *he*—it is my father!"

And she trembled with affright, and leaned shrinking upon the arm of the Duke, while her fair blue eyes dilated with a strange expression, and her glance was fixed in one wild dread look upon the darkened air.

"It is done!" exclaimed a voice breaking from the vacancy of the air; "*It is done! Fair daughter of mine, thou art Duchess of Florence—the coronet is on thy brow— all is fulfilled!*"

"Holy Mary, save me!" shrieked Annabel in a low whispered tone; "an icy hand is pressed upon my brow. It is like the hand of death."

And as there she stood upon the throne of gold, her form upraised to its full height, her eye fixed on vacancy, and her fair white hands trembling with an unreal fear, a feeling of terrible and overwhelming AWE over-shadowed each heart, and paled each face, while the solemn tones of the spirit voice broke on the ear of the lovely bride.

"In life thou wert my ambition, and in the solemn walks of death, amid the fear that may not be named, and the gloom that may be dared, thy father, maiden, is still the evil angel of all who wish thee harm, or do thee wrong."

A low moaning sound broke on the air, and again the words of the spirit voice came to the Lady Annabel—

"The last behest of thy father—the parchment scroll, and the phial of silver confided to thy hands—hast thou obeyed the dying words of Aldarin?"

The cheek of the Lady Annabel became pale as death, and her eye grew bright with supernatural lustre. The hurried words of the scroll, written in the blood of the doomed man, the fearful request, the dark hints at the re-vivification of his mortal body, by the action of the water of life, all to be accomplished by the devotion of his daughter——flashed over her brain at the moment, when the gloom of the presence of the dead, darkened the joy of the living, and the Ladye turned to Adrian, and murmured with a whisper of hollow emphasis—

"The corse, Adrian, the corse of my father—where doth it rest?"

"It hath no place of repose on earth," was the solemn answer. "Given to the invisible air, the mortal frame finds nor home, nor resting place in sacred chapel, or in wild wood glade; but mingled with the unseen winds, floating in the atmosphere of heaven; on, and on forever wanders the earthly dust of the Scholar, denied repose on earth, refused judgment by heaven, condemned to the eternal solitudes of the disembodied spirit; on, and on it wanders seeking companionship with the mighty soul of Aldarin!"

And a low and solemn voice, speaking from the invisible air, murmured the words—"It is finished,

IT IS FINISHED!"

FOOTNOTES:

[1] There have been one or two persons, who have made themselves merry with this passage. These persons, however, belong to that large class of literary pretenders who are always in the market, as the phrase goes, willing to edit anything, publish anything, take one side to day, another to morrow, for a little notoriety and a little bread. Their criticisms, do not demand an answer. You can have their good opinion for a dollar, and be adored by the whole tribe, for the gift of a dinner.

But, a word is due to the candid reader, in regard to the Doomsman's description of Capital Punishment in the olden time. *The author is not responsible for a single line, word, or comma.* He has left a wretch, embrated, nay, demonized by spectacles of carnage, to describe the slow agonies of a horrible death, in his own way.

In the same manner, in another work, the author has introduced the Moloch of modern law,—the Hangman,—who but the cowardly instrument of a cowardly vengeance, puts a rope about his defenceless victim's neck, and in a dark jail yard, chokes him slowly to death, while Ministers of Religion stand by, and approve the murder, with copious texts and learned references.

The author is no more responsible for the ravings of the Hangman, than he is for the ravings of the hireling critic.

[2] The word which we have written "Postillion," in the ancient MSS. indicates a Courier, a Messenger; "one who carries letters from place to place." This personage, whom we here designated, "Francisco the Courier," is not unfrequently styled "Cisco the vagabond," in the original manuscripts.

[3] With his own peculiar abruptness, (to which the reader is by this time accustomed) the Chronicler of the Ancient MSS. changes the scene to the Valley of the Bowl, noticed in Chap. 3. Book. 3.

[4] The story changes to Albarone again.

[5] It will be seen that the Chronicler of the ancient MSS. goes on to picture the events of the previous night, in the succeeding chapter.

[6] It is observable that the chronicler of the ancient MSS. applies the word Alembic to an open vessel resembling a crucible in shape.

[7] Ibrahim Ben-Malakim (Arabic) "the Son of the Kings."

[8] This song is taken from an old Monkish Chaunt, and makes no pretensions to poetic beauty.

[9] The Chronicler of the Ancient MSS uses the phrase as a general and comprehensive term, to designate the '*man of the feudal times.*'

Milton Keynes UK
Ingram Content Group UK Ltd.
UKHW012254110624
443988UK00006B/433

9 789361 479366